Atahualpa's Mummy

The Harrogate Chronicles
Book 1

Nan Sampson
Susan Wachowski

This is a work of fiction. All of the characters, places, and events are the product of the authors' imagination or are used fictitiously.

Printed in the United States of America

Published by Leaping Clouds Press

Thank you to our families. You put up with our weirdness during the creation process--Steve, Art, Cassie, Cody, Sean, and Jaden. Special thank you to Sandee, Sue's mom, who donated her home, occasional meals, and sage life advice to get us through this. To the rest of the Hive, (Carol, Chris, Kristine), thank you so much for your support as writers and as good friends.

We hope you all enjoy this one, because we're finishing up book 2 and have ideas for a few more...

Chapter One

Damn. Late again.

Esmeralda Elizabeth Eggerton, née Huddlestone, and by marriage now Countess of Harrogate, picked up her skirts and ran in an unladylike manner up the carpeted steps of a little used stairway in Buckingham Palace. She gulped air as she hurried. Damn Cooper. If her automaton hadn't taken the time to force her into this bloody corset, she'd have been here half an hour ago. Now, when she needed to run the fastest, she felt confined.

She paused at the top of the steps and braced her hands on the railing. Bending forward at a wholly unnatural angle, she sucked air into her burning lungs. It took a full minute to stop gasping. When she could straighten, she mopped the moisture from her face with a lace-trimmed handkerchief and crossed to a short corridor.

Two familiar royal retainers stood outside Her Majesty's Private Drawing Room as she approached. "Lady Esme to see Her Majesty, please."

The one on the right, a man named Carl, looked her up and

down, winked, and gave her a nod of approval. "Her Majesty is expecting you, my lady."

She allowed herself a small sigh of relief. She would pass muster. He opened the door, and Esme forced a slow and measured pace. Victoria abhorred tardiness, but not as much as a breach in decorum.

Her Majesty sat on a settee, back straight, a slight frown on her round face. Her hands were in her lap, and her small but observant eyes followed Esme as she performed her curtsy and greeted her sovereign.

"You are late, Esmeralda."

"I'm sorry, Your Majesty. I encountered an accident on Grosvenor Crescent involving a hansom cab and a lorry." She stopped. Experience had taught her that the queen did not want excuses. "Yes, Your Majesty. Forgive me. It won't happen again."

"It better not." She waved her hand. "Please sit."

It wasn't a suggestion. Esme took the chair indicated, spine erect, ankles crossed and to the side, arranging her long skirts so that the requisite plethora of annoying petticoats did not show. Only then did she become aware of another presence in the room. A figure stood in a curtained alcove beyond which lay the queen's private office. Esme didn't dare check who stood there, yet she found it highly unusual. Her meetings with the queen were usually private. She had not been invited here to have tea, make small talk, or share court gossip. She'd been summoned because the queen had another favor to ask. Another 'little adventure' to send her on, an adventure of a clandestine nature that was critical to the Crown, and outside the pale of the official auspices of the government.

Esme's lips were dry, her mouth parched, and she felt a trickle of sweat slide slowly down her back beneath the beastly confines of the corset. She wanted to get this over with. She wanted to chivvy the queen to tell her what had been so important that Esme had been forced to cut short a perfectly lovely evening with a Russian count from whom she was winkling state information.

The queen gave her a cool, unflinching visual inspection. "How is your husband, Lord Harrogate?"

How odd. Victoria never asked about old Egg. Had the queen somehow known about the dinner with Volkorsikov? Esme knew the queen didn't approve of the rather fast and loose way she lived her life, or of the unconventional relationship she and Egg espoused. Yet, it all worked in the queen's favor. Being unchained from the more usual wifely duties left Esme free to pursue the queen's errands as required. Besides, Esme loved old Egg, in her own way. He had been her teacher and mentor and finally her savior. If he hadn't married Esme when he did, her life would have become a nightmare. She felt that old frisson of panic and quashed it. No, she'd never hurt Egg.

She laced her fingers together in her lap to keep from fidgeting. "He's well, Your Majesty. He's left for Yorkshire and Harrogate Hall for the school break, although he'd be better off here. The cold is so hard on his rheumatism."

Victoria nodded. "And you? You have been well since you returned from Our little errand in Turkey? We had heard that you were injured."

"I'm quite well now, thank you, Your Majesty." Injured hardly covered it. Six months ago, she'd been shot through the shoulder, the bullet narrowly missing bone. The wound still twinged in cold weather.

Victoria pursed her lips. "As We are sure you are aware, there are serious matters afoot, both on the Continent and in the Colonies."

The queen's usually rigid back slumped a little. Esme

remained silent at the rhetorical comment, imagining the queen suppressing the urge to sigh. In a controlled voice, Victoria continued. "Albert claims Bonaparte the First could not have built his Empire if we had won at Waterloo. I am not so sure. Yet now that his land-grabbing grandson controls most of Europe save for Spain and Greece, We are in danger of losing India." Her shoulders grew stiff again. "The situation in the Colonies is even more dire. I fear with the help of the French, the New England Treaty will break and the land will fall to the native Confederacy. Word came this morning of a devastating attack just west of the Hudson River. There is deviltry in that place..." Her brows furrowed, her lips pressed together in distaste. "Magic."

She fixed Esme with a look as sharp and pointed as a hat pin. "All of which makes the favor We have to ask of you more important than any other you have performed for Us."

Esme remained silent and respectful, waiting for the proverbial other shoe to drop, a little excited, a little nervous.

"Normally, for something this important, We would go through the usual channels, but there are extenuating circumstances that require Us to ask for your help."

As if Esme could say no. Not that she would, of course. She rather enjoyed Victoria's little errands. The danger, the intrigue, the exotic locales, the tall, dark handsome gentlemen. It gave her life shape and form and interest. The knowledge that she could die merely added spice to the dish. Why bother living if you didn't give it all you had? "I am always honored to assist Your Majesty in whatever small way I can."

"I have no patience with false modesty, Esmeralda," the queen snapped. "This is important. The very fate of our world hangs upon the outcome. Bonaparte must not be allowed to win again."

A serious woman, Victoria's face rarely expressed joy

unless in the company of her husband, the much-adored Prince Albert. Her love for her husband had, if possible, become more ardent over the past decade, since he had narrowly survived a brush with stomach cancer. It had been the newly invigorated science of alchemy which had saved him, causing Victoria to become passionate about scientific research as well. Today, however, neither of these happy things occupied her thoughts. A scowl replaced her usual frown. Esme pressed her lips together. "Forgive me, Your Majesty. How can I help?"

"We need you to travel to Ecuador, to an area outside of Quito." She nodded toward the figure concealed in the alcove. "We believe you remember Doctor Rafael Navarro Cabrera?" The use of the man's full name, including the matrilineal suffix of Cabrera, showed unusual respect. The amity between England and Spain grew daily, it appeared.

Esme swung to face the dark-haired Spaniard who approached. Dapper as always, he wore a charcoal gray waistcoat with pale gray stripes, and a silk, dove gray cravat. His chocolate brown eyes bored into hers, and his full lips, lips she remembered the feel of only too well, curved into a gentle, hesitant smile.

Esme felt a stab of pain. She might just as well have that metaphorical knife blade of betrayal still vibrating between her shoulder blades. She curbed the desire to spit on his shoes. "I do." She looked away, even as those warm eyes sought hers. How could she forget? They'd been partners for two years. Until he'd abandoned her.

"There is a certain object We need you to find in Ecuador. The details are in the envelope Doctor Navarro has for you. Also included is a map, recently obtained from the archives of the Vatican."

Esme desperately wanted to ask, why is *he* here? Not a

question one posed to the queen, especially as it dripped with venom.

As if reading her mind, the queen gestured to Rafael. "Doctor Navarro will also be arranging for a guide who will meet you in Quito to take you into the mountains."

"I don't need Doctor Navarro's help in that, or in any other regard, Your Majesty. I would prefer—"

The queen's frigid expression made Esme close her mouth. "He is doing Us a great favor, Esmeralda." The unspoken "don't be rude" sparked in Her Majesty's pale blue eyes.

Esme's stomach churned with bile as she forced herself to face Rafael and give him a polite nod. "Of course, Your Majesty." She turned away quickly. He attempted to communicate something to her with those liquid chocolate eyes of his, and she refused delivery of the message. "May one inquire what object Your Majesty wishes found?"

"A gruesome artefact. A mummy. Apparently, the mummy of a man named Atawala—" She made a dismissive gesture. "We simply cannot wrap Our tongue around it. Rafael?"

Rafael? Just how far had the bastard insinuated himself?

"His people called him Atahualpa, Your Majesty." The Spanish accent that had once graced his speech had virtually disappeared, making her wonder how long he'd been in England. "The last great ruler of the Inca people."

Accent aside, his voice sounded much as she remembered it, though it had been nearly five years. It brought back a flood of memories, of passionate nights, of days on the Costa del Sol soaking in the sun, soaking in each other. The scent of roses and mimosa, lavender and sweet Spanish wine. But also the taste of ashes, of standing in the freezing rain on the deck of a fast packet that would take them to the New World and a new life. Standing alone, searching the gas-lit dock for his tall, lithe form, searching the darkness for the man who had stolen her heart. For the man who never came.

She swallowed bitterness, her breathing shallow and rapid. Her face burned, and her heart pounded so loudly in her ears she hardly heard his continued response.

"There are those who believe that if his body is found, the remnants of that once proud people could use his mummy to foment a revolution. They say it emanates a supernatural power that will cause an army to be invincible."

She spoke without thinking. "Who cares if those poor natives take back a strip of rocky land along the Pacific coast that should probably be theirs anyway?"

The queen's gaze froze her again.

Rafael's gored her. "Because the Inca are not the only interested party. There are others, some of them not so far from Britain or Spain who would use that power to dominate more than just, as you say, a little strip of rocky land along the Pacific."

He didn't have to name the other interested party. Bonaparte III, Emperor of France, who controlled a bloody huge portion of Europe and always hungered for more, would love to get his hands on such a object. Not only could he annex Spain, Austria, and Britain, but he'd have the means to fulfill three generations of Bonapartes' desires to conquer Russia.

She didn't look at Rafael, couldn't get lost in those eyes. Instead, she focused on the frowning face of the queen. "There is evidence that this thing, this mummy, truly possesses this power?"

"The Vatican didn't safeguard the map without reason. The Church aside, however, there are other, shall we say, indicators that the legends of this object's power are real."

Esme marshaled her attention on the task at hand with difficulty. "So I am to retrieve this cadaver?"

"Retrieve." The queen paused. "Or destroy."

Rafael interjected. "The critical thing is that it not fall into the wrong hands."

"In other words, any hands but yours," Esme shot at him.

His lips thinned. "Ours."

How interesting. Did he speak for Spain, or did Rafael now work for Britain?

The queen made a small noise. "We have other matters to attend to. Esmeralda, please take the envelope and read its contents at home. Arrangements have been made for you to sail on a ship leaving two days hence for Panama. From there you will travel via airship to Quito. The details are in there as well as a generous allowance to cover your incidentals. Professor Burroughs, as usual, will be sending you a package of tools specific to the task at hand in tomorrow's post, including something he calls a 'containment net' in which to transport the grisly remains safely back to Us. Should you need anything else, please send your request to my Secretary, Lord Farrington." She fixed Esme with a stern look. "Fail in this, Esme, and you fail Britain."

She'd been dismissed, leaving her no choice but to rise and curtsy. "I shan't, Your Majesty. Thank you."

Without knowing how it had gotten there, she found the envelope in her hand. Backing her way to the door, as one did not turn one's back on the queen, she discovered Rafael there ahead of her. He opened the door and followed her through it with a deep bow. Once out in the corridor, with the door closed by Carl behind her, she began to stride off, but a warm hand on her arm halted her.

She spun on him, poised to slap his face. Anticipating her move, he caught her wrist before her hand could land. Damn, but he knew her well.

"What do you want?" Esme snarled.

"Esme, please. I would speak with you. I need to explain."

Fury boiled up. She forced the words out one at a time lest she explode. "You need." She echoed him. "You need? It is too late, *Doctor* Navarro. I need nothing from you, least of all your explanations."

"Esme, *por favor*, I need you to understand—"

"Oh, I understand perfectly." She yanked her hand away, saw Carl take a step from his post by the door. "I understand that you are causing a scene, Doctor. I have nothing to say to you, and you have nothing to say to me that I am interested in hearing. Good night."

He had no choice but to let her walk away. She wanted to run, God, how she wanted to run, but she stalked away instead, with dignity and fierce, flaming pride, as Cooper had taught her. Not until she reached the safety of the waiting carriage did she permit herself to sag back against the padded cushions and let out a long litany of invectives no lady of her station should know. Some women might have cried, but she'd run out of tears years ago.

Her driver, used to such language from her, paid her outburst no mind and urged the horses on to Belgravia and Harrogate House. When she'd run through the most foul words she could think to call that perfidious Spanish peacock, in all eight languages she could curse in, she squared her shoulders and turned her attention to the envelope in her lap.

She'd find this accursed mummy for the queen. And she'd do it without Rafael bloody Navarro's utterly unnecessary help.

Chapter Two

Kinzalynn, faeleath and Shadow agent for the queen of Tír na nÓg, straightened the silver embroidered cuffs of her pale green silk tunic into place, then stood tall and composed under the glare of the guards barring the doors to the seat of Fae power.

She shouldn't feel so nervous about this summons from the queen. It wasn't her first time in Her Majesty's presence. But no one else waited in the antechamber. No one waited in the hallway behind her. Every small detail swept through her thoughts. She named each dusty painting on the walls. Counted each flutter of a moth in the corner. Identified the speaker of each murmur from the servant hall. Counted the wild beating of her own heart, mixed with the faster patter of Trell's.

Trell purred at the nape of her neck where the small dragon, called a drakkeki, wrapped his long tail around her in a necklace of intricate gold scales. With his wings folded tight, he'd buried himself beneath the wide braid of her long dark red hair. His warmth and support, as well as sharp claws and teeth, came in handy on their missions. She'd been wary at first when presented with him over three decades ago, but not every Shadow was given a shape-shifting drakkeki like Trell as bond companion. His presence now calmed her. She sent him a grateful nudge through their mental link, and he tickled her ear with a flick of his serpent tongue. She sent him a poke through the bond and refused to move a muscle as he tickled her again. *Beast.*

Kinzalynn turned her thoughts back to her surroundings. Both guards wore the bright green and silver livery of Queen Airmed, confirming the king's absence, or she'd have faced one guard each for King and Queen. She'd worked very hard the past few days to learn all she could about His Majesty King Bres of House BanAnor's secretive absence, along with a dozen lords and ladies of his retinue, discovering enough to understand the importance, as well as the danger of the king going to North America. She'd been drilled in the wisdom of any faeleath in her position as Shadow, to understand the schemes and plans of the Fae around them. Surprises could be deadly.

She shifted her attention to the here and now, from one guard to the other, feeling their sharp scrutiny like an itch she could not scratch. Tension crept down her spine. She longed for her comfortable leathers, her curved draiglann blades secure in her grip. Add in a cloak to hide within as she traveled the shadows, and she was fully in her element, prepared for anything. Here, she felt defenseless with only a small blade hidden in her rarely used dress silks.

The ornate doors opened slowly without sound as Belaron, the King's Right in warm brown and gold, stepped aside and beckoned her to enter the throne room. "You are summoned, Faeleath Kinzalynn. Enter and approach the throne." The trueborn Fae sneered at her as he usually did.

She missed the Queen's Right, a gruff but affable elder Fae

woman who traveled with the king as the queen's representative. Kinzalynn kept a firm smile on her face, having had plenty of practice at control when around Belaron. She'd overheard him once explain to the king that faeleath were no better than prized humans and smelled far worse. Kinzalynn knew many courtiers thought Belaron himself employed far too much oil of juniper to mask his addiction to human tobacco. The stench reached her even now.

Kinzalynn took heart in the fact that the queen did not share in his contempt of all things human.

She bowed to him, as expected. "I am summoned."

Loose tunic and pants flowing and flapping around her legs, Kinzy set out toward the throne with Belaron a step behind. His loyalty tied him to his king first, the kingdom second, himself third, and the queen somewhere below that. He hated faeleath, and would stab her in the back, by blade or deed, at the slightest nod from the queen.

Belaron knew full-well Kinzy's own vows tied her to the queen only. If the queen ordered her death today, she would accept it. When Master Shabao took Kinzalynn for warrior training on her Day of Choosing, she took vows wrapped in magic to serve only the Lady of House Flaeryn, Her Royal Majesty Queen Airmed.

The magic of Tír na nÓg may have chosen Airmed and Bres for the throne, but theirs was not a traditional marriage, more a melding of two circles of power into a whole that supported the realm. Few Fae marriages had held up since The Breaking banned the Fae from Earth. Since then, Fae could no longer procreate and discovered they could only create children in Tír na nÓg through pairing with a human. Marriage made way for a human concubine if a Fae desired progeny. They openly claimed their children if they possessed the ability to touch their magic, making them trueborn Fae, but faeleath offspring, who had no ability to use magic though born with the core of magic within, were relegated to be raised in *creis* and chosen by a trade or position within a House. Any poor babe born without a core of magic simply joined the House's human slaves, servants, and concubines.

Those close to the thrones knew the ceremonial joining of King Bres and Queen Airmed had nothing to do with love or children, and everything to do with magic and power. When both were present, they ruled together. With the king away, the queen held the power of the throne. Kinzalynn guessed the queen had an important new blossoming scheme that needed the help of a queen's Shadow, but was it for the House, or for the throne?

The possibility existed that today Her Majesty had something dire in mind for Kinzy, and perhaps she'd nod to Belaron, and Kinzy would cease to be. Her stomach clenched in fear, but with a deep inhale and slow controlled breath she moved forward into the cavernous room. No courtiers stood in attendance. Other than the queen, Belaron, two guards behind the throne, and herself, the ornate room stood empty.

She walked down the promenade, lined on either side with vine-covered stone pillars shaped as trees that grew majestically from the floor, their tops lost in the dark ceiling above where stars twinkled and shimmered. Kinzalynn longed to touch the carved bark of a pillar, remembering how real, how alive it felt. Yet, for all the beauty of magical stone, today the throne room felt bathed in quiet loneliness. She hoped that came from the king's absence affecting the realm.

No current plots involved Kinzy in any way, at least at this time, and she wondered why the queen had summoned her in this hasty manner to a private audience. She'd never been brought before the throne like this before.

Kinzy's duties through the decades had led her to steal,

arrange trade, provide information, and yes, even kill. As long as she was dutiful to her queen, she would be a leaf on the tree of whatever Queen Airmed plotted and planned. While the Fae could not normally leave Tír na nÓg–and rumors reported that the king's journey had taken the realm's top master mages to accomplish–faeleath could travel in the human realm on behalf of their Fae

Houses.

Kinzalynn served her small part as the Fae played their dangerous games of houses and power, trapped in this land of magic and perpetual light, but she worried at the plans in motion now. Any weakness seen by the Fae would bite her in the future, so she kept her nervousness deeply buried. Her mind still ran in circles, though, trying to pluck at clues and work out what was coming.

The guards on either side of Her Majesty had firm grips on their halberds, and their chest armor shone with the intricate silver work of the queen's seal. They glowered at her as she knelt, head bowed before the queen.

"Rise, Faeleath Kinzalynn." Queen Airmed's soft voice echoed through the huge stone hall. "Be at ease, child. I'll not kill you today. You may rise."

Kinzalynn kept her face carefully neutral as she remembered the day she'd been brought before the queen as an exhausted teenager covered in bruises and sword cuts. Queen Airmed announced that the young faeleath would not be killed for her insolence to a trueborn, and Kinzy had fainted away right there in front of the throne. The queen never let her forget that inauspicious moment, though Kinzy had proven herself again and again since then.

"Your choice, My Queen. I work better when I'm alive."

The queen laughed, the movement rustling her blue velvet dress as dark as the midnight sky on the ceiling above them. A silver and sapphire crown sat amid the carefully tumbled mass of pale blonde curls that framed her porcelain face. The slim fingers of her hand rested for a moment on the necklace at her throat, a large sapphire surrounded by white diamonds bound by intricate silver filigree.

"Since you are not fainting today, I have for you a mission of importance to the throne."

"I am your servant."

"Do not speak of this to anyone. Not even Master Shabao. No one is to know, beyond those present. Do you understand?"

"Yes, my queen." Kinzalynn could not help being intrigued at the request to keep a secret from her own mentor, the queen's Master of Shadows. He kept the queen well informed of everything going on within the court and the realm. Shadows like Kinzy passed their information to him, and he to the queen's ear. Flattered to have direct access to the queen on her own merit, caution made her wary at the implications of keeping information from Shabao, her own Master.

"You will travel by human means to Ecuador, a colony of the Spanish in the South American region, and seek the desiccated remains of Atahualpa, last leader of the Inca Empire. He will be found, still guarded, within the Andes Mountains inside a secret tomb. There is a power that lies within him that has come to my attention. Naturally, other Houses opposed to the throne desire such power, or want it for their allies. It is reputed to make an army invincible. I have decided that no House or human government should hold such a thing in their keeping. You will prevent anyone from obtaining this power and bring it directly back to me. If not possible, you will destroy it by any means necessary so that no one can claim it."

"Do you know which Houses may actively oppose my mission?" If others knew of such power, they'd certainly have their own agents on the trail.

"House DonClannagh. They have been known to work with the French government, where others of our Shadows have learned of this power and its importance. The Court has been told I am sending you to finalize a trade deal for certain exotic fruits of this distant region. Has your drakkeki ever tested its ability to portal from so far away?"

"Trell came to me already well-experienced and trained, Your Majesty. I do not know how he feels about the distance, but I will surely use him to send messages to you along the way."

"I trust that if it becomes too much for him, he shall find his way to me somehow and let me know of his distress. See that he does, this moment, understand his duties."

Kinzy nudged Trell to come out. She stroked his golden head between his small horns and down along his neck ridge. He gave a rumbling purr and settled on her forearm, his focus on her. She looked deep into his amber, cat-slitted eyes and slipped along the life bond between them. Drakkeki lived a very, very long time, and she was honored to be his third bonding.

He sent her the distinct feeling of impatience. *This meeting has already gone on too long. I am hungry.*

You understand the distances? You will port to the queen and no one else. Secrecy is primary.

He bowed his elongated head and sent back his assurance that he understood. Trell then turned to the queen and bowed to her as well. A tiny creature as polite as any courtier. Many dismissed their intelligence, but she knew Trell was much more than a useful pet. He preened smugly.

"Trell should also be able to assist you in locating your objective although once close enough, your own senses should show you the way."

Kinzalynn could feel the magic running through her, a

conduit of power that allowed her to sense magic energies, though she could not use magic, not like the Fae and those true-born. This is what made her faeleath, having the magic within, yet forever cut off from using it.

Trell snuck back behind Kinzy's neck as Queen Airmed dismissed him with a flick of her fingers. Her Majesty gestured to Belaron. He handed Kinzy a plain leather satchel. She bowed to Belaron as she received it. He didn't bother acknowledging her, but quickly turned away to stand again beside the queen, radiating his disapproval.

"Inside are the papers to complete the trade agreements in Panama, as well as funds for your use. Fare thee well, Faeleath Kinzalynn. Be safe and quick about this."

"I shall, Your Highness." Kinzy bowed lower than she had to Belaron and backed away from the throne as the doors once again opened. She turned after the required ten steps back, and quickly strode out of the throne room with her satchel and strange mission.

Kinzalynn walked with a measured step down the hall, her smile hidden from the guards. Once again, she had brought a blade to the throne room despite the laws. It was one of Master Shabao's rules, to never be without defense. Another of his rules suddenly came to mind: *a smug faeleath was a dead faeleath.*

Trell hissed in her ear, catching her worry.

"I'll be fine, my friend. A grand adventure to a new place that few, if any, of the Fae have seen. I heard it is warm in South America. You will like it, I think," she whispered. He rubbed his snout against her jaw in response. They could handle this mission together, face anything that blocked their way. They would not disappoint the queen.

Chapter Three

Esme stormed through the front door of Harrogate House at a quarter of midnight, startling the dozy footman, a young man named Bart who minded the door late at night. Cooper, her housekeeper, waited for her in the vestibule, her recently detached head held in the crook of one shiny bronze arm. She wore a starched white apron over her high-necked dress, pristine despite the overpowering smell of clockwork oil. Hieronymous, Professor Burroughs to most, must have been here, working on the reattachment. The fact that the automaton still carried her head about, sans her usual wig, meant that the inventor still had not been successful in whatever improvement he'd attempted this time.

To some, finding a headless housekeeper might have been an alarming sight. For Esme, it had become a not infrequent occurrence. Unfazed, she removed the pins from her hat and set it on the marble-topped mahogany table where the mail sat on its silver salver.

"So still no success with the new neck coupling?" She flipped through the calling cards on the tray and the two or three letters that had arrived while she'd been out, but none were important.

Cooper grumbled. "Not yet. I asked him, quite politely mind you, to just put the old one back on, but you know how he is. It isn't my place to tell Himself what to do."

Esme patted the automaton on the arm. "I'm sorry, Cooper. It's my understanding that he can't do that, or I'd have had him do it before now." The most disconcerting part wasn't that Cooper's eyes were on the level of Esme's ample bosom, but that Cooper didn't have on her auburn wig, and her shiny, metal pate stood in stark contrast to her very human dark blue frock. "Why don't you ever wear red, Cooper?"

"I beg your pardon, Miss?"

"I said," Esme replied as she divested herself of her overcoat and gloves, which were whisked away by young Bart, "Why don't you ever wear red? Or green?"

"Red and green are not suitable colors for a housekeeper."

"Nonsense. With that lovely auburn hair, you'd look fabulous in green. Or even purple."

"Purple is for royalty. Besides, I quite like dark blue."

Esme retrieved from the hall table the envelope she'd received from the queen and stalked into the parlor. "I need a whisky. Then we've got packing to do."

Cooper followed her. "I've already had Bart bring your trunk down from the attic and I've laid out a number of traveling suits, but as I wasn't sure of the destination, I didn't know whether to pack the heavy wool or something lighter."

"Cooper, you are a marvel." Esme poured a splash of whisky from the decanter into a cut crystal glass. "I'm going to Ecuador, so no need for fancy dress, just my trousers and my two expedition hats."

Cooper sighed, the sounds of her bellows-like lungs, making an exasperated wheezing sound. "You will need evening wear for shipboard dinners, and several decent day dresses for the voyage. You are the wife of an earl, no matter you're wife in name only. You have appearances to keep up."

"Dear old Cooper. Always looking out for my reputation." She flung herself down on the velvet fainting couch and held the envelope in her lap in her free hand. "You know I adore him. Our arrangement works for both of us. As for clothes, you can just—" She looked over at Cooper, standing there with her head in the crook of her arm and a disapproving look in her green eyes.

How could she take Cooper with her to Ecuador and hike who knew how many miles into the backcountry with the automaton carrying her head? Her stomach gave a little flip. She'd never been on one of her expeditions without Cooper. The automaton stood like a rock at the center of her world. She'd been with her since infancy, first as her nanny, then as her governess, and lately as her housekeeper and ladies' companion. She relied on Cooper.

"What is the weather like in Ecuador, my lady? Should I bring my parasol?"

The envelope in her lap suddenly felt heavy and burdensome. "Cooper, I think perhaps this is one trip on which you should not accompany me."

Cooper pulled herself up, impossibly stiffening her steel spine even further. "Why would that be, my lady?"

Esme considered Cooper's head. "It will be heavy hiking, Cooper. In the mountains. You'll be rather at a disadvantage given your current, er, affliction. If you were to stumble, you'd fall to your death."

"I have always accompanied you. Who else is going to keep you from doing something foolish and dangerous?"

Esme set the envelope on the couch and crossed to Cooper, laid her hands gently on her beloved automaton's arms. "You hate travel, you always have, and Ecuador is not a place for polite ladies. It's a wild country, full of rough people with strange customs and even stranger food. They eat rodents, you know. Furry and adorable little creatures with short tails, but they're rodents nonetheless."

Cooper gave a shudder but continued on bravely. "I'm perfectly capable of taking care of you. I can carry my head in a net bag hung from a belt. Being thus afflicted hasn't stopped me from doing my duties around here, now has it? I've supervised the kitchen staff, seen to the provisioning and the marketing—"

"You better not have gone out in this rain! You'll get water in your fittings!"

Cooper didn't quite meet her eyes. "I am perfectly capable of managing all aspects of this household, Esmeralda Elizabeth Huddlestone Eggerton, with or without injury."

Oh, a direct hit! Her former nanny had used every one of her names. Esme tried a conciliatory tone to diffuse some of the hurt and anger. "Of course, you are, Cooper. But even I wouldn't go on a quest for a decaying, mummified Inca Emperor in the heart of the Andes Mountains without my head attached. It would be suicidal." She paused, realizing her statement sounded more nonsensical aloud than it had in her head.

Cooper steamrolled over her, understanding the intent if not the actual words. "The devil you wouldn't! More importantly, Esme, you cannot traipse around the world on your own, unaccompanied. The scandal—"

Esme shook her head, tried to get them back on track. "Cooper, give me a little credit. I am sometimes foolish, but I am not stupid. I would not dream of traipsing around the Andes with a serious injury."

She felt a frisson, a sudden chill, and a voice whispered in her ear. "You would." The hair on her arms stood up and her scalp rippled. She shivered at the sound of her mother's voice. As a child, she'd been told that her mother's frequent ghostly presence represented nothing more than grief and an overindulged temperament. After the events in Turkey, where her mother's frigid, translucent apparition physically shoved her out of the way of an oncoming bullet so that it only passed through her shoulder instead of her heart, Esme could no longer deny the spirit existed outside her fevered dreams and childish hopes. She also knew that discussing it with anyone would likely lead to one of the current barbaric treatments for female hysteria – to wit, having her female organs surgically removed.

At the spirit's sarcasm, her lips quirked up.

Cooper tipped her nose in the air. "Well. If you're bent on relegating me to the scrap heap, like a rusted, worn out pile of cogs, then who *will* go with you?" She scowled her displeasure and Esme felt like a recalcitrant toddler again.

"My dearest Cooper, you are not being relegated to anything. I depend upon you. If anything happened to you, I would be utterly bereft. You're irreplaceable."

"Hmph. You didn't answer the question, young lady."

Esme rewound the conversation in her head. "You mean, who will I take with me?" Oh, how she dearly wanted to say nobody. But that wouldn't do. "I, uh, I suppose I could take..." She scrambled through a list of potential companions and came up blank. She had few genuine friends, and even fewer of her own sex. The two she thought capable of giving up conveniences and roughing it through the journey were unavailable. Constance and her husband had taken off for Greece on holiday, and Lillibet was in confinement with her second child. All the other females of her acquaintance were fluff-headed annoyances.

"When do you leave?"

Esme could literally hear wheels turn in Cooper's head. "Thursday."

"Thursday next?"

"No, day after tomorrow."

"Good heavens! How am I supposed to—" Cooper stopped. "Never you mind. I'll handle it. Just like I always do."

"Thank you, Cooper. I would be lost without you."

"You would indeed." The features of Cooper face, made of a remarkably malleable material, relaxed a bit. "An Inca mummy, you say? What on earth would Her Majesty want with a disgusting piece of corruption like that?"

"It's supposed to be capable of making an army invincible." Esme breathed a sigh of relief as she sensed she had at least won this round.

"Stuff and nonsense."

Esme shrugged. "Nevertheless, that's the assignment." She considered what she might need on this trip, other than the corsets and petticoats and evening dresses she knew she could not stop Cooper from packing. "I'll need my vest with the knives, both pistols and assorted rounds of ammunition, my trusty Derringer, oh, and that pearl necklace that Hieronymous made for me for the South Africa expedition."

"The one that exploded when you threw it in the fire as we ran away from those treasure hunters?"

"Ah. I had forgotten we used that. Still, it did its job, exploding. The beads contained nitroglycerin." She sighed. "I don't imagine there's a way to have him quickly make another one."

"I doubt it." Cooper scoffed. "Ecuador. You are a young woman of substance. I do not understand what Her Majesty is thinking, sending you off on these affairs."

Esme gave a shrug, inwardly grinning. "We all must serve as we are able, and one cannot turn down a direct request from the queen." She tossed back the drink although it failed to wash away the taste of ashes and bitterness that seeing Rafael had left in her mouth. As Cooper's frown deepened, Esme got up and poured herself another.

"As if you would." The automaton paused. "What is it you're not telling me?"

Esme turned her back on Cooper, went to pick up the envelope. She imagined she could smell him on it, his distinctive cologne. She stared at the writing, wondering if he had penned the several sheets of information that had been included. She could still see clearly in her mind's eye the few words he'd written on the note he'd left with the night porter at the hotel, the night he left her standing there on that damned ship like a young, lovestruck fool. 'I'm sorry.'

Still facing away from Cooper, Esme replied, "Nothing."

Cooper's hand came to rest on her left shoulder. "Child, don't lie to me. I know when something is troubling you."

The anger burned off and tears stung her eyes. No, damn it, she would not cry, not for him. Not again. Her shoulders shook, her body betraying her.

Cooper gathered her in, turning her into her shoulder. "There now, luv, what's caused all this? Come and tell me about it."

Esme let herself be led like a child to the settee. Cooper sat, placed her head carefully on her neck then pressed a handkerchief into Esme's hands. Esme took in a shuddering breath and, imagining stabbing Rafael in the kidney, managed to bring herself back under control. Dabbing at her eyes, she sniffed, straightened. "I'm being foolish is all. I saw someone tonight, and I let him get under my skin again, but I'm fine now."

"Saw who? That devil of an uncle of yours or that pederast he tried to force you to marry?"

Thank God for Cooper, the one person in her life she knew

she could count on. "No, not them." The drinks tray called to her, but she knew another glass of whisky would make her maudlin.

"Then who?"

She breathed the name she'd sworn never to speak again. "Rafael."

"Ah." Cooper didn't speak for a moment and when she did her voice took on a hard edge. "What did he say to you after all these years?"

Esme folded the now damp handkerchief into succeedingly smaller triangles. "I didn't let him say anything. There is nothing for him *to* say. God willing, I won't ever see him again."

Something flickered in Cooper's eyes, something neither hard, nor cold, nor angry. "What should I tell the staff if he comes to the door?"

"Tell them they may grab him by the collar and belt and toss him to the curb into the nearest pile of horse dung."

She thought that might make Cooper laugh but her mechanical confidante still had that sad look in her eyes. "As you wish, my lady." She stood then, tucked her head back under her arm and smoothed her starched apron. "I should tell you that your *friend*, Piotr, had to leave some while ago."

Esme felt a warmth spread through her middle. They'd been having such a lovely evening, her and the count. "That's a shame. She hadn't quite got him to the point of revealing what she'd been asked to find out about the Russian. "Then I guess I'll just have a late supper in the kitchen before retiring."

"It's late for a meal, Esme. You'll have indigestion."

"I'll be fine. You go on up. I'll retire shortly."

Whatever you could say about Cooper always being in her business, the automaton knew her place and, more importantly, when she'd been dismissed. "Very well, my lady. I'll bring your tea at eight a.m., as usual. We'll have a busy day tomorrow, making the necessary arrangements for your departure."

"Yours too, Cooper. You'll go and stay at Harrogate Hall while I'm abroad. Hieronymous can come work on you there."

"Harrogate Hall! Way out in Yorkshire? I am perfectly—"

She cut off Cooper's objections or they'd still be discussing this at bedtime. "Yes, you are, but I would sleep much more soundly if I knew you were where you could be looked after. Just in case there is any trouble with your head."

Cooper huffed.

"Besides. Egg will appreciate the company." She paused, gauged her automaton's sour look. "That's an order, Cooper."

Her former governess's green eyes flashed, but she kept her lips pressed shut.

Esme grinned and then bussed Cooper's cheek as she went past. "Sweet dreams, Cooper."

If Cooper had a rejoinder, Esme didn't hear it as she exited the parlor on her way to the kitchen to see what she could scrounge from the larder to replace the romantic supper she had missed.

Chapter Four

"Don't bother telling me your lies, Faeleath Kinzalynn." The familiar gruff voice barked.

She paused as she passed by the arched entry of the large training hall in the Queen's Wing on her way to her room. Master Shabao, Master of Shadows to Her Majesty, scowled at her from the center eye of the sparring circle, his well-muscled tanned arms crossed over his dark leather vest. He'd gathered his mass of long black braids at the back of his head with an ornate silk band of deep green and gold. Kinzy did not miss the more extensive streaks of gray in his glossy hair and beard today.

She altered course to stand at attention before him. "I did not faint before the queen, Master."

Shabao's green eyes sparkled with amusement as he looked her up and down, lingering on her left boot. "You did not stab anyone either."

"*Never be without a weapon.* I continue to learn the value of your lesson every 50 years or so."

"You are overdue. The last time was 80 years ago at the

Albion Mills fire. A good day for retribution upon the lying human industrialist scum that sold us iron-tainted flour and sickened so many. On Blackfriar Bridge, wasn't it? You dropped your knife in the river during the scuffle and Trell had to bring you another."

"I was so angry, I made the opposing agent drop his knife in the river, too. He did not heed one of your other rules. *Always have another option.*"

Shabao leaned forward, glaring. "Remember that this mission. This is important."

A prophetic twinge accompanied her solemn nod. Extras would be a good idea, going so far from home.

"There's a travel trunk in your room, as well as items that may help you. Inside that satchel from Belaron you will find your ticket for the human ship from London to Panama. Do not fail in this mission. We need more regular shipments of banana, mango, tobacco, and the cacao." His eyes narrowed. "And do not underestimate age-old corpses."

"Belaron *is* looking like a corpse. He must have had quite a party recently. I promise not to underestimate him." Despite the queen's insistence that no one know of Kinzy's mission, Master Shabao certainly hinted at more than he should. She wouldn't play this game and confirm anything for him, he'd only scold her for revealing too much. Her orders had been clear. "I'll bring back a nice bunch of bananas for you."

Shabao uncrossed his arms as he laughed. "Good, do not let slip any secrets."

She put an edge in her voice, "You test me like a novice." In truth, she would always feel like a student around the elder faeleath. He'd been Shadow Master for over a thousand years and he would always have something more to teach her, but his constant nudges grated on her today.

He simply took off with a brisk stride back out the archway.

Kinzy raced to keep pace as they headed toward her room. Shabao held back as they neared her door, and she stepped forward to unlock it. How polite of her Master to unlock her door and lock it again. Still, she made a quick search of her room to make sure there was no danger. Trell scampered down her arm and onto the top of her desk as she tossed the satchel next to the pile of things to pack that lay on her bed. Her Master had done it neatly, at least.

Shabao grabbed the only chair and sat in the corner, watching her sort through what he'd gathered. He'd included a number of divided walking skirts and dresses, two sets of leathers, and her largest backpack. Though she saw many warm weather items, she found a heavier coat and cold-weather gear at the bottom of the pile. Exactly what she would have chosen herself for the Andes.

"Stick to the shadows as you've been taught." Shabao wagged a finger at her. "Bite deep when challenged. Be a pleasant mouse of a human when you must."

"In this?" She held up the deep green velvet gown he'd laid beside the more every day human traveling skirts and coats. The heart-shaped neckline and short puffy sleeves tapered to a simple pointed bodice and modestly full ruffled skirt. "This is hardly the gown of a mouse."

"You will travel first class aboard ship on a long voyage. You will need to present yourself well at dinners and other occasions. *Being prepared and flexible—*"

"*—can save your life and your mission,*" Kinzy finished. "I would never question adding a few gowns, but why this one?"

"You look lovely in it, and green is my favorite color. What would you have chosen?"

"Possibly the light blue dress, with the lace collar. Though it's harder to keep clean, it's a more current fashion."

"The pale blue will show sweat marks if things get athletic."

"Agreed." She carefully folded up the green dress and slid it into the travel trunk beside the bed, "Is there another reason you're here, Master? I am capable of packing my own things for this trip."

The chair creaked behind her, and Shabao spoke so quietly she almost didn't hear. "When you return, I'm naming you a Master."

She turned to find him right behind her, always fast and silent in his ways.

"Hold out your right hand."

Holding out her hand to him, he slipped his Master's ring on her index finger. The bright silver filigree and symbols encircled her finger perfectly.

"The ring's magic shapes itself to the wearer. When you find a worthy successor one day, you will pass it on to them, just as Master Merlin did for me, Master Kinzalynn."

Shock grabbed her hard, but she shoved it down deep beneath her outer shell. She wasn't ready to be a Master. She should be decades away. His youth gone, Shabao still had the strength and cunning of the best of the faeleath. She wondered if he would be stepping down, though she could not imagine such a thing. A faeleath in the autumn of his prime, he kept his students on their toes for all of the *athletics* he put them through.

"Master of my chambers? Master of poached eggs? Ah, Master of the Green Gown." She tossed the comments at him as she studied the ring's silver runes.

He didn't rise to the bait. "I may be sent to assist the king. The decision is not yet confirmed. My successor should be clear before I leave."

"Jolen has been your student years longer. He will object."

"Jolen has no subtlety for the human shadows as you do. He hates all humans. You do not. He will never play among the Houses as a Master Shadow. You are the best and will be named my successor as Master of Shadows."

She bowed to him. "I am honored, Master. Do others know?"

"I told the queen when she asked me the question of who to send on a very important mission."

Kinzalynn turned back to pack her extra blades, various additional cases holding instruments, herbs, and gear. If the queen knew, then so did the King's Right, and the Queen's Guard. That might account for the sharpness of their gaze during her audience.

"Trell," Shabao held out his arm and her reptilian friend quickly leaped over to him. "You must travel in the human world, so please choose an aspect that is both cunning and appropriate enough to fool the humans."

Trell tilted his head and ruffled his golden leathery wings, one eye on her and one eye on Shabao. Suddenly a brown speckled mongoose sat on Shabao's arm. The beast sprang to the bed and dug himself into the satchel. A few items were kicked out by furry paws as Trell buried his nose in the very bottom.

"Trell, stop that!" she scolded, even as Shabao gave a grunt of amusement.

Hunting treats, Trell spoke with a distracted voice in her mind. Behind his words, Kinzy felt a giddy and playful wash of complex emotions from him.

She swept up the tickets and wallet, tucking them back inside the satchel, and dragged the mongoose out onto the bed. As soon as she released him, he raced to another small bag and wrapped himself around it playfully.

She gave up herding her small companion and changed

from court silks to a rather drab brown traveling skirt, tunic, and matching embroidered jacket. Her relief escaped in a pleased sigh when she could finally don her good sturdy Fae leather boots. She'd give up many things, but Fae boots hugged her feet in comfort like nothing else could. Partly magic and partly fine workmanship, no one made boots like the Fae. She usually skipped human shoe fashion on assignments. She quickly put her hair up in a simple bun and added a nice deep brown hat with lovely feathers and ribbon. Shabao grabbed the worn, but upper-class traveling cloak on the hook by the door and held it out for her.

"Do I look the part of a human woman of middling to upper means, ready to make trade deals and feed her incorrigible pet mongoose?"

Shabao laughed and gave a nod of approval. "Trell shall guard your satchel of mongoose treats with his life, brave and wise drakkeki that he is. There are a variety of useful British coins, along with a few Spanish *reales* and *escudo*s to provide your monster with nibbles."

Trell settled once again behind her neck, wrapping his long brown furry tail around her throat. When she checked in the mirror, he looked almost like a fur collar.

"Be careful, Kinzalynn." She could see the concern on her Master's face as she glanced back at him in the mirror. "The French Emperor has sent his agents hunting, and House DonCladdagh supports them. The Bonaparte family is struck with illness, and a man preserving his family, or defending the family of his sovereign, has little to lose. They will walk across your dead body if need be, then let House DonCladdagh stomp you into dust."

"DonCladdagh has truly allied with the French?"

"Napoleon's grandson is a man who is being led down a

more dangerous path than his grandfather. You know the shadows well. Safe hunting and safe return, by the Light."

"The King's Right seems to have little trust that I can complete this mission."

"Belaron cannot think past his powdered nose and dueling blade. But he is completely loyal to the throne in the end."

She turned back to him, swinging the satchel over her shoulder. "Anything from the shadows regarding the king's project?"

"There is not, which worries some amid the Houses, but not the queen. This was part of the plan, to be without word for a time. You will be well south of them, they will not interfere, nor can they help."

"What must it be like to be so far away from Tír na nÓg in the human world? The stretching of the link must be so painful to the Fae in the expedition, even with the magical assistance of a great stone."

"The Fae can be comfortable enough, even halfway around the world, with the quantity of great spells laid in preparation by the king and his clan. Have no fear, we faeleath do not suffer any difficulty being so distant from our home realm."

"I have no fear of that for myself but wondered at what the expedition must be dealing with. May the expedition be blessed in the Light as they do their duty for the king."

"We will step forward into the Light of the true sun and rejoice with our king someday. For now, we have not yet been officially told anything of the king's expedition. Know when to ask your questions and when to remain silent." His countenance changed from serious scolding to lackadaisical lecturing. "No slicing off the fingers from the roving hands of human men of rank."

Kinzy grimaced. "That was over 100 years ago, Master. My

first solo mission. I didn't understand humans well enough then and expected a mayor to be more polite to his trade partners."

"An educational experience for you, so I kept my mouth shut and let you handle your first trade deal with the humans, just as the queen ordered. She has not always been pleased with your resolution of some assignments. On this mission, do exactly as the queen commands, or face her terrible temper. She can destroy you with an angry flick of her hand." Shabao held her shoulders to face him. "I have trained you well in the Way of Shadows. Our queen and our very House depend on you right now. Keep your focus there. What happens to the king and his project is none of your concern yet."

"I won't faint on you either, Shabao."

"Good! Now let's get you to London."

He summoned two human servants to carry her trunk to the wagon in the courtyard, then they rode through the living forest, Kinzalynn breathing in the magical air and feeling the connection of the trees to the ground and the dawn sky still dark enough for the brightest stars to be visible. They soon reached the standing great stone at the very center of the realm.

This single tall stone rooted the only gateway into Tír na nÓg, but the Fae had spelled standing great stones in a network across the British Isles, and even some on the continent. It took special casters and a lot of magic to create the link, and the further away, the more magic that creation took. The king's absence involved just such an endeavor, one of the human servants had told her after a suitably large bribe. The servant would be punished soon and sent to the stables for revealing what he should not. King Bres indeed sought to build the first gateway stone link to North America. She had already discreetly investigated when she noticed the sudden disappearance of many prominent Fae most loyal to the king. Master Shabao and the queen herself expected Kinzy to find out on her own and keep it to herself. The queen's mind often worked that way, so Kinzy kept abreast of all plans and personages around her at the Fae Court. That was a Shadow's duty.

She led the way into the central glade of Tír na nÓg, a beautiful circle of blooming white roses surrounding a clear swarth of green grass. Kinzy breathed deeply of the rose-scented air and caught the faint whiff of old stone magic emanating from the 10-foot-high sarcen stone in the center. The Heart of Tír na nÓg. The Keeper of the Stone abruptly appeared out of nowhere in front of her, as he always did. Kinzy bowed to the keeper, a very old familiar Fae. The intricately embroidered flowers on his pale cream robes swept the grass as he stepped forward.

The old man regarded them with a friendly gaze and smile beneath his white shaggy eyebrows. "I have prepared the way to the London townhouse, Faeleath Kinzalynn. Do you cross as well, Master Shabao?"

"I am simply here to ensure she does not forget my teachings, Keeper Visanye." Shabao bowed low, almost as low for the keeper as he would for the throne.

Of all the Fae she dealt with, only Keeper Visanye never had a condescending word, never a cruel comment. He was always the last she saw of Tír na nÓg when she left on assignment, and always the first to welcome her home. He seemed to know some secrets, though she never determined how. There were no shadows around the Keeper of the Stone.

"Your student knows her shadows and her light, Master Shabao. Let the young bird fly. May the Light keep you safe on your travels, Faeleath Kinzalynn."

"May the Light keep you safe while I am away, Keeper

Visanye." She turned to Master Shabao with another deep bow. "I promise to remember your teachings, Master. May the shadows hold you safe between the Light and the Dark."

Her master chuckled. "So somber, little bird. Keeper, perhaps the magic can change her humor as well as her location?"

"If it cannot change yours, it will not change hers." The Fae smiled amid his white beard and mustache. "Time to go. Touch the stone and the trunk to go with you."

Kinzy laid her hand on the travel chest, felt Trell's claws dig into the back of her neck and shoulder, and closed her eyes as she lay her hand flat on the gray, crystal speckled stone. After a flash of bright light, she felt the cooler breath of wind, *real wind*, on her face. Opening her eyes, she found herself and Trell in front of a standing stone in the middle of a large, well-tended English garden of roses and lilacs. An older gentleman in an impeccable black morning coat stood nearby and snapped his fingers at two lads next to him. They immediately grabbed Kinzy's trunk and hurried out of the garden.

"my lady, your carriage awaits out front. The human driver has orders to take you to the docks and see you and your luggage settled."

"Thank you, Master Kip, I appreciate the assistance. Is all well here? Your weather has certainly turned cold." Kip, a faeleath who lived mostly in the human world, had this London townhouse to manage, as well as all communications and the necessities of the traffic through this stone. She had been assigned to him as household staff as a young girl first learning the ways of the human world.

"The autumn air nips in the mornings and evenings, but nothing terrible yet. You remember how cold it will get in the winter months."

"I miss the wind and breezes here, no matter how cold, Master Kip." She smiled as he raised her hand to kiss.

Trell kneaded her neck for attention. She ignored the predictable beast. He just wanted the treats that Master Kip kept in his coat pocket. They used this stone often.

Master Kip led her through the garden, the house, and out the front door. He assisted her into the carriage, and then held out a small treat. Trell snatched it from Master Kip's fingers with a small chirp of relief, as if he thought he might have been forgotten. Kinzy felt his warm fur cradle her neck as he happily chewed the small bit of jerky. The carriage door closed, and they were soon on their way down the busy streets of London.

Despite the importance of her mission, she felt her heart lighten at being in the human world, feeling the true sunlight, as well as the smells, even the odors of the poorer neighborhoods of London they drove through. All around her were the scents of life and living, nothing like the light sweet scent that permeated all of Tír na nÓg. The intensity and variety of London thrilled her in a way nothing else could.

As she walked up the ramp and onto the ship, the sea breeze played with the folds of her cloak and kissed her cheeks with a breath of cheerful energy. Humans did not appreciate this kind of natural magic enough.

Trell nibbled her ear in disapproval. *The port smells of too many dead fish and waste water.* He sent her a flash of a wrinkled nose and the intense need for flowers. *Good fish-hunting out on the ocean though.*

"All you think about is your stomach," Kinzy softly muttered, scratching under his chin. Trell chittered and resettled his tail around her neck.

Kinzy always did enjoy traveling by ship. She felt truly free on the ocean, though she preferred a schooner or something with sails as opposed to the steamship she was on. She would still enjoy the journey to Panama. From there, recalling her geography, she would need to find an airship to cross from Panama into Peru and Ecuador. Most importantly, here in the human world, she would need a cover story suitable for a young lady traveling alone. That, she sighed, would take some thought.

Chapter Five

Esme dragged herself into the airless, enclosed space of her cabin aboard the Spanish airship *Doña Isabella*, unpinned her hat, and flung it into the corner before flopping down onto the narrow bed. She wanted more than anything to strip down, unfasten her corset and pour the contents of the washbowl over her head, but it would have taken far too long to resume the accursed garment when she'd be required to go to the saloon for tea.

Another point of irritation had been the companion Cooper arranged for her, a second cousin on her father's side, Cecily Houghton-Smythe. She had *not* worked out. The first week aboard the *HMS Oceanic*, Cecily'd been confined to their cabin with seasickness. The second week, she'd contracted a catarrh and moped around after Esme in sniffling misery. The third and final week, Cecily managed to perk up, but no matter how Esme tried to teach her, the girl remained completely unable to learn the rudiments of either chess or Senet or Parcheesi, Each night, after she thought Esme had fallen asleep, she sobbed into her pillow from homesickness. By the time they'd arrived in Panama City, Esme had arranged with ship's staff to find Cecily a companion of her own, an elderly governess on her way back to England, and paid for her return trip. Cooper would be unhappy, but Esme had penned a letter to the automaton, explaining that Cecily had tried her best but that not everyone could withstand the privations of international travel. She'd also written that she would find someone else to be her escort when they arrived in Panama, although she had no intention of doing anything of the sort.

Cooper would know it for a lie, but there wasn't much the automaton could do about it now. The only drawback was the damn corset and she had determined that after the formal first evening's dinner aboard the airship, she would just do without the bloody thing, and let tongues wag as they would.

Her trunks had been brought aboard earlier, but unlike a luxury liner where the stewards unpacked for you, and since she now had neither maid nor companion, she had to unpack at least a few of her belongings herself, a task she would not ordinarily have minded performing but for the stifling heat.

Well, at least she could remove a few layers while she unpacked. Having purposely brought dresses that she could do-up herself in a pinch, some of which she'd had designed specially to fasten up the front, to the chagrin of her dressmaker, she stripped off her dress, her much-hated bustle, and two petticoats, leaving her in her corset and bloomers. She even took off her stockings, which were soaked with sweat anyway, then set about hanging up two formal dresses in the wardrobe, placing her bandolier of throwing knives and a box of ammo for her pistol into the top bureau drawer, over which she arranged a spare corset, some small clothes and her lace trimmed stockings. She also placed the containment net there, a six foot by six foot swath of shimmering gossamer netting folded up into a square the size of a man's handkerchief, inserted into a clear stiff envelope. The net looked like you could shred it with a thought, but Hieronymous's note assured her that it could withstand the blow of a machete. He also cautioned her against opening the envelope until needed, a piece of advice she would heed. Hieronymous's inventions sometimes came with unintended consequences.

She fastened her pistol holster to her left thigh then strapped the Vatican's map, in a silver, waterproof tube, to her right. Both would be nicely concealed under the bulky and insufferable bustle and petticoats society forced her to wear. Finally, she fastened the filigree Egyptian-style bracelet to her wrist that Hieronymous had sent her. About an inch and a half wide at the broadest point, fine bronze chains connected it to a ring on her middle finger. A large piece of lapis lazuli occupied the center, carved into a scarab. It looked like a typical piece fashioned by some jeweler trying to make a pound off the current Egyptological fad. According to Hieronymous, however, it served as more than just decoration. The note delivered with the bracelet explained that it would help her find the mummy, or rather its magical emanations, when she got within ten feet of it.

However, coming over on the ship, it had gone off on three separate occasions. Either it didn't work the way Hieronymous designed it to, which had happened before, or there had been another source of magic on the HMS *Oceanic*, which Esme had a hard time crediting. Still, she couldn't be sure, so she'd kept the bracelet on. At least it hadn't accidentally set her hand on fire or exploded unexpectedly. Unfortunate things like that had happened before with some of his more radical 'helpful' devices.

Thusly accoutered, she went back to the trunk. A few more *toilette* items went on top of the washstand, but the rest of her equipment, things used for forging documents, picking locks, and other assorted useful items, she left inside. She'd only be aboard four days.

Flushed with heat and most assuredly past the point of 'glowing', Cooper's euphemism for sweaty, she sat back down on the bed, across from the open port hole, hoping for a breeze. It lacked a half an hour yet before tea, so she leaned back against the pillows and allowed herself a few minutes of respite before going to the saloon to meet her fellow passengers. *Oh, Lord, let there be someone worth talking to for the next four days. Or if not interesting, at least pleasant to look at.* With a quirk of her lips, she closed her eyes and drifted into a sweat-soaked doze.

A small crowd milled about the saloon when Esme entered. She scanned the passengers. Almost all men, which might have been promising, but sadly, almost all were either portly Spanish businessmen or rumpled local plantation managers. There were two ladies present, one the wife of one of those businessmen, who wore a poppy-colored gown and hovered at her husband's elbow like some sort of clinging parasitic flower, and a tall, lithe young woman in a charming blue afternoon gown who sat aloof in a corner with a book in her lap.

Esme sighed, resigning herself to more days of tedium. At least she'd have plenty of time to finish several books she'd brought with her on the Inca and their last great ruler, Atahualpa, most of which, she thought, provided little more than conjecture. Rafael's long dead countrymen had done a thorough job of eradicating those proud people and all traces of their culture, although to be fair, she felt sure the English would have done the same. Two hundred years ago, the French and British had engaged in wholesale slaughter of the indigenous peoples in North America to establish a foothold in the virgin territory. She found it to be poetic justice that now somehow the tables had turned, and England could hardly keep hold of Her colonies in the New World. Still, the result of sending hale and hearty young men into the fray across the Atlantic meant a whole generation came back shell-shocked and broken by what they had endured. In some ways, she thought, the current war ranked higher on the scale of atrocities than had the bloody fight for India.

She pushed that aside and went to the bar, ordered a whisky to the delighted astonishment of the handsome barman who had eyes like warmed brandy and whose flashing grin and wink promised at least a little entertainment, then took her drink and wandered over to her only contemporary.

"Good afternoon," she said as she approached, smiling at the red head bent fixedly over a book. "I'm Esmeralda Eggerton. It seems we'll be traveling together."

The woman had a shrewd look to her. Green eyes, and that porcelain complexion that often went with red hair. Esme cringed internally, knowing her own hazel eyes, often ruddy cheeks, and easily tanned face could not possibly compare, were they to compete for any man's attention.

"Kinzalynn," the woman responded. "A pleasure to meet you."

Esme pointed to the adjacent chair. "Do you mind?"

"No."

Esme sat down, and suddenly the bracelet on her wrist began to heat up in the tell-tale sign of the presence of magic. She kept her eyes level with the exotic-looking girl, kept a pleasant look on her face, but found the growing heat from the bracelet distracted and concerned her. Could it be the girl or something else? Or nothing at all. "What brings you to this part of the world?"

"I'm visiting a relative."

Esme tried to place the girl's accent and couldn't. Shades of the British Isles, certainly, but also something else. Breton? Folks there lilted a little like that. Or maybe the Orkneys. Some of her father's relatives had that sing-songy dialect. "How nice for you. Such a long way to travel, though. Have you been enjoying the experience? My poor cousin Cecily, who planned to accompany me all the way to Quito, found she simply loathed the experience. I had to send her home when we arrived in Panama City yesterday."

"It's been pleasant, thank you. And you?"

"Me what?"

"Why are you traveling to Quito?"

"Oh, my husband is interested in Inca culture, but much like Cecily, he abhors travel, so I do his artefact scouting for him. It entertains me and keeps me out of his hair." Esme read the title of the book, printed across the top of the page, in Kinzalynn's lap. "I see you are reading up on the Inca yourself."

The woman's eyes didn't leave Esme's face. Esme felt judged, exposed. Cooper looked at her that way when she found her manners or dress wanting. "Yes."

Great. She'd hoped for someone to at least have a conversation with, but Miss Monosyllable here would not be that distraction. If not for the bracelet, she might have gone in search of more entertaining company. The zinging heat might simply mean a malfunction, but it could also mean something about the girl set it off.

Time to find out, she thought. Tossing back her whisky, she gestured with the glass. "I think I need another before dinner. Can I get you anything?"

A wrinkle appeared between the young woman's remarkable eyes. "No, thank you."

Another moue of disapproval followed. Cooper and this woman were cut from the same cloth. "Pardon me, I'll be right back."

She moved away to the bar, noting that the bracelet cooled down almost immediately when she left the woman's vicinity. Well, wasn't that interesting? She ordered another whisky and this time the barman left his hand on the glass as he passed it to her.

"You are the Lady Esme, *si*?"

Cheeky bastard. She granted him a nod. She liked cheeky bastards. "Have we met?"

"You sailed on the White Star Line last year. To Egypt. I worked the dinner shift."

She took a closer look. Mediterranean complexion, classical features, beautiful eyes with long lashes, and something just slightly effeminate about him. Memory gelled. "Diego! I remember you! You always made sure I had a full glass of wine at dinner." He'd been most attentive, she recalled, and not in a lewd way. She didn't think her charms had anything to offer someone of his persuasion. No, he'd simply been delightful company. Chatty, well-informed and almost preternaturally aware of what she wanted before she herself did. "What on earth are you doing on this bucket?"

His eyes and his lips turned down. "A small disagreement, you understand, with the management." His Spanish accent charmed her, a weakness she regretted. "They say," and here he rolled his eyes heavenward, "I make unwanted advances on a lady."

Esme giggled. "Well, *that's* ridiculous."

"You see? But they would no listen to me. And now, *madre de dios*." He gestured around him. "I am here."

He released her drink and she took a sip. Good and strong, just the way she liked it. God knew, she'd need the fortification. "I don't suppose there's much in the way of entertainment onboard?"

Diego plopped a cherry into a cocktail glass with a flourish. "Knowing you, I think you will find diversion enough to pass the time. It is a short trip. But I urge you to be careful. There are snakes aboard."

"Snakes?" Someone onboard had live reptiles?

"Not *that* kind of snake. The other kind. The sneaky kind." He gestured at the young woman Esme had been talking to. "That *señorita* may be one. And there is another, one that I think will interest you more."

"And why would I be interested in sneaky people, Diego?" She kept her voice calm, curious.

His teeth shone, white and perfect. "It is no for me to say, my lady. I am just a simple bartender."

Esme shook her head. He was a simple bartender the way she was a simple tourist. He returned to his drink making with a wink. She murmured her thanks and made her way back to the chair she had vacated. On her wrist, the bracelet heated up again. Curiouser and curiouser, as Lewis Carroll might have said.

Esme raised her glass. "The queen. And may true Britons never be without her likeness in their pocket." A standard enough toast, and even though the other woman lacked a glass with which to reciprocate, Esme expected some sort of response. Instead the other woman just looked at her.

Taking a drink, Esme settled herself in the chair, while the bracelet on her arm began to burn. Why couldn't Hieronymous have made it turn cold instead? "Do you play chess, Miss Kinzalynn?"

"Yes."

"Oh, excellent! Poor Cecily never grasped even the rudiments. The sea voyage seemed dreadfully long." Time, Esme thought, to do a little digging into who this creature might be, especially if she had roused the suspicions of Diego. "Dare I hope that you also play Senet?"

"I do."

Oh ho! Now that was most definitely odd. Senet was an ancient Egyptian game, probably the world's first board game. Few men outside the dusty realms of Egyptologists had ever heard of it. "Truly? How unexpectedly delightful. But I must ask, where did you learn? I only know it because my husband is a professor of Classical Civilizations at Cambridge."

A brief pause. "A neighbor taught me. A university professor."

"Really? Where does he teach? Perhaps he's one of old Egg's fellows. Seems like all we do in the summer is host shooting parties for Egg's raft of teaching friends."

The cool young woman avoided making eye contact. Esme wondered if the girl lied. "I am not sure. It was a long time ago, when I was a child."

"Oh." Esme let her face fall. "Well, it looks like we'll have plenty of ways to keep each other occupied during our time aloft." She cast around for another topic of conversation. One, she thought, where she might get more than two or three-word answers. She still couldn't place the accent. It wasn't quite like anything she'd ever heard before.

"Have you been long in Panama? I had so little time between when my steamer arrived and when this airship departed, I didn't get a chance to take in the sights."

"I have just arrived myself."

"Ah. Well, perhaps there will be time for it when I come back this way. Will you be in Quito long?"

"No." She expressed no emotion. Just sat there, book on her lap, spine erect.

Good gad! The woman's reticence felt like sand in Esme's bloomers. Didn't all normal women chatter? At home, with her so-called typical female acquaintances, Esme could never get them to shut up. The question of her identity aside, why did the girl make the bracelet heat up?

The door to the saloon swung open and a gentleman strode in, dressed in the latest Fleet Street fashion, a dark brown morning coat with a dapper bronze and brown satin waistcoat. A daring claret-red cravat adorned his neck. He paused a moment, ostensibly to survey the room, but also, Esme thought, to make sure he had been noticed.

No flicker of recognition lit the young woman's eyes, but Esme sensed that the newcomer had been quickly sized up and found lacking, although lacking in what, she had no clue. He certainly cut a dashing figure, and his face, while unadorned compared to most Britons, who were most partial to their facial hair, bore strong, finely chiseled features.

She fancied that his eyes were a deep blue and that he'd be charming, both traits she enjoyed, so she afforded him a nod of greeting. He crossed to the bar, ordered something and waited while the bartender fiddled with sugar cubes and other ingredients. After a time, he turned around carrying a milky green drink in a stemmed glass. Absinthe, that affectation of the idle and outré young nobles. He made his way across to them and bowed as he neared. "*Bonsoir, mesdames.* Allow me to introduce myself. I am Jean-Paul Reynard, le Comte du Chassard. Whom do I have the pleasure of addressing?"

He struck a bit of a pose with his glass and Esme stifled a chuckle. Oh, he really thought a lot of himself. On the other hand, at least he was pleasant to look at and had already spoken almost as many words in one sentence than Miss Kinzalynn of the mysterious magical presence had in the past five minutes. Still, caution was in order. French spies, in her experience, always came in attractive and charming packages. He could be after the same thing. While Britain and France were not as yet at war, the relationship remained chilly at best. She had to prevent Napoleon from obtaining the mummy, for the good of both Britain and the bits of Europe Napoleon had not already conquered. She lowered her head and peered coyly up at him through her lashes, deciding to play the game with him. After all, better the spy you could see than one you could not.

"I am Lady Esme, and this is Miss Kinzalynn..." She realized she had never learned the young woman's full name. The girl did nothing to correct the situation and there ensued an awkward pause. She glossed over it quickly. "A pleasure to make your acquaintance, *Monsieur le Comte.*"

In a deep, rich baritone he said. "Please, call me Jean-Paul, my lady."

Cooper would have been scandalized, a stranger asking a young woman to call him by his Christian name. Then again, the man was French. She sidestepped the issue. "Miss Kinzalynn and I were just discussing board games. Do you play chess, *Monsieur?*"

He'd been blessed with dimples, a trait some women would have swooned over. His eyes, which were indeed a startling blue, crinkled a little, pegging him a little older than his smooth, tanned, skin and trim physique might suggest. "I do indeed, my lady. Perhaps this evening, after dinner, you would consent to joining me in a match?"

She caught a note of danger in his tone, something a little wolfish, she decided, but she didn't let it worry her much. She could take care of herself. They would play in a public space and she knew how to reveal nothing about her true purpose. Besides, she had her little pistol strapped to her thigh. "I would be delighted." She turned to Kinzalynn, who watched them the way a scientist studied a new species of insect. "Perhaps Miss Kinzalynn could play the winner, then."

Kinzalynn shook her head. "Thank you, but no." The woman's attention returned to her book, dismissing them both.

Reynard's eyes widened a little and his lips twitched. Esme's responding shrug went unnoticed by the young woman and she smoothed her skirts. "Well, then, we'll leave you to your reading, Miss Kinzalynn. Perhaps we can speak again at dinner."

Esme turned to Reynard. "It is so warm in here, don't you think?"

He offered her his arm. "Perhaps a stroll on the deck would provide a breeze? I understand we won't be lifting off until after dinner."

"That sounds delightful. I must admit, I did not realize it would be quite so warm here."

"It will be better when we get to Quito. It is in the highlands and while not so cool as it is in London this time of year, it is not so hot as Panama."

"That will most certainly be a relief."

"You will be staying long in Quito?"

She dithered, looking up at him coyly under her lashes. "I'm not sure. Dear old Egg, that is to say Lord Harrogate, has set the itinerary."

They strolled through a set of double doors and out onto the deck. "Ah, I see. Will he be joining us for dinner, then, my lady?"

She gave a little titter. "Oh no, Egg despises travel. He leaves it to me to manage most of his business abroad. I'm on a hunt for certain antiquities and historical documents this trip. How long it takes me to find what he's looking for in Quito will determine how long I need stay."

"He must value your judgment highly if he sends you on these trips. But surely you and Miss Kinzalynn are not planning to wander the streets of Quito on your own?"

Oh, such a sly one, this Reynard. Interesting, but predictable, that he assumed she and Kinzalynn traveled together. At the moment, she saw no reason to disabuse him of the notion. "Oh, certainly not, *Monsieur*. That would be foolhardy. No, we will be meeting a trusted guide in Quito. Someone well known to my, er, husband." Or at least well-known to the man who might have become her husband. Apparently, Rafael trusted the guide he had selected with his life, and more importantly, as he had written in his letter, with her life, which he declared he still held as dear to him as ever. Smarmy bastard. As if she would believe that now.

She looked up into Reynard's piercing blue eyes. Yes, definitely a bit of a rake, but most Frenchmen of her acquaintance were. In any case, he would certainly be a diversion, provided she could stay one step ahead of his advances, the first of which would come during the evening's chess game. Could chess be a game of seduction? How very Tom Jones.

They walked on for a minute more and then heard a bell. The captain's voice came over a speaking tube, announcing that dinner would be served in thirty minutes.

Esme released Reynard's arm. "I must go and attend to my toilette. Thank you for a lovely stroll, *Monsieur*."

He bowed over her hand. "It was my pleasure. *À tout à l'heure, Madame*."

She gave him a little finger wave and swished back inside and to her stateroom. How far, she wondered, would she let him get over their chess game and what might she learn about why he traveled to Quito? He might be exactly as he appeared; a dreadfully rich, frightfully bored French nobleman. Yet Esme suspected his true purpose mirrored her own. She grinned. She so loved the chase, the exhilaration of the game. Little Miss Kinzalynn would be a harder nut to crack. Intuition, or perhaps the subtle voice of experience, told her the young woman hid motives just as devious and dangerous as Reynard.

Best all around that Esme not trust either of them.

She entered her stateroom with a sigh. Persistence would be the key. In any case, at least the next four days would prove more stimulating than the previous three weeks, and for that she was profoundly grateful.

Chapter Six

Quiet and solitude for Kinzy became more difficult to find on the airship. While on the great passenger ocean liner, Kinzy had many hundreds of people to help her blend in, with plenty of nooks and crannies from which to hide and observe. The airship *Doña Isabella* had, at best, twenty passengers, mostly men and one married couple. She could already tell by the occasional side glance from the crew that speculation had begun regarding this young woman traveling alone with a mongoose. The Captain demanded he be kept in her room. When she needed some fresh air away from an unhappy Trell, she decided to keep the humans at bay with the book Master Shabao left in her trunk. If she was unsure how much he knew before, the book *Incidents of Travel Along the Incan Trails of the Andes, Volume 1*, gave him away.

Yet, just when Kinzy would find a quiet corner of the saloon, or a deck chair on the promenade, one particular passenger repeatedly sought her company and insisted on striking up a conversation. Book or no book. At first Kinzy had thought it natural for the woman to seek out another young woman traveling solo. The two of them did make a natural pair on the small airship, as there were no other women traveling alone.

The incidents had now increased to the point of intrusive predictability. No sooner would Kinzy sit in the saloon with a sandwich and a cup of tea, hoping to read her book, when lady Esme, with that pasted-on smile and sharp eyes, would arrive and ask about her day. The woman was certainly not faeleath of an opposing House, unless she had an impossibly subtle glamor to keep her hidden from Kinzy's sharpened magical senses. She'd touched the woman and felt nothing definitive in the way of magic about her. As far as Kinzy could ascertain, the relentless woman was human. Kinzy opened her book to continue reading about an expedition lost in the Andes of Ecuador for weeks during a native insurrection.

Right on cue, Lady Esme arrived and sat next to her.

"And how are you today, Miss Kinzalynn? I simply adore your hair. I can only imagine how popular it must make you among all the young gentlemen at home. A pretty thing like you must receive a constant influx of invitations from your many suitors. What do they think of you gallivanting about South America alone?"

"Nothing." Kinzalynn didn't even lift her head from the book. She'd learned that if she didn't provide some response, Lady Esme would babble on for an hour about the inconsequential business of the other passengers. Although forced to answer, Kinzy kept her comments brief so as not to encourage additional inquiries. It was possible the lady was an agent on behalf of one of the human governments. There was a sharp mind behind the constant attempts to discover why Kinzalynn travelled to Quito. An impressive, subtle, interrogation. The woman was certainly a determined hunter.

"Oh, you poor dear! Well, then surely your family must be worried about you. Do you write them often? I had to pen a long missive to my dear old Egg last night after dinner. He simply adores hearing about all the different people I meet. What kinds of things do your family enjoy hearing about?" The Harrogate woman gave her a wink. "I assume you don't tell them everything. I don't. Cooper would be appalled at some of the less savory elements one must perforce encounter, so I don't write as frequently as I probably should. How often do you correspond?" The woman learned early on that Kinzy would not willingly engage in conversation, so Harrogate rarely asked a question that allowed a simple answer.

Of course, when Kinzy had once asked questions of her, the lady's answers were obvious subterfuge. Looking for historical documents and artefacts for her husband was a half-truth at best. The incessant woman was a plague on her journey whether an agent or not.

"I don't, unless necessary." Kinzy's short reply, delivered with a glare of disapproval, did not deter the stubborn blighted female.

"You read books, so I assume you *can* write?" the woman asked her with a hint of exasperation.

"Yes." Kinzy reveled at the breach in the woman's composure at the simple reply, and nearly drowned in relief to see the other passenger she worried over, *Monsieur* Reynard, coming up behind Lady Harangue-to-Death.

The flirtatious way Harrogate acted around the Frenchman, most likely an agent for Bonaparte himself, hinted at them being co-conspirators at worst, or seduction between them for some nefarious purpose at best. The confidence the woman employed when alone with Kinzy quickly evaporated in a puff of perfumed smoke as soon as Reynard arrived. The lady dissembled before Kinzy's eyes into a flighty female, playing up to his masculine prowess and domineering ways. Without his presence, the lady became a carefully honed blade inching closer to Kinzy's neck. Kinzy kept her pleasure at seeing him to herself.

"*Mademoiselles*," Reynard swept a bow, then plucked the lady's hand to bring it up to his lips for a lingering kiss. "I have arranged a tour of the bridge of this excellent airship with the captain. Would you care to join me?" Scandalously, he still had not let go of the woman's hand.

The lady laughed in a coquettish fashion, hand upon her breast. "Why *Monsieur* Reynard, we'd be delighted! Right, Miss Kinzalynn?" The woman's raised eyebrow dared Kinzy to take the leap and be sociable.

"No." Kinzy had other ideas for her time free of the two passengers. A perfect time to slip into the woman's suite and make a thorough search. She'd handle Reynard's cabin if the opportunity presented itself. As the captain led Lady Esme and *Monsieur* Reynard through the door for airship staff only, Kinzy closed her book and quickly left the saloon.

She flicked the locked latch on the door to Lady Esme's room with a tool she tucked safely back into her cuff. The room was neat and tidy, which meant the woman was either normally obsessed with cleanliness, or all the important things were squirreled away. Time to work.

Nothing on the bed stand, not even a jewelry box or hairbrush. In the desk, there were no letters to family and friends, no diary or journal, no notes or documents. Frustrated, Kinzy turned to look at the trunk. It was well-kept yet showed some wear. Kinzy searched through the pouches and drawers, where she found a lock pick set in a secret pocket. Finally, something that did not fit the story of a young lady of fine family on a simple journey. There were knives, a pen case with various inks and nibs, as for forgery. Kinzy herself had a similar set. Other items of a shadowy nature confirmed Kinzy's suspicions and drew her deeper into the trunk. Under a few trousers and two pith helmets, she uncovered a strange firearm along with unusual ammunition and a strange-looking handkerchief that made her shiver from an enchantment laid on it. Something to charm a potential lover, possibly? It was curious, but she set it aside. The weapon held more immediate interest. She pulled it out for a better look, bringing it closer to the light of the porthole.

It had a barrel with a wide bore and an intricate loading mechanism for only three rounds of the overly large ammunition. Given the size of the barrel and unfamiliar bullets, it would put an enormous hole in whatever it hit.

The door clicked.

Kinzy whirled, her free hand holding one of her knives, and the gun in her other hand now pointed at Lady Esme.

"That particular gun would do a great deal of damage and certainly bring unwanted attention." Esme closed the door behind her, calm as a cat. Kinzy was certain the woman's tail would twitch constantly if she had one. The lady's expression was hard and her eyes steel. She took a ready-for-action stance, and Kinzy wondered what weapons the human's petticoats might hold.

Lady Esme's words were probably worth heeding, though. Kinzy laid the weapon down on the bed, watching Harrogate closely. The silence between them lingered overlong. Kinzy recognized the tactic of making your opponent blurt out something useful, and finally gave in with an impatient sigh. "Lady Esme, if that is your real name, who do you work for? Why do you pester me?"

"May I sit?" Lady Esme asked. "It's been a long day in these blasted heels, and I have similar questions for you. We may as well be comfortable while we sort out our whys and whos and whats."

Kinzy waved her knife and indicated the chair for the woman as Kinzy sat on the bed, the pistol kept near her hand and as far from Harrogate as possible.

Esme sat on the small settee and slipped off her shoes, although her attention never left Kinzy. "You, Miss Kinzalynn, are a contradiction. Something I cannot abide."

"As are you, Lady Esme. I hoped to discover your full story with a quick inspection of your luggage. I learned only more specific questions I need answered."

The lady looked incredulous. "Are you looking for a signed letter, confessing my mission and plans? It's never that easy. And you," Esme pointed at her forcefully, as if she might pin Kinzy in place, "you are rummaging in my corsets. Please, steal them all, for I despise them."

Kinzy straightened her shoulders and glared. "We are two competent women. Let us speak plainly, as humans seldom do." Kinzy put away the knife and faced Harrogate, hoping she was not wrong. She did not believe the woman would harm her.

Esme's hands rested lightly in her lap, belying an intense readiness. "I suppose it is pointless to pretend now, but you must realize I am not foolish enough to reveal anything substantive. Let us simply say I am on an important mission for a certain interested and highly-placed party."

Kinzy raised an eyebrow. "I am on an important mission, as well. This is ridiculous. Are we caught in a comedic play or a tragedy?" How much could she tell this woman in exchange for her information? On one hand, she was sworn to secrecy and such orders had weight and substance to those of the Fae, especially having been sworn to Queen Airmed. On the other hand, Kinzy needed to know if this woman stood in her way.

Esme fanned herself. "At the moment, I'm hoping for a

comedy, although a brief one. No long, drawn-out monologues and utterly preventable miscommunications. Preposterous circumstances that could have been avoided if two people spoke simply and honestly to each other." The other woman tilted her head, challenging Kinzy with such a daring proposal.

Tell the truth? How could she?

Kinzy felt in her gut that she needed this woman on her side, even if only for a short time. "If we're telling the truth, let me answer further, as I am obviously on the wrong side of your door. I go to Ecuador to find an important Inca artefact for my benefactor, who desires to keep it safe from others of—" Kinzy paused, not willing to give away too much, "of Reynard's nature."

Kinzy caught the twinkle in the lady's gaze. She would not attack Kinzy anytime soon. "For my part, Miss Kinzalynn, I am not working with Reynard, and the certain personage I work for desires to keep the Inca artefact I seek safe, or at least ensure the French do not acquire it."

Kinzy felt the two of them were matched in many ways, but which personage did this woman work for? Kinzy's hunch was Queen Victoria, and she knew the Fae had no direct treaty with the Brits, though their queen was aware of the Fae on a limited level. She was unsure if this woman was privy to such deeply held secrets as the existence of the Fae. "How about a different statement that can break this tie?" Kinzy spread her awareness around the room. She could sense no one listening at the door or the porthole windows, but she lowered her voice anyway. She must either join forces with this woman, if their goals were the same, or keep her close.

Squaring her shoulders, Kinzy whispered, "*Atahualpa.*"

Chapter Seven

Esme rolled the backgammon dice. Doubles, and the win. That meant Kinzalynn had to answer a question about herself. The winner of whatever game they played could ask a single question.

"So how did you acquire a mongoose?" She leaned back to relish the answer but Kinzy showed no discomfort at the interrogation. The woman was a clam.

Leaning forward to close up the backgammon case, Kinzy took a breath. "A gift, a reward of sorts, though he sometimes thinks it's the other way around and I am his reward." The case snapped shut.

They played a game of Senet after tea. Esme won that as well.

"Who taught you Senet?" she asked her enigmatic Sphinx.

"A close friend, Mr. Shabao. A teacher." The girl's inscrutable expression softened and Esme burned to know who the man could be to cause that hint of warmth.

Nothing more was forthcoming. Asking about Mr. Shabao

would take another game win. Damn it, Esme wished she'd never suggested this strategy.

They played cards after dinner. Kinzy, earning her win, asked about old Egg with a curiosity in her eyes that intrigued Esme. So she chatted amiably about her eccentric husband, his teaching, the old pile of a manor house out in Wessex, and his eclectic historical pursuits. Kinzy's interest had a hunger to it that Esme couldn't understand but was happy to slake.

Another round, another win for Esme. Diego came past and turned up the gas lamps as darkness gathered outside the wide saloon windows. Esme tossed her cards in a pile on the table. A full day of this and neither had spilled much. It grew tedious. Esme wanted real answers. Blowing out a breath, she leaned forward. "Will you try to kill me when we reach our target?"

Her opponent's head snapped up. Her hands, which had been gathering up the cards, stilled. She sat back in her chair and squinted at Esme. Irritation? Esme almost cheered. Finally, a reaction.

"Maybe. One of us must reach the target first and walk away with it. That is the mission. Even you cannot avoid answering this same question in your own mind. How can either of us know the truth of this answer. It's in the future."

Esme sagged back. There were no easy answers to the big questions. Not even in her own mind.

Over the next two days, they bartered more snippets of information with each other about their missions and backgrounds. They played endless matches of chess, Senet, cards, and backgammon. By the afternoon of the second day, they found themselves relaxing in each other's company. The games became a pretense to continue their conversations. Although it might have been wishful thinking, Esme felt as though Kinzy craved egalitarian companionship too. They appeared to share similar professions, and she sensed a loneliness in the girl, despite her cool and aloof demeanor. God, how refreshing to speak with a woman whose intellect and adventurous spirit matched her own. Still, they continued to avoid the bigger question. Only one of them could have the mummy.

Another bright light turned out to be the ship's bartender, Diego. He treated them to small indulgences with delightful Spanish charm. His interests lay outside the female gender, and none of the current crop of fat, middle aged South American passengers occupied his attentions, leaving him free to dote on them, and dote he did.

The last evening aboard, as Esme and Kinzy sat over the remnants of a passable supper, he sauntered over to them and placed a honey-sweetened tisane of mint and chamomile in front of Kinzy, and a snifter of highly aged Courvoisier for Esme.

Diego bowed to Esme with a flourish and a wink. "The *pièce de la resistance* for you, my lady."

Esme clapped her hands. "You are a magician, Diego. Please, join us and tell me where you managed to acquire a bottle of Courvoisier? That bastard Bonaparte has had a lock-down on the stuff for a decade now!"

Diego dropped into an empty chair. "I have my ways. It is good to be able to satisfy the desires of my charges."

Esme sipped her cognac, watched the young man's face. He looked smug as the proverbial Cheshire cat. "You seem quite pleased about something."

Diego leaned towards them. "I might have something else of interest, my lady. A small morsel of information."

Esme put her small evening bag on the table. "I see. In my experience, interesting information never comes without a price."

He tsked. "Oh, I would never ask for something so gauche as money, my lady. Your husband, I understand, he has interests in a number of businesses."

"Many."

"I am thinking of one in particular, a line of airships. If I were to provide you with certain information about another passenger, I would be grateful if you could put in a word for me and arrange for a position on a more, how you say, salubrious ship and route. Say, over *España* perhaps."

He wanted a job. Esme toyed with the beading on her purse. It would be easy enough to arrange. "I daresay I could speak to Lord Harrogate. I cannot, of course, guarantee anything. And the information would have to be of a significant nature."

Long, tanned fingers spun a knife in circles on the table. "Oh, I think the information will be highly useful to you. Just as the information I provided to you on last year's trip to Egypt proved useful."

He *had* given her some good intelligence in addition to excellent service. He had a knack for gaining people's confidence. "I had nearly forgotten about that."

He waved a dismissive hand. "It was nothing. I was unimportant then. I hope to change that." He paused. "If I can improve my situation, that is."

"I cannot possibly help you until I know what it is you offer."

He leaned forward again. "Very well. I will show my hand. There is a gentleman aboard who is in possession of a sealed document signed by Bonaparte himself." He made a gesture as though to spit. "It makes mention of some kind of map, and a treasure. Bonaparte desires both these things."

Esme remained aloof. "And how do you know this?"

"I helped this gentleman unpack his luggage, while he strolled about on deck with a lady of wealth, privilege and certain elegant charms." He examined his nails. "Seals are not so hard to deal with, if one has the skill."

Next to her, Kinzy sat stone-faced. Uninterested, or did she already know all this? Had her new ally also searched Reynard's cabin as she had searched Esme's? Esme licked her lips. "I need more, Diego. What specifically did the document say about this map and this alleged treasure?"

"That the treasure lies somewhere east of Quito, high in the mountains, and that the gentleman should seek a man named Tomàs, as he can lead him to the tomb containing the treasure. It also said he should use whatever means necessary to gain this information."

A shock ran through her. Tomàs was the contact Rafael instructed her to consult as a guide when she arrived in Quito. A man Rafael counted on.

She took a sip of her cognac to cover her surprise. Diego had actually provided information worthy of what he wanted. She nodded slowly. "It is fortunate you have such skill. That is indeed interesting news."

He betrayed no eagerness, through either voice or action, yet she sensed it. She nodded to him. "I will wire Lord Harrogate when we reach Quito. It should be an easy enough thing to arrange. Eustace McWhirter owns the Pegasus Line and he is always looking for resourceful, ambitious young officers."

He released a breath. "*Muchas gracias, Señora*. I thank you. Truly. The oppressive heat, the dingy surroundings, the unendurable boorishness of these colonials. It is almost too much to bear."

She laughed. "Are all good-looking Spaniards such peacocks?"

He struck a pose, hand against his forehead. "The lady believes me to be good-looking! I am the most fortunate of men." He slithered to his feet, white teeth flashing. "I must get back to my duties now. Is there anything else I can do for you, *Señora? Señorita?*"

"No, no, we're fine, and thank you for the cognac. A most thoughtful gesture."

He turned to go then paused, spun back, stuck his hand into his pocket. "Oh, one more thing, Miss Kinzalynn. I thought your little pet mongoose might like these. They are called peanuts. A local South American snack food. You crack the shells and there are little round nuts inside."

He poured a handful of the unappealing lumpy brown things onto the table in front of Kinzy, who looked surprised. "I thank you."

Esme could almost hear the 'I think' after the spoken words.

With a little finger wave, Diego ambled off to check on a few other passengers who lingered over their supper, leaving Esme and Kinzy to puzzle over the information.

A cool breeze caught tendrils of Esme's hair and tugged them out of her hastily prepared coif as she and Kinzy strolled onto the promenade after dinner. Tonight would be their last night on board and their carefully maintained and increasingly comfortable detente could be coming to an end once they reached Quito. Esme would be sad when the moment came. She enjoyed the feisty redhead's company and under other circumstances thought they would have made a great team. It wasn't often that she encountered another woman who could keep up with her, not just on a game board and in general conversation, but also at the larger game they both played. Both worked toward the goal of keeping Atahualpa's mummy out of the hands of the French, although Esme still had no clue which government the woman worked for.

In the end, however, they would be at cross purposes. Esme had been tasked to bring the dusty pile of bones home to England and Kinzy's job was to do the same for someone else. Esme had even considered that Kinzy worked for no government at all, but for the Vatican. But if so, why had the Vatican given the map, which Esme now kept on her body every moment, waking or sleeping, to Victoria? Could the Pope be playing a double game, sending multiple agencies out after the thing and waiting to see who turned up with the goods? It infuriated her and she'd spent many sleepless hours spinning it all round and round. She simply didn't have enough information to put a clear picture together. Her assignment remained clear. Get the mummy, or destroy it, to keep it out of anyone else's hands. Anyone else now had to include Kinzy, and of course Reynard, even if he had been an attractive distraction.

The sun smudged the western horizon with coral and lavender as she and Kinzy stood at the starboard railing, the ship moving gently beneath them as the wind buffeted it about. The ship now anchored over a small habitation, as they did each night. Esme hesitated even to call this one a village, as it appeared to be little more than a collection of mud daub structures with roofs made from local enormous leaves. Few residents could be seen — one dozy fellow on a donkey, a couple of men who appeared through her opera glasses to wear some sort of military uniform, and an old woman sitting cross-legged beside the door of one of the buildings with a basket in her lap. Surrounding the encampment rose up an endless sea of swamp and jungle.

As the sun sank, the twilight deepened, and the stars popped out in a sky scattered with wispy clouds.

Esme smelled Reynard's cologne before she heard his approaching footsteps. He leaned on the railing next to her. "*C'est magnifique, non?*"

"The stars? Yes. But that?" She gestured at the landscape below them, turning inky black as the light bled away. "Endless miles of swampy jungle. I read they can't even build a road in this region, there is so much muck."

"The naturalists argue there is money to be made from some of the plants that grow there, but my sources say there is no way of realizing any sort of profit. It would require industrialization and that is impossible due to the lack of infrastructure." He pointed down. "That little enclosure was built strictly for airship travel. A resupply depot along the Panama-Quito route. They have a devil of a time staffing it, and there aren't even any native villages around to provide, er, entertainment."

Esme refused to dwell on what sort of entertainment a garrison of bored men might enjoy. No wonder the captain forbade anyone to disembark. She tried peering again through her opera glasses at the old woman, but it had grown too dark to see now. "I had hoped to see, I don't know, more native life, the way one does in Egypt, from the deck of a *dahabeeyah.*"

"You and the lovely Miss Kinzalynn have been to Egypt, my lady?" He turned sideways towards her, one elbow on the rail, his hands clasped across his stylish black and grey satin vest, accentuating his flat midsection. His charm seemed benign, but she knew the game. He dug for information again. Then he answered his own question with an arched eyebrow. "But of course. On another of your husband's antiquities hunts, *non*?"

She inclined her head, allowing him to assume without her ever admitting anything. She truly didn't like to lie if she could help it. "You have traveled there, *Monsieur*?"

"Oh, many times. I am a bit of an antiquarian myself, although not formally trained. My older brother runs the family vineyards and prefers to do so without my help. Alas, this means I have more free time than is probably good for me. So I have taken to traveling, pursuing this and that, as my interests sway me."

"How lovely for you, to have such freedom."

The conversation flagged. Kinzy, who studied the terrain below as though she could see something of interest there, left Esme to manage the conversation with the Frenchman, per usual. Tonight, however, Jean-Paul Reynard held little fascination for her. Tomorrow they would arrive in Quito, and she had a great deal to consider before that. Much as she enjoyed sparring with Reynard, she really wanted a whisky and her wrap, which she'd foolishly left inside. "It is a bit brisk tonight. Kinzalynn, if you wouldn't mind, perhaps we could go inside, if you've had your fill of sight-seeing."

Kinzy abandoned her fixed inspection of the scenery and turned towards her. "If you wish. I believe—"

A gust of wind brought a noxious smell wafting upwards and the air filled with the sudden, loud noise of an engine. Before Esme could react, an airship rose in a rush from below them, and shouts floated across the ten or so feet that separated the two ships.

She heard Reynard say, "What the devil—" as three large grappling hooks thunked into the railing.

In a matter of seconds, three sailors from the other ship swarmed like dark, deadly monkeys, across strange webs that filled the gaps between the grappling hook lines.

Reynard shouted, "Pirates!"

Esme reached beneath her skirts for her pistol, but Reynard shoved her behind him, throwing her off balance. As she struggled to get to her feet, one of the sailors struck Reynard in the side of the head with a club. He slammed into the bulkhead with a thud and slid bonelessly into a heap onto the deck.

The sailor now grinned and lunged for her. Esme again reached for her pistol but found herself flung down onto the deck. The uncouth brute straddled her and pulled a dark cloth sack from his belt, which he tried to place over her head.

She fought him, trying to twist out of his grasp. Her magic-sensing bracelet caught in the man's belt. It tore away from her arm and skittered across the deck.

"Damn you!" Angry now, instead of merely irritated, she yanked his arm to her mouth and bit down hard. He shrieked, rearing back. She scrambled out from under him. While he still knelt clutching his arm, she clenched her fists together and brought them down hard on the back of his neck. He slumped, giving her the time she needed to pull her pistol out from beneath her cumbersome skirts.

He staggered to his feet, swearing vilely in Spanish, and lunged again. Bracing herself, she aimed her little revolver and fired into his chest.

The sailor spun backwards. Her small caliber revolver was more of a deterrent than a death dealer, so she did what any self-respecting British woman would do. She raised her skirts and gave him a roundhouse kick in the solar plexus. The sailor issued a satisfying oof and went ass over tea kettle, cracking the railing. The webbing between the grappling hooks sagged then tore, and the hapless sailor fell down, down, down, towards the ground below, his screams echoing then fading away.

How many more to go? Surely she had seen three sailors scramble across from the other ship. The sun set and darkness fell like a sodden blanket. Other than the few lights along the superstructure, the deck lay in shadows. Kinzy faced off with another of the goons a few yards away. The exotic young woman had two curved blades, one in either hand, and she and her opponent circled one another. Kinzy's teeth bared in a feral grin. Esme watched transfixed and impressed as the young woman lashed out with her weapons. Steel blurred in a flurry of blades.

Assuring herself that Kinzy could hold her own, Esme searched the shadows for other assailants. Where the hell were the crew of the *Doña Isabella*? Surely someone heard the shot she'd fired.

Across the way, she could see other sailors on the pirate ship, waiting for something. None of them seemed to be moving.

Too late, she sensed someone behind her. A hood went over her head and strong arms wrapped around her body, pinning her arms to her side. Blinded, she kicked his shins, but this assailant proved stronger and smarter because he didn't let go. A hand over her mouth and nose and she struggled for air as the man dragged her across the deck. She clawed desperately at his arms, scoring his flesh with her nails. The lack of oxygen made her lungs burn and her vision gray. Her feet scrabbled futilely against the deck. A beehive buzzed in her ears and she fought for even a hint of oxygen. Her last thought, as the blackness claimed her, was how angry Cooper would be that she'd died without her good, whale-boned corset on.

Chapter Eight

Kinzy's draiglann flashed at her attacker's face, each small curved blade a perfect extension of her arms. She slashed with one and then the other, hoping to catch him off-guard. She forced him a single step back. The worried look on his face was heartening, obviously they'd not expected such resistance. She dared not look to Esme's fate, but trusted that one given such a mission would have skills in defense. Kinzy's opponent seemed to be a determined thug, not a warrior, without armor, attempting to subdue her with a simple club. His attacks lacked subtlety or calculation. His predatory grin lacked teeth.

He swung at her torso. She sucked in a breath, arched away, then her blade cut cleanly through the man's leather vest and the filthy shirt beneath to draw a line of blood across his chest. She carried through with the second blade in and up as he hunched into his wound. Her draiglann whipped up into his jaw and laid it open to the bone.

She ducked and rolled low as he screamed and swung wildly. Her claw-blades sliced across his legs, opening one of his kneecaps. He howled. Staggered in shock. Kinzy leapt up and knocked him back with a solid kick in the stomach. With an extra punch, she toppled him over the rail into the net stretched between the grappling hooks.

Kinzy cut the ropes attaching the hooks along the railing and watched her opponent fly backward into more pirates ready to climb over from the black airship. They yelled and clung to the flapping severed net.

She whirled back for her next target, to see Esme being dragged towards the railing and the pirate ship, kicking and squirming. A black sack around the woman's head and shoulders muffled her outraged cries. As Kinzy rushed to her aid, the pirate landed a blow square on Esme's jaw and she fell limp. Kinzy leaped, but before she could slash at the man's arms he turned and brought Esme's drooping body between them.

Suddenly Trell appeared out of thin air in drakkeki form and flew into the man's face. Claws raked the bastard's nose and cheeks. Kinzy hoped no one was looking, as Trell's true draconic form was forbidden in the mortal realm, with dire consequences for breaking that rule and leaving live witnesses. The pirate dropped Esme and drew his own blade as blood dripped down his face. Trell hadn't blinded him, but he'd done some damage and made the man angry. Shouts around the ship could be heard now. That meant help and, oh *bloody bright bane*, she grimaced. Witnesses.

She swept her leg low and caught the side of his knee. He toppled onto his back and struggled to rise. She was faster and slammed a draiglann into the man's chest. He died, wide-eyed, blood bubbling from his lips. Trell swooped in with claws and sharp teeth to make sure the man was dead.

Kinzy hissed. *Back to the room before anyone sees you!*

The drakkeki disappeared with a snarl in her mind. A mongoose the humans might understand, but word of a small winged dragon would spread across the Andes by morning. If word reached the queen, there would be dire consequences.

She tucked her blades into the secret pockets of her skirt as the last of the pirates scurried back to their ship. She knelt by the pirate to search his pockets. Empty. A strangled noise came from behind her. Running to Esme, she ripped the black sack from the woman's head. They stared at each other, breathing heavily as crewmen and the captain raced around the corner.

Kinzy pointed toward the railing, "Pirates!"

The captain and his men fired shot after shot at the retreating airship, but they had little effect. The night and the jungle soon swallowed the black ship whole.

The captain returned to their side. "Are you ladies all right? Any injuries?"

Esme coughed and wheezed, leaving Kinzy to explain. "We're bruised and a bit battered, but alive. *Monsieur* Reynard was struck heavily on the head."

They watched as a crewman rolled Reynard over.

Esme gasped. "Is he dead?"

"Unconscious," the crewman proclaimed.

The captain called for men to carry Reynard to his stateroom.

"My bracelet!" Esme clutched her wrist. "Help me find it. Please, it's important!"

They searched but the bracelet had vanished. Esme still gasped for breath, so Kinzy, with the help of the captain, forced her into a deck chair where she could catch her breath.

"I am truly sorry about the bracelet, Lady Esme." The captain called for water to be brought to them. "It must have fallen overboard. Please accept my apologies, I am deeply sorry for this experience!" He ordered the deck cleaned and the passengers who'd come to see the ruckus herded back to the saloon. "We have never before been beset by pirates on this route. The brazen scoundrels will be reported as soon as we get to Quito. We will double our watch crew tonight. Let me assist you to your cabins."

Kinzy looked back at Reynard, who groaned as two men carried him off. "Will *Monsieur* Reynard be taken care of?"

"I will have a crewman stand watch over him. The blow is superficial. He'll recover with nothing worse than a headache and a bruise, I'm sure. Come, let's get you settled into your cabins?"

Kinzy nodded her thanks.

"Send for whisky." Esme stood with Kinzy's help. "A bottle and glasses for two, to my cabin, please. Come along, Kinzy."

Kinzy resigned herself to sharing a whisky with this woman. "Captain, may we also get water and towels? I will need to wash off some blood." Kinzy caught the sideways looks of the crew as they carried away the body of the pirate she'd stabbed in the chest. Esme's arms and chest showed a constellation of red splotches, and speckles across her face. Kinzy guessed her own had a similar splatter.

Back in the room, after water, towels, and soap had been delivered, Diego dropped off a bottle of whisky and two tumblers, along with a platter of crackers, cheese, and olives. Esme thanked him and waved him out as she popped the cork on the whisky.

"Get out of those clothes," Kinzy cautioned, "and wash yourself before you drink too much. I have something in my room that will help get the blood out of your dress, unless you have something I could use?"

"I never overindulge. And what blood?" Esme examined the front of her dress. "Ah, that was why they looked at us in such shock. I thought it might be simply because two women fended off a pirate attack by themselves." The woman drained the whisky in one gulp, then refilled both glasses. "Top right drawer in my chest, the small gray box. Cooper swears by the stuff and never lets me travel without it. There is also better skin soap in there in the pink satchel next to it. Cooper says it contains calendula and lavender, good for soothing the skin and keeping it soft to the touch."

Kinzy met Esme's glass with her own in the clink of a salute, then downed her own in one gulp. It burned all the way to her stomach. Her eyes closed as the warmth spread. She put the glass down for Esme to refill while she retrieved the soaps.

Esme obliged and sat down, the glass clutched in her hand. "Cooper is my automaton. She was my nanny when I was born. My father's uncle, a brilliant inventor, created her and provided her to my mother to help look after me. She has been my constant companion, serving as my governess after I was out of the nursery, and now as my housekeeper." She frowned, as though remembering something unpleasant. "We were briefly separated, but now that I have her back, she is the closest thing to true family I have. Outside of old Egg, anyway." A sparkle showed in Esme's eyes. "If Cooper were a real woman, I think old Egg might have married her instead and just adopted me." With a shake of her head she raised twinkling brown eyes to Kinzy. "Make no mistake. Cooper is a *force majeure*!

"A remarkable ally to have by your side. She did not come with you this journey?" They had heard of automatons in Tír na nÓg, but there were so few in the world that Kinzy wondered how such a woman came into possession of one. Human science amazed her, though the thought of a mechanical being made her uncomfortable. Yet Kinzy did not blink at magically animated servants.

Esme cleaned herself of the blood, setting aside her soiled garments as she undressed. "She had a problem with her neck coupling and is currently carrying her head around under her arm. She wanted to come and planned to carry her head in a mesh sack, but I couldn't let her." She sighed. "She can be so stubborn." She took another sip of her drink. "Is there no close companion in your life?"

"One. My Master trained me since I was six." Kinzy twirled the ring on her finger. "Trained me well enough to know, Esme, that those men were there to take us. Not Reynard. *Us*."

"You believe they were sent to stop us from completing our missions?"

"One or both of us, yes. But who they work for, I don't know. We should join forces, protect each other, or neither of us may succeed in finding Atahualpa." Kinzy thought about what she was about to reveal. Allowing Esme to continue by her side without the full story invited disaster. "For better or worse, we're allies. I need you to listen carefully and learn what you may face."

"Allies, agreed. I shudder to think of what would have happened to Cooper or that silly git who was my former traveling companion if they had been here this night instead of you. I owe you my life, Miss Kinzalynn. Whatever you tell me, I swear I shall keep to myself alone."

"Do you know of the Fae?" Kinzy watched the British woman for any hint of subterfuge.

"What do fairy tales have to do with this?" Genuine confusion crossed Esme's face.

This woman could help her complete this mission, but she had to know fully what opposed them and what the capabilities of her new ally might be. Kinzy sighed as she thought this through. She was about to tell Esme a secret very few humans knew.

Kinzy sat across from Esme and told it all as simply as she could. "The Fae live in Tír na nÓg, where I am from. I am faeleath, a half-human, half-fae, in the service of Queen

Airmed. I am her agent in the human world, as I believe you are a British agent. Queen Victoria?" Esme gave a single nod in affirmation. "I am not human, Esme. I am not a full trueborn Fae either, but I do have some abilities that help in my missions."

"You are fast, I'll give you that. Faster with those blades than anyone I have ever seen." The British woman stood and paced for a few steps, then crossed her arms over her bosom and narrowed her eyes at Kinzy. "Just how different are Fae from humans?" Then she muttered, "I cannot believe I am having this conversation."

"I don't need much sleep, speak about eight languages, and sense magic. I cannot cast, so am only faeleath, but the energy still runs through me."

"You are able to feel that kind of power? Amazing." Esme crossed the distance between them. "You can detect Atahualpa? Sense him?"

"Yes. I need to be close enough, but all faeleath can, including those that may have been sent to stop us. It is not just the French I fear."

"Here I thought I was at a disadvantage, losing my bracelet. I believed it might be faulty as it kept going off and telling me *you* were the thing it reacted to. It was correct all this time. Hell and damnation! I don't need the blasted bracelet, I just need you!" The woman's chin jutted up in triumph. "How do you feel about joining forces with a human?"

Keep enemies close, Shabao had drilled into her. "Easier with an ally to reach the mummy, in terms of resources and safety. Traveling as two women together is much less conspicuous."

Esme stood, arms akimbo. "Agreed. So we work together until we reach the mummy and defeat all other comers. Then what happens?"

"That all depends on our circumstances when we get to that point. We have to get there first." Kinzy kept her own turmoil within. Esme's life was now forfeit for knowing the secret, but she could put that truth off until the mission was assured. She would not kill unless she must.

Esme stuck out her hand in that uniquely human gesture. "Deal."

Kinzy firmly shook the woman's hand. "As allies, we need to clean these clothes. I only hope they will dry by tomorrow when we land in Quito."

Esme chattered as they got to work cleaning the blood from their skirts and bodices in a second basin of water. "When we reach Quito, lodgings and a guide have been arranged for myself and a traveling companion. They do not know exactly who that traveling companion is, so we'll just pretend it's you. I won't even have to lie to Cooper when I tell her I found a replacement for Cecily!" She grinned. "We'll be all set. The guide should meet us at our lodgings. We can set off as soon as we are suitably rested."

Esme removed her petticoats, showing the straps along both thighs where a pistol and what appeared to be a silver scroll case were secreted. At a scratch on the door, she hurriedly shoved the scroll case in a bedside drawer. The two looked at each other, then each grabbed a weapon as Kinzy, the one still dressed, went to answer. She was the traveling companion and lady's maid now, she may as well play the role.

She heard another scratch at the door, low to the ground, with a faint chitter. *Let me in too? I brought an herbal ointment.* Kinzy pulled open the door and flung out a hand to stop Esme's aimed pistol.

Trell, in mongoose form, chittered angrily as he swirled around Kinzy's feet with a small leather bag in one paw, then raced up her skirts and bodice to slide around her shoulders.

Kinzy felt his worry and anger at the pirates and she sent him reassurance as she stroked his furry head and ears and took the small bag he offered her. *Calm down, my friend, all is well. We have an ally now.*

Esme slid the pistol back into the holster on her thigh. "Your mongoose breaks out of your room and brings you things?"

Kinzy held up the bag. "This is a good ointment for bruises and scrapes. The scamp around my neck is the third member of our new team. This is Trell. He's my own traveling companion. I use him to help send and receive messages from home. He is not quite what he seems." Trell reared back in mid-chirp, turning a wary eye on the human. Kinzy purred at him. *She's going to help us get to the mummy. We've formed an alliance, and she needs to know your basic capabilities.*

He slithered out from behind her neck to sit on her shoulder and studied Esme. *If I show her my true form, her life is forfeit to the Fae, you know the law.*

Yes. She's our means to get to the mummy, though, and you should not be a surprise that might cost us the mission. She felt Trell concede the point. She'd figure out just how much of an ally this woman was before the end.

Esme gasped. A winged golden lizard now perched on Kinzy's shoulder. Wings of iridescent scales shifted as Trell's golden claws dug in to steady himself. He extended his neck toward Esme and flicked his tongue at her.

"What is that? This is still Trell?"

"He is a drakkeki, a small creature of infinite wisdom and a hunger to match." Kinzy grabbed a piece of cheese for him off the plate. He snatched it and swallowed in one fast gulp.

Then crooned for more.

You're all stomach, aren't you?

I am a growing young hatchling.

You're an ill-mannered imp and older, even, than I am.

Trell crooned again, a pitiful warble. *You should worship your elders, faeleath.*

In your dreams, you winged belcher.

"May I?" Esme asked, reaching for another piece of cheese.

"He understands English, among other languages, just fine. He's not quite as smart as a human, but he understands much more than you think."

Esme held the cheese out to him, and he reached for it with his front claws, giving a trill and small bow in Esme's direction.

"He says thank you. You may pet him if you like. He loves his eye ridges rubbed and behind his ears and horns."

They spent the evening attending to their wounds, washing clothes, and feeding Trell most of the plate of food and none of the whisky. They finished that themselves.

Chapter Nine

The next morning, Esme had just poured herself a cup of coffee from the tray the steward brought when there came a knock on the door. She opened it cautiously, the steaming coffee pot still in her hand, then pulled the door wide to let in her new friend.

"Good morning! I trust you slept satisfactorily. Coffee?"

"Thank you, yes. Is there sugar?"

Esme poured a second cup and pointed to the tray on the table. "I'm still trying to put myself together." Stepping behind a screen, she removed her dressing gown and put on a loosely laced corset, taking time to do up the front and adjust it into some semblance of comfort. "I hope you are recovered from last night's little adventure?" She came out from behind the screen and grabbed one of the less frilly petticoats. "Men are so lucky. I cannot wait until we are out of the city and I can be done with all this blasted feminine frippery." She reached behind her and tugged the corset lacings tighter before tying them. It wasn't as tight as Cooper would have made it, but at this altitude breathing took precedence over having a wasp waist.

"I am not injured, but we were fortunate." Kinzy added at least three sugar cubes to her cup before sitting on the bed.

"I like to think we are skilled. What I want to know is who set those pirates on us. Clearly those thugs are in the employ of someone else." Esme spent a moment donning her favorite blue walking suit, consisting of a high-necked white blouse with a ruffled jabot, a lovely pale blue skirt and darker blue velvet jacket. She picked up a matching, broad-brimmed hat, hesitated. "I suppose the hat can wait until after breakfast, don't you think?"

Kinzy simply shrugged. The fae girl had on a pale green and white striped damask dress that suited her complexion and coloring, trimmed with ecru lace, and set off by a rose underskirt. She was a petite creature, with a naturally tiny waist that Esme envied, made more so by her tightly laced corset. Somehow, she managed to sit comfortably despite the small bustle in the back of her frock. She possessed a grace about her, an ease in her own skin that Esme coveted. Esme knew herself to be a plain woman. She had a distinctive Roman nose, her eyes were dark brown instead of the favored blue, and her hair a sort of mousy color. The only time she felt comfortable was in her working clothes. She preferred her canvas pantaloons, her sturdy boots, an open necked blouse and traveling waistcoat, which contained a number of pockets for storage whilst hugging her figure and enabling her to divest herself of her corset.

She sighed, let go of the envy. She'd made a good life for herself with Cooper and dear old Egg's help.

Kinzy's shoulders remained stiff, her eyes shifting like a soldier on alert. "They must have been employed by Reynard," she replied to Esme's question.

"I suppose he is a natural choice, as we are both sure he is working for the Emperor but remember he did try to save us. I heard his head crack against the bulkhead. He didn't fake that."

Kinzy didn't look convinced. "There's a possibility that other Fae are on the hunt as well, though I doubt they would use pirates, and I have not detected any aboard ship."

Esme raised her eyebrows. "Really? The game becomes more interesting all the time."

She took a look in the mirror, tucked a few tendrils of hair back up under a hair pin, then felt satisfied that Cooper would have frowned only a little in disapproval. She pulled her pistol holster, the containment net, and the strap for the map tube out from under her pillow. Setting the net down on the bed, she unscrewed the top of the silver scroll holder. With a gentle tug, the parchment map pulled free of the velvet lined tube and she unfurled it. "Before we go to breakfast, I wanted to share a few things with you. If we're going to be partners," she amended.

Kinzy leaned over to take a look, first at the net and then the map. "What are these?"

Esme gestured at the net. "This, according to the inestimable Professor Burroughs, is a containment net. My instructions are to wrap the mummy of Atahualpa in this in order to contain his magic and to bring him safely home. It is made from some kind of newly developed fiber, thin as silk but strong as iron cabling. One of his alchemical inventions."

Kinzy snorted. "Feels more like Fae magic."

Esme raised her brows. She knew some of the things Hieronymous had demonstrated dabbled in magic outside the alchemical realm. Could he have contacts in the Fae world? She was beginning to think she was the only one in the queen's little spy circle who had been kept ignorant of their existence. She picked up the thin square and slipped it into the pocket of her skirt proprietarily before pointing to the map. "*This*, according to the Vatican, is a map from a priest who traveled with a group of Spanish conquistadors sent to follow the loyal Inca who skedaddled into the hinterlands after the execution of Atahualpa. In this learned priest's journal, from which this map was taken, he says they believed the natives would lead them to a horde of gold."

Esme joined Kinzy as the woman examined the map. The Fae's slim finger traced the route, a winding black line from the circle marked as Quito, past what looked like a volcano among little triangles that must represent the surrounding mountains. Then came a rectangular marker of some sort of warrior with a headdress, brandishing a serrated club marked at the crest of a hill. *Demon Warriors*, read the Spanish translation. The trail passed a waterfall, across a river labeled *Green River* via what appeared to be a bridge between the steep sides of hills or canyons. The black line then wound around a lake with an elaborate snake in the middle. The Spanish note beneath it translated to *Place of the Snake God*. The trail then wove through two carefully drawn twin mountain peaks. On the far side of those lay a strange rock formation that looked like two faces in profile, facing one another, beside which had been inked a jumble of large rocks. And just beyond that, at long last, the trail finally ended at what Rafael and the queen believed to be their destination: a village or city on a plateau, snugged up against a taller mountain, dotted with thatched roof buildings on successive tiers, surrounded by a tall stone wall. The familiar symbol of the sun god, Inti, blazed above the place.

The few words in Spanish had probably been on the original map this had been copied from, but the English translations had been added in a different hand. Esme recognized the writing. Rafael. Treating her like an idiot, despite the fact that he knew she could speak and write Spanish like a native. Men.

"What was down here?" Kinzy pointed to where the trail entered the map on the lower right, just below Quito.

Esme leaned in. "One presumes that the bottom half of the map showed the route the Inca, and the conquistadors who followed, took from Cuzco to Quito."

"So this is not the original?"

"No, it is a copy. Although I am assured by the person who provided the map that it is an exact replica."

Kinzy arched an eyebrow at her. "You trust this person?"

Esme thought about that. She took a sip of coffee, found it bitter and unsatisfying, and wished she'd ordered tea instead. "With these details, and my safety, yes."

Kinzy shifted, stiffened. Distrust blossoming again? "I sense a reticence."

Esme swallowed her bitterness. "Let's say that the informant and I have a personal history. History that will not affect the information he provided." Esme paused. She could see that her answer wasn't completely satisfactory and felt relief when the girl dropped the topic.

Instead, Kinzy asked, "So we are to head north and east, towards the coast?"

"Yes. We didn't discuss it, but do you have suitable clothing for hiking? It will be colder, especially at night and when it rains, which I am assured it does frequently at those elevations."

Kinzy nodded. "I am well prepared."

Esme found herself warming to the girl. "I really do like you, Kinzalynn." She let her hand fall to the map. "We can of course study this later tonight, however, if you are done for now, I will put it away and we can carry on to breakfast."

Kinzy straightened. "I've memorized this. I will not need to see it again."

"You have an eidetic memory? Oh, you are a delight!"

"I am a trained observer. Where I come from, it is always best to commit things to memory, as a note or a document could be discovered by one's enemies."

Replacing the map in its case and strapping on both it and her little pistol, Esme smoothed her skirts. "I wonder if *Monsieur* Reynard will be joining us for the morning repast. I must admit, as much of a scoundrel as he is, I harbor some little concern for his well-being. He earned his injuries honorably last evening."

Kinzy's face betrayed not one iota of concern for the Frenchman. In fact, she gave away no emotion at all. Did she not find the man even a tiny bit attractive? Perhaps things were different for the Fae. She made a note to ask the young woman about her own situation. She found herself desperately curious about how the Fae arranged their personal lives. Did they marry as humans did or what?

She held the door open for the young woman and they started off towards the saloon.

Fae. She'd heard Egg and Hieronymous muttering in hushed tones about magic, about help from far away places. Could they have been talking about Kinzy's people? Could the kind of magic she'd read about in story books actually be real? She'd seen the little mongoose transform into a tiny dragon. She'd hunted for artefacts that held strange powers in the service of the queen. Now, walking beside this strange girl who seemed to be the embodiment of a real life fairy, she felt her whole belief system straining. And if the old tales were true, and the Fae held little love for humans, just how far could she trust her new friend?

At least as far as breakfast, she decided. Then it would be one moment at a time.

They entered and led to their accustomed table by the windows, while bright morning sunlight streamed in and glinted off the silver tableware. Oh, but the world was a wondrous place.

Their last meal aboard the airship had to count as one of the best. Freshly squeezed orange juice accompanied two lovely coddled eggs, perfectly browned toast, creamy butter, and four crispy pieces of bacon. Either the cook had improved radically overnight, or perhaps Esme's close brush with death the night before made even ordinary food taste better. At any rate, she attacked her breakfast with less than lady-like gusto.

She'd tucked into her second perfectly coddled egg when Jean-Paul Reynard walked stiffly into the saloon and approached their table. He wore a dark green suit this morning, with a burgundy satin waistcoat, but the deep emerald fabric did little to improve his pasty complexion. He had not shaved, and his cheeks appeared gaunt and his eyes hollow. As Esme looked up at him, a sense of recognition filled her, as though she had seen that haggard face before.

He eschewed a bow, ran long, manicured fingers through his dark, tousled curls. Esme's fleeting memory dissipated like fog in the sunlight. "Good morning, *Mesdames*. I would like to offer my abject and sincere apologies."

Esme gestured to a chair. "Whatever for, *Monsieur* Reynard? And please, do sit. I live in fear that you will fall prostrate to the deck at any moment." She wondered if Kinzy's instincts were correct. Could he be the man behind last night's attack? She knew he had to be a spy, that more lay behind his trip than what he shared, but she could not coax another jot of information from his well-formed lips. She inspected him, looking for signs of guilt or secrecy, but his eyes looked pained and she could detect no trace of dissembling.

He nodded his thanks and collapsed into a chair opposite them. "I failed you miserably last night. I thank the good Lord that you escaped your ordeal uninjured, no thanks to my efforts. I humbly beseech your forgiveness."

"Nonsense, *Monsieur* Reynard. No forgiveness is required. You behaved quite valiantly, throwing yourself in front of that blackguard and we both applaud your chivalry and courage. We were terribly worried about you, even after the captain assured us you had only suffered a mild blow to the head and that you would recover." Kinzy, she noted, looked not in the least concerned.

He reached across the table and touched Esme's fingers with his own. "You are too kind, Lady Esme. I remain your most devoted servant." He sat back as the waiter brought him a tisane, something pale yellow in color. From the smell, Esme identified it as chamomile. He added a dollop of honey, stirred his cup with a tiny silver spoon. "It would appear I am once more in your debt." He raised his cup to her as if in toast then brought it to his lips.

What a curious statement. The waiter interrupted before she could ask him what he meant, bringing several dishes to Reynard, including a croissant, a cup of yogurt, and a little plate of fresh fruit. Reynard stared at the food, then pushed the plates away. "I am afraid I have very little appetite this morning."

"You should eat something, *Monsieur*, or you will regret the lack of it later." She harbored genuine concern. She'd spent time working as a nurse shortly after her marriage. She knew that head injuries were nothing to trifle with and of the importance in keeping up one's strength. "Have you your man with you? I am thinking you should be monitored today, lest your injury prove more serious than the captain thought."

Reynard waved away her concern, his charm a little thin this morning. "I will be fine. I am meeting some people later this morning. Friends of mine. I will be well taken care of, but I thank you for your kind concern."

The rest of the meal passed pleasantly enough, although Esme kept her eye on him. The gaunt, pale countenance of the man kept tickling her brain, like a glimpse of a dream she couldn't quite remember. She'd seen a man like that before, but had no idea where. Two years at Bishopsgate Hospital, taking care of the young men coming back from the fighting in the Colonies in the New World, had created a blur of pale, haunted faces. Perhaps he simply reminded her of those poor young soldiers.

Kinzy, who never did more than pick at her food, sat with her hands in the lap of her pale green, lace-trimmed frock, gazing fixedly at Esme. She could almost hear the young woman's thoughts.

"Are you ready to go, then, Kinzalynn?"

She saw a flicker of relief in Kinzy's expression before the girl said pleasantly, "If you are quite done, Esme."

Oh! A little barb. Esme chuckled as she examined her plate, barren save for a few yellow smears of egg yolk. "Thank you for your forbearance. I was unaccountably hungry this morning. Who knew that being attacked by pirates could create such an appetite?" She stood, and Reynard stood with them. "It was a pleasure sharing this journey with you, *Monsieur* Reynard. I hope you enjoy your stay in Quito and thank you for your most gallant defense on our behalf last night."

"*Avec plaisir, Madame.* I only wish I had been more useful."

She allowed him to take her hand, which he bowed over and bestowed a very chaste kiss upon. She could sense Kinzy's inner consternation over the gesture and almost felt as if Cooper were here.

They said their goodbyes and swept out of the saloon.

Once in the corridor outside, Esme turned to her new friend. "Why does he irritate you so?"

"I don't trust him."

Esme laughed and paused in front of her cabin door. "Neither do I, dear, but he is the only entertainment available." She winked. "And you certainly can't fault his manners."

Kinzy shook her head and continued down the corridor toward her own cabin to pack.

Chapter Ten

Ready to play her role as traveling companion, Kinzy followed Lady Esme down the ramp leading from the airship to the massive steel docking tower in Quito's main square.

The captain waited at the bottom. "Thank you for traveling with us, ladies, and once again, my apologies for the terrible tragedy you endured. We've already sent for the local constables, so your return trip will be much safer, I assure you."

As Esme politely thanked the man, going on about the deplorableness of pirates, Kinzy caught Reynard's stride already below them on the ground crossing to a group of men by the line of carriages waiting for the airship passengers. She would give much to know what the man really wanted in Quito. She'd never gotten to his room to search it for answers, and though the man had taken a blow in their defense against the pirates, her stomach twisted whenever he was near. She did not like his furtive looks, his ingratiating manner. Trouble, for sure.

Trell snuggled closer around her neck. *The man hides beneath the gentleman.*

It's what he hides that has me worried. We were never able to get into his chest of secrets. Though not for lack of trying. The timing just never worked out. Diego's discoveries were all they had.

Do what we can and leave the rest to the Light. Works for everything. Except snacks. You need to work on those more.

Kinzy closed her eyes briefly and took a deep breath. Would the drakkeki's stomach ever cease to be a major issue with them?

Porters with their luggage joined them on the platform of the docking tower, then a crewman pulled the metal gate closed behind them with a loud clatter. The hiss and sputter of steam increased to almost a whistle, as the platform slowly traveled the fifty feet down to the solid ground. She'd been told by a kind crewman that airships had a tradition of never touching ground, but Kinzy couldn't be sure if that was true. Though with humans involved, she could not dismiss the absurdity.

The vibration beneath her feet increased, traveling up her spine in a disconcerting way. She didn't quite trust the mechanism as a screech became the grinding of metal on metal. Trell covered his small ears and noted they were obviously not free enough with lubricants here. The platform lurched to a halt at ground level, and Kinzy caught a glimpse of the sunshine splashed across Quito's main plaza, the airship above conveniently blocking the bright sun.

They walked through the drifting hiss and cloud of steam onto an expansive cobblestone plaza filled with people walking here and there, the sound of Spanish music played somewhere off to their right down one of the side streets. Impressive stone buildings surrounded them on all sides. Old Spanish churches and palatial mansions interspersed with seemingly mundane eateries and run-down shops. People filled the plaza, traversing the market stalls and strolling by the line of carriages and wagons waiting for the passengers and crews of the airships.

Here in the upper elevations of Quito the air was crisper, the sun brighter, and the magnificence of the churches and other buildings rivaled what she'd experienced in Spain. Kinzy marked the Ecuadorian influence in the darker, smaller people selling Inca masks and carvings in the closer stalls, but the wealthy patrons that shopped and strolled throughout the square would have been lauded as the height of fashion in Madrid.

This colony had done quite well, despite a foundation of bloodshed and war, as she'd read in the book Master Shabao had left in her trunk. The Spanish and their conquistadors completed a brutal subjugation of the native peoples here beneath these very cobblestones. She supposed groups remained in Ecuador that still lived the old ways, that may still honor the old Incan Empire. An empire and people the Spanish had destroyed with the execution of King Atahualpa, and the complete destruction of his capital here on this site. Her heart suddenly ached for the ancient ones lost.

Some elders counseled greater Fae involvement in countries like Spain and France, to curtail human bloodlust and destructive expansion, even so far as demanding the Fae defend the natives of all lands. Kinzy had to admit her people had much in common with these natives. They themselves had been pushed out of their comfortable homelands on Earth into the realm of Tír na nÓg long ago, yet they yearned for a return to the Earth realm. She'd heard the king's whispers of alliances that would curtail the European expansions into North America. More secrets surrounded his mission, but an alliance with the many tribes stood at the heart. European's dreams of colonies and expansion had been thwarted by the indigenous peoples with the help of the Fae.

Her queen, however, wanted Kinzy's focus here. The Andes mountains towered around them and hoped she and the British agent could remain ahead of the French on those rocky slopes. They had a better chance together than they did working at odds. She looked around the carriages as they climbed into theirs but could not see any sign of Reynard.

"We will be staying at La Casona house near La Ronda. The arrangements have been made by, well, made on our behalf. It is not far, and we could walk, though the altitude makes some tired and less likely to want that walk, I am told. Have you had any indications of altitude sickness?"

"I should be fine." Kinzy laid her hat on her lap and looked through the window on her side. At the market stall across the way, Reynard stood in heated argument with another man. She sat back so as not to catch his eye. The carriage shook as their trunks and gear were settled in place. "Where do we find our guide?"

"Tomàs will be our guide and should meet us at the house. I will send word of our arrival as soon as we reach La Casona. There will be a light staff, as the family who owns the house is off traveling."

Suddenly Reynard's upper body leaned inside the carriage as he placed his hand on the carriage door before the driver could close it. "*Mademoiselles*, will you need any assistance in your search for artefacts? I have many contacts in Quito and could escort you without any bother at all. There are unsavory sorts in and near the city. I would hate to see anything happen to either one of you."

Kinzy felt the sudden urge to slap the man's hand and close the door herself, but Esme laid a staying hand on her arm.

Esme replied with aristocratic cool. "Thank you for the

offer, but an escort has been arranged for us, Monsieur Reynard, so you need not fear that we shall be well taken care of. I do hope you have a pleasant stay in Quito."

Kinzy caught the flash of annoyance that crossed his face, but the man bowed his head in acceptance of Esme's refusal and closed the door, much to Kinzy's relief. Her palms itched for her knives. The driver hopped up onto the driver's seat and the carriage engine coughed to a rumbling start. The inadequately padded seat beneath them bounced and a belch of steam shot out behind them as they pulled out smoothly from the line of carriages.

Kinzy looked back out the window to see Reynard staring after them, a frown on his face. He waved for a man and pointed their way. "I believe that Frenchman has the nerve to send someone to follow us."

"Perhaps you've captured his heart. He is persistent."

"You're the one who played games with the man. Did you bed him?"

"Reynard?" Esme laughed. "Good heavens, no! First, he is a wealthy French nobleman. The Revolution has not been kind to that country's nobility, nor have the Bonapartes. Any man with a title who still has both his head and his wealth in Bonaparte's court is a survivor and should be considered dangerous."

"And second?"

"Second, if you take them to your bed, the game is over. They think they've won and will not continue to play." Esme's tone lost some of its flippancy. "Besides, I'd never do anything to hurt old Egg. He saved me from a life of utter revile and abuse. Only twice before have I taken a lover. Once because I was a fool, and the other time because it was required to save a life." She shook her head, stared out the window at the passing throngs. "For all that he is old enough to be my father, my husband is very dear to me. Despite or even because of our unorthodox arrangement, this life suits us both."

The carriage stopped at their destination with the hiss of released steam from the engine. The driver hopped down and opened the door for them, setting out the small step stool for their ease of egress. He handed them down from the carriage, then began unloading their luggage.

The narrow street was still the same cobblestone of the plaza, and as far along the street as Kinzy could see, stone pediments sat over large dark wooden doors carved with intricate patterns, and small stone balconies with marble balustrades strung in a line above their heads. The street sloped downhill, and from here the view stretched across the city. A much larger city than she'd realized.

A smartly dressed gentleman, clearly the household's butler, waited for them near the grand home's front door, with an older woman and a young footman, who immediately took charge of the luggage. The butler welcomed the ladies to La Casona and introduced himself as Alejandro, and the housekeeper as Lucia.

Esme passed a piece of cream-colored stationary to the man. "Please see that this is delivered right away. We will expect our guide to attend us immediately."

Alejandro nodded and the tiny housekeeper with eyes as dark and bright as a bird curtsied and gestured for Kinzy and Esme to follow her. In highly accented English, she asked, "*Señoras*, would you like to rest after your trip, or would you prefer a small meal?"

Meal? Trell raised his head and chittered hungrily. *Yes, that sounds absolutely necessary.*

"Ayee! What beast is this? I thought you merely sported a fur collar!" Lucia put a hand to her chest as Trell purred at her.

"He is a well-trained mongoose and will be absolutely no

trouble beyond extra food on my own plate." Kinzy glanced at Esme for support. Her companion gave the petite but commanding lady a polite and respectful nod. "We've eaten not long ago, but I daresay we could use a few minutes to refresh ourselves after the exertions of disembarking. The creature will behave and should give no cause for alarm. He'll remain in our rooms this evening."

The housekeeper pursed her lips, but led them forward through the house, gesturing as she went. "Ballroom, dining room, and kitchens are all on the first floor. Library and billiards room are on the second floor. Your rooms are on the third. You have freedom of the house, except for the family rooms on the fourth floor, and the servant quarters. I would kindly ask that you not bother the cook, Rosa Maria, unless you are in dire need. She speaks only Spanish and considers herself *la reina de la cucina*."

Esme laughed as she followed Lucia into an elevator. "I promise that she may remain *la reina* of her domain. You may also tell her that I intend for us to go out for dinner this evening. In the meantime, we will go up and refresh ourselves until our guide arrives. Please install him in a suitable place to meet with us privately."

"I shall send word to *la cucina* of your plans, though we will ensure that a selection of fruit, cheeses, and bread are available on the sideboard in the dining room. What is the name of the guide, your Ladyship? So that I can inform the footman."

"*Señor* Tomàs Gonzalez."

"That scoundrel?!" The maid crossed herself, then turned back to them. "*Lo siento mucho, my lady*, I have spoken out of place."

"Knowing who hired him on our behalf, I expected nothing less. Still, I am told he is the most suitable for our plans and trusted by our benefactor."

Lucia showed them to elegant bedrooms with a connecting door between, and lavatory across the hall.

They all turned at the sound of the bell.

"*Señoras*, your guide may have arrived. I will have him wait in the front parlor for you until you are ready to meet with him."

The ladies saw Trell and their luggage settled then freshened up before going downstairs. Once Lucia led them to the parlor, they could see why she had called the man a scoundrel. The tall Spanish gentleman was handsome, although a scar marred the left side of his face. It had been a day at least since his jaw had seen a razor but his luxurious mustache was well-oiled. A loose mess of dark hair hung about broad shoulders, and he wore a full-sleeved shirt with a well-worn waistcoat. Both had seen better days.

He also took them in from head to toe. His smile broadened, Kinzy certain he liked what he saw. He had the confident stance of a rogue, and the playful smirk of a boy ready to get away with something. Upon introduction, *Señor* Tomàs Gonzales bowed with a flourish and pressed his lips to the back of their hands.

Chapter Eleven

Esme wiped her hand on her skirts and frowned. "Impudent, aren't you?" She ignored Kinzy, whose eyes widened almost imperceptibly.

Tomàs tried another grin. "Only with the most beautiful of ladies."

Esme blew out a disgusted breath. Spaniards. "In any case, thank you for coming promptly." Esme gestured to the settee. "Please, sit and let us discuss our plans." She brought out the map, set it still folded on her lap. Rafael had assured her she could trust this man with it, with their route. She hated sharing critical information, but if this rapscallion was entrusted with leading them through the mountains to their goal, he could hardly do so in ignorance.

The fellow lowered himself carefully onto the cushion, perhaps mindful of the dirt on his trousers."*Señora*, first let me assure you that all is prepared for our departure."

Esme frowned at the impending argument implied in his pause. "But?"

A little of his cockiness skittered away. "This place you

seek. Many have looked. All have failed. They go, but never come back."

She tapped the parchment. "The others did not have this."

He scowled at the map. "A piece of paper, even one from such a holy place, will not save us from the perils that await."

"You know of these perils from experience? Know what dangers we face?"

The Spaniard shook his head. "No, *Señora*. I only know what other men say. Ghouls and monsters guard the route, controlled by the spirit of Atahualpa himself. It is not safe. And Rafi, he will have my head if one hair on yours is harmed."

God damn it. She would not let Rafael bloody Navarro try to control her life from half a world away. Noting the gold crucifix that hung around his neck, she chided him. "*Senor* Gonzalez, you are a Catholic. The Church does not allow for the existence of ghouls and monsters."

He touched the talisman, perhaps not quite trusting even God to protect him. After a moment, he shrugged fatalistically. "If that is your decision." Not quite a question, not quite an agreement.

"It is." She started to unfold the map and he raised his hand.

"I do not need to see your map. I know the route. My chief porter Mani and I have discussed how we will go. We will follow the old roads, make many offerings on the way. *Si Dios quiere*, we will make it to your hidden place all in one piece."

God willing, indeed. She offered him a smile as he crossed himself and brought the crucifix to his lips. He cleared his throat and, resigned to his fate, some of his smug charm returned.

"*Bueno*. All is prepared. A carriage will arrive here at dawn tomorrow morning and take you into the hills above the city where the pack animals and our mounts will be waiting. We will push hard tomorrow to get to our first campsite before the rain and darkness falls. The mountains are treacherous at night."

"Good. We will be ready."

"There is only one thing left to do. This afternoon I will seek a blessing from the Church. We will need God's grace on this journey." Abruptly, he switched gears, all professional guide now. "How many trunks will you be bringing?"

"Just one small trunk apiece. This is not our first foray into the wilderness. We are neither of us wilting flowers."

"Ah, that is good. I will not need to acquire more llamas. And you are not sick with the altitude? No sick stomachs or headaches? You know about the coca leaves, yes?"

She knew he asked only reasonable questions, but his appearance and his condescending attitude grated on her. He reminded her far too much of Rafi. No matter how hard she tried to ignore it, seeing that bastard again had stirred up the bitter stew of the past. "We are well aware of the precautions, thank you."

"*Muy excellente, Señora,* it is settled then. May I inquire as to your plans for the afternoon and this evening? I was instructed to see to your comfort and entertainment while you are in Quito." He looked at one, then the other. The two women hadn't yet spoken about plans to sightsee, and Esme had been so focused on perusing their map and contemplating the journey ahead that she'd been remiss in her research on the city itself. Whatever they did must be efficient. She needed to stop by the British Embassy and arrange for some communiques to both Egg and Her Majesty, and dawn would come earlier than she liked.

"Well, Miss Kinzalynn?" Esme turned to the Fae girl. "Shall we see some of what Quito has to offer before supper out?" To Tomàs, she said, "No offense to you, sir, but I fear this will be the last chance for a fine meal until our travels are over."

Kinzy's eyes sparked with interest, although whether polite or feigned, Esme couldn't tell. "I would love to see more of the city."

Tomàs gestured expansively. "*Bueno*. I will make reservations for you at La Plaza Grande. It is where the important people go."

She ignored the subtle dig in his voice. "Thank you, that will be lovely. You are the local, Tomàs. Given that we have limited time, what do you suggest we see?"

"Ah, you must come to the *San Francisco*, my church. Many hundreds of years old. It is the most beautiful place Man has ever built on this earth. *Esto es un milagro,* a miracle. Let me show you the paintings, the view from the bell tower, and if you are brave, even the catacombs! From heaven to hell, the church gives you all of Quito! I myself am going there this afternoon for a blessing." His voice rang with pride. "Padre Rodriquez would be happy to provide you with a blessing as well, *si permites.* "

Esme relished the man's fervor, the first thing about him she liked. "I have heard of the lovely goldwork and *retablos* there, and I could use a few vials of holy water to travel with if they would oblige us."

"It is *muy impresionante, Señora*! I will wait here for you to, how do you say, refresh yourselves, then I will show you beauty beyond belief!" The man raised his arm in the air with a flourish and a stamp of his leather boot. Yes, another damned dramatic Spanish peacock, but the gesture also allowed her to glimpse the pair of pistols strapped under his coat. A peacock, but a careful one. Perhaps Rafael had chosen well after all.

Minutes later they were on their way. Where Tomàs would have preferred a languid saunter through the fashionable neighborhood the embassy inhabited, Esme forced a bustling pace. Perhaps she mightn't have noticed the rat-like man dressed in ragged trousers and a brightly colored poncho who stepped into doorways or turned to face away whenever she looked directly at him if they'd taken a leisurely stroll, but the man had short legs and he scuttled madly after them like a frenetic land crab to keep up with them.

So. They were being followed, and by Esme's estimation, rather inelegantly. It could be Reynard behind it. Or some other interested party. Without being able to question the man, she would never know.

As they neared a tall building behind iron gates upon which waved the Union Jack flag, Esme faced the fellow, who immediately bent to adjust his boot. She put a hand on Tomàs's arm and leaned close. "Do you know that man?"

He glanced at the land crab, shrugged. "No. Could be a pickpocket. The city is full of them."

Possible, but Esme doubted it. "When we go inside, follow him. Find out where he goes, who he sees."

"Him? Why? He is nothing. Just one of the city's poor, looking to prey on the wealthy to feed his family."

"He's been following us." When Tomàs just stared at her, she gave him her best Lady of the Manor sneer. "Is this the kind of help we can expect from you in the days to come?"

He scowled. "*Bueno*, I will go, but do not leave here until I have returned."

Kinzy slipped something out of a hidden pocket of her skirt, something small that glinted in the afternoon sunlight. "I will go."

She shouldn't have been surprised. "No, it's too dangerous." She stopped, shook her head at that obviously inaccurate statement. The woman dispatched pirates on the airship like they were paper dragons. "Fine. Go. Just remember that we have dinner reservations at eight and there is still the church to visit. Do not let him lead you on too merry a chase."

Kinzy's glance shot upward at a small shape flying high above them and a wicked gleam appeared in her eyes. "We will return in twenty minutes. With answers."

Ah, Trell. The two of them would be more than a match for the skulker.

Esme would have liked to join them. She enjoyed the thrill of the chase. Yet the queen required her communique, and Esme felt the woman's stern influence from an entire continent away. In addition, she'd promised Diego she'd contact the Pegasus Airship Line on his behalf. With a disgruntled sigh, she made a dismissive motion with her hand then turned and walked in through the gates of the embassy to do her part.

Chapter Twelve

Kinzy grabbed their guide's arm before he raced off after the quarry. "Let him get a little ahead. You take one side of the street and I will take the other. Don't be obvious, look like you're doing errands. If he catches one of us then the other follows."

"*Señorita,* this is my city, let me do this. No need to—"

Kinzy leaned in close with the knife poking through his shirt into his abdomen, but not hard enough to draw blood.

"I see. He's about to turn a corner, *Señorita.* Shall we?"

Tomàs didn't look back but set out on the far side of the street, leaving her the near side. Kinzy quickly took off her jacket and turned it inside out to show the contrasting color of her travel dress. She set out at a brisk pace, removing her hat and a couple pins from her hair bun to change the style. Their tail would not see what his mind expected and slide right past her. She kept one eye on Tomàs, a fair hand himself at following unobtrusively, and her good eye on the target. Their former tail seemed in a hurry to get somewhere. Kinzy wondered for a moment if there was another tail left waiting to see when Esme would emerge from the embassy and follow her. Tomàs had asked Esme not to leave til they returned but he did not know Lady Esme as well as Kinzy did now. They needed to return as soon as possible.

The man became furtive suddenly, checking over his shoulder Tomàs's way. Their guide had been spotted. Tomàs ducked into an alley and gave her a jaunty salute. She followed the small sneak around another corner and lingered at the window of a bookshop, leaning over and turning her face away from the gentleman. In the glass she saw him continue on, still at his frantic pace. He must think someone needed to know where they had gone.

Tomàs spoke from behind her right shoulder as she moved along, "He's heading toward a few well secured areas, *Señorita*. If you want him, we need to catch him before he gets there. We have a few minutos, but not many."

"Which places?"

"The *policia* headquarters, the *Embassy de Francia*, and a certain gentleman's club that enforces its territory very well."

"Let's get our man then." She could simply ask the man who he reported to once they had him.

She sped up as their former tail turned forward again and sped off. She picked her skirts up, hating such frippery for this work. In her leathers, she'd have had him by now. Tomàs strode past her as the man turned another corner.

Tomàs twirled around and mouthed "Embassy" to her.

She turned the corner and understood. Four guards stood in front of the large ironwork gate, the entrance to the French Embassy that spread across the entire block. Their target raced past the men and inside with a minimal wave of his hand. He'd been expected. She stood for a moment on the opposite side of the street, stretching her senses across and into the building. The place had no Fae, but she caught the brief flash of a face in the second-floor window. Jean-Paul Reynard, *le Comte du Chassard.*

"*Señorita*, shall we wait for him to come out?" Tomàs stood beside her, his back to the *guardia.*

"No, Tomàs. Let's retrieve Lady Esme. There is nothing more to see here."

Shall I continue to circle? Trell asked in a bored tone.

Kinzy considered it, but there seemed little point. *There's nothing here but some French complications. You can head back.*

Tomàs took them another block away and grabbed a waiting steam carriage for hire. They stopped briefly to pick up Esme. Kinzy gave a shake of her head when Esme raised a hopeful brow.

The steam carriage was barely adequate to the task of making it up and down the hills of Quito, but they soon pulled up in front of the main steps of a huge stone cathedral built on the other side of the central plaza where they had disembarked that morning. Their airship had already departed on its run back to Panama City, and the docking platform towering above the many market stalls was empty.

The church's double steeple in the baroque Spanish style reached gracefully to the sky, the grey stonework edifice a massive presence in the city. They climbed the half circle of steps to the massive wooden doors which arched high above them. Tomàs led them through the wicket gate, a smaller door inset within the larger entry.

"Of all cathedrals in the New World, you have come to the biggest and best. No one should leave Quito, *Señoras*, without seeing this." He swept an arm before him.

As they followed Tomàs slowly into the heavily gilded nave and under the central dome, she suddenly felt homesick for the first time in her many travels. Above her the faraway circular ceiling was deep blue amid exquisite woodwork, skillfully painted to seem an endless twilight sky. She had never paid much attention to the few small churches she had been in, but none of them had been so close to her homeland and the throne room in Tír na nÓg. She ached at the lack of magic around her. She could not feel the sense of life and nature in the stonework and carved wood here as she did in the throne room, but she admired the lavish artistry the Spanish humans had given the temple of their god.

"*Bello, si, Señorita* Kinzalynn?" Tomàs stood beside her, leaning in close to whisper in her ear. "It is said that if you stare long enough you might see into heaven itself."

"It reminds me of home, *Señor* Tomàs, enough to make my heart ache."

A gentleman in church robes waited patiently for them. The two men greeted each other with a friendly handshake.

"*Padre* Rodriguez, this is *Señora* Harrogate, and her companion, *Señorita* Kinzalynn. They will be traveling with me soon. I have told them this cathedral was the most beautiful thing man has made on earth and they could not leave without seeing it. After the blessing, may I show them the choir and bell tower?"

"*Si, claro,* Tomàs. Welcome, *Señoras.* Make sure he shows you the courtyard gardens in his grand tour. What brings you to Quito?"

"We are here at my husband's request. He teaches at Cambridge and as he is not a good traveler, I am often sent to gather research material for him. artefacts, documents, first-hand accounts."

"May your endeavors be successful. Would the *señoras* care to receive a blessing along with Tomàs? You will surely need it, and as you can see, they work, as Tomàs is still with us."

They followed the priest to a small chapel on the other side of the elaborate gold central altar staged impressively to face row upon row of pews for the human sheep.

Kinzy often mused on human religion being a form of herding, and sheep even featured in their Christian stories and lessons. The Church attempted such great good in the human world, though she loathed the fact that it too often used bloodshed and manipulation. Human lives being so fleeting, it was no wonder they would forget the wars, the battles, the relentless persecution of those who thought differently and worshipped other gods. Such was the human way. They could not see that the world was all. Life was the purpose, not a commodity.

The Fae revered life, and yet, as Kinzy thought about the king and his project, she wondered if they would go to war over their beliefs as well. Since the creation of Tír na nÓg, the only way to create Life and give birth came through a human mate. Fae needed the natural earth and sky ties of the original realm, now the human world.

The priest had them kneel, but Kinzy hesitated. "I'd be honored for the blessing, though I am not a Catholic." She wanted to be sure of the protocol for such a thing and thought it best to be honest.

The priest gave her a wink. "Let us view this as a simple request for His grace and protection as you all face the trepidations of spirit and the vagaries of life in the harsh mountains of Ecuador. Have no fear, my child."

Kinzy bowed. "*Gracias, Padre.* I am happy to share this blessing in the face of danger."

"Well, life would not be as much fun without a little danger." Tomàs wiggled his eyebrows as he grinned at them.

The priest gave an exasperated sigh. "I fear, *Señoras,* that it will take more than a blessing to survive the wit of Tomàs."

Tomàs gave an exaggerated look of affront. The priest did

not even pause as he read from a small book and Esme laid out her strange pistol and ammunition, and Tomàs laid out his own pistols, knives, and sword.

With a few moments of ceremony, *Padre* Rodriguez paused by each of them and laid a hand on their heads, and over their weapons. He then finished with "May God bless you with every heavenly blessing and give you a safe journey; wherever life leads you, may you find him there to protect you. We ask this through Christ our Lord."

Tomàs and Esme replied, "Amen."

Esme then requested a few vials of holy water, and with a large donation, the small bottles were turned over to her.

As they thanked the priest and followed Tomàs to the choir and various places of note in the beautiful church, Esme whispered to her, "I thought perhaps you might burst into flames. Is that why you would not kneel?"

"Could you trust your soul and kneel to a god who would burn unbelievers and destroy the world in his name?"

"I bet you would kneel for your queen."

"I trust her to execute me if I don't."

"Ouch, harsh queen."

"Is yours any better?"

"Touché."

"Let's leave it at, your god and I agree to disagree, or at least leave each other alone and hope each follows a bright path in this Life."

Tomàs cleared his throat and they quickly caught up to him in the choir loft, where the back walls were covered in art of a most unusual nature.

"Are each of these a murder?" Esme asked as she peered closely at the nearest wall.

"Not murder, no. Each Saint is pictured at the very moment of their martyrdom, the miraculous moments when they sacrificed their lives for the glory of the Lord." His well-formed mouth quirked up in a smile. "A little gruesome, I admit, but beautiful nonetheless."

"Gruesome I can accommodate. What I find difficult to understand is why the violence has been brought here."

"*Padre* Rodriquez says that these *retablos* show that which the Saints endured to hold the darkness at bay and allow us our chance for redemption in the eyes of the Lord. You see the violence here of man, so we may better admire the beauty of Life around us."

The nearest carved scene showed a man hanging upside down, blood dripping onto the ground while angels hovered in the corners watching. "That is a profound outlook, *Señor* Tomàs." Kinzy gave him a small bow for his reverence. She had seen that look, eyes bright and a wildness deep within, in the eyes of the Joyous Ones. They were Fae who focused solely on reverence for the energy of Nature and Life, fulfilling a similar role to that of priest.

Tomàs simply shrugged. "If my life had been different, perhaps I would have been a priest." He turned back to them. "Now let me take you to the bell tower. We will soon see if you can indeed handle the steepness of the mountain trails."

At the top of the low-ceilinged stairs and through an arched wooden door, they stepped up into the tower. Kinzy knew she should be amazed at the view, but she instead felt as if the city spread out around them like an infestation upon the mountain, a colorful jumble of rooftops, streets, and smoke, where people swarmed like small scavenger ants, spreading themselves voraciously.

The history of this place, as she'd read in the books Master Shabao had packed for her, repelled her with a strength she had not expected. An entire Inca capital city lay beneath the cobblestones and dwellings of Quito. The subjugation of the

Inca empire had been complete and brutal, perpetrated by men this church supported because it gave them places to build more churches. She shook her head to clear the negativity building inside.

"Kinzy, are you all right? Is it the altitude?" Esme laid a gentle hand on her arm, making Kinzy realize she'd clenched her fists.

"I am fine, just taking in the view."

Esme moved to the railing.

"Tomàs, in what direction are we to travel? Toward that mountain there?" Esme pointed into the distance.

"We will journey that way." He took her arm and moved it a little to the left. "Our trail leads between those two majestic peaks."

Their guide's attention dropped to Esme's ample bosom. Esme arched a critical eyebrow at him as she recovered her arm and stepped away. "I would advise you to keep your eyes focused on the trail from here on out, *Señor* Tomàs."

He looked only a little chastened. "Of course, *Señora.* Forgive me. I was just admiring the scenery."

At his suggestive tone, Esme's face hardened. "This particular scenery is not yours to admire."

Tomàs swept her a courtly bow but could not quite wipe the grin off his face. Kinzy ignored him as his gaze fell on her. "Of course, *Señora.* There is always magnificent scenery elsewhere."

In a blink, Esme twisted his hand up behind his back. "Your sole function on this trip is to keep us on the correct trail, Tomàs. Is that quite clear?

Tomàs did not struggle. "Rafael said you were a handful."

Esme pulled his arm up further until he yelped with the pain. She put her lips to his ear. "I'll thank you not to mention that man's name again. Is that also clear?"

The smugness drained away. "*Si, Señora! Claro!* I will not mention my cousin ever again. I swear!"

Esme released him with a frown. "Rafael is your cousin? Well, that certainly explains both your cavalier treatment of women and a certain physical resemblance."

Kinzy was unsure what Rafael meant to Esme, but he was certainly someone important. There was pain in her, and although Esme had said she trusted the man who arranged their travel with her life, Kinzy had to wonder what transpired between them. She vowed to speak of Rafael later. From a safe distance.

They continued the tour, Kinzy noting Esme's contrived smile, and Tomàs glancing their way with narrowed eyes when he thought they were not looking. There were fewer comments from the Lady, and more frequent impolite mutters from their guide. She was certain Esme could not hear, but Kinzy stored them for future use.

Although dinner that evening at La Plaza Grande was wonderful, disturbing thoughts of the history of Quito plagued her. The two of them each helped the other out of their corsets once they'd made it back to their rooms, allowing Lucia to go to her bed. Esme tossed them in a small trunk of gear they would leave behind. Kinzy felt again the soft velvet of her green gown, and then tossed it in and locked the trunk. Tomorrow she would wear her leathers under her travel dress. She always found it wise to listen to her instincts, and her gut told her something was disturbed here, something dangerous.

Chapter Thirteen

The Cloud Forests of Ecuador ranked as one of the most miserable environments Esme had ever trekked through. She shivered in her mist-dampened clothes, waiting for the pale sun to burn off the morning's chill and concentrated on putting one careful foot in front of the other, ever mindful of the fact that they hiked along a narrow precipice on the side of a mountain. Kinzy, who walked behind her, seemed utterly unaffected by the cold or the damp, forcing Esme to keep her complaints to herself. She would not be out-adventured by some wispy little chit of a girl, Fae or no.

Tomàs walked ahead of them, while their train of porters consisting of a number of locals and four rather unpleasant llamas, brought up the tail. Abruptly, Tomàs veered left, away from the ledge, disappearing for a moment around the vine and grass covered side of a vertical cliff. Esme followed and found the face of the mountain was actually a stone wall. A few steps more and she realized they had passed through an overgrown entrance to some Inca building, hidden by hundreds of years of determined vegetation.

Someone had been using the place. The vines had been cleared from the doorway, and empty food tins lay scattered in a corner where blackened pavers indicated someone had built a fire. Tomàs slipped off his pack and let it drop to the stone floor, remarkably dry thanks to a sturdy roof of thatch that covered a portion of the space.

The entire group of them fit comfortably inside with room to spare, even the llamas.

"We will rest here for a few moments," he said, eyeing Esme, who tried to straighten under the scrutiny.

They'd only been walking a couple of hours, although it felt like an eternity since breakfast. "Why on earth didn't we just push through last night so we could have slept here?" Her tone sounded more strident than she meant, but her *joie de vivre* was running low. The previous night had been spent under a leaky tarp in a pouring rainstorm without a fire. Not even a single pair of dry socks remained in her pack, and with the unpredictable weather, she held little hope of ever having some. Even the stifling, breath-stealing heat of the Sudan felt more congenial than this place. At least in the Sudan the air contained oxygen.

"Because, my lady, that trail is slick as the devil when it rains. Even the llamas, sure-footed as they are, might have slipped. I could not risk a mishap."

He squatted in front of the ring of stones that had been used as a fire pit and poked the ashes with a stick. "Cold." He called to their head porter, a congenial Quechua man with a quick smile who barely stood an inch taller than Kinzy and whose deeply tanned face indicated a life spent in the sun. "Mani, let's get a fire going." Tomàs looked up at Esme and Kinzy. "We'll rest here for a bit, have something warm to drink."

Esme removed her pack, which contained her spare

clothes, her journal, her bed roll, a canteen, and her own supply of coca leaves and *ypta*, the alkaline substance that activated the leaves. She slid into an unladylike squat against the stone wall. The altitude had caught up to her, she thought. She did not normally feel such fatigue. Her head pounded and she felt nauseous. Yesterday she'd vomited. In front of Tomàs, of all people. Now the nausea threatened to return, and worse, breathing had become like sucking air through a straw. Although it galled her to be seen taking it, it was time for more coca leaves.

Kinzy, of course, didn't seem to be adversely affected by either the altitude or the weather, which annoyed Esme to no end. She felt a strong sense of competition with the girl that did her no credit. Cooper would *not* approve.

Esme rested against the smooth stone wall, trying to appear as though she were not gasping like a beached fish, and focused on the work that had gone into forming the wall out of large and somewhat irregular blocks. They were put together without mortar yet fit so snug she could not have gotten a nail file between them. How many men, she wondered, had it taken to carry the blocks of stone to these heights from wherever they were quarried?

When Tomàs handed her and Kinzy each a tin cup filled with hot coffee, she took hers gratefully. "Thank you, Tomàs." She gestured around them. "It appears this place has been used by more modern people."

"The Inca trails are still used by the descendants of the Inca, as well as by those of us who lead expeditions into the highlands." His smirk filled in what he didn't say: *for tourists like you.*

Esme regarded his scruffy, bearded face, wavy disheveled hair, black as a raven's wing, and those impenetrable dark brown eyes. Rafael's letter had said he trusted their guide like a brother, yet she could not imagine the two men together, they were so different in personality. Rafael was refined, courtly, with a wicked but genteel sense of humor. He'd been well-educated, with a degree in medicine, conversant in both science and poetry. The traits he and Tomàs had in common could be contained in a teaspoon, yet they shared a physical resemblance. The high cheekbones, the jaw line, the shape of their mouths; all were similar enough that they could have been brothers.

"Forgive my impertinence, Tomàs, but how did you come to be a guide in these regions? Your accent tells me you are from Basque country, so you did not grow up here."

He shrugged. "I am suited to it. I enjoy the highlands, enjoy the solitude, the peace of the ruins. If I could live without having to work, I could happily spend my life up here." He spread his hands, shrugged. "Alas, even here in the Andes, one needs money to survive. So I escort people on their little trips and earn my daily bread."

Mani, who squatted on the ground not far away, gave a gentle chuckle. "The worst crime among my people is indolence. The guide work keeps Tomàs from being lazy, as he makes a poor farmer. The *apus* are pleased, and Tomàs does not need to eat his meals at my table *every* night."

There was a lot in that sentence for Esme to unpack. She started with the most unfamiliar thing. "Mani, what are these a*pus*?"

"They are the spirits of the mountains. Each mountain or lake has its own *apu*. Each morning, we make offerings to the *apus* and to Pachamama, the earth mother. *Chicha*, tobacco, maize."

So that is what the little group of porters did as they huddled together at dawn. She had seen them pour some liquid onto the ground and lay things out on a blanket before chewing coca leaves and recognized it as some kind of ritual but had no idea of the purpose. "How lovely!" She sipped at the coffee and relaxed in the warmth of the fire Mani had coaxed to life in the fire pit. "Thank you for sharing that."

Mani winked and sketched a bow. "Of course."

Tomàs drained his cup and stood. "Please excuse me for a moment, *Señoras.*" He stood and stalked off, disappearing around one of the structure's external walls. Esme allowed herself an eye roll. "Is he always so charming?"

Mani chuckled again. "You must not judge him so harshly, *Señora.* He has many bad memories. Like bad spirits, they trouble him, day and night."

Esme wondered where the man had fought. If he grew up in Basque country, perhaps he'd been involved in the Carlist revolt. It had been Spaniard against Spaniard then, brother against brother. Or maybe he had fought in defense of Spain against Bonaparte's most recent invasion attempt. God, there were just too many wars, too many places in the world where young men suffered. "I'm sorry to hear that. He finds some measure of peace here, in the mountains?"

Mani nodded. "It helps. I tell him he needs to find a woman. Make a home. But he no listen. He never listen." Mani made a face, shrugged.

Esme frowned, having heard that argument all too many times herself. "Marital domesticity is not for everyone, I'm afraid, Mani."

He didn't have the impertinence to ask her the obvious question, but she could see it in his eyes. Instead he gestured at her cup. "You like more?"

She shook her head. Between the caffeine in the coffee and the coca leaves, her whole body jangled with energy, even while her eyes drooped from fatigue. "More and I'll not sleep a wink tonight."

"You just wait. The day after tomorrow is a holy day. We will have a special dinner after which we will drink some *chicha*. You will have some *chicha* with us and you will sleep nice."

"What is this *chicha*?"

"It is from maize. Like your beer, only strong. It is a sacred offering to Pachamama also. You will try it. You will like it." He laughed again, his eyes crinkling. "But you must not like it too much!"

She laughed. "I promise, I won't."

Mani stood easily, tossed the rest of his coffee on the ground. "I check on llamas now. Good day, *Señora*."

She sat back against her wall and watched him wander over to where Kinzy stood talking to the natives. She'd become quite apt with their language. Esme browbeat herself for not making more of an effort in that regard, but she just didn't have the energy at the moment. Right now, she decided, she'd enjoy the brief respite, the warmth of the fire, and the blessed sensation of not climbing up another damn hill.

They hiked the rest of the day. In the afternoon, the path turned to the east, leading onto a huge plateau that sloped gently upward. They passed more tumbled ruins as they went, most little more than piles of stones amid hummocks of grass. Esme's breathing eased a bit after more coca leaves, and for a few lovely hours the clouds dissipated and the sun shone brightly, if not warmly. She paused half way up the slope and pulled out her map. Kinzy came up beside her, peering down at the parchment as well.

"Look. These ruins, that enormous hill. It matches this spot on the map." She tapped the heavy duty paper. "There is also a symbol of a warrior. Do you suppose there was a battle here with the Inca, during their flight from the conquistadors?"

"It is possible." She raised a hand to shield her eyes, scanning the hill covered in tall grasses that waved hypnotically in a constant breeze.

The sun began westering and clouds swept in again. Soon thunder rumbled in the distance, a promise of more rain.

Tomàs dropped back and grumbled a few words with Mani in low tones, then paused until the ladies came even with him.

"We'll camp early tonight. The storm may pass us but I would rather be prepared. There is a place just ahead that will provide better shelter. It is a *pucara*, an Inca watchtower, and it is in decent shape. No roof, but we can pitch our tents inside, out of the wind, and rig a tarp over yours to protect you further from the rain."

"Thank you, Tomàs." She wanted to ask him about the *pucaras* and how they had served the Inca, but he strode rapidly away. She snorted. "Perhaps I should have made eyes at him, as I did Reynard, instead of yanking his arm behind his back. He seems to have become sullen and taciturn."

Kinzy raised her eyebrows. "You did seem to find fault rather quickly at the church. Is it his class that made you react so? A common man versus a wealthy one? Or because he mentioned his cousin, this Rafael? Rafael and Tomàs seem to be your allies, and yet you treat mention of Rafael's name as if he were your enemy."

Esme's breath caught in her throat. She kept her countenance blank, but her heart beat a little faster at Rafi's name. Damn it, she should be over him by now. It infuriated her that just the sound of his name sent the blood thrumming in her ears and twisted up her insides. "I would appreciate it if we dropped the subject of Tomàs's cousin."

"Did he commit some crime against you?"

"Crime? No. He simply loved himself more than he loved me. Hardly a punishable offense, and yet." She shoved all those feelings deep down inside her. Time to let go of old business. Again. She had outgrown her childish infatuation. She'd become an adult woman, a woman of experience and wisdom. "I was young. Foolish. I gave my heart without thinking. Rafael made his choice, and for a long time after I resented him for it. I let myself believe that his feelings were the same as mine, that a man could be capable of feeling for me what I felt for him." She sucked in a breath, picked up her pace, needing to burn off her anger.

Kinzy sped up to keep pace with her. "I am confused at these relations between humans, especially between men and women. I fear I will never understand them. The word love is whispered with both longing and dread. What is love?"

Esme considered. "Love is an ideal. Young girls fantasize about a man who will worship them, be handsome and dashing, brave and bold, and above all things, be kind and loving. Love should be unconditional, not given only upon reciprocation, or obedience. Love is partnership, sharing, the true meeting of two souls traveling different paths, but always together." She paused, swallowed hard against the lump in her throat.

"But it is a feeling. What does love feel like? How do you know when you feel love?"

"Once upon a time, I thought I knew." Her lips compressed. "Apparently, I was wrong." She stopped and faced Kinzy. "What I can tell you, with absolute certainty, is that men are incapable of that kind of love, Kinzalynn. I am convinced, and not without cause, that they do not have the same capacity that women have to love unconditionally." She looked away from the intently curious Fae woman. "A lesson I learned the hard way. Now, I only give as much as I can reasonably expect to receive, which in the case of most men is little enough indeed. I suppose I should thank Rafael for teaching me that."

"His name still makes you angry."

Esme waved her hand dismissively. "Angry at myself mostly. I hate to be reminded of my mistakes." She paused, shielded her eyes with her hand, taking in the low grassy hill they climbed. In the distance stood a tall stone structure surrounded by more tumbled ruins. "That must be the pucara Tomàs mentioned. We should get there soon." She forced her expression to soften. "Let's hurry. I would love a sponge bath before we retire tonight. I feel as though I have the dirt of the centuries in every crevice."

"On that, we are in complete agreement." Kinzy gestured for Esme to precede her up the trail.

Gratified that the young woman let the subject drop, Esme hurried up the hill toward the *pucara*, fueled by anger and the gritty coca leaves.

Chapter Fourteen

Trell chittered and bobbed his furry head in impatience.

Let me finish setting up our tent, and I'll be ready. Kinzy tied her final knot and tested that corner with a quick tug on the pole rope. The tent would hold up to the winds and rains at this height on the mountain, though it did little to keep out the damp and chill. She reveled in the power of the storms and wind, but she preferred dry leathers and a nice fire on this expedition.

Around her, the others were also well into the routine of setting up tents and a cooking fire, taking care of the llamas and other necessities. Esme collapsed by the fire where Mani would soon start the evening meal. The coffee pot was already heating. Kinzy found this moment the best time to leave the others, telling them she and Trell enjoyed hunting to supplement their supplies. She always completed her duties first, though, so no one would miss her, and she tried to be back before dinner. She would catch whatever small game she found to supplement their stores. But someone needed to check their backtrail and scout further afield for any sign of danger.

Inside the tent she shared with Esme, she quietly arranged their cots, blankets, and laid out their clothing for bed, but she could not decide just what she would report to Queen Airmed today. The expedition had travelled well up into the Andes, everyone seeming to accept the story that she was Esme's lady's companion. She had already mentioned Reynard to the queen, and his overt interest in their affairs and travel plans, but there was no sign of him or any other parties on the mountain, faeleath or human. No one else seemed to be hunting for the mummy, or for her.

The quiet unnerved her.

She stopped by the fire on her way out of camp. "Esme, the tent is ready."

"Thank you, Kinzy. I'll set up my things as soon as I've had some coffee." Her new friend tightly gripped her tin cup like a lifeline.

Esme sounded more tired each day. Kinzy worried about the effects of the numerous coca leaves the woman had consumed. Tomàs warned them about the signs of altitude sickness, and though Esme seemed fine, Kinzy watched over her just in case. She needed Esme and this expedition to reach the Incan city high up in the clouds, the resting place of the ancient bones Queen Airmed was so concerned about.

Trell ran through the legs of the llamas who snorted and stamped, barely missing the tail of the mongoose annoying them.

"Stop bothering the llamas, Trell!" She waved at the porter on sentry duty near the pack animals. "Heading out to hunt, I should return near dark."

Trell changed form as soon as they passed beyond the camp and the watching eyes of Tomàs and the others, his wings whipping out with a snap as he launched happily into the air. He was faster at checking the backtrail from high above, and more difficult for enemy eyes to notice in the clouds that formed in the late afternoon. Kinzy checked for tracks and other signs, and they both hunted small game to better explain their absence from camp.

At a spot along the rockface near the trail, Kinzy lithely climbed above to see more of their surroundings from higher ground.

The late afternoon sun headed toward the edge of the volcano across from them. Much of the valley below lay in darkness already. The air felt cleaner than Quito. Here in the Andes, the air was pleasantly cool, crisp, with shades of earthiness. She could delightfully breathe in to her fullest. She sensed natural earth magic around them, but nothing out of the ordinary for such an old and extraordinary place.

Trell dropped another small furry creature he'd killed next to her. She tossed it with the others in her game bag. Mani had shown her the best way to skin and roast them, and Trell had become fond of chasing the little beasts.

No more, Trell, we have enough. No sense having them think we are too good at hunting.

I'm going to find one more to snack on. Maybe a present for the queen.

Kinzy laughed as she pictured Trell dropping a furry bomb in the lap of the regally dressed queen.

Settled on a large outcrop with her legs hanging over the edge, she brought out her pen, a small scroll of paper and the message harness for Trell. While he soared above her, keeping watch and an eye out for his snack, she carefully crafted her report.

. . .

Your Majesty,

The mountains are wetter than imagined. The game is different but makes a good roast. We are proceeding, no sign of others. Our guide, Tomàs, estimates it will be at least 6 more days. The coca leaves do help with the effects of the altitude, though I am not as affected as the humans.

Yours to command ~ K

She called to Trell through their link and fastened the harness on him with the report tucked safely in the message tube.

You don't need to take a gift to the queen. Straight to Her Majesty, come back when you are able. I will wait for you.

Trell leapt from the ledge and disappeared, to wing his way to Queen Airmed with a flash of disappointment at her for missing out on a good snack.

Kinzy closed her eyes and experienced the quiet breezes as they brushed along the tall grasses and played in the rock faces around her. They swept down the mountain with a touch of determined power as they did before the rains came with the dampness and smell of the cold water drops to come. This is what the Fae had lost, being trapped within Tír na nÓg. They no longer experienced the power of real weather, its natural energy.

She could not stay long, or there would be too many questions. She'd give the game bag to Mani and he'd have it skinned and ready to roast for tomorrow's breakfast. For now though, the setting sun bathed the volcano opposite her perch in an orange-gold haze. Esme's map had shown an Inca Warrior marker next. That could mean a place of a famous battle, a training location for Inca warriors, or simply where the conquistadors and priests had found and slain some of the Inca they followed. *Study the future well, a shadow always looks for hints*, her Master taught. She sat deep in meditation until Trell returned. He wrapped his tail around her neck and snuggled in.

Your breath smells like bacon and ... plum pudding?

The queen is much more generous than you are.

Kinzy reached back and removed the message in his harness.

My dear K, watch all your circles. The shadows tell me little of the French human agent other than he has Fae friends. We do not know the full nature of their relationship or what assistance they give, but the French want the artefact. No word of Fae agents on the southern continents at all. Bonaparte's temper rises with each telegram received. ~ A

Circles usually meant a training circle to Kinzy, or a circle of friends, but the queen would not say it unless it meant something important. Some days Kinzy wished the queen would just speak plainly and be straightforward. Elder Fae seemed to abhor such practices, though. Perhaps the magic within them caused the need to be enigmatic, or maybe they reveled in giving others a headache.

But Kinzy's eye went to the silver ring on her right hand that she played with, spinning the silver circle around her finger. A Master's ring with history and power. She felt nothing active from it, though she could sense other pockets of natural magic in the area. It felt as if the ring slept, but what deep magic must be involved that an object *slept*? Someday the ring would awaken and she anticipated something special and subtle.

Esme's bracelet was another circle she'd dealt with along her journey. On the airship, the bracelet had truly bothered her. Esme had been able to tell the magic resided in Kinzy, and yet Kinzy had detected no magic in the bracelet. That puzzled her. She had mentioned it in her report to the queen, but without the device to study there were few clues she could give the mages who desired more answers to all of their questions.

Kinzy breathed deeply of the mountain air and stretched her senses around her, another circle.

A different magic zipped closer to her, she opened her eyes and swung around to see a small glowing dot of essence floating toward her, ignoring the wind, weaving in and out of the tall yellow grass on the hill behind her. It swung around to hover before her, happiness and curiosity stemming from it's core. A will-o-the-wisp. Kinzy held out her hand and it sat in her palm, an impossible thing outside of Tír na nÓg. She'd been taught that when the Fae were banished from this world, they took all magic with them into Tír na nÓg. Natural magic could grow within the earth still, but without purpose, without intelligence, it was just essence. This glowing ball of fairy dust lived, recognized her kinship, and with a sweet kiss upon her palm, continued its playful path down the mountainside.

The wisp should not exist here. Trell whispered in her mind, perfectly still around her neck.

No, it should not. Kinzy wondered what other surprises these mountains held, but she would watch all her circles for magical interference, as well as human, with her mission.

Time to get back to the others, my friend.

Time for dinner?

Yes, you flying stomach.

They made it back just as Mani started dishing out dinner for everyone. He'd even saved a small rodent, a cuy, for Trell, which the drakkeki took gingerly with a thankful bob of his furry mongoose head that made those around the fire laugh at his cuteness. They just had no idea.

What? I'm cute! Cuter than you.

Kinzy ignored him and ate her meal, the day's revelations running in circles in her mind.

Chapter Fifteen

"Esme! Wake up!" The voice hissed in her ear, a sound so familiar that when she opened her eyes she expected to see her mother.

Instead, a hulking, bare-chested native loomed over her, looking for all the world like the pictures she'd seen of Inca warriors. He glared at her with loathing.

Behind him, no, *through* him, Esme saw another figure and cried out to Kinzy, even as she reached under her pillow for her pistol.

She brought it to bear too late. The man raised a long, broad sword-like thing, with jagged serrations on either edge. She fired as the blade arced down towards her, hoping Kinzy heard the warning in time to save herself.

Icy pain sliced across her torso, the cold burning from the inside out.

The Inca stumbled back. He howled. His translucent shape shrunk into a black cloud which collapsed to a point and vanished.

Esme shivered, put her hand to her torso. Ice crystals coated her clothing. She searched for a wound but found none.

Another warrior stepped into their tent. The lack of a wound became irrelevant.

Kinzy stood in her leathers, blades out and combat-ready, staring around like a blind woman. The Inca raised his weapon, ready to cleave her in two. Esme shouted another warning, but the girl didn't seem to see the warrior standing right in front of her. Kinzy slashed at the air, but her draiglanns passed right through him.

Suddenly, Esme understood. The sudden cold, the translucent nature of the things. The things were just like her mother, creatures from the other side of the veil. "Kinzy, they're spirits! Inca spirits!" She aimed her pistol at the warrior, but Kinzy stood in the line of fire. Trell screeched and leapt from Kinzy's shoulder into the face of the Inca, claws outstretched.

The spirit wailed. He flung up a hand, but it passed right through the drakkeki's body. Esme wondered if he experienced the same painful, supernatural cold she had. Her whole body ached where she'd been struck.

Trell opened his mouth and although Esme couldn't hear a sound, she felt the vibration in her head and a stabbing pain in her ears. Just as before, the warrior turned vaporous, condensed into a black point, and winked out of existence.

From outside the tent came blasts of gunfire. The piteous shriek of an injured llama. Men yelling and screaming.

She looked at her gun. Remembered that the priest had blessed her weapon before they'd left Quito. Could a Catholic blessing repel an Inca spirit? She had no other explanation.

Kinzy stared at her, while Trell clambered back onto the Fae woman's shoulder and chittered in her ear. "I cannot see them, though Trell says they are there." Kinzy stroked the head of her small companion.

"Consider yourself lucky, then. They are terrifying."

"How is it that you can see them and I cannot?"

Esme paused. Her belief in the existence of those who'd passed on typically earned her ridicule. She wasn't sure she felt ready to discuss her beliefs with Kinzy, nor was now the time. Beyond the tent a battle ensued. "I've always been able to see spirits. Some people have a gift for it." She pointed outside as she stood. "You ready? There are more."

"I am, but I have no weapons to use against such things."

Gratified the Fae woman had not questioned her abilities, Esme gave a manic laugh. "Yes, you do. You have him and I have *this*." She held up her pistol. "A gun with blessed bullets. Knew they'd come in handy." Brandishing her weapon, she raced outside.

Two Inca spirits waited for them, weapons raised. Beyond them, through them, Esme saw Tomàs struggle with what appeared to be two flesh and blood attackers. They were dressed like the spectral warriors, but Tomàs's knife proved their humanity. Both bled. On the ground nearby, Mani straddled another, beating his fist into another attacker's face.

Esme aimed, careful not to hit one of their own men. In that moment, the spirit sliced into her with his weapon.

She staggered. The spectral blow spun her and pain lanced through her chest. Dropping to her knees, she gulped for air. A third blow hit her across the back of her neck, spears of invisible ice slicing into her. She touched her throat, amazed her head remained attached. A glaze of ice coated her skin where the spectral weapon passed through her.

Energy drained out of her like blood and she collapsed. She didn't think she could withstand another blow. Rolling over onto her back, she fired upward.

The spirit cried out and dissipated before his fourth blow connected.

Esme fell back again, too weak to hold her head up. She shivered, no longer able to feel her fingers and toes. Her pistol fell from her hand. The battle raged on around her, lit eerily by the banked fire, but she felt as though she were miles away. The people around her moved as though through treacle. With a deadly grace, Kinzy stabbed one of the mortal attackers and Esme could count each drop of blood that fell from the curved blade as it withdrew.

A mist descended and the world blurred.

A weight thumped down on her chest. Through heavy lids, she saw Trell, his amber eyes, with their odd, vertical pupils, fixed on hers.

A warmth suffused her, and the mist evaporated. In a literal beat of her heart, the world resumed its normal pace.

She didn't know what the little winged creature had done, but it had saved her life. "Thank you, Trell. You are a scholar and a gentleman."

The creature trilled and preened, then raced off to his mistress, who dispatched her next human foe with her usual alacrity. Esme clambered to her feet and cocked her pistol, thrilled to be back in the fight. Across the small enclosed space, Tomàs had his back against the broken wall of the *pucara*, eyes wide in terror as one of the spectral warriors impaled him.

She couldn't shoot, she'd only hit Tomàs, but if her blessed bullets dispelled the spirits, then maybe holy water would as well. She hurried back into the tent, found the three vials she had filled from the font at the San Francisco church, and uncorked one as she ran towards Tomàs.

Tomàs screamed and raised his hands against the spirit's invisible attack. The blow should have severed his torso. Instead it left a trail of ice and frost across Tomàs's shirt and arm. Esme shouted at the thing to get its attention, not knowing how much more Tomàs could take.

The warrior turned towards her and raised his blade.

"Be gone! This is not your world any longer!" With her words, Esme flung the contents of the vial at the spirit.

The spectral warrior shrieked as the holy water sizzled through it. With a pop, and the warrior vanished like the others.

Tomàs gasped and slid to the ground. Esme paused to make sure he still breathed, then turned as she uncorked another vial. She scanned the small enclosure, saw Kinzy also looking around, her blades dripping with blood. The own men, their porters, were gone, probably hiding in the darkness or dead. Five real Incan attackers, dressed just like the spectral warriors, lay bloodied and unmoving around the central campfire. Other than Kinzy, who turned slowly in a circle herself, and Tomàs, who lay panting on the ground, nothing else moved.

Esme regarded the carnage. "Dear God in heaven." She stooped over one of the attackers, closed his now unseeing eyes then turned back to Tomàs. "Tomàs? Can you hear me?"

His eyelids fluttered. "Oh, *Señora*, am I dead or alive? I am cold like the grave."

Why were Spaniards such dramatic idiots? Esme took his hand and rubbed at the thin layer of ice. "You are very much alive, Tomàs."

He took her hand and pulled her towards him, pressing his face against her chest, covered now with only her own chilled, damp blouse. "Please, hold me close, I am so cold."

Esme had been genuinely worried a moment before. Now she pushed him away. "Kinzy, I believe Tomàs is in need of a blanket." She turned towards the woman, saw one of the spectral warriors with his large bladed weapon held high over his head, ready to strike.

"Kinzy, behind you!"

Esme leaped up and threw the vial of holy water at the

Inca, but not before it brought the huge spiked weapon down through Kinzy's head.

The Fae dropped as though she'd been clubbed. The screaming warrior did not fade into black smoke. Esme had missed. The thing made a low, vibrating sound that might have been a laugh and stalked slowly forward, his eyes now focused on her. She fumbled in her pocket to find the third and final vial. Her chilled fingers plucked futilely at the cork. The vial dropped to the ground, rolled away. "Damn it!" She fell to her hands and knees, searching the rocky, grass-covered stones of the *pucara's* floor, but she couldn't see in the dim light. Shadows writhed in the flickering firelight making it even harder.

The thing stood over her, lips pulled back in a frightful rictus.

Esme groped through the matted grass while staring up at the spectre. "You are not wanted here. This is no longer your home."

He raised his weapon overhead. His voice rasped like a quill on parchment. "You are the one who is not wanted. Death to those who would violate the resting place of the king!"

Her fingers finally closed around the smooth glass of the vial. She hurled herself at the creature and broke the glass vial with her bare hands, dousing both her and the spirit with the water.

The warrior hissed and she passed through it, stumbling to her knees, engulfed by numbing cold. In a shrinking cloud of black smoke, the Inca left the mortal realm with a bang.

Esme gasped for breath, juddering with cold. She jumped when she felt a warm hand on her shoulder.

Kinzy squatted beside her, peering down into her face. "Are you okay?"

Taking stock of herself, Esme realized that other than being chilled to the bone, her only real injuries were the cuts on her hands from the broken vial. "I'll live. Although I may never feel warm again. What about you?"

Kinzy shrugged. "I too ache with cold."

Tomàs struggled to his feet and helped Esme, then wrapped his arm around her. "I can help you with that, *Señora*."

Esme turned a baleful look on him and he dropped his arm, but not his wicked grin. In that moment, by the light of the fire, he reminded her of Rafael more than ever. "We have more important priorities, like seeing to our men." She looked her friend up and down. "How much of that blood is yours?"

Kinzy spent a moment examining her leathers. "Some, but not much. A small wound on my arm, a nick above my eye." She shrugged in her characteristic self-effacing manner. "I've had worse."

Esme nodded. "I wager you have."

Kinzy nodded at the blood on Esme's own hands, caused by the breaking of the vial. "And your wounds?"

"Shallow cuts. They'll heal soon enough." The smell of the dead, of blood and the stink of one whose bowels had released in death, drew her attention. Familiar if awful smells from her time as a nurse. "We'll have to find a way to deal with these strangers. Heathens they may be, but I will not leave them to be scavenged. What's happened to our porters? Were they killed?"

"Two of them ran," Tomàs said. "The last I saw of Mani, he fought with one of the bastards—" He stopped. "Forgive me. He fought with one of the fellows. I do not see him here now." His brow furrowed.

Esme heard a scuffling sound at the edge of camp and she rose, scrambling for the pistol she'd dropped earlier.

Mani limped back into camp, propelling one of their porters with repeated shoves. His left leg dragged. "I found this one running. Pedro is rounding up the others. They went and hid in the ruins to the south. Something attacked them there, something they could not see, and left them covered in frost." Mani crossed himself and spat on the ground. "But they are not injured and he will bring them back."

"Well, then. One problem solved." She shot a sideways look at Tomàs, and said under her breath, "Until the next thing frightens them."

Tomàs wore a grim expression. "I will deal with them, *Señora*. Trust me."

She saw again that stubborn, angry, retributive look she had seen in Rafael's eyes when he learned of someone's betrayal. She had to look away.

"Coffee. We will need coffee to restore us." She looked up at Kinzy, grateful to have the woman as an ally. At least for now. "Then we need to discuss how best to prepare for tomorrow." And what to do if the spirits returned.

Chapter Sixteen

Trell scurried through the tent flap in the wee hours of the next morning and hopped into Kinzy's lap as she sat cross-legged on her cot. She'd stayed alert through the night with a constant light touch on Trell's mind while he scouted around camp for any further danger. She'd sharpened her knives and meditated. She had even tried reading, but once she realized her book glorified the atrocities against the Incan empire, she worried even more about the ghostly Incan warriors defending against their expedition's invasion of the mountains. The priest who created their map must have faced the ferocious warriors as well. She had felt their animosity, the anger at their expedition's intrusion. Though it meant they followed the right track, it also meant danger ahead.

After the attack, the men set a double watch, and finally the camp settled down to a restless sleep for the remaining hours til morning. Esme's snores were erratic, dreams of the horrific assault most likely keeping her from a deeper sleep.

It was quiet outside the tent as the rising sun allowed the men to build a cairn in the rocky soil for the porters who had succumbed to the ghostly attack. Trell had led Mani to another ice-covered dead porter just two hours ago. Mani sat in the twilight of pre-dawn next to the body for a long time before he called out for others to help him carry the man back to lay with their dead.

Kinzy stayed out of the way inside the tent while their guide and the remaining porters prepared for their ceremony to appease the *apus* of the mountains and say their final prayers for their dead.

Faeleath taken by the Light received little if any ceremony. Not like the elders and trueborn Fae, who were attended to by the Joyous Ones as if their spirits and those left behind depended on such attention. Warrior faeleath though, had a simple tradition passed from masters to students of blood vows from the living to avenge or hold the departed in the Light. It acknowledged the sacrifice of the dead.

Trell arched his back and shook himself, his fur drenched in morning dew and condensation. Kinzy's face and leather armor now dripped. He softly chittered, miserable at the wet fur, and made sure she knew it. *But a moment in my true form, to feel clean mountain air against my slick scales, and I could be dry again.*

We're in enough trouble. No more shifting form. She used a shirt from her pack to wipe off her face, and then dried Trell with a rough scrub. *Sit still, weasel butt. You've not done enough damage already, that you had to soak me, too?*

Your suffering is nothing compared to mine. He gave a smug snort as she dried his face, then he flopped down on her legs and laid his bedraggled head on her knee. His weariness radiated down their link, and his worry echoed her own.

Kinzy took a deep breath to center herself. *You changed without permission in front of the humans. I am supposed to report that to the queen. But you also saved us from an icy death.*

She felt trapped. The queen could end Trell for breaking Fae law, or the queen could reward him for saving the mission. Her Majesty would know nothing until Kinzy sent a report. If she sent that report.

Trell shivered as she ran her hand down his fur, but he sent love and reassurance through their bond.

Kinzy listened closely, her eyes closed, as Tomàs ended his spoken prayer for the dead and Mani and the others followed with an *Amen*. Then the muttering began.

"*Señor*, it was *el diablo's* work last night."

"*Si*, the spirits rise against us, we need to turn back."

Kinzy could hear the deep breath Tomàs took before answering his men. "I gave my word that we will complete this expedition. You will start packing and after breakfast we will continue forward."

Angry mutters and complaints were met with fury from Mani. "*Basta!* We know these mountains best. Listen to Tomàs, he has never let any of us down." The men went back to their chores, but the disquiet was palpable, a warning of trouble to come.

Tomàs clapped a hand on Mani's shoulder. "Thank you, my friend." He moved among the porters. "Come now. We have made our sacrifices to the mountains, we have given extra prayers. The spirits are now appeased. If you are not satisfied, then I promise an extra pouch of gold to each man!"

A few still muttered and Kinzy noted whispers about the devil-on-wings come to take them. Others questioned if they had appeased the mountain *apus* enough. Still, the men went about their business.

They traveled two days, past a beautiful waterfall that had not changed the mood of the party. The subdued porters muttered and quarreled, a disturbing shift in demeanor from when they'd first left Quito. Trell frequently expressed his disgust with the condensation on his mongoose fur, and then just as frequently would race off into the bushes having spotted or smelled something interesting. He would soon catch up with her, satisfied with whatever he had found, his fur soaked again.

The men stared at the mongoose as it raced here and there, and she worried at the fear on their hard faces. They had seen Trell's true form the night the Inca had attacked, although she'd passed that off as drunk hallucinations of the evening. She thought they had believed her, but still they made the sign of the cross as their gazes followed him.

Kinzy worried often about what price this mission would ask of her. The ancient war that forced the Fae to give up life on Earth and flee to a land of their own magical creation, Tír na nÓg, had made secrecy their primary defense. She'd been asked to assassinate such witnesses to Fae marvels before. To complete her mission, though, she needed Esme, Tomàs, Mani and the men to get her to this place in the lost wilds of the Andes upper slopes. She'd come to like them, even the rogue Tomàs who told indelicate jokes one moment and brought the ladies an extra blanket to ensure their comfort the next. They were, all of them, good people.

She sent no further messages to Queen Airmed, and though she tried to believe it was because there was little to report, she had to face her own fears. She did not want Trell to come to harm, nor any of the others on this expedition. It was very human of her, she knew, but she could not resolve it one way or the other in her mind. Duty warred with her heart.

She studied Esme walking in front of her, pulling out another coca leaf to chew. Kinzy paused to take a leaf from her own satchel and made a show of chewing it herself. She didn't need it, but it helped keep up the appearance of being as human as Esme.

The two women shared a common goal, tasked to acquire

the mummy if they could. Kinzy well knew she must lay claim to it before Esme, as Esme wouldn't simply allow Kinzy to walk away with Atahualpa. Lady Esme was a determined woman, neither stupid, nor used to taking second place. Kinzy would keep her close, but she must make plans to leave the British woman behind.

Kinzy decided to send a brief report on their progress up the mountains and say nothing of Trell's part in repelling the attack of the Incan spirit warriors. Once the mission was complete, no one would care what these men had seen. It would simply be more whispers about the mysteries of the Andes.

Decision made, she felt a moment's relief.

Trell clambered up her leg and around her neck. His furry nose rubbed the side of her jaw. *You grow, young faeleath.*

She reached up to rub around his ears, but her hands came away covered in shed fur. She wiped them on her leather pants. *You shed your wisdom upon me?*

If you allowed me to change, I would be dry and not shed.

It's too dangerous, my friend.

She had learned Fae history long ago, how humans had feared the Fae, yet craved their magic. Master Shabao always said that if you lived long enough, history repeated itself. Human memory was short, their lives fleeting. Though their books taught them of events that had come before, humans continued to pursue the same war-laden paths. The Fae were right to fear re-discovery by the humans.

Drakkeki do not fear humans!

With a brief squeezing of his claws on her neck, Trell was off again, clambering up Esme's walking skirt and begging for a treat. Esme laughed and produced a bit of jerky to appease the smug little devil.

Chapter Seventeen

More days of trekking up and down broad, grass-covered hills had dampened Esme's enthusiasm. The daily downpours and the lack of oxygen drowned her spirits and weighed down her legs. When they arrived at the spot Tomàs had selected for their camp that night, Esme groaned in relief.

While the rain blew sideways, sluicing down her face into her collar, she kept out of the way as Mani and the porters erected a roof tarp. When they finished, she helped Kinzy set up their tent while the porters turned to setting up their less luxurious accommodations. Esme laid out their sleeping rolls in slow motion, chilled and exhausted. Moving out into the common area, she slid down the slick stone wall of the pucara, ignoring the growing puddle of water beneath her. What did a puddle matter when she was drenched to the skin already? Kinzy, still utterly unaffected by the altitude, bustled about, assisting Tomàs to start a fire under the newly-erected tarp.

When Tomàs squatted down next to Esme, a cup of hot

coffee for her in his hands, her eyes snapped open with a start. She realized with shame she had drifted into a doze.

"Take this, *Señora*. It will warm you."

Esme wrapped her stiff, icy fingers around the warm cup and took a grateful sip. She sputtered realizing the cup contained more than just coffee. The liquor burned delightfully and a little of her *joie de vivre* returned. "Thank you, Tomàs."

"*De nada*."

The flames crackled in the ensuing silence.

"You are not—" Tomàs began. At the same time Esme said, "You look like—" They both smiled, and Tomàs gestured for her to continue first.

She started again, examining his face in the firelight. "You look like him, you know. Rafael."

He snorted a laugh. "Me? No. Rafael *es muy guapo*. It was Rafael that all the young girls chased, like hens and the rooster. His father had much land, much money. I am merely the son of a candle maker." He pointed to the puckered scar that disfigured the side of his face. "And this did me no favors." He leaned back on his elbows and stared into the flames. "Still, if not for Rafael, I would be dead. The scar now seems a small price to have paid."

She wanted to ask how he'd gotten the scar. Before she could think of a polite way to ask, he went on, more reliving the memory aloud than for her benefit. His voice took on a dreamy, contemplative tone.

"I was ten, Rafael was twelve. It was the year after the troubles started again with the Carlists. The capital grew to be a dangerous place for loyalists, and *Don* Mateo, Rafi's father, sent Rafi to spend the summer with Mateo's sister, my mother." He took a drink from his cup which she surmised had even less coffee than did hers. "We were playing *soldados*, soldiers, as boys do, down by the stream. Rafi was teaching me some of the things he had learned from his fencing instructor when three men in the Carlist colors rode down the opposite bank and forded the water. They were on us before we could run. One grabbed me by the collar and hauled me up onto the horse. I think he meant to carry me off to join the Basques militia. I tried to fight back, but I dropped my sword.

"Rafael grabbed the reins, slashed at the man's legs, and the man lost his grip on me. I fell down onto the grass, while the man on the horse spun around and pulled his sword."

Esme watched Tomàs's face, reading anger and fear and humiliation there. She let the man go on, not daring to interrupt.

"It was a sight to behold. Before the man's sword cleared the scabbard, Rafael pierced the blackguard's side. The *villano* tumbled from his saddle, cursing in Basque. I don't think the wound was mortal, but as he landed, I heard the crack as his head hit the ground. He didn't move again.

"I remember scrambling out of the way as the other riders came at us. I pulled the dead man's sword, attacked the one who came at me. I missed, nicked the horse instead. It screamed. God, what a sound. It reared, and that man too fell. He did not hit his head though. He ran toward me." Tomàs paused, looked away. "We played at soldiers, Rafi and I, but I had never seen a real battle. I was just a babe in arms when the first Carlist revolt happened. We played." He drank more, cleared his throat. "When I saw the man three feet from me, ready to drive his blade through my heart, I screamed like my sister. I fell on my ass."

Lost in the past, he stopped speaking and stared into the flames.

As the silence lengthened, her curiosity got the better of her. "How did you survive?"

Tomàs lay back and propped his free hand behind his head, booted ankles crossed, mug on his chest. "Rafael stabbed him through the heart, from behind. When the bastard fell, his sword caught the side of my face, tore open my cheek."

More silence. "And the third rider?"

"Rafi fought with him, wounded him in the shoulder with a thrown dagger. When he saw I was in trouble, he broke off and came to help me. The other man must have thought the odds were no longer in his favor. He turned his horse and rode off upstream."

He raised up onto an elbow and lifted his cup in a toast. "To Rafael, who saved my life."

Esme, reluctantly, raised her own cup as well, although she refused to verbally enjoin the toast.

Tomàs chuckled, took a swig, then said, "And who never ever lets me forget what I owe him." He emptied his cup and tossed it aside before reclining once more.

"He's like that, yes." Esme found her own cup empty.

Tomàs turned his head to look at her. "He was most insistent I escorted you personally. You are important to him. He told me he would cut off my—" He paused, a wicked grin on his face. "He told me bad things would happen if any harm befell you."

Esme bit back a knee jerk scathing retort. "I hope he is at least paying you well."

A shrug. "You are not what I thought you would be. Rafael's women have always been, how you say, ornaments. Like a fancy sword belt, for show. You, you are different. You are the sword." Another laugh. "Sharp. Perhaps even deadly."

She didn't know who to be angrier with, Rafael for his predilection for useless, decorative women, or Tomàs, who'd just insulted her in the same breath he'd given her a compliment. "I am many things, Tomàs, but foremost, I am a woman with a job to do. I need—"

He held up a hand. "No, do not tell me what you need. I do not want to know more than I do. I have seen your map, I know where you want to go. I don't want to know why, or what you seek there, or for whom you seek it. You and Rafi, you are two of a kind. All the secrets, all the foolish missions, all the ridiculous plots and schemes. For what? What changes in the end for the people? We work like dogs every day to feed ourselves, to feed our families." He gestured at Mani, who sat with the porters at their own fire, a little distance away. "The wolf still howls in the darkness beyond our door, waiting for one of us to grow weak, teeth bared and ready." He reached for his abandoned cup, found it empty, scowled.

Esme straightened, her anger heating up. "You're wrong. What we do *does* matter. I spent two years treating the wounds of the young men, no, boys, who came back from the fighting in the colonies. Broken, shattered, bodies mutilated by the natives, half-mad from torture, from killing, from watching others be tortured and killed. We are the only ones who *can* stop it, Tomàs. If not us, then who? Why do you think I do what I do, why Rafael does what he does? I might hate him for abandoning me, but in the end, he did it for the same reason I now help my own government. To stop all of this. To find a way to bring peace, a world without a despot like Napoleon. If the wrong people got their hands on what we're looking for, the whole of Europe would fall. Bonaparte would set flame to Spain and England like the Visigoths burned Rome."

She clutched at his arm, dug her nails into his flesh hard enough to reach through his alcoholic haze. She saw misery in his eyes. He'd seen battle. The horrors of whatever war he fought in made him flinch, made him look away.

"Tomàs, if you don't help us, then even more young boys,

like Mani's sons, will die pointlessly, suffer horribly. If you love your cousin, if you love Mani's children, you must help us. You must get us to our destination."

Alcohol dampened Tomàs's anger, instead of inflaming it. He lapsed back and stared up at the stars showing through the quickly clearing clouds. "Talk is cheap." He grunted, pried her hand from his arm. "Still, I give Rafael my word. I will see you there and back. Not because I think that the grandson of that Corsican upstart is more of a monster than any other man. No, I do it because Rafi fought alongside my father at the battle for San Sebastian. Because he saw my sister married to a good and honest man. Because he paid for my mother to be buried next to her brother, something I could never have afforded to do. But mostly." He staggered to his feet, retrieving his cup after two faltering swipes. "Mostly, I will do it because he saved my life when he could have left me to die of my own cowardice." He flourished the empty cup at her. "So do not fear, *Señora*. I will keep my word." He lurched a few steps. "I may be a coward, but I am still a man of honor."

She stood herself, watching him as he wove his way over to the fire where the porters sat, worried he'd fall over and hurt himself. Could she trust, when push came to shove, that his word was worth the breath it cost him to give it? Not knowing came hard. She could only trust Rafael's judgment, which was harder still.

Chapter Eighteen

Kinzy stepped cautiously to the edge of the cliff and looked down, then leaned out further to peer at the river, snaking through the gorge a thousand feet below. This must be the Green River marked on the map. It did look more green than the normal blue of water. The priest had depicted the bridge accurately as well, though he failed to convey a height that would give anyone ample time to consider the vagaries of life and death before they met their end.

"We are not crossing *that.*" Esme jabbed her finger at the way ahead. "It's a death trap."

They had followed a trail of stone steps up to an Inca rope bridge, hung precariously across the chasm. Kinzy could see the ancient stone trail continue on the other side.

Kinzy turned as Mani laid a hand on her arm, concern on his face. "*Por favor, Señorita,* step away from the edge. *Es muy peligroso.*"

Kinzy nodded and stepped back to consider the rope bridge. "Is that contraption as dangerous as Esme believes?"

"For those bridges that are no longer repaired by a Bridge

Master, *si*. They hold the secrets to making and repairing them. This one look like no Bridge Master for many years."

"Will it hold?"

He squinted his eyes at the bridge. "We will take a llama across first. If the bridge hold for the llama, it hold for us. We make extra prayer to Pachamama."

Soon the first porter, holding the llama's head down with a tight rope, led the beast, step by careful step. Kinzy could see why llamas were used in these mountains, as it took to the straight and narrow rope the same way it took the tight ridges and trails — quick and easy. The bridge swayed, but it held. Mani and Tomàs yelled encouragement that echoed through the gorge, and the rest readied their llamas for the crossing.

Cheers rang out when the porter reached the other side. Tomàs smirked at Esme and swept his arm in invitation. With a tight expression, Esme preceded him onto the bridge, gripping the shoulder high handrails, placing her feet on the thin band of ropes at the base. Kinzy followed Tomàs, her step light and sure.

Trell soon gave up his patience at their pace, leaped from Kinzy's shoulder to the rope railing, and scampered ahead. Esme startled at the unexpected creature skittering over her hand. She scowled at the unrepentant beast, squared her shoulders, and carried on. Kinzy and Tomàs called words of encouragement until Esme turned and told them both, in that sharp yet polite voice, to shut up. Once Esme and Tomàs faced forward again, Kinzy allowed herself a small grin.

When all arrived safely on the other side, the porters took a break for food and water. Kinzy led Esme to a stone to sit on so the woman could recover her breath and have a coca leaf and some water. The woman refused food. It did not look like Esme would be laughing anytime soon.

Tomàs strolled up to them after a moment. "You have recovered from your spell of vapors, *Señora*? We must go."

Esme picked herself up and wordlessly stalked ahead of Tomàs, who winked at Kinzy and followed.

They came to the top of yet another pass and Kinzy chewed on a coca leaf as she looked out on a small rocky grass valley with a lake at one end. Late afternoon had come, the sun would soon hide behind the Andes peaks and the night would turn cold and clammy, and rainy, as always. She'd hoped they would be further along, but even she found the long hikes to be hard on her legs and back.

Esme's breathing turned heavy, focused on the trail as she stepped past. Kinzy had to reach out a hand to stop her and pull her aside. The woman needed to rest, or she might make a false step and slide down the skree and into the dark waters of the lake.

"Few have seen these sights, Esme. Take a moment to look ahead and see where our road takes us. This must be the lake marker on the map." She held out a coca leaf, and the woman shook her head.

Esme rubbed at her eyes, the dark circles there evidence of how much the woman pushed herself, which included the days of long hikes, as well as the horrors they had faced in the dark a few nights ago. So many of the men also showed the effects of the loss of friends and trauma of the attack. Esme spent each night restless and turning, crying out in her sleep. The human put her hands on her hips as she took in some deep breaths and leaned over to look down the sharp drop off on the far side of the trail.

The woman let out a quiet whistle. "Why is it that such beauty lies hidden away in the middle of nowhere?"

"It is beautiful *because* it is in the middle of nowhere. If it wasn't, there would be hotels and houses taking advantage of the view, and steam engines and rails would cut across the slopes to help bring in more supplies for those that enjoyed looking at the beauty. The lake would be filled with boats. It would cease to be as beautiful."

"You certainly paint a bleak picture of human encroachment on nature." Esme sighed. "But you are likely right."

"Colonization comes at a price." Kinzy paused, thinking of the king's plan to make a new Fae colony in North America. There would come a price, and she feared what the Fae might be called to pay. Colonization at its simplest, became a cascade of impositions and destruction of one thing for another. As Nature cast its madness of hunger on all mortal things, that must then eat other things to survive, so humans and their tribes, their communities, their countries and factions, all hunted and destroyed.

She could not ignore that the Fae, too, travelled on a perilously similar path. Kinzy shook her head and simply stepped back onto the trail to continue on, no doubt leaving Esme confused. Kinzy's head roiled these days with too much time to think and dwell on the negative. She tried to focus on the beauty around her, the valley ahead where they would most likely set up camp for the night. But she could not shake a small unsettled part of her mind. Whether by something here in the valley, or the train of her thoughts, she could not tell.

Their trail wound across the mountainside, down to and around the edge of the lake, the shore dotted with a handful of stunted trees and scrub. The water looked calm and peaceful, but her sense of dread dogged each step closer she took down the slope. Kinzy stopped to replenish her canteen as they crossed a small rocky stream falling down from the upper slope and dropping in a waterfall cascade below them into the lake. The water brought a freezing chill up her arm and into her body. The slow creeping cold threatened to engulf her. She snatched her canteen back and sniffed the water in it. It seemed clean, but the ache remained in her very bones as she stood up. She felt pulled toward the lake. Staring at the glassy surface, she knew something was wrong here. Moving on, Kinzy flushed the cold from her, but it seemed familiar in a way. A flush of magic pooled within the valley. She felt ... *power*. A presence that should not be here in this world.

Tomàs called a halt as soon as they hit a flat area near the bottom of the valley between the trail and the lakeshore. Huge boulders, tumbled down from the mountains above them, piled in a way to leave a cave opening beneath the pile where two hunks of stone met, big enough to pitch some of the tents out of the wind and out of sight.

Kinzy set down her pack near where Mani indicated their tent would go and scurried up on top of the rocks. From there she could see across the lake, the valley, and up into the peaks beyond. The lake still tugged at her. Something had claimed this valley, but nothing like this should exist outside Tír na nÓg. She kept watch on the still lake until Esme joined her on top of the largest boulder, as Tomàs organized camp for the night.

Esme had proven herself very unlike the Ladies of her culture. She had skills on the trail, despite her current fatigue, and she never complained. The men treated her like a Lady, but she often laughed that off, at least she had before her physical condition made their courtesies much more necessary.

Then she accepted it as her due, but with heartfelt gratitude as well.

The lake reflected the blue sky and fluffy white piles of cloud that drifted lazily above them. Their rocky path led through the grassy debris the mountains had shed, with the side of the trail falling sharply a good ten feet to the water. Tomàs cautioned them to have a care not to stray too close to the edge.

Esme shaded her eyes from the late afternoon sun. Esme shaded her eyes from the late afternoon sun. "This must be the lake on the map."

Kinzy studied the far shore. "The shape is right. An "s", like a serpent. It looks deep."

"I hope no more spirit warriors come climbing out of it. We'll have to post guards tonight." She peered into the sparkling blue water. "I wonder if there are fish in it? We could bolster our supplies a bit. A little change in the menu would be welcome."

"I'll get my line and hooks. Do you fish?" Kinzy asked, curious, as she knew of no other Lady of the British Empire who stooped to fishing.

Esme wrinkled her nose in disgust. "*Worms.*" She gave an exaggerated shudder. "Scorpions, tarantulas, even poisonous snakes I can handle. Worms give me nightmares. So wiggly and squishy. And that smell!. I will, however, keep you company and we can see what you can catch. Tomàs should know what's edible here." She paused. "Is it just me or does this place, this lake, feel eerie?"

The thought of getting closer to the lake made Kinzy's own stomach churn, and she wondered what affected them. She'd never felt anything like it. Possibly just more Inca Guardians, ready to attack, but this felt different and came from the lake itself. She wished her instincts were more revealing. She would consult Trell, but he napped around her shoulders still. He'd been scouting behind them for most of the afternoon to make sure they were not being followed. He deserved his rest.

As the two women made their way down from their rocky perch, a loud splash came from the lake and a man cried out. They raced around the rocks to see the head and neck of a long blue-green scaled beast rise out of the water.

"*Monstruo*!" Mani flung out an arm to hold the women back, then he strode towards the beast, his machete raised to strike.

Tomàs swore from the beach on the far side of the monster. "Mani, get back!" He ran to cut off his friend. "It struck fast like a snake! Everyone get back!"

The creature's webbed feet and claws dug deep into the slope and slithered further up the bank and closer to the tents. Its head snapped down and seized Fernando with its massive, toothy jaws. The man's cries died with a sickening crunch.

The beast tipped its head back and swallowed the body whole, then turned its snake-eyes on Tomàs who still shouted for everyone to get back. In a flash of iridescent deep teal scales, its jaws opened wide again and shot straight for Tomàs. He jumped to the side at the last moment and struck at the beast's head with his saber. His blade bounced off the scales without effect.

Kinzy woke Trell abruptly with a shout in his mind. She leaped at the beast, her sharp blades slashed across the long thick neck. It reared back with a screeching cry, then turned to take another strike at Tomàs. Her blades dug in deep and ripped through the scales as it lunged. One blade caught and yanked Kinzy off her feet. She stumbled to the ground as she worked her blade free.

Scrambling up, Kinzy moved in to crouch below the monster's head. Using her blades like grappling hooks, she swung up onto the top of the beast's head. She yanked out her draiglanns and used one to pierce an eye. The other she drove into its neck for a handhold and swung back down to the ground.

Trell screeched, suddenly in dragon form, and dove toward the other eye, claws forward like a golden raptor. The beast shook its head to the side and Kinzy rolled away. Trell circled around for another strike.

"My blades will get through his hide," Kinzy called out. "Normal blades will not! Stay back, get behind the boulders!"

Their remaining porters fled back up the trail screaming for everyone to run. Kinzy briefly wondered which they were more afraid of, Trell or the magical beast they battled?

Tomàs and Mani both remained. Tomàs unholstered his pistol and took aim.

Kinzy held back instead of going in as planned, and whistled to Trell, the signal for incoming danger.

Trell flew to her but didn't land on her outstretched arm or shoulder. He winged his way in a tight circle around her and landed at her feet. In a flash of tightly controlled anger, Trell sent a picture of the full beast that he could see under the clear water from up above. Magic radiated from the monster, unlike anything Kinzy had felt before. Trell expressed similar confusion with a snort, then added, *it's not our magic, where is it from?*

Tomàs pulled his trigger, and though he hit, the hide of the beast proved impervious to bullets. The beast roared, and she realized Tomàs had stepped too close.

"You can't help, Tomàs! Get back!" She ran, knowing even she could not reach them in time. The men had made a stand they could not win.

She nearly tripped as Trell, who had run at her side, grew in size with each step until he matched the beast head to head. Kinzy gaped. She'd not known he could do that. She was more than happy to have him on her side right now, no matter the no-shifting law. But he'd been keeping secrets.

Tomàs reloaded and aimed again as the serpent stepped closer to him. Mani shoved his friend aside, out of the way of the open jaws. For a moment, Kinzy thought the beast had missed them both, but when it raised its head, it held Mani by his leg. The beast whipped him back and forth until Mani went limp, then tossed him into the lake like an abandoned toy.

The serpent screamed a challenge that echoed through the valley. Trell trumpeted in reply as he leaped with Kinzy, each of them with claws out to slash and puncture, doing as much damage as they could. The serpent cried in pain. Trell latched onto the creature's neck with his hind claws and dug his front claws into the head, claws now as sharp and large as Kinzy's own draiglanns.

The frenzied serpent snapped its head back and forth, trying to dislodge Trell, both eye sockets dripping black ichor. Over and over Kinzy darted in and cut, until the beast slowed. It flailed one more time before it toppled like a mighty tree trunk. The ground shuddered. Trell leaped high into the air with an exultant cry then dove into the lake. When he surfaced, his body had shrunk to his normal size. He shook himself off in mid-air, showering Kinzy, before landing on her shoulder.

He trilled and rubbed her cheek. *Bad magic. New magic. Dead now.*

We need to talk about this new growth trick of yours later.

He bobbed his head. *New tricks. Time for dinner now?*

Predictable. Fell a monster, time for treats. She reached into her bag and complied. He resumed his mongoose form and settled around the warmth of her neck. She purred back and strode toward the monster.

Tomàs and Esme raced to the edge of the lake, calling for

Mani. They searched for several minutes but could find no sign of his body. The lake had gone still as a mirror, showing the blue cloud-spotted sky.

Having confirmed the beast was truly dead, Kinzy carefully made her way down to the water, dousing her blades. She wiped them on nearby grassy tufts to remove the ichor that clung to them. When she rejoined the others, Tomàs glared.

His voice choked with grief and anger. "This is your fault. Mani is dead. My friend is dead, and you are to blame. You brought us here. What are you, you and your little winged friend, eh *Señorita*? I do not think they teach such skills in London schools for ladies."

Esme started to reach out then pulled her hand back as he turned that glare on her. "I'm so sorry about Mani, Tomàs. He was a good man."

"He should not be dead. He gave his life for me." He turned away, fists tight and shaking.

Esme's tone remained calm. "His sacrifice will not go—"

Tomàs spun, dark eyes flashing. "Rafael should have warned me of such things. Take these women into the mountains, he said. Keep them safe. He said nothing about monsters. About *demonios*." He pointed at the serpent, his hand shaking. "This *monstruo*, it is not natural." Then he pointed at Trell. "And that creature is another demon." He looked down his nose at Kinzy. "I do not know what *she* is."

Esme took a breath. "Trell is not a demon, Tomàs, and neither is Kinzy."

"Then what?" He narrowed his eyes as his anger turned back to Esme. "You knew, didn't you? Did Rafael know?" He huffed a breath. "Damn you, *primo*."

"None of us knew about the serpent, Tomàs. Nor about the spirit warriors. That, I swear to you."

"What will be next then? What horrors from hell lie upon

our path?" He shook his head. "We go back to Quito. *Ahora.* Start packing."

Kinzy didn't know what would sway the Spaniard, so she spoke more to Esme. "I don't sense any further danger here in this valley."

Esme turned back to their grieving guide. "Tomàs, we cannot turn back. There is too much at stake." She stepped closer to him. "Rafael entrusted you with this mission. With our safety. You are the only one who knows these mountains, who can help us follow the blasted Vatican map and get us where we need to go. I am asking you, begging you, please help us."

He groaned at the mention of his cousin's name. "We will die."

"Perhaps, but the alternative is worse. We need to retrieve an artefact that must not fall into the hands of the Frenchman, Reynard. He would give Bonaparte the key to his war against the world. There would be nothing anyone could do against his armies. I am so sorry about the men we have lost, but more will die if we do not get there in time."

Kinzy thought it a gamble to explain even that much to the man, but they did need his help to make it through the strange trails and passes of the Andes. "We have come so far already, with no sign of being followed or of the Frenchman ahead of us. We know he must be somewhere, but I'm betting he searches in the wrong direction. We cannot turn around now. It's too important."

Tomàs watched the mirror-still surface of the lake and was silent for a time. Finally, he sucked in a breath, blew it out. "I will take you. I will do as I promised Rafael. But after this, I am done. I owe him nothing more."

Esme gave a relieved sigh. "Thank you, Tomàs."

"You will not thank me when we all die. Best you make

your peace with God." He frowned, watching the spot on the trail where their porters paused. "We must finish making camp before darkness falls. I need to get the rest of them back down here. Stay away from the lake." He strode away, spine stiff, his hands still clenched.

Kinzy and Esme watched in silence as Tomàs yelled in Spanish back up the rocky trail behind them, his arms waving and frequently putting hands to his hair as if to yank it from his head.

A porter yelled back to Tomàs that the expedition was cursed by the spirits of the mountains. Looking around, Kinzy realized the porters had taken all their llamas and everything still on them. They'd been left with some food and their packs.

"Get back down here and set up camp! We have our own spirits of protection!" Tomàs threw his arm out angrily and pointed toward Kinzalynn and Trell, but the men made no reply.

"At least leave us some more supplies!"

The porters, with their llamas, continued back up the trail until they were out of sight.

Tomàs lowered his arm, then spun around and stalked toward them. "Is what they say true? Are we cursed by the Spirit of the Mountain?"

Kinzy could feel the wave of anger and frustration coming from him, and ached for his loss. Mani and the porters had been cheerful guides and support for this expedition, until the dangers had engulfed them all. Tomàs deserved better. So had Mani. "I know nothing about the strange serpent we fought, but I assure you that though Trell is a creature you are not familiar with, he is still a friend who has defended us. I assure you he is not a danger to anyone but our enemies. Trell is willing to retrieve Mani's body. You can bury him properly. We can help."

Trell leaped from her shoulder and Kinzy narrowed her eyes as he grew in size once again. Tomàs and Esme silently followed his winged flight as he circled the quiet lake. Trell soon dove toward the water, claws held out beneath him. He snatched at something below the still surface, a circle of ripples extending outward as he rose up with strong flaps of his wings. He gently laid Mani's body in front of them.

Thank you, my friend. I do not know if anyone else will say so.

He was always good about giving me treats. He was wise and kind.

Esme laid a hand on their guide's shoulder as he hung his head. "I am sorry, Tomàs. Mani was a good man."

"I will lay him to rest, and then we should return to Quito."

"We must reach the tomb. You do not have to come with us, though. This is our mission, not yours."

He stabbed the air with his finger. "I *will* not leave two women alone in the Andes mountains." He faced them with tears in his eyes, then walked away to arrange his final farewells to his best friend in the world.

Esme turned to look back up the trail where the others had gone. "I hope they make it home," she whispered, then turned to help Tomàs.

Kinzy hoped so as well, though she cringed at the heartless thought that came to her mind next. She was relieved she would not have to decide his fate.

Grabbing her gear, Kinzy let Esme know she would hunt and check their perimeter. She'd return shortly, but would give them peace to lay Mani to rest. Tomàs ignored her.

Trell hunted more of the furry cuy not too far out as they scouted for any further dangers. She'd take on the cooking, as without Mani someone would need to.

The mountainside remained rocky with grasses and stubby

plants amid the ledges and boulders. The trail faded in and out from the dirt and stone, but it continued on in the right direction. Having found nothing to alarm her, she'd made it almost all the way back when she spotted Fae boot prints. Hers? They headed in and out of their camp, but in a direction she did not remember traveling. She stood and let her senses float out from her but found no unfamiliar magic or presence. She must still be addled by the drug. They had to be hers, there was no other logical explanation.

She returned to camp, and worked on a more pleasant fire to cook with as Esme and Tomàs finished burying Mani beneath the stone pile. The two spoke with their God, and Kinzy could not help but give her own silent words for the man who had taken such good care of them all. Mani had been a wise man.

May the Light grant you a dreamless sleep, Mani.

As she went to their packs to gather items for dressing the small furry *cuy* she'd found and ensure their dinner stew was ready as soon as possible, she found Mani had pulled out one of the bottles of *chicha*, probably preparing for the porters' ritual of thanks to Pachamama and God both. She'd not tried the alcohol during the trip, but she left the bottle by the fire, a small tribute to Mani and his ways.

Chapter Nineteen

That evening, the campfire did little to raise their spirits. Esme sat massaging her feet, wishing for their little canvas bathtub, but it had been on the llamas and she doubted she would see it again. She spent a frivolous moment fantasizing about a lovely steamy soak in her claw-foot tub, soothed by the imagined scent of lavender and rose petals.

Tomàs shuffled over and sat across from her, a cup of something in his hands. "I could rub those for you, *Doña.*"

Accustomed now to his manner, the risqué suggestions, the little flatteries no longer bothered her. They probably worked well on more malleable women, even women of her own rank. His attentions were harmless, however, and she found she was starting to enjoy the game a little, now she could see that he was indeed a gentleman. "My feet hurt badly enough that I might be tempted to take you up on that offer. I am sure, however, that it would lead you to behave inappropriately and I am too exhausted to break your arm."

He chuckled, although shadows veiled his eyes and his

smile became grim. Stretching out his long legs, he leaned back on one elbow and sipped from his cup. "Your loss."

Kinzy suddenly rejoined them, stepping into the circle of firelight. She had disappeared some while ago, wanting to scout the area with Trell. Tomàs let her go without so much as a fare thee well. As brave and intrepid as their guide had proven himself, the man stayed well clear of the little mongoose since their encounter with the water serpent, and eyed Kinzy with deep suspicion. He refused to talk about what he had seen, but every time Trell came anywhere near him, he crossed himself, muttered a prayer, and moved away.

Esme knew that Kinzy worried about Tomàs and what he had seen. They'd discussed it in that succinct way Kinzy had. Few words, but full of intensity. What that meant for Tomàs remained unclear. Esme understood there were things Kinzy needed to keep secret. For that matter, there were things that Esme needed to keep secret. Yet they needed Tomàs, not only to get to the site of Atahualpa's tomb, but to get home afterward. Unless, of course, Kinzy had some magical way to return to Tír na nÓg that didn't involve the arduous trek back. In that case Tomàs's fate appeared grim indeed. As, in fact, did Esme's.

The Fae woman's face looked young, even innocent at the moment, but Esme had seen her in battle three times now. The grisly determination on the girl's countenance as she dispatched one and then another foe, those deadly blades flashing scarlet, had burned itself into Esme's memory. She killed as easily as she played chess, and Esme felt certain she did not spend her nights in an agony of guilt over those who had died by her blade. So what would happen when they reached their goal? Would Esme face those same curved blades? She had no wish to kill the girl, provided she could, even in self-defense.

As Kinzy sat down beside her, looking fresh-faced and

open. Like a friend. Trusting? Or did the girl really trust anyone? Esme felt a shiver of foreboding, yet, there was nothing to do about it at this moment. She faced her friend, noting Trell's absence. Perhaps she had him patrolling. Now that they had no porters, and with poor Mani gone, Trell could wander the perimeter of the campsite in his own true form. Yet, even though Tomàs had seen him thus, Trell maintained the fictive disguise of a mongoose. Esme shrugged. Maybe he liked being a mongoose. Either way, she still rubbed him behind his ears on the occasions when he crawled into her lap.

Esme gestured at the cooking pot over the fire. "The stew is nearly ready."

"I am not hungry."

Tomàs sipped again from his cup, kept his eyes on the fire, studiously avoiding the Fae girl. "I told you making so much was a waste."

Esme kept her tone light. "We can carry it with us and save the trouble of making a meal tomorrow night." She sighed. "How much longer will it be until we reach the area where you think the tomb is?"

He scowled, evaded. "I wish to God I had never agreed to this trip. It has cost me far too much."

Esme pulled out the map and stared at it, wondering how to judge distance and time. The unusual symbols and names she had noted back on the airship, like *Place of the Snake God* and *Demon Warriors*, now made sense in the light of their recent experiences. Kinzy looked over Esme's shoulder. Sliding a slim finger along their route, she pointed to two rounded peaks between which their trail passed. "Tomàs, are you familiar with these two very tall mountains?"

Tomàs grunted. "Have you not looked around you, lady? There are mountain peaks in every direction."

"Come now, Tomàs," Esme chided. "You have looked at the

map as often as we have. It shows two very distinctive peaks, and the legend beneath says *The Good Mother's Paps.* Is there no folk tale that talks about two mountains like this?"

He drained his cup, crossed himself and spat. "There is. Do you think I am leading you on a wild goose chase?" He sighed. "I know where we must go." He sipped from his cup again. "If you still insist on continuing, as you always do, then we will get to the pass that leads between the Teats of Pachamama maybe the day after tomorrow. Depending on how late in the day that is, we would be wise to camp there for the night. There is a flat spot, but no pucara or other ruins to stay in. The wind can be fierce there. There might be storms."

"You make it sound delightful. Whyever is there no resort there?" Esme shook her head. "I think you are making excuses for not going. Tell me, you have been through this pass before?"

"Never. Up to it, yes, a long time ago, but never through. It is not a good place to go. The weather is very bad. Even the locals do not go there."

Kinzy tapped the map. "Just beyond the pass is this village or whatever, at the center of which is this raised platform. Presumably, that is the tomb, yes?"

Esme blew out a breath in frustration. "It would have been so much easier if the blasted priest had just put an X to mark the spot. I have never understood why these types of maps cannot simply be clear and instructive."

Tomàs stood and wandered over to his pack from which he withdrew a stoppered clay jar and two more tin cups. "I do not know. What I do know is that there better be treasure there at this tomb. Enough treasure that I can take some back to Mani's widow and children." He came back, dropped down again onto the mossy stones that paved the little ruin they camped in. He unstoppered the clay jar and sloshed some of the contents into all three cups. "Here. I found this near Mani's pack. It is *chicha,* a kind of local beer. Mani used it as an offering to the *apus,* and we will save some for the spirits at the Teats of Pachamama, but tonight, tonight we drink to Mani." He passed them their cups and emotion choked his voice as he raised his high.

"To my friend Mani, who took me in, shared his home, made me family, and gave his life for—" He couldn't continue. Instead he slugged back the contents of his cup in one go.

Esme raised hers. "To Mani." Then she followed suit. Kinzy watched her then did the same.

After a moment of tortured silence, Tomàs came over to sit next to them and refilled all their cups. While the fire crackled, and the stars winked in the crystal clear sky above, they drank in silence, remembering a man who had given them good companionship, warm smiles and ultimately, his life.

By the time Esme staggered to her own bed roll hours later, the jar of *chicha* was empty.

She was dreaming. She knew she dreamed because Rafael complained about her pistol being in the way, and he'd never done that. They both had a habit of going to bed armed, so love making frequently involved avoiding weaponry. She could feel his hands sliding down her body, his breath on her cheek, the weight of him as he positioned himself over her.

"Wake up, *puta*. Tell me where it is."

"Where what is?" she murmured.

"The map, *chicha*. Where is the map?"

"Silly man." She was having trouble forming words. Her

head spun and she could hardly open her eyes. "You gave it to me," she mumbled sleepily. "Why do you need it back? Don't tell me you didn't make a copy."

Another voice, more cultured, said, "Look under her."

She tried to open her eyes, found them gummy, the lids impossibly heavy. "Rafi, go away. I'm tired."

Someone struck her across the face. "Tell me where it is!"

The dream-Rafael faded like morning mist, replaced with the foggy and wavering images of other men, one of whom knelt over her. Men with faces she didn't recognize. A native, his black eyes gleamed cold and flinty. He leered at her, gap-toothed.

Then the man's face morphed grotesquely and she looked up into the face of the odious lech her uncle Neville had tried to force her to marry. Just like he had all those years ago, Everett had snuck into her bedchamber to lay hands on her. She tried to sit up, found herself pinned beneath him, his knee on her thigh.

"Don't move, little dove. Just lie back and enjoy it, you know you always do. Stop fighting me."

No. She would not let it happen again. She'd been weak then, a young girl. She had strength now, cast off the pall of obedient victim her uncle and Everett had forced on her. It took all her energy to make her limbs move, but she managed to swing at Everett, her fist connecting with the side of his head. He yelped. Curling her fingers, she raked his face, his neck, his arms, anywhere she could make contact.

Her vision swam as Everett grabbed her wrists. Then Everett vanished and became the dark man again. He had her wrists in one strong hand, gripping them so hard she thought her bones would break, and in the other she saw the glint of a knife.

Another blow landed across her cheek, but she ignored the

pain and lashed out again, wrenching one hand away. She grabbed the hand that held the knife, but he broke free and slashed her shoulder.

Then Everett returned. His face hovered over hers and his smooth, oily voice trickled into her ear, words straight from memory. "You want to play? That's fine with me. I like it rough."

Another voice spoke. Uncle Neville? No, it didn't sound like him, although it was familiar. God, she was so confused. She couldn't think, couldn't concentrate. Couldn't wake up. The world swam in and out of focus. Whoever stood behind the native man shouted. "Enough, Miguel, just find the damn map."

She screamed for Cooper. Cooper would help her.

A hand clamped over her mouth and a blow to her midsection took her breath away. As she gasped for air, as hands groped her body, a chill stillness came over her. Looking up, the image of Everett wavered and in its place was the face of the swarthy, gap-toothed man again. Beyond him, however, she saw the filmy apparition of her mother.

Hush now, Essie, she heard in her mind. *Be still, close your eyes and let them think you have fainted.*

But Mama—.

Shh. I will protect the thing you hide. They will not find it.

No. Everett hurt me, Mama. I won't let him do it again.

He won't. I promise you. I could not reach you then, but I am here now. The spirit, tinted blue like the chill it imparted, settled over her and wrapped its arms around her. Esme felt herself enclosed by her mother's loving embrace, felt tears come unbidden to her eyes. *I miss you, Mama.*

And I you, my darling. Now hush and be still. Close your eyes. When you awaken, they will be gone.

She did as she was bid and soon felt the weight of the man

lift off her, although the voices of her uncle and Everett came to her as though from a great distance.

"The map is no here."

"Are you sure?"

A filthy laugh. "Trust me, *Señor*, I search her everywhere. Even between her legs." How odd that Everett sounded like a Spaniard. Was this still a dream?

"You are a disgusting cretin, Miguel. *Bien.* Perhaps the guide has it. Come."

"I join you in a few minutes. Now I finish what I start."

She heard a sharp blow, a grunt of pain. "You will come now, and you will not touch her again."

"Fine. But you will pay me more now."

The voices faded and she heard her mother, low and crooning, singing her a lullaby, just as she had when she had been alive. Snuggling into her mother's frigid embrace, Esme drifted off to sleep.

Chapter Twenty

Kinzy jerked awake, a blade in her hand. She felt a wrongness, in herself and her surroundings.

Her bones ached in a strange way, and she battled to rally her thoughts through a throbbing head. She pulled on her Fae boots and her hand grabbed for her satchel, but it was gone. In the faint glow of morning light through the canvas of the tent she realized their trunks were missing and the place had been ransacked. She tried to swallow away the terrible taste in her mouth, akin to a burnt lemon, as she looked around and listened. A few clothes and empty satchels were scattered, but not enough to be all of their gear. The camp was quiet and still, except for her own breathing and, thank the sky and wind, Esme's.

Kinzy crept over to wake her tentmate, whispering in her ear. "Stay silent, someone robbed us in the night."

Esme struggled to sit up.

Kinzy exited the tent with a cautious step and searched the camp. Most of their supplies and food were gone. All that remained were their cots, blankets, a few scraps and sundries, and the clothes they wore. Kinzalynn mourned the loss of her extra knives and warmer cloak from her missing trunk. Inside Tomàs's tent things were strewn about in similar fashion, but Tomàs was nowhere to be found. A small pool of blood congealed on the ground by the head of the bed. There had been a scuffle here, a fight. She listened hard outside the tents again, turned a full circle. Nothing but the natural wind and the cry of a bird in the air above them.

"Tomàs?" she called out. No answer but the breeze that whipped at her hair.

Adding up the state of their camp and the horrid metallic sting across her tongue, Kinzy raced back to find Esme still on her cot, staring at her hands.

She kneeled next to Esme, her tone worried. "Tomàs is missing. There is blood, but not enough for a death blow. The camp has been ransacked, our supplies stolen. And the net your queen gave you to wrap up the mummy, that is gone too." Kinzy saw no sign that Esme even heard, but there were bruises forming on the human's face. She put a gentle hand on the woman's shoulder but pulled back when the human flinched. "Esme, I think we were drugged last night."

Esme held out her arms in fascinated horror. "I think I was attacked last night. It's all so jumbled in my mind. Did I dream it all? My mother was here, singing me a lullaby. And Ev-Everett." She stumbled over the name. "I mean, some man, some native, grabbed me. There's blood under my nails, Kinzy, but it was a dream. Am I still dreaming?"

Kinzy gently prodded the large swollen red bruise on the woman's cheek. "I'm fine, but we need to check you from head to toe. You may have other injuries."

Esme's eyes widened as she scrambled up from the cot on wobbly limbs. She stripped out of her nightclothes, mumbling, "Please check my back? I feel quite ill, and I can't tell if I've been injured or if it's simply the after effects of the drug."

Kinzy made a head to toe inspection. "I'm here. You are able to stand, and you're going to be right as clover soon."

"Rain. Right as rain." Esme's voice steadied.

"Just as right as clover, and drier, I suspect."

A dark bruise purpled across Esme's shoulder and one side of her jaw was swollen. A split lip left a streak of dried blood down the side of the chin. The woman was struck more than once. Kinzy turned over Esme's arms. Scrapes bled along the woman's inner forearms and knuckles. She'd defended herself against an attacker. A few fingernails were broken, with obvious blood under the others, so there'd be gouges on whoever had attacked her.

"You remember nothing?" Kinzy kept her tone soft while cataloging bruises and checking for broken bones and cuts in need of a bandage.

"It was a dream." Esme swayed and Kinzy steadied her.

Across the top of one thigh a huge bruise was forming. Someone used a knee to hold Esme down. The other thigh still had on the strap and sheath with the map — there was no sign of any injury on that leg. Puzzling. Using water from her canteen and a ripped-up skirt, Kinzy washed away the blood from Esme's lip, arms, and hands. Scrounging through their scattered clothing, she found something relatively clean for the woman to wear.

Esme gasped when they buttoned her vest. "I may have to add a bruised rib to my litany of injuries. But I wasn't ... I don't think they..."

Kinzy understood her fears. "No, dear lady, I do not believe you were violated, but they searched for something here and on your person. All is torn apart and scattered, and the trunks and satchels outright taken."

"They were after the map." Esme swayed again, but there was more fire in her eyes now.

"But why didn't they take it? They obviously had you at their mercy and you fought them like a wildcat. The map is untouched, not even a drop of blood."

"Mother would not let them." Esme rubbed her eyes then gathered up her dark hair and attempted to pin it up. "That's ridiculous, of course. That must have been part of the drug dream. Wait," she dropped her hands and faced Kinzy. "Did you say Tomàs was gone?"

Kinzy worried about Esme's state of mind. The woman had been through something, and Kinzy was furious that she herself had been incapacitated. It had to have been more than the alcohol in that *chicha*. Kinzy had drunk more alcohol than that before and never felt such effects. The *chicha* must have been drugged, though she could not yet recall any substance that would affect Fae as well as humans and leave such a bad taste.

She sat Esme down and gave her more water, then searched more closely for signs of who might have done this. She gathered what they could still use. The ammo for the special pistol was still wrapped in a skirt shoved in a corner where they had obviously dumped the items from Esme's trunk and just not gathered and taken everything. Only most of the things. They had both of their canteens and a day's ration of jerky and stale bread. Kinzy always slept in her leathers and knives and those had not been taken, nor had she herself been touched. Even more puzzling. She scowled to think their enemies discounted her entirely because she seemed simply Esme's companion or lady's maid. If so, that meant that their enemies knew only the role Kinzy had adopted on the airship.

That was when she realized something else was missing. "Trell!"

Not finding him in their tent, she shoved aside the tent flap.

"Trell! Tomàs! Where are you?" She called out with both voice and mind.

All signs pointed toward the offenders having come and gone hours ago. Had they taken Trell along with Tomàs? Trell was her lifeline to her homeland, a companion entrusted to her care. If anything happened to him, she had no way to contact home or the queen. He was her friend, out there somewhere, possibly in the hands of their enemies.

Esme came out from the tent as Kinzy circled the camp. "Let me help you widen the search."

Kinzy appraised her sharply. "You are with me now? Your mind is here? Aware?" If still dazed, there was no way she could let the woman traipse across the mountainside and possibly add a broken leg to the list of her injuries.

Esme visibly drew herself up. "I'm fine. You go left, I'll go right. Trell and Tomàs have to be out here somewhere. Call out every minute or so. That way we can each hear the other, just in case."

The two called for their missing companions as they covered a wide area around the camp. Kinzy discovered tracks where she believed men in heavy boots had come into their camp, then exited in a different direction, moving down the mountain.

Just as the women swung around and could see each other, a scaled yellow tail flopped out of a stand of thorny brush and rock between them.

Kinzy raced to Trell's side. He lifted a groggy scaled head toward her, eyes barely open, tongue hanging out along with a bit of drool. He was his new larger size again, as he'd been with the Water Serpent. Kinzy hugged his neck tight. She'd been afraid he was dead. The drug could've killed him. Or he could've been taken or killed by their attackers. Her tears fell onto his scales as he snuggled into her shoulder, slowly growing smaller until he once again fit in the crook of her arm. He purred and hummed, and Kinzy sighed as the anxious rush of her fears faded.

Breakfast? It will help clear the drug. Larger helps too, but means bigger breakfast needed.

You shape-shifting woofleheimer, we have to search for Tomàs, first.

Does he have breakfast?

"Is he all right?" Esme scratched Trell's eye ridges and he leaned into her touch.

"He seems fine. The drug affected him as well, but it looks like he was hidden by the bushes and never found, thank the Lords of Light. Becoming larger helped lessen the drug's effects." Kinzy stroked his tail as the drakkeki crawled up around her neck.

"One down, one to go. Let's widen our circle. Perhaps Tomàs is out here too, having wandered away. He could be injured." Esme swayed unsteadily, enough that Kinzy eyed her carefully. She certainly was not yet fully recovered.

"You go back to camp, pack what's left of our supplies. Trell and I will search for Tomàs."

Esme nodded and returned to camp. Kinzy covered the mountainside. She studied the tracks, trying to glean what she could from them. Speed, number, how laden they were. She found what might have been signs of a scuffle, drag marks. More interesting, however, one particular set of prints. Prints made by a pair of Fae boots. She followed them back to the camp, into the tent she shared with Esme. Her instincts all told her these attackers knew what they were after.

Trell placed a paw on her cheek. She looked deep into his eyes and saw mental images of Tomàs, unconscious, thrown over the shoulder of a bleeding man, and a brief glimpse of that blasted Frenchman, Jean-Paul Reynard.

I am certain I can track them now the drug no longer clouds my mind.

Then let's get packed and moving.

And breakfast.

If it's not drugged, yes, breakfast.

Esme had laid out their blankets on which she'd piled the pitifully small amount of supplies.

"We're in luck, Kinzy! We have my shaded lantern, my timepiece, and my telescope. The leftover stew is still in the pot." She paused, considering. "Do you suppose it was the stew that was drugged?"

Trell hopped down and jumped onto the rim of the stew pot, tipping the lid away. He dipped his beak toward, but not into, the stew. Kinzy waited for his conclusion. He finally dunked his head in and ate a piece of meat, licking the gravy from his snout with a long, forked tongue. Then he ate a few more.

"It wasn't the stew. Thank you, Trell." He chirped back at her and took off into the air after licking his claws clean, circling high over the camp, scouting. She turned back to Esme. "They have Tomàs. Tracks lead down the mountain and ahead. These men have to know what we are after. Reynard was with them, Trell saw him. It's likely they plan to use Tomàs to lead them to Atahualpa and believe that we will be lost in the Andes without him."

Esme sighed, shoulders sagging. "If they are after Atahualpa, it will be nearly impossible to get there ahead of them now, even with the map."

Kinzy sat down beside her, looking over Esme's gathered goods. She'd done well, but was the human over the effects of the drugs? How had these men attacked her and yet not taken her map? "Tell me what you remember from last night."

"The last thing I remember clearly is drinking that awful

liquor that Tomàs offered us. The *chicha*. Then I thought I was dreaming. First came Rafael. Then he turned into Everett." The woman must have seen the confusion on Kinzy's face. "Everett was the bastard to whom my uncle affianced me. He was a vile, manipulative degenerate, and if it weren't for Cooper and Egg, I would have known nothing but abuse and misery." She brushed at imaginary dirt on her shirt sleeve then raised her chin and waved the past away with a slim hand. "Anyway, Rafael became Everett, but then it changed into another man entirely. He looked like a native, with bad teeth and foul breath." The next words came out in a rush, and from the look in Esme's eyes, Kinzy judged she was loath to speak them. "My mother's spirit came then and told me she would protect me. Which she did."

"You mentioned your mother's visitations before. Very few among the Fae have the magic to touch the spirit realms, beyond the veil between life and death, but this is not unheard of." Kinzy felt a tinge of jealousy rise in her. This human had more magical ability about her than Kinzy ever would.

Esme appeared relieved. "Thank you. No one else has ever believed me. Not even Cooper. Most people do not see ghosts. The majority believe they are little more than figments of the imagination. Although there is a burgeoning Spiritualist movement, most of the practitioners, the so-called mediums, are shams and charlatans, preying on people's grief."

"You're speaking to me, a creature connected to magic, part Fae, and think I would not believe you? The mortal world should be without magic, yet I find it everywhere on this trip." Kinzy considered how much her queen knew of the touches of true magic in the world, or how much technology humans had that could be used against the Fae. When Kinzy gave her final report on all she had seen and experienced, would relations between Fae and humans be better knowing just how much magic the mortals had access to? Or would this only widen the gap between them?

Esme's shoulders relaxed as she slowly exhaled, gathering her wits. "None of what happened makes sense, really. I am not sure what was real and what wasn't."

Kinzy knew Trell had seen Reynard, but Esme had not mentioned his presence. Her mother was obviously akin to the spirit warriors, able to touch the mortal world. Through Esme at least. "It could be another attempt of the Inca spirits to defend their secrets."

Esme shook her head. "I don't think so. I believe that we dispatched them all the other night, although I suppose more may have been summoned. Still, if what you believe is true and Tomàs was taken alive, then it could not have been more spirits. Plus, I have real injuries. Why leave us alive? That doesn't make sense. More importantly, why did they not find the map?"

Kinz shrugged. "So Reynard and his men drugged us and stole most of our supplies to give them a clear shot to Atahualpa's tomb. They took Tomàs because he is our guide here in the mountains. They may not even know there is a map. They do not know where they are going, not like we do."

Esme scowled. "Well, then, we will give chase, and I am not slow."

Kinzy watched the woman straighten her blouse and pull herself together, despite her pale and sickly complexion. "Let us eat and finish packing what we can carry."

They shared more stew with Trell, who returned to let them know he could find no trace of the attackers or Tomàs. Then Kinzy took one of the rolled blanket bundles made with rope from the tents and followed Esme, who set a quick pace with her own bundle slung over a shoulder. Trell flew ahead and above. No need to be a mongoose anymore. They needed his aerial surveillance.

"He won't challenge our attackers on his own, will he?" Esme called over her shoulder as he swooped past.

"No, but he will let me know if danger lies ahead. I can hear him in my mind even if he gets miles away."

"Hah. Soon those bastards will learn the meaning of danger from behind. Now stop dawdling, and for once let's bring the fight to them."

Chapter Twenty-One

They hiked for six hours, following tracks and trail signs Esme could not see, but that Kinzy claimed were clear as day. Despite the coca leaves, Esme's legs felt like lead weights and her lungs burned.

As the weather turned and clouds crowded the skies, they both agreed to stop for the night. Esme discovered putting up their tent without the help of the porters more difficult than she'd expected. She blamed it on the fact that tents on previous expeditions had been smaller and easier to manage, although in truth, she still felt groggy and fat-fingered.

The world felt more unreal than her nightmares. She couldn't imagine how she had slept through being attacked. The drug she, Kinzy, and Tomàs ingested must have been powerful indeed. Who could have done such a thing? Reynard headed the top of the suspect list, but she could not imagine how he could have accomplished it. The drug must have been in the stew or the *chicha*. Reynard would have needed an accomplice and Esme had an even more difficult time believing that accomplice could have been Tomàs. Still, toasting Mani had been his idea.

No, it didn't feel right. Besides, Tomàs and Rafi were cousins, and whatever Rafi's failings, she knew her former lover would not have sent them into the hands of someone who could have committed such perfidy. Not even Rafael, no matter how he had betrayed her personal feelings, was that rotten. Especially not when working for the Crown.

Unless Rafi played a double game and only pretended to be working for Victoria, when in truth, his allegiance still belonged to Spain.

God, it all made her head hurt.

She rubbed her eyes with her bruised and swollen hand then rummaged through her backpack for a handful *chuñios*, one of the few food items they'd been left with. These she put in a pot of water over their fire, something they'd risked even though it meant they could be discovered. They needed the warmth at this altitude. She'd no intention of dying until they'd achieved their goal.

Kinzy disappeared, as she always did early in the evening. If the Fae woman stuck to her routine, she'd be gone for some time. Needing a breath of air, Esme took a walk around the camp as the overcast afternoon darkened, meaning only to walk a bit, stretch her legs. Not being a fool, she brought her pistol, gripped loosely in her good hand. Thirty or forty yards from the tent, she heard an odd pattering noise, like rain on leaves. Except the rain hadn't started yet. Curious, she moved toward the sound, which came from beyond a small, mist-shrouded hill.

Cocking her gun, she crept up the slope and peered over the top.

Her stomach lurched at the carnage before her. She swallowed bile then lost the fight, vomiting violently. The heaving continued for some time. When she could pull herself to her feet, she staggered down the hill towards the grisly sight.

Tomàs hung by his feet from a tall improvised stake, an enormous pool of black, congealed blood on the churned-up grass below him. He'd been stripped of his clothes and dozens of cuts covered his body. Both of his ears were hacked off, along with several fingers. A deep gash to the throat had nearly severed his head from his body. She badly wanted to cut him down and tend to him, but there was no urgency. The stickiness of the blood and the stiffness of his body told her he'd been dead for hours. Esme prayed he'd been unconscious by the time the *coup de grace* had been committed.

She searched the area as Rafael taught her, working in an imagined grid. Here, unlike at the campsite, there appeared to be only one pair of footprints in the rain-dampened ground. Large prints, sunk deep into the soft earth, and strikingly familiar in appearance. She knew those boot prints, they were unique. They looked just like the prints made by Kinzy's tooled leather Fae boots.

She felt dizzy, blamed it on the drugged *chicha*. It wasn't the sight of the body, she'd encountered violent death many times, though she hoped she'd never become inured to it. She had seen more than enough mangled bodies during her years as a nurse, much less the adventures that had come later. What galled her was the thought that her companion, a woman she had just begun to like, and worse, to trust, could have committed such a heinous act. Tomàs had been tortured, at length.

She tried to convince herself it couldn't have been Kinzy. After all, the woman bore none of the scratch marks that, judging by the skin and blood under Esme's fingernails, she had clearly inflicted on her attacker. Plus, Kinzy had drunk the *chicha* just like Esme had.

Or had she? Had Esme actually seen her take a sip? She couldn't recall. The Fae woman also didn't have a mark on her, leading Esme to wonder why their attackers hadn't assaulted her.

The final damning piece of evidence hit her like a blow as she stared at Tomàs's body. Kinzy's weapons of choice were her razor-sharp draiglanns, and the wounds on his chest and arms had clearly been made by an exceedingly sharp blade. Nothing so crude as a machete or common hunting knife had made those almost surgical wounds.

Her head buzzed with the noise of a thousand bees. She had been an idiot. Again. She had given her trust, almost blindly, as she had done with Rafael, and now she paid the price. Kinzy's friendship, the saving of her life on the airship, it had all been a ploy to gain her confidence. She'd once again been a fool, not only because she had fallen for the pretense, but because she had fallen so willingly. She'd grown so desperate for friendship, so lonely for the companionship of an equal, a woman of like mind, that she'd walked blindly into treachery. How utterly pathetic she was.

Her face grew hot, and she clenched her hands into fists as she stepped up to Tomàs's body. Swallowing bile, she closed his eyes then walked a few feet away. Beyond reach of the incredible stench of blood, she paused, bracing hands on knees, and sucked in a few deep breaths. "I am sorry, Tomàs," she said to the dead man. "This is my fault. They were after me and I am sorry you came to such an end. I promise, I will avenge you."

She knew now what she needed to do. Victoria had sent her on a mission and she had a duty to not only her queen but to the whole of the free world to prevent Napoleon and now this strange Fae empire from acquiring the gift, or curse, of Atahualpa's mummy.

She hurried back to camp, relieved that Kinzy remained absent on whatever mysterious errand took her away from camp each night. This meant she could abscond without confrontation. She packed half of their remaining food and water, unable in good conscience to leave Kinzy without enough for survival, no matter what the Fae woman had done. Then she stuffed some clothing in her blanket bundle and re-secured the map to her thigh before leaving camp.

She struck out to the east, heading toward where she believed the pass through the Paps of Pachamama lay. She imagined Kinzy even now meeting or communicating in some Fae means with the men who attacked them the night before, the men Kinzy had let paw and maul Esme while she lay drugged and unable to defend herself.

Fury and humiliation burned like acid in her stomach. Adrenaline pushed her to climb further up the snaking trail between the two peaks they had been heading for, long after the sun had set, and the stars began to glitter in the sky. She let anger and determination fuel her through her growing exhaustion, marching up the narrow-paved path that Inca hands had created hundreds of years before. She would find Atahualpa first. She would either claim it for England or put a torch to it. She didn't much care which, as long as Kinzy and that maniac despot on the French throne never got their hands on it.

The moon rose but the faint light did little to keep her on the path. Three times she had to backtrack when she discovered nothing but dirt and grass under her feet instead of Inca stone. Her eyes were gritty, her feet cast in iron, and her head pounded from lack of oxygen as she climbed higher. Every injury she'd accumulated on this trek, from minor cuts, to a swollen hand and bruised ribs, felt magnified in her exhaustion. At last the trail veered, winding up the side of one of the peaks, instead of between them.

She trudged on doggedly, knowing Cooper would be proud of her. Despite having been tricked, she would succeed. She didn't need anyone else, she'd do this on her own, damn it. She imagined Victoria's smiling face, imagined perhaps receiving some clandestine medal at Prince Albert's hands, something she could never wear, but that she could keep in a velvet box and look at in quiet moments.

She saw in her mind's eye the shape of the fictitious medal. She smiled. She was smiling still as the ground underneath her right foot crumbled and gave way. She toppled sideways, arms flailing, and plummeted off the path and down the mountainside. Rocks and lumps of earth and branches poked and jabbed at her as she careened down the steep slope. A stiff but yielding wall halted her descent.

A wall that smelled of mildewed canvas.

A man shouted and she heard people running toward her. A flare from a lantern blinded her. Groaning, she struggled to sit, every muscle in her body screaming at the fresh abuse.

Someone with strong hands hefted her to her feet. She blinked against the lantern light and stared into a familiar face.

"My dear Lady Esme. Whatever are you doing in such a nasty place?"

Her eyes traveled from his smug face to the gun in his hand and then down to his boots. Boots almost identical to Kinzy's boots. Except larger.

He followed her gaze and his jaw clenched. His Fae allies were no longer a secret, at least to her. She had to get this intelligence back to Victoria somehow. He made a motion with the gun and two men stepped out of the shadows and grabbed her arms. "Take her inside my tent and tie her up."

She struggled to free herself, used every dirty trick she'd ever been taught, to no avail. In moments, Reynard's men bound her hand and foot and secured her to the central tent pole. She wriggled, but she might as well try to uproot a tree.

Reynard entered, sat down on a camp stool and poured something from a canteen into a tin cup. "Are you thirsty?"

She nodded. Better to stay hydrated, even if it made her look weak. Pride had no place right now.

"What a pity." He sipped from his cup, watching her smugly over the rim. "Where is your young friend?"

The bastard. "She's not my friend."

"*Vraiment*? So you have had a falling out? How convenient." He reached over to his cot, pulled a long, curved blade from under his pillow, and rested it on his thighs. "I think it is time you and I had a frank conversation." He leaned forward. "An intimate and honest one."

The weapon in his hand filled her vision. It had a silver filigree hilt and otherworldly etching along the curved blade that glowed in the lantern light. Just like Kinzy's blades. More evidence of his complicity with the Fae. Other Fae. "I have nothing to say to you."

Oh, how wrong she had been. It wasn't Kinzy who had betrayed her. Those weren't Kinzy's boot prints around Tomàs's body, and it hadn't been Kinzy's draiglann that had been used to torture and kill Tomàs. Self-loathing churned in her already acid-filled stomach. She'd misread it all once again, and her temper and her habit of jumping to conclusions had put her right into the hands of her true enemy.

Reynard's blue eyes glittered. "I think you'll talk. You are but a woman, whereas your guide was a man. A man perhaps used to such abuse. Where he was silent, you will not be."

"You're a butcher."

"On the contrary. If I were a butcher, I would have slit him open like a prized deer and let his innards spill out of him while he was still alive. That was the fate you saved me from all those years ago, you know."

"I don't know what you're talking about." Truly, she didn't. He acted as if they knew each other, but for the life of her she couldn't remember him.

Hurt flared in his eyes, then dulled to resignation. He shook his head and raised the draiglann. "It is of no consequence. Let us return to the topic at hand. I am aware you are in possession of a map. The Vatican's map. Tomàs provided me with some information on where to go, but I suspect he was leading me, as you British say, down the garden path." He leaned forward, the curved weapon in his hand, and placed the tip on her collarbone. "Where is the map?"

"I don't have it."

He tsked. "Esme dear, cease the prevarications." The sharp point of the blade rested more heavily on the bone. "There are some who say that women have difficulty lying successfully, that they must look away. Personal experience has taught me that a woman is perfectly capable of looking a man in the eyes while telling the most outrageous untruths. So let us stop this pointless back and forth. Tell me where you are hiding the map and this unpleasantness will be but a fleeting memory."

Everything ached, like she'd been beaten with a cricket bat. She pressed her lips shut when he eased the point of the blade forward to prick her skin. A warm trickle of blood slid down between her breasts.

Tomàs had suffered under this same blade and had not broken. She could do no less. Since she knew she hadn't the strength to fight Reynard and his goons physically, she needed cleverness. A trait men routinely discounted in members of her sex. Reynard considered himself a gentleman and seemed to feel some connection to her. She would make use of it outside of the game of sexual attraction they had played. She hung her head and used her own feelings of stupidity and humiliation to produce enough tears to fill her eyes. They ran down her cheeks and dripped off her chin. "I don't have it anymore." She let her lower lip tremble before looking up and meeting his eyes. "Tomàs took it. He was the one guiding us, so he insisted on it. He believed me to be incapable of keeping it safe." She sniffled. "Clearly he was right."

Reynard scowled. "I warn you, lady, lying to me is a dangerous affair. Your pretty tears will not move me."

She tossed her head, raised her chin. "I'm not lying! He took it for safekeeping. He kept it in the bottom of that grungy backpack of his. At least that's the last place I saw it." She tried a diversion. "Didn't your men find it when they searched the camp? They certainly took everything else of value, including, I might add, my dignity."

His eyes flashed as he stood. "No one touched your dignity, I assure you. I would not have allowed that."

"Well, they certainly came close. I have a bruise on my thigh the size of a crumpet."

He gave a snarl. "That was Miguel, not me, and I stopped him from further abuse."

Esme ducked her head. "I thank you for that." She sighed. "Maybe one of them found it in his backpack but didn't know what it was."

He spun and stalked out of the tent. She heard him yell for Miguel. There followed an explosive diatribe in Spanish and Miguel left to search every man's possessions for the map. After a moment, Reynard came back and flung himself on his cot, throwing an arm over his face.

"I now have a splitting headache. You are an infuriating and vexing creature, Lady Esme. I am at a loss as to what to do with you."

"I don't suppose letting me go is an option?"

He chuckled, the sound somewhat muffled by his shirt sleeve. "Sadly, no." He leaned back on one elbow and clasped his hands. "I gave you every opportunity to turn back. I thought the pirate attack might frighten you off, but no. Even the night I raided your camp, I left you unmolested in a drugged stupor. You could have abandoned this foolish quest to best me then, yet you did not. Now I am left with no choice but to behave in an ungentlemanly fashion. And wait for Miguel to find this apocryphal map."

"What if one of your men found it and is trying to keep it for himself?"

He removed his arm and raised his eyebrows. "If he is, then he will be dealt with, but I am almost positive that this is not the case. One wonders if your comment was meant purely to create dissension."

Esme tried her best to look cowed. "You give me too much credit, although now I wish that had been my intent." She paused, allowed more tears to flow, not hard given her level of pain. "What then? If you find it, will you kill me?"

"Oh, I think I can find a less violent way of disposing of you, my dear. I am a gentleman after all. I do have an ace in the hole, as the colonials say." He pulled something from his pocket and dangled it in front of her. It was her bracelet, the one Hieronymous had given her to help her locate the mummy. "With this, even without the map, I'll find what I'm after in the end. The map would merely make it easier." He sat, rubbed his face. "No, I will not kill you. I cannot, my honor won't permit it." His eyes lit. "However, I do know of a sultan in Arabia who would love to add a charming English rose to his harem."

She watched silently as he sighed and stood. Pulling a soft, woven blanket off the end of his cot, he brought it and a cup of water to her. When she'd drunk her fill, he tucked the blanket around her.

"There. That is as comfortable as I can make you, I'm afraid, *cherie*." His fingers lingered a moment on her cheek before he straightened. "Such a pity you would not cooperate. We might have made an interesting pair."

He snuffed out the lantern that hung over her head. "I will move to Miguel's tent to preserve your precious reputation. He will have to find other accommodations for the night." He grabbed his pillow and strode to the door, turning back to her as he raised the tent flap. "But make no mistake, my lady. If you so much as squeak or wiggle your toes, the men guarding this tent will see to it that you neither squeak nor move again. *Comprenez-vous*?"

She nodded, looking suitably chastised.

With a gallant bow, he bid her goodnight and let the tent flap drop, but not before deliberately allowing her to glimpse the boots of the two men on either side of the doorway.

She squirmed a bit, carefully, trying to create a gap between the rope and her skin, but she had been trussed tightly. If she struggled too much, the whole tent would shake. Damn, but she was truly stuck.

Maybe Kinzy would find her. Or maybe, in a much more likely scenario, Kinzy would rightly assume that Esme struck out on her own to reach Atahualpa's tomb. This in turn would cause the young woman to race to beat her to it. Even as Esme sat here, tied up in this bloody tent, Kinzy was probably using her magical senses to find her way to the Inca Emperor's final resting place.

Esme squeezed her eyes shut, furious with herself. It seemed like every decision she'd made on this trip had led to disaster. Maybe she wasn't cut out for missions of true importance. Maybe she should just go home and pop out the requisite heir and a spare and spend her days embroidering and inviting other foolish and obedient women to tea. That brought real tears to her eyes.

She lost herself in misery, not caring that the men outside could hear her sobs and sniffles. Drowning in the darkness, she dropped into a restless and uncomfortable sleep.

Chapter Twenty-Two

As far as Kinzy could see along their backtrail, no one followed them. She put down her gathered fistful of grass she'd used to cover Esme's tracks that day and spread the drying blades around in a natural pattern. Kinzy's own tracks were difficult to discover already, a product of her Fae boots and her training.

Trell flew in wide circles, his wings outstretched and playing with the mountain winds. *All clear,* he chirped in her mind. His joy in full flight drew a rare smile from her.

They seemed safe enough for now, but she had believed they were safe the night before. She'd been terribly wrong. Tomàs was missing, and they'd been drugged and robbed in the night. There was no magic for as far as she could sense, many miles for certain. The Inca Spirits had not taken people before, not cared about objects and luggage. They'd just attacked. She doubted their involvement in this conundrum. No, a human predator pursued them, and number one on Kinzy's suspect list was *Monsieur* Reynard. Or an agent of his. It was nearly impossible for a human to hide from her senses, and yet out here she felt they were alone on the mountain, just as she had the evening before on her self-appointed duty checking their back-trail. She could find no traces at all. She felt lost, unable to depend on her own senses. She'd give anything to know how they were hiding from her. They must be out there somewhere.

She still tasted the drug in her system, a bitterness on her lips and tongue that nothing washed away. Even poor Trell still felt the effects of the drug that had been used on them, an effect rare for their kind. It had to be more than the drug affecting her senses to hide from her.

One more task and then she could quickly return to the fire and Esme's company.

She gave a quiet whistle, and Trell turned back toward her. *It's time, dear friend.*

He landed on her shoulder and rubbed his head along the side of her jaw. *Time to hunt for dinner?*

Always thinking of your stomach. No, time to return to the queen with my report of the serpent, and the attack last night. I have done my best to make you the hero of the tale. I can only hope the queen will see the necessity as well, and that you shall feast in Tír na nÓg tonight.

She brought the scroll out from her belt pouch. The weight of the words had distracted her as they hiked through the day. During their brief rests, she'd rewritten them thrice to try and get the tone and details of her message just right. She'd done her best. She swallowed her fears regarding the instructions the queen would send in response to Esme's knowledge of the Fae, as well as how Queen Airmed would react to Trell's true form displayed for the entire party to ogle as he fought the serpent and saved them all. If she didn't give the queen a chance to give those instructions, Kinzy would not have to obey them. But she could no longer delay or she risked the queen's anger for that. In dusk's cold light, it was the mission that was important, no matter what the queen decided about how Kinzy accomplished it.

They are good words, my bonded. Do not worry and waste your thoughts and energy on what may come this day. Do the deed and then let it play.

Kinzy went over the words in her head anyway as she put on Trell's harness and secured the scroll.

Your Highness,

A giant water serpent of unknown new magics attacked, killing Mani and another. During the attack, Trell revealed a new manifestation of his draconic form: increased size to match the full-grown serpent. With his help and my draiglanns we killed the beast, but the entire party witnessed that their weapons did not affect the serpent in any way. Our remaining porters fled, taking the llamas. We did not pursue.

Esme, Tomàs, Trell and I toasted the dead last night with a local alcohol that affected all of us, yes, even myself, causing a drugged sleep. Trell now senses a magic component, though last evening we sensed nothing. We woke to find Tomàs taken, our camp ransacked, and the supplies scattered or gone. The Vatican map is safe, thanks to Esme. A curious track was clear, a Fae boot, and yet I sense no other Fae. A human Fae agent must be involved against us.

Esme and I push on. She has my complete trust, as does Tomàs. The Light hold Tomàs safe, whoever has him. Trust me in sharing the secret of Fae existence in order to complete my mission. I believe Lady Esme can assist us more in the future.

. . .

~*K*

Although humans who discovered the truth of the Fae were normally assassinated or spelled to forget, Esme was different. The queen would see that. Lady Esme held a unique position to help Kinzy with this mission and in the future. They closed in on their target, and the attack proved someone else was here with the same goal in mind. Kinzy hoped that partnered with the Lady Esme, they would win out over whoever their opponents were, and reach the mummy's tomb before them. Kinzy shied away from thinking what happened then, but she knew her duty. Her queen wanted that mummy, and she shall have it.

"Ready, my friend?" She stroked his neck for what might be the last time. "Safe winds," she called out as he rose into the misty air with a flap of his leathery wings, and vanished.

Time to return to Esme, whose passion for the mission matched her own, and whose sensibilities soared above most of her peers. Kinzy took a deep breath and faced the truth. Esme must be left behind at some point in order to take the mummy for the Fae. Or the queen might order the woman's death, no matter what Kinzy counseled.

It would be a shame. Esme deserved better.

Their back trail secured, and her report sent, Kinzy's next duty was to stand watch as Esme slept. The human would certainly feel better with a good night's sleep to purge the last of the drug from her system.

She stepped lightly and quickly along the combination of Inca stone road and steps, with breaks in the overgrown brush and grasses that covered the hillside in a thick thatch. The sun sank below the mountains to the west, painting the sky lavender and pink, and the valley between the mountains became dark as Kinzy arrived at their camp for the night.

Just beyond the tents she stopped. No sound. No cooking fire, though Esme had planned one. The camp seemed deserted as the darkness deepened. Kinzy's heart clenched.

She circled around and noted only Esme's tracks in and out. Within the tent, Esme's bed roll and clothes had gone, half the food and water missing. Everything else remained neatly in place, unlike the disappearance of Tomàs.

Esme had taken off into the night. Without her.

Kinzy immediately followed Esme's older tracks out of camp. She had to find out what had happened to her friend in the brief few hours Kinzy'd been gone. The attackers may have found the camp again. She studied the footprints, noting they were Esme's normal stride, until deeper indents in the dirt showed where the woman had stopped briefly before resuming with a stealthier, lighter step, each one placed with care. Kinzy could faintly hear animal noises over the hill as she tracked Esme up the slope and through the tall wild grass and stone. At the top she dropped down on her stomach and peered over the hill into the small rocky bowl below. There she looked down on a horrendous sight.

Poor Tomàs.

He hung upside down from a dried wooden limb shoved into a rocky crag wall with a slight overhang shielding it from above. The mountain breeze swung him above a darkened circle of dirt and gravel where his blood had soaked in. Two winged scavengers squawked and fought over a bit of entrail pulled from the hole in his stomach. Kinzy aimed a stone at the beasts as she came closer, and they flew a short distance away. She'd not kill a scavenger for only doing what was natural—to consume the dead and thus perpetuate life in a never ending circle.

Tomàs had clearly been tortured, then chewed on. The slices across his torso looked deep but curved, and clean.

Closer examination confirmed they seemed to be draiglann cuts.

Kinzy looked around, hoping for more clues. Esme had obviously lost the contents of her stomach over the matter, off to the side. Closer to the body, where the torturer had circled his prisoner, only one other set of prints showed. Fae boots, much like her own. Putting her foot side by side with the new prints, these were a bit bigger, a bit wider than her own, but the smooth, round impression of the familiar Fae heel and sole were clear. The walk had much more awkward weight shift than a Fae, and that meant a human made these strides. Likely working with a Fae clan to possess such boots. The human had tortured Tomàs after kidnapping him the night before. A human with ties to House DonClannagh, most likely. Queen Airmed had mentioned them as an enemy in this particular game, working with the French.

By the temperature of the body, this happened hours before they even arrived at their campsite. Kinzy searched Tomàs for anything his family might want back, but found nothing in his shreds of clothing. Esme had come close to the body, then left with a quick, erratic stride. She'd made a decision, one that involved running back to camp.

Esme found the body and saw the Fae boot prints, much like Kinzy's own, belonging to the torturer. The boots. Esme had stood near the prints the longest. With Kinzy being the only Fae Esme knew, the only one to possess such footwear, she must have leapt to the assumption that Kinzy had something to do with Tomàs's death. It hurt to think Esme considered her capable of such betrayal and brutality. Esme had raced back to camp, packed, and left to continue on her mission without Kinzy. She must believe Kinzy to be a threat.

The attackers must have been after the map. It was the only item of real consequence. It had somehow remained hidden on

Esme, despite how she'd been assaulted. The person who'd taken Tomàs likely believed that because Tomàs was their guide he knew the location of the map, where they were heading, and what they would find there. She could only hope Tomàs had been so badly tortured because he refused to give any information to his captor.

Fae boots. Apparent cuts from a draiglann. Her insides clenched in fear. *Reynard.* Checking the area again, the boots went on ahead, and Esme had clearly gone back to camp in a hurry.

She cut the body down, then Kinzy drew her blade along her thumb in a shallow slice and smeared her blood on Tomàs's bloated face, as she would for any faeleath warrior.

She spoke aloud in Spanish, the language Tomàs and his God would understand. "*Enfrenta la Luz final con coraje y fuerza.*" *Face the final Light with courage and strength.*

Staunching her blood flow with a brief moment of pressure, she gave Tomàs's body a final nod, then raced back along Esme's tracks.

Back at camp, she quickly packed everything she could, except the tent. Time was of the essence, as was her carrying capacity. From the signs around camp, Esme had left, on purpose, and on her own. The woman had not even finished the food in the pot over the fire, still slightly warm. Fear had pushed Esme to leave quickly. Even so, she had honor enough to leave Kinzy with food and water. Kinzy's chest tightened with a deep ache. She had to catch up to Esme, make things right between them. Esme had taught her so much about being human, about friendship, and trust. Kinzy needed to learn more of human ways, something she could never learn from the Fae. The queen would say Esme was simply a tool to be used and set aside when broken or no longer needed, but deep down,

Kinzy recognized that she still wanted Esme's trust and companionship.

Kinzy took a deep breath as she swung her pack onto her back. Under the darkened sky with a rising moon, she followed the British woman's trail into the night, hoping to find her before Esme found the true enemy out there. An enemy Kinzy could not sense, hidden behind some glamor veil.

Esme's tracks seemed erratic in places and Kinzy suspected altitude sickness. The woman rushed dangerously in the dark, following the Inca stone steps Tomàs had believed led through the Paps of Pachamama, the marker on the map. By the time the fingernail moon was high in the sky, she still had not found Lady Esme.

Kinzy watched her own footing and studied her surroundings for any signs of the enemy or her friend. Trell had not yet returned, and she missed him and his ability to scout overhead. She hoped he returned. Soon. This was the longest he had ever been away from her. Considering all she had sent in her message, worry gnawed at her.

She scanned the tall grasses upslope and down, as she rounded a curve of stone. There was no sign of Reynard or anyone else. Her worry increased, as did her pace, until she caught sight of newly upturned stones and dirt alongside the steps. Yes, her friend had slipped here. Judging by the mashing of the earth and broken blades of grass down the hillside, Esme had gone over the edge of the jagged stone and down the mountainside.

Kinzy crouched low on the cold Inca stone. A camp was well hidden among the grass and large outcrops below her. Four tents, and a small fire. She counted two men but was certain more rested inside the tents. No alarm had been given, so no one had seen her come around the curve of the mountainside. She needed to get in closer. Esme's fall down the mountain led straight into the camp below, and Kinzy had no doubt her friend had been captured. *Light above grant you're safe, you frustrating woman.* She slowly backed up along the Inca trail and finally found a good spot where she could crawl down to the same level as the camp. She needed to know how many men she faced inside those tents, and how best to rescue her friend, if Esme was still alive.

As she crept closer, Reynard himself came out of one of the tents, his smug face clear in the firelight and weak lamps.

"You two, guard this tent," he called out to his men around the fire. "No one is to touch the woman. No one in or out without me. Do you understand?"

The men rose and went to stand in front of the tent. His orders being followed, Reynard grabbed a dish of food from a pot on the fire, and walked into a tent on the far side, opposite the one being guarded. The camp settled into quiet again, the fire dying and the men drifting off to sleep. Soft sobs came from the guarded tent. At least her friend was alive. Once the man walking the perimeter was on the opposite side of camp, she quietly moved to the back of the tent where they held Esme, cut one of the ties that held down the canvas wall, and crawled inside.

All was silent as she crouched and waited for her eyes to adjust.

Bright light flared and she flinched. When she could finally see again, there was Esme, tied to the center pole. Reynard held a draiglann to the woman's arched throat. Well, they'd confirmed he was indeed the bastard hunting them. Not only did he wield a Fae blade, but he wore the Fae boots as well.

"Careful, *Mademoiselle*." Reynard seemed pleased with himself as he grinned and drew the blade across Esme's neck, causing a trickle of blood to run down to her collar bone. "I find the knife to be exceedingly sharp and needing only the slightest pressure to split the skin to the bone. Hands above your head, please. Miguel?"

Kinzy stood up straight and did as he asked. Someone came under the tent wall behind her and grabbed her knife as he leaned in close to breath into her ear. "I take that now, *Señorita.* No weapons allowed at this *fiesta.*" Miguel smelled of too much alcohol and the stench of sweat. She flinched away. "We're going to dance soon."

He kicked the back of her knee and she collapsed with a cry. As she struggled to rise, he struck her on the head and darkness closed in.

Chapter Twenty-Three

Esme spent the majority of the night chafing at her bonds and wishing she could at least take Kinzy's pulse. Her friend's face took on the color of unrisen dough in the lantern light and her breathing had been shallow and raspy for some time after they'd been left alone. Esme worried that the Fae girl was in shock and that the knock on the head had caused a fracture, or worse. Before leaving them, their 'gallant' French host had graciously deposited Kinzy's unconscious body on the cot. He bound her hand and foot, which seemed an absurd precaution. Any idiot could see that Miguel's blow to the back of her knee had done serious damage. Neither of them were going anywhere.

The long dark hours passed in a fugue of worry. Kinzy didn't move, didn't make a sound, and the woman's pasty coloring and unnaturally deep sleep made Esme fear that her head wound would prove fatal. Fear and self-loathing churned in Esme's stomach like wash water in Cooper's self-agitating laundry tub. Esme couldn't shake the sense of guilt. If she hadn't jumped to the wrong conclusion, if she'd just waited to talk to Kinzy, gotten her side of the story, they'd be free. Kinzy wouldn't have been so grievously injured, and they'd likely be on their way to finding Atahualpa's mummy. Now, Reynard would find it, and she and Kinzy would either be killed outright, or, well, she didn't want to dwell on what the 'or' might be. In any case, both she and Kinzy would have failed their mission.

By the time a line of faint light appeared between the door flaps of the tent, she had convinced herself that Kinzy had fallen into a coma from which she would never awaken and that any moment, Reynard would come in and have Miguel slit her throat. When Kinzy stirred and moaned, Esme nearly wept with joy.

"Kinzy? Can you hear me? Thank God you're not dead."

"Not yet." Kinzy lifted her head then let it fall back onto the cot with a groan. "Water?"

"We don't have any. Although I'd be hard pressed to give it to you anyway. I'm trussed up like a Christmas goose."

"Someday you need to explain Christmas. And why one ties up a goose." She shifted, and Esme saw her wince. "For now—"

Esme rushed to fill the awkward silence. "I'm sorry. I never should have believed what I did."

Kinzy's lips pressed together and her hands clenched. "I would never have done that to Tomàs."

Esme leaned forward. "I know." Her voice cracked. "I mean, I should have known. You're not capable of that kind of horror. But when I saw the boots, and the shape of the wounds, it seemed a logical conclusion." She squeezed her eyes shut for a moment, remembering other times she'd jumped first and thought later. "I am forever jumping to conclusions. It's my worst trait, and I've made a fool of myself before. I'm truly sorry. I was an idiot, and now we're stuck here, trussed up—"

"—like Christmas geese. Yes." Kinzy shook her head carefully and winced again. "We are indeed stuck, but the fault is also mine. I should have known Reynard would watch the tent, and I should have been prepared for a counterattack." Kinzy snorted in frustration. "I should also have mentioned to you that I came across Fae boot prints that I could not immediately account for after Mani's death. I ignored them as I could find no Fae presence but my own. If you had known that, then you might not have made the assumption you did."

Kinzy recounted the story of the prints and finished with, "I am not used to working with a partner, with sharing information with anyone."

"Neither of us are. I haven't worked with a partner since Rafi and that ended with me standing on a dock in the rain, alone and heartbroken." The damp, mildewed canvas walls closed in on her, a cage as stale and confining as her own life had become. She'd tried to break free of the walls society placed on her sex by becoming Victoria's agent, but in doing so she'd created a life of secrets and lies that left her confined and even more alone. She grimaced. "This business, this vocation we chose breeds distrust. A necessity, but it makes for a lonely life." She bit her lip, wishing she could travel into the past to alter her assumption, or fast forward to a time when she and this remarkable woman no longer competed for the same prize and could be friends. "I really like you. I wish things were different."

Kinzy's shoulders drooped. "I wish this too." The unspoken, that things were not, might never be, different, hung in the air between them like the chill morning mist.

The tent flaps parted. Reynard strode in, looking annoyingly refreshed and impeccably dressed. "*Bon matins, mesdames*! I trust you slept well?" He stepped aside to allow one of his men, who thankfully was *not* Miguel, to bring in a fully loaded tea tray.

Esme glared at him. "We slept not a wink, as I'm sure you know. Kinzy is not well at all. I studied nursing, please untie me so that I can see to her."

"I may untie you, in time, but there is something I must do first, something of burning importance." He crossed to Esme, kicked her feet apart and knelt between her legs. He snapped his fingers and pointed to her right foot and the man who had carried the tea tray knelt down also and held her foot, narrowly avoiding a kick to the face. Meanwhile Reynard grabbed her left foot, quickly unlaced her boot and removed it. Then the men switched places and Reynard robbed her of her right boot as well. Thus having deprived her of her footwear, he slowly slid his hand under her skirt and up her bare legs.

Esme shuddered. Did he mean to ravish her here, in front of everyone? In broad daylight? "You are a deplorable bastard!"

The gentle brush of his fingertips up her leg stopped at the elastic strap that held the map cylinder in place on her thigh. He grinned then, his eyebrows arching, an amused twinkle in his eye.

"Well, well, what do we have here?"

"If you move your hand one inch farther, you'll have my foot in your face."

"Why do you think I removed your boots?" He chuckled. "I am well aware of your tricks, my lady." His fingers tiptoed up her bare skin. Then, with a fierce yank, he pulled the map holder and its attached holster out from under her skirt and held it high in triumph. "I knew you still had it!" He chucked her under the chin. "*Ma petite dinde*, did you really think me so base as to assault you here, now, in front of this motley audience?" He tsked, then stood. "Miguel!"

The sadistic native man entered, leering. "*Si, Señor?*"

"Untie this pretty little idiot, and release *Mademoiselle* Kinzalynn's hands so that the ladies can have their morning tea. Perhaps they will be in a more cooperative mood after that."

"I need her left leg untied as well. I have to examine the knee that your goon here damaged last evening."

Reynard blew out a frustrated breath. "Fine. Release the girl's leg as well."

"We will also need a wash basin, soap and time to freshen up. Alone."

Reynard's hands clenched. "*Madame* Eggerton, this is not Claridges and you are not on holiday."

She stared him down, determined to get at least a few moments of privacy. "Sir, there are personal matters to attend to. Surely you do not expect two ladies of our station to relieve themselves under the rude stares of your men."

He huffed. "Fine. Miguel, when they are finished with their tea, come and fetch me. I will stand watch out front and you will stand out back." He turned to Esme. "Will that suffice, your Ladyship?"

"Yes." She appeared to relax. "Thank you."

He tapped the map tube against his palm. "*Bon.* Miguel, you will watch them like a hawk while I am gone. Do not underestimate either of them. Do you understand?"

Miguel grinned maliciously. "*Si, Señor.*"

A small victory, and probably best she could hope for. There would be no escaping right now, especially considering how ill Kinzy looked, but maybe a few moments of privacy would allow them to plan their next move.

Reynard nodded and held up the map tube. "*Eh bien.* I have a map to study. Enjoy your tea, ladies." With an elegant bow, he left them to Miguel's not so tender mercies.

The next hour passed grimly. Kinzy's kneecap had been displaced by Miguel's blow. Esme set the kneecap back in place and despite Kinzy's stoic nature, the pain of that action wrenched a cry from the Fae woman's lips. Esme tore up the bed sheets from Reynard's cot, then wrapped the knee tightly to provide support and to reduce the swelling. Any future locomotion would require Esme's help.

Miguel grinned through the whole procedure, seeming to enjoy Kinzy's discomfort, making Esme almost glad for the presence of the second guard. She didn't trust Miguel, and if they had been alone with him, Esme had little faith he might not have done them even further damage, no matter Reynard's wishes.

After settling Kinzy as comfortably as she could on the cot in a sitting position, she fetched the tea things and they shared a cup of now tepid tea and a couple of hard, scone-like things that frankly tasted like sawdust. At least the tea helped wash the damn things down and provided warmth. By the time they had finished their paltry repast, Kinzy's color had improved a little and when Esme tracked her eye movements and vision, she seemed to be unaffected by her head wound.

Finally, Esme turned to face Miguel, hands on her hips. "You will leave us now and bring a wash basin with warm water and some soap."

Miguel puffed out a derisive breath, glancing at the tent flaps. Thinking of Reynard, Esme judged. He muttered under his breath and turned to the other guard. "Luis. *Traer jabón y agua. Agua caliente.*"

Esme nodded at Miguel's order to bring soap and hot water. "*Gracias.*"

"I will stay, while Luis goes." He stabbed a finger at Esme. "You. Sit on the cot. Next to the other one."

She crossed her arms over her chest. "I will not."

He took a step closer to her and drew a knife from his belt. "*No?*"

Esme swallowed. Reynard might be a bastard, but this man curdled her blood. She took a step back, then another, until her legs encountered the cot, not wanting to turn her back on him. She lowered herself gingerly onto the cot, so as not to jostle Kinzy's leg. "Fine. I will sit here until Luis comes back with the water." She hoped her face didn't show the fear she felt. "Then you will leave us to our toilette."

With the knife still in his hand, he leered at her. "I can help you with that. The Frenchman, he is no real man. Me, I have *huevos*." He palmed his crotch.

She kept her expression steely. "You and your *huevos* will wait outside."

He shrugged as Luis bustled in with a large wash bowl, some towels and a bar of lavender scented soap that had to belong to Reynard.

Miguel shooed Luis out, then went to the door flap. "Maybe not today, but soon you and I will dance."

He had the audacity to wink at her before disappearing outside.

Esme shivered. Sucking in a breath, she fetched the water. Kinzy looked exhausted, the pallor of her porcelain complexion marred only by the dark smudges under her eyes. She needed rest. Passing her friend a towel, dampened at one end with warm water, she quickly wiped her own face and arms, careful not to expose any part of her she didn't want seen. She had no faith that Miguel wasn't watching through some crack in the tent walls.

"How are you feeling?"

Kinzy tried to sit up a little straighter. "I will live."

Esme knelt next to her and dropped her voice. "Now that Reynard has the map, he will want to head out to the ruins today. I'm sure of it."

"You are not wrong."

"I am so sorry."

Kinzy brows lowered. "Esme, stop apologizing. You made an assumption. An erroneous one, but I can understand why you came to it." She looked away for a moment. "It hurt that you thought me capable of such a thing, but given the boot prints and the nature of the wounds, it's understandable." Her chin came up. Pride, Esme wondered? A rejection of the perceived insult? The woman was so damned difficult to read. "But I would never torture anyone like that."

Esme swallowed hard. "I know now. I think I knew it then too. I was just so shocked. And, yes, frightened. I have made mistakes before, trusting people. Believing what they told me, accepting them at face value, only to have them betray me. I let those experiences color my judgment."

"You couldn't have thought too badly of me. You left me food and water."

"It was the least I could do." She paused. "After I left, you surely realized I had deserted you. You must have thought I'd gone after the mummy alone, casting you aside." She looked up into Kinzy's face. "I have to ask. Why did you come after me?"

"I knew that whoever had killed Tomàs was out there, and that you were in danger."

"Even though I deserted you?"

Kinzy's expression softened. "Isn't that what friends do?"

"But you had an unfettered opportunity to go after the mummy."

"Your life was more important than Atahualpa at that moment. He'll still be waiting for us when we reach his tomb. I couldn't leave you to face our enemies alone. It felt right to find you first."

Esme blinked rapidly, not wanting the unbidden tears to spill down her cheeks. She reached up and squeezed her friend's arm. Her friend. "Thank you. I am so—"

Kinzy held up her hand and chuckled. "Don't say it again. It is a thing of the past. Right now, we need to figure out how we're going to get out of this. Reynard may keep us alive until he finds the mummy, but after that, he will kill us."

Esme nodded. "He *is* a bastard. Still, at the moment, I don't see how we can escape."

Kinzy began scanning the objects in the tent, stopped on the washbowl. "Perhaps if you called Miguel in here, you could be waiting to trip him and I could hit him over the head with the bowl. It is large, heavy."

"And just how would you stand up long enough to clobber him?"

Kinzy's jaw jutted out. "I am not crippled."

"No, but you're seriously injured." Esme picked up the bowl again, and the water sloshed. "Besides, it is not so heavy as all that. Cheap, porous. It would shatter but do nothing more than annoy him with a few cuts." She frowned. "You are weak and frankly, I am hungry and exhausted. There are many of them and even if we succeeded in coshing Miguel over the head, the minute we stepped outside the tent they'd be on us."

"So what do you suggest?"

Esme prided herself on being able to think on her feet, of being able to get out of almost any kind of trouble. This time, however, no brilliant plan occurred to her. "Nothing comes to me immediately, except to wait." She held up her hand to Kinzy's objection. "Reynard is wary of us right now, he will have someone watching, waiting for some kind of escape attempt. I think we should bide our time. If they think we are compliant, they will drop their guard and when that moment comes, we'll be in a better position to take advantage of it."

"You say that as though you think there *will* be a moment of distraction. What if there's not?"

"Then we'll think of something else."

"Unless we are already dead."

Esme straightened her spine and held her head high. "We will not be dead. We will find a way. Reynard told Miguel not to underestimate us. Well, we shouldn't underestimate ourselves either." She patted Kinzy's arm. "Come on. Have a little more tea and another of those horrid cakes. We need to build up our strength. God only knows when we'll get fed again."

Kinzy took the hard, tasteless cake and bit off a corner. "You'd best not be wrong about this."

Esme took a breath and squared her shoulders. Was she trying to convince Kinzy or herself? "Trust me."

Kinzy nodded. "I do."

Esme had never felt so honored. She resolved to be worthy of that trust.

Chapter Twenty-Four

"Vamos, viejas!" Miguel barged into the tent in the twilight of morning with a glowing lantern and kicked Kinzy in her injured leg with a smug grin.

Kinzy bit back a cry and nudged Esme awake before the man felt the need to kick her, too. After Reynard led them further up the mountain, they'd been tied hand and foot for the night and tossed on a single cot. Kinzy doubted breakfast was any more forthcoming than dinner had been.

Reynard strode in with a feral smile. "Oh, how I do love mornings here in the Andes. I trust you slept well? No? I am saddened that you were not as comfortable as you are accustomed, but I am sure you will sleep well once my mummy is found."

They were given a brief few minutes to attend to their toilette, as Esme kept calling it, before they were forced onto the trail with hands tied in front of them. Kinzy did her best to ignore the pain, the hunger, but Esme kept glancing back and asking how she was doing. Esme looked terrible herself. Kinzy tried again to reach Trell, but she could only tell that he still lived. Their bond usually gave emotion and connected their thoughts, but nothing came through at all. He was alive. That would have to do. She wasn't in any position to help him now.

The hike through the mountains became torturous, but at least it provided something to keep her mind off what the queen might have done with her drakkeki friend. Esme's stories of her travels also helped. She did not know much of the people the woman spoke of, but she could hear the love and affection Esme had for Cooper, for old Egg, and another gentleman named Hieronoymous. The words gave something else for Kinzy's mind to latch onto and pull herself along. A counterpoint to the crackle and snap from her knee, and the sharp pang of her ribs. Her body healed, but the trail made it difficult. She let her mind drift as they traversed the mountain.

She had been walking a moment ago, but she became aware that she now sat in a disheveled heap on the ground beside Esme, who berated Miguel for his treatment of them yet again.

"Back on the trail in two minutes!" Reynard told his men as he walked down the trail among them.

"One won't speak, and the other won't shut up. Why keep them at all?" Miguel grabbed Reynard's arm as he walked past where Kinzy and Esme had been shoved to the ground.

"Just do as I tell you and give them water. Save your breath for the trail." Reynard yanked his arm from Miguel's grasp and continued on his way, preparing the men to take to the trail again.

Miguel, who muttered under his breath about the Frenchman and his arrogance, tilted a water bottle in each of their mouths. Kinzy silently swallowed what scant liquid she could.

Esme, however, continued her tirade after her brief swig. "You could at least untie our hands and give us a proper drink. That wasn't enough to wet a toe nail." The woman held her back straight and chin up. "We also require a brief respite and privacy to attend to our personal needs before we can even think of going any further."

Miguel bent down, his face directly in Esme's. "You can piss over there by that rock like everyone else. Less drink means fewer stops for your personal *necesidades*."

"You will provide us some privacy."

More harsh words between the two ended with a bare amount of privacy accorded as most of the men guarding them briefly turned their backs. Reynard fumed at the delay, and as soon as the women were finished he had them moving again along the side of the mountain.

The rest and the water helped clear her mind, allowing Kinzy to study Reynard and his men as they traveled. She was almost certain it was House DonClannagh who had backed Reynard and supplied him with the boots and draiglann. Did they know she'd been assigned to thwart them? Reynard's men were all local Spaniards who owed Reynard no loyalty beyond the promise of money when they returned with what he sought. Miguel was the one who controlled the men, who enforced Reynard's orders, but even he held little respect for the man. Reynard better watch his back as he led them along the ancient trail that continued up around the mountain.

In places the trail was difficult to find, stones having slid down the mountain and covered the Inca stone path. Thick grasses in great swaths across the mountain refused to give up any secrets. More often than not they waited while some of the men were ordered to scout about, looking for a place to once again pick up the track. Unlike earlier trails on their journey, Kinzy surmised that the Inca had meant for these trails to be harder to follow. The map had shown places of importance and concern for the *conquistadores* as they traveled. They had to have been of more concern to them than the Inca, it was a matter of perspective.

Kinzy ignored the ache in her leg, but without better wrappings and rest the long trek had made it worse. She could still outlast these humans, but she wasn't as sure about her speed. They were all going to the same place, though. Her journey proceeded, though more harsh than she would have liked.

Ahead of her, Esme stumbled for the third time in the last few minutes. The woman needed a longer rest, and had become too dependent on those coca leaves. Kinzy deliberately stepped wrong and tumbled off the trail, though she did not get far before Miguel had grabbed her and straddled her while she lay on the ground.

"Halt!" Reynard yelled and carefully made his way down to them.

Though Kinzy watched Reynard's approach, she also spent some time looking at the sky around them. Trell would come soon. Unless the Queen had been angered and Trell imprisoned. Or worse. But their bond lay quietly there at the back of her mind. He still lived, though not a whisper crossed her mind. She had called to him, in the long quiet of the night, wishing for a sarcastic comment about her sad state. Even a derisive snort for how easily she'd been captured would be welcome.

"These *mujeres* slow us down, *Señor* Reynard." Miguel grabbed her jaw, his fingers digging into her hard enough to bruise, his cold eyes promising dire consequences if he had his chance.

Reynard tugged on his coat and glared at her. "Perhaps I need to come up with ways to renew your enthusiasm, *Mademoiselle*?"

Esme's voice came from the trail above, "You injured her leg and forced us on this rocky track and then expect her to move like a thoroughbred on a flat grass track? You are insane, *Monsieur*. She needs rest. Let us camp and I can attend to her leg so she may hike the trail more easily tomorrow."

Reynard turned to once again argue with Esme, but Kinzy barely noticed their conversation. At the corner of Reynard's rucksack strapped snuggly to his back, a bit of the containment netting Esme had been given had worked its way out to hang down and wave in the breeze as if to say hello. So it was not gone. Reynard had it still.

They needed to be free of these men, and grab the backpack. Easy as, what would Esme say? Oh yes, *easy as cutting cake.*

Chapter Twenty-Five

Clouds the color of bruises massed above the jagged, scrub-covered peaks ahead of them. A mist settled down over the trail, chilling Esme. Her clothes hung heavy and wet after a close encounter with the spray from a plunging waterfall a couple of hours before. Now their trail snugged close to a frigid mountain stream, following the rivulet between steep slopes, the paving hidden beneath an overgrowth of grass. Every couple hundred feet the edge of the path crumbled into the cut bank of the stream.

She eyed the narrowing sides of the valley, hoping the trail wouldn't become one with the stream bed before long. Rolling hills had given way to sheer walls of rock that loomed over them menacingly. Or so it felt. Esme had the sense they were not wanted here. Did that mean they were close?

The trail veered to the left, away from the stream and the way narrowed further. Fist-sized rocks and stony debris littered their path. Esme offered a steadying hand to Kinzy, who rejected it.

Esme kept her voice low and gestured subtly with her chin.

"Do you see that formation ahead? The way the slopes both jut out over the trail?"

Kinzy nodded.

"Does it remind you of anything?"

Silent, the faeleath examined the trail ahead with those preternatural eyes. "Two heads? Facing each other?"

"Indeed. Like the two faces on the map. Just before the X that marks the spot." She didn't want Miguel to overhear the word *tomb*.

"Ah. I believe you are correct."

"And the pile of rocks." The next symbol, inked in the same fashion as the Inca warrior and the serpent. Another danger point. She shivered, the weight of the threatening walls of rock pressed ever closer. "A pile of rocks? Or a trap."

Kinzy answered with a subtle lift of her shoulders.

A breeze parted the mist and a ray of weak sunlight shone through the gathering clouds, spotlighting a flatter patch of green some distance ahead, higher up. A plateau of sorts. For a brief moment, she thought she saw a line of pale stone against the darker green. Inca walls? She strained her eyes, even as the light faded, seeing what appeared to be more terraces further up, more lines of stone. Before her eyes could properly focus, the mists obscured her view again.

The parade of porters and llamas, with Reynard striding close behind clutching his ill-gotten map, snaked single file up the path. None of the men gestured or remarked on what she had just seen, making her wonder if she'd imagined it. A glance at Kinzy and her intense scrutiny of the spot Esme had been examining reassured her. Esme raised her eyebrows, asking wordlessly, *You saw?*

Kinzy blinked an affirmative.

They labored up the trail for a few more minutes, the low hanging clouds shrouding them like walking corpses. Esme's nerves jangled in anticipation. They were close, she knew it. The map had been spot on so far. Something lurked out there, something waited for them, she just didn't know what.

A sharp crack like a tree branch snapping rang out, followed by a low rumble. A vibration started in Esme's feet and traveled up through her spine. She stumbled. Fear fluttered in her chest, a sort of reptilian panic, the same feeling she'd had during the earthquake in Thessalonika last fall. She grabbed Kinzy's arm, yanked her to the side into a shallow depression in the slope.

Reynard shouted, another man screamed. Then all other sounds were drowned out by the cascading crash of a ton of rock filling the pass like a deadly flood.

It took several minutes for the cacophony of shattering rocks and the shrieking of men and llamas to cease.

"Esme, let me go."

She released her death grip on Kinzy, listening to the rain of pebbles rattling downslope. "That was close. Do you suppose--"

"You did this!" Reynard pushed Kinzy aside and jerked Esme to her feet. His breath was hot and rank as he gripped her shoulders.

She'd faced more than one irate male threatening violence. "I did not do this. Whatever this was."

"Then she did." He jabbed a thumb at Kinzy. "Her kind are anathema. I'm sorry the Emperor ever agreed to an abominable partnership with these creatures. It is a deal with the very devil himself."

Kinzy hobbled closer. "You are a fool. I could no more have caused this avalanche than could Esme."

Reynard scowled, breathed raggedly through his nose, fists clenched. His face was so red, Esme feared an apoplectic fit. Slowly the color faded and his breathing returned to normal.

His glance flicked to Miguel, who struggled up the slope toward them, trousers torn, knees bleeding. The gash on his cheek looked like it would leave another unattractive scar. Esme almost smiled. Reynard stepped back onto the trail, pointing toward the rockfall with the ragged map.

"Gather everyone who is still alive. We need to clear that rockfall. We are close now, this was meant to block us from reaching the city." He peered upwards with a manic fury. "Nothing will stop me now."

The avalanche filled the six-foot wide path that led upward as completely as a dam. The rubble rose eight or nine feet high. Even their nimble pack llamas could not be expected to clamber up and over.

Miguel swore in rapid-fire Spanish. "*Esto es ridiculo*! Impossible. We cannot dig through that."

Reynard poked a finger at Miguel. "You can and you will. Dig me a path through that. The tomb lies up there." He gestured toward the plateau Esme had glimpsed. "Somewhere. You have been paid more than enough, and if we reach our goal, there is more to come. More than you can imagine." He placed his hands on his hips, spoke through his teeth. "Get. It. Done."

The venom in Miguel's eyes never made it to his lips. He spat, wiped some blood from his face, then stalked off to gather up the other men to begin the work. "You are blinded by greed, *Monsieur*."

He brushed dust off his waistcoat before facing her with a cool smile. "I am a patriot, *Madame*. I am serving my country as you serve yours." The smile became smug. "It is a pity you are not as proficient in your duties as I." He made a sweeping, come along gesture. "Now if you will, please precede me. We must all pitch in. I *will* reach the city tomorrow."

"You cannot expect Kinzy and I to dig. Kinzy is injured."

"Yes, yes, so you keep insisting. And you would have me believe you are a delicate female, and that is a lie too." The smile faded entirely. "Let us end the pretense." Pulling a pistol from his pocket, he waved it at them. "*Allez.*"

Nowhere to run. Not that Kinzy could anyway. And there was no way Esme would leave her now. Squaring her shoulders, she gathered the folds of her walking skirt and marched up the trail, Kinzy limping at her side.

Chapter Twenty-Six

Kinzy awoke the next morning to the throbbing of her knee. Pearl pink light colored the soft clouds of the early sky in contrast to the hard rocks digging into her spine. More debris had fallen on Reynard's men as they labored to clear a path wide enough and stable enough for llamas and men to reach the other side. Reynard called a halt as the stars shone against a coal black sky and the men seemed near mutiny at the dangerous work under a moonless night.

No tents had been set up. She and Esme had slept on the scree from the avalanche, watched over in turn by Luis and Miguel. No campfire smell tickled her nose in the night, nor this morning. Reynard's hired thugs now grumbled about lack of hot food and sleep, even as Reynard ordered them back to work shifting the rocks.

Eventually the man named Luis brought Kinzy and Esme a hunk of stale bread and a cup of water apiece. While they ate under close scrutiny, Kinzy watched for a chance to break free, but Miguel, surly and on edge, ensured that chance never came. *Have patience and know when to strike*, Master Shabao always said. Maybe Reynard's own men would kill him.

Half-hearted cheers went up, and Miguel and Luis once again tied their hands in front of them and prodded them through the new gap in the rockfall. Kinzy sent desperate calls for Trell, but the silence between them persisted.

The morning passed as they climbed the steep peak, continuing to follow the ancient Inca's trail. As they came around a sharp cut in the rock, the view became much more interesting. Kinzy was not the only one who slowed their steps and stopped.

Carved from the mountaintop before them, terraced levels lay upon each other like stacks of dishes askew, reaching up to the top of the peak. The levels spread wide like a raptor stretching its wings to catch the rush of wind across the rock-face. Greenery covered each terrace, amidst stone buildings and steps, creating the look of a green and dark grey scarf draped along this side of the peak. They'd reached the Inca city. Somewhere up there, Atahualpa's mummy waited to be found.

"Move along, ladies." Miguel shoved Kinzy forward into Esme, almost tumbling them down the slope. His evil smile promised no apology.

Reynard pushed them faster and faster, his mood growing more manic by the moment, laughing one second, shouting the next. The closer they came, the more treacherous the trail, until they found themselves on a precarious ridge between the peak they'd climbed and the one on which the long-abandoned city beckoned to them.

When they reached the first broad terrace, the porters guiding the llamas stopped, refusing to go another foot without a rest. Reynard shouted, swore, promised money, but it was wasted breath none of the humans had to spare. Kinzy dropped gratefully next to a gasping Esme onto the softer ground of what once must have been an agricultural field.

Miguel brought them water then stood, pistol pointed at them, while they drank. Reynard wandered over and stood in front of them, making a show of eating bread and what appeared to be dried meat of some kind. Even Kinzy's stomach rumbled.

When he was finished, he squatted in front of Esme. "I looked over your Vatican map again. Next to useless now that we are here. Your bracelet from Hieronymous is also useless until we get nearer the tomb itself. This means, my dear Lady Esme, you must have been given further directions to help you once you reached the city."

Esme sat up straighter. "Bring us a meal and release our hands so that we can eat. I'll not tell you a thing otherwise."

"Oh, how I could accommodate you, *ma petite*, but my men need to eat, and we'll need every ounce of our food to make it home again. Now where is the tomb, *cherie*? Be a good girl and admit I have won."

"I admit nothing. And I was given no further instructions." She snorted. "You know what I really think? I think this whole trip is pointless. A lie, a fairy tale. The map, the rumors, everything."

Reynard's hand shot out and held her jaw in an iron grip. Esme struggled and cried out in pain. His fingers dug into her already bruised jaw. "Where is the tomb?"

"You will get nothing from me." Esme spat at him.

He backhanded her and snapped her head to the side. Shoving her backward, he turned his attention to Kinzy. There was no smile of any sort for her. He sneered in contempt, holding her in place with just his gaze while unsheathing his draiglann.

"Mademoiselle Kinzalynn, I do hope you choose to be more

reasonable than your friend. Have you been taught ways to ignore pain?" He kicked her injured leg then slashed his knife along her arm. Kinzy could not hold back a gasp, though she tried hard not to give him the helpless reaction he wanted. "Ah, so you do feel pain. Tell me where the entrance to the tomb lies and we shall see all your injuries attended to." He smiled now, as if he offered her a hospital bed just down the road.

The smile of the snake. Kinzy wondered if he truly thought they would tell him anything or help him in any way. "Do you always talk so much?" she taunted him. If they delayed the man long enough, Kinzy hoped Trell would come back to rescue them. If the queen had left him alive. No matter what, Kinzy's duty was clear. Stop the Frenchman.

Reynard's face purpled and he waved the knife. "Which one of you wants their throat cut first? I swear I will spare the one who shows me the entrance."

Esme spat. "Spare what? Spare the knife cut in favor of a bullet or a fall off a high cliff?"

"You are too young, *Madame*, to be tossing your entire life away. I can ensure you are comfortable and alive, if you will help me find this tomb." He loomed over Esme.

It seemed Esme tensed, ready to kick him, but Miguel cocked his pistol and put it to her head.

Reynard pulled Esme to her feet by her hair and pressed the knife against her throat. "Show me the entrance. Now. Or you die."

Esme remained silent, but her breath quickened. The blade bit, drew blood.

"Wait!" Kinzy could not watch Esme be harmed. "I am the one who can find the entrance, not Esme. Leave her alone, and I will find it for you." She held his gaze, letting fear for her friend show on her face. He needed to believe her.

Reynard held the blade firm. "*Vraiment*? Is that why Esme

brought you?" He turned his head and assessed her with a sneer. He let up on the knife. "I wondered at such a strange companion. Not Esme's usual sort."

"I have been given a device that follows the aether trails of the spirits that flock to Atahualpa's bidding, a device tuned only to me. It will take time to search the city and locate the aether flow that leads to the tomb."

He wiped his knife on Esme's canvas skirt. "A magical device, I suppose. Where did you acquire such a thing?"

"You know I am faeleath. I bear enough magic to work the device. I assume you know about me and my kind, given your own accoutrement." She stared pointedly at his boots.

"How could I have forgotten. Very well then, let us see you do so. You have until noon to find our entrance, or your dear Esme will suffer."

"Kinzy, no! You mustn't!" Esme struggled in his tight grip.

"I swear that I will search for the entrance to the tomb for you, if you will, in return, swear that Esme will come to no harm and make it back to Quito alive, whole and free." Kinzy put every ounce of her determination into that vow, and she felt the Fae magics take heed. It was one she could truly give and not violate her honor. At this point, it was the only play she could think of to keep them both from being killed.

"I shall so vow." Reynard smiled triumphantly and waved at his henchman. "I told you they would be useful. Tell me, *Mademoiselle*, where is this device?"

"It is my ring, enchanted by my Elders." If anyone else here could sense magic, the ring would indeed appear magical, but it would take a full Fae to discover what the magic actually did. She felt nothing magical outside herself, no other faeleath in the camp.

He clapped delightedly. "*Bon! Tres bon!* Let us begin our

search pattern before the sun rises a degree higher toward noon."

The men gathered, ready to follow wherever she led them. Reynard refused to untie her hands. Closing her eyes, she pretended to commune with the magic and turned in a slow circle with her arms held out ahead of her, fingers splayed.

"Which way?" Reynard growled at her.

She needed to buy them time. Opportunity would come eventually to get rid of this madman.

She opened her eyes and gave him a scathing glare. "You must give me time to access the magic and sense its subtle pull. This takes more than a moment of concentration."

She closed her eyes again and heard Esme's even breathing, and the scuffling of the men as they waited. She must delay this motley crew of cretins on the edge of violence. She knew she could free herself, grab her knives, now sticking out of Miguel's belt, and slay at least a few of them in an instant. But Reynard held Esme tight, the knife at her throat once more. Esme's life might be forfeit if she did so.

She turned in a circle and picked a direction, opening her eyes and pushing her hands out the same way. "There. The entrance is that way. Let us go that direction for a short time and then I shall use it again. I'll need to do some triangulation."

They traveled the crumbled stone stairways and paths of the city for a few minutes, before Reynard pulled them to a halt and demanded she use the ring again to adjust their path. Kinzy led them higher, pretending to stumble on the steps, forcing one of the men to assist her. She weighed the possibility of grabbing a knife from the man's belt, but the angles were wrong. She walked slowly with her arms held forward, as if warming them by a fire.

When she came in direct line with the arched stone entryway of a small square tower built into the side of the mountain, Kinzy felt a strange sensation run up her spine, something she had never felt before. As if a string pulled her, the feeling yanked at her from her very core. Her head swiveled of its own accord, and she paused. Paused too long. Her gut clenched as she realized what she'd done. She slowly turned in the opposite direction as if nothing had happened and limped forward again.

"Stop!" Reynard grabbed her upper arm and hauled her back toward the doorway. "What was that you did? This is it, isn't it? I knew you would try to mislead us, but I have been watching you closely. Inside we go! Miguel, light the lanterns and grab torches."

Miguel led the way inside with a lantern held high. The walls were intact and although there was open sky above them where a wooden ceiling had once sat, the shadows seemed dark and menacing to Kinzy's eye despite the bright sun. Not a chink could be seen in the stacked stone walls around them. A dry and dusty oval-shaped cistern sat in the center of the back wall, going down below floor level at least eight feet. If it had been filled with water, no one would notice the wide tunnel below, cut into the solid rock of the mountain, leading into the darkness.

Reynard jumped down into the pit. "How curious. One of the aqueducts, no doubt, but it's certainly much bigger than the others." Reynard shone his lantern inside.

The circular tunnel looked about two and a half feet wide and seemed to slope up toward the mountain peak. The aether trail Kinzy could sense led into that tunnel. Somewhere through there lay the mummy of Atahualpa.

It must have been a beautiful place once, the water running fresh from the snowmelt above the city and into this pool, the rushing sound bouncing around the walls. She turned away, trying to distract Reynard. "It is not this way."

His lips quirked up in a parody of the charming smile he had used on them on the airship. "You lie. Miguel will go first, then myself and the ladies. The rest of you, behind."

Kinzy saw her own expression mirrored on Esme's face. "You cannot mean to go through that! It could collapse."

Reynard examined Esme's costume, his eyes falling in disgust on her canvas split skirt. "It is fortunate for your modesty, if not your fashion sense, that you wear that unwomanly walking skirt instead of petticoats. You will be able to crawl faster."

Esme looked to Kinzy, but Kinzy could not meet her gaze. She didn't dare acknowledge Esme's unasked question. Esme huffed and moved closer to Reynard. "This is just an aqueduct. I refuse to crawl through a death trap for nothing."

"You are clever, but not clever enough. I've seen you crawl through worse."

Twin furrows appeared between Esme's eyes. "I beg your pardon?"

Reynard waved a dismissal. "Come. No more delays."

He slashed through their bonds with a warning to behave themselves. Kinzy had to trust that the Lords of Light would find a way for them to be rid of Reynard somewhere ahead, and that Trell would return soon to help them. She and Trell had never been so long apart since their bonding. She hoped for his return, though a small portion of her heart wailed that the queen had followed through on the death penalty.

Kinzy ignored the throbbing pain of her injured knee as she crawled inside after Reynard. The height of the tunnel made walking upright or crouched impossible. She struggled along as best she could up inside the mountain, Esme right behind. She soon lost feeling in her hands as the cold stone leeched all heat, and her knee swelled with a sharp pain that traveled up her leg each time she set it down and pushed forward through the tunnel. She tried to spare her injury as much as she could.

Esme kept up a constant whisper of encouragement to her while the men grunted and gave sharp commands to hurry up. Kinzy felt they would never reach an end, that the tunnel would go right through the entire Andes. The weight of the mountain pressed in from the ceiling, a suffocating miasma of earth energy. If they tripped some sort of trap, sending water rushing through this tunnel again, they would all be swept back down. Drowned like rats, and cold as ice.

Miguel shouted and the lantern ahead dimmed. Kinzy peered around Reynard, and saw the tunnel finally opened up. Reynard slid through, then held out his hand for her to grasp. She almost wouldn't take it, but the sharp knee pain won out on the helping hand side. He pulled her out and set her on her feet, steadying her when she put weight on her knee.

He then turned to Esme, already half-way out, who rejected his help. With a scowl, Reynard turned away from them and directed his men to tie their hands again.

The light from the lanterns could barely reach the faintly glittering heights above them. They moved forward along a trench-like channel cut into the floor of the cavern, a conduit through which ice melt could flow. The channel led to a square cistern much deeper and wider than the one where they had started. Kinzy judged it at least eight feet across, cut into the stone itself without fancy edging, just sheer smooth walls straight down. The lantern reflected off dark water at the bottom, no telling how deep. At the far end of the chamber, a stone arch led further into the mountain.

Reynard skirted around the dark hole and darted over to the archway. He stooped to pick up an object on the rocky ground and held it up close to his lantern. The half-moon shape of a royal pectoral, like the ones Kinzy had seen in her reference books, glittered in the light of the lantern with the unmistakable ruddy hue of ancient gold. The men whooped with excitement and began scouring the cavern for more gold. A few more trinkets revealed themselves between the tunnel they had crawled out of and the dark archway that beckoned them on.

Reynard walked toward Kinzy and Esme waving his small prize triumphantly. "I believe this is where we part company, *mes cheries*." He nodded curtly. A hand shot out and Esme windmilled over the edge of the cistern. Before Kinzy could react, she felt a shove from behind. Miguel's feral laugh echoed through the cavern as she fell.

Chapter Twenty-Seven

"We must stop falling into things." Esme lay half-submerged in the freezing cold water at the bottom of the cistern, with Kinzy atop her. The Fae woman groaned and rolled off, gasping as she hit the chilly pool.

"We?"

Esme sat up, inclined her head. "Very well. I must, then. Did you re-injure yourself? Hit your head?"

Kinzy struggled upright and the frigid water swirled around her calves. "I'm fine, although I might not have been if you hadn't broken my fall."

"I'd say that was foresight on my part, but it would be a lie." She looked up, saw Reynard leaning over the edge, holding a torch. "You are a right bastard, Jean-Paul."

"Now, now, my dear Esme," he called down to her. "I am only doing what you would have done, if you'd had the upper hand." He dropped down to one knee, and she could see his eyes sparkling in the firelight from the torch he held. "You know, all of this could have been avoided if you had worked with me instead of against me, *cherie*."

Esme climbed to her feet, water dripping off her sodden clothes. "Fool. I wouldn't work with you if you were the last man on earth, you gormless worm."

He reached inside his vest and pulled out the map, now folded instead of rolled. "You are the fool, my dear, as well as a tease. Now that I have this, and we have located the tomb, I have no need to suffer you any longer." His face darkened. "I lost an entire day because of you and that Spanish *couchon*! Sending me on a wild gooses chase all over the countryside."

"The phrase is goose chase, and you are the one who is a pig. If you've no further need for us, then do the honorable thing and let us go."

Reynard laughed. "Do not mistake me for an idiot. Only one of us will walk away rich and victorious today, and I fully intend that to be me." He shrugged. "And France, of course." He stood now. "With the power of the mummy, your kind," he jabbed the torch at Kinzy, "will finally be beaten back, and those savages you've been nursing along in North America will fall like trees before a storm." His eyes glittered like crystals. "France will take its rightful place as custodian of those endless tracts of resource-rich lands, and I will be the Governor of a sizable portion of them."

He stared into the middle distance, lips curving. Then he snorted, and adjusted his cravat beneath his once-pristine white shirt. "And so I must leave you. I am sorry about the conditions. My Emperor would have me kill you, but once, long ago, you saved my life, so I owe you yours in return."

Esme knew he had seemed familiar, but she still couldn't place him. "How? Where?"

"Am I so forgettable, then? Ah, but I was half dead from torture, hunger, and fever when you and your comrade dragged me and my fellow prisoners from that damp, miserable cell in Austria and hurried us onto that boat."

Damn it, she couldn't remember him. There had been any number of rescues she'd been involved in over the past seven years and at that moment they were all a blur in her mind.

He continued. "Still, it wounds me that while your angelic face was seared into my memory, I am nothing to you. Much as your husband must feel, I suppose, as you go traipsing about the world, making love to strangers."

"I do no such thing!"

"Don't you?" He looked at her from under raised brows. "I've heard of your exploits, both in Europe and further abroad, you and that abomination you usually travel with."

Anger burned in Esme's gut. "Cooper is not an abomination! She's certainly more human than you are."

"That thing is not human in the least. It is unnatural and an affront to God." He jutted his chin at Kinzy. "Now you have picked up another one, in the personage of this unholy creature."

Esme wished she had something, anything, to throw at him. "I'm sorry I saved your pitiful life."

His lips quirked up. "Ironically, I am not." He waved away her growing fury. "At any rate, while you are wet and cold and most-assuredly uncomfortable, you are not dead, at least by my hand. I am sure this cistern will hold you long enough for me to find this much sought-after corpse. Perhaps I will even send someone back here for you, when I reach civilization again." He chuckled. "And to prove that I am a gentleman, I will even leave you this torch to keep the dark at bay. For a time, at least." He wedged the thing between two loose paving stones near the lip of the cistern.

"No gentleman pushes a lady down a well, you pigeon-livered ratbag!"

"Such language!" His eyes hardened. "You are correct, no gentleman *would* push a lady down a well, but *you*, my dear, are not by any man's definition a lady." He straightened. "*Mesdames,* perhaps we will meet again one day." The man had the audacity to tip his hat. "Or, perhaps not. *Adieu.*"

Beside her, Kinzy tensed. "Wait! You gave an oath that would see Esme freed and safe in Quito. Your word."

He paused then shrugged in that peculiarly Gallic fashion. "Ah, but you lied to me. Therefore, I have no obligation to keep that oath."

Before Esme could respond with anything other than a string of expletives, he strode off, taking with him his motley crew of thugs.

Kinzy leaned against the wall of the cistern. Her face was composed, but Esme could well imagine what was going through her mind.

"Don't say it. Just don't."

Kinzy shrugged in that phlegmatic way. "I told you he—"

"I said don't!" Esme snapped. "What a fine pickle we're in."

"Are you hurt?"

Esme shook her head. Although she shivered with cold and her bruises from the other night now had companions, on the whole, they'd survived the ten-foot fall relatively unscathed. Her hand looked like a balloon, making it hard to make a fist, and her ribs burned when she sucked in a deep breath, but she'd suffered worse. In fact, the shoulder where she'd taken a bullet last year ached as well, as if in sympathy with the other wounds. On the positive side, the foot or so of water in the cistern had helped cushion their fall even as it leached warmth from her body. "I'll live."

Kinzy sighed. "Then it must be you that stops him. You will have to climb out." She gestured at her knee. "I cannot."

The Fae had just handed her the solution to her conundrum. Kinzy stuck down in the well, unable to capture the mummy for her own queen, leaving Esme to win the day for Britain. Fate had handed her the perfect opportunity. So why wasn't she trying to scramble up the smooth, stone block walls of the cistern?

She turned back to Kinzy. "Let me ask you this. If it was me that was injured, would you go and leave me here?"

Kinzy frowned. "It solves the problem we both face, doesn't it?"

"I bet you could make it up that wall if you really wanted to."

Kinzy shook her head. "I cannot."

"I don't believe you. Or perhaps, I don't believe you wouldn't at least try, although you'd probably fall and split your skull open in the process. You are still none too steady." She put her hands on her hips. "So why are you removing yourself from the equation? Do you know something I don't? About Reynard? About the mummy?"

Kinzy leaned her head back against the stone, winced as she shifted her weight then sighed. "What I know is this. The power contained in that mummy should not belong to anyone. Not to Tír na nÓg, not to France, not even to your beloved Britain." The woman paused, and Esme felt the weight of their respective onuses. "I also know this. You are an honorable woman. I do not believe you would sacrifice the world in order to satisfy your queen. And I would rather you have it than Reynard."

Esme watched the woman's face twist up, as though she were in pain. Seeing any emotion on the Fae's face surprised her, much less pain. "Then you believe what the legend says. That Atahualpa's remains truly can make an army invincible."

Kinzy nodded. "I do."

"And you're willing to sacrifice attaining the thing."

"I have never been disloyal to my queen before. To my Master. To my people." Again, that look of intense discomfort. "But this is far too important. Esme, no one, human or Fae, should get hold of that Light-bereft thing."

"So you want me to carry on and leave you behind? An acceptable loss?"

She shrugged, spread out her hands. "If I am so injured that I cannot get out of this hole, and you scaled the wall and were able to defeat Reynard, then—"

"Then you have plausible deniability." Esme couldn't help smiling. "I have a better idea. How about we *both* get out of here and defeat Reynard and then you and I can come up with Plan C."

Kinzy looked defeated. "What would Plan C entail?"

"I have no idea. Yet. Right now, we need to figure out how to get both of us out of this damned well." She went to stand by her friend. "Together."

"Do you have a plan for that?"

Esme peered up at the flickering glow from the torch and shook her head. "No, but I think we have about an hour to figure it out."

A distant, blood-curdling scream drifted down to them. "Maybe less."

More screaming reverberated off the cave walls then abruptly ceased. Esme exchanged a look with Kinzy. "That doesn't sound good."

Kinzy's lips compressed. "Such a shame. They appear to have run into some trouble."

Esme felt a chill that had nothing to do with the ice-cold water. Her voice dropped to a whisper. "More of the spectral warriors that attacked us that night?"

"Esme, I cannot see them, but you can. I don't suppose you have any more of that holy water?"

Esme shook her head. "But remember that Trell can see them. And fight them."

Kinzy frowned again. "Trell is not here." She addressed Esme like a parent to a particularly thick child. "He hasn't come back from taking my last message to the queen."

Esme blew out a breath. "Okay, first things first. Let's get out of this hole. Then, we'll figure out a way to deal with the trouble ahead." Esme stared up at the flickering torch, thinking, while part of her brain listened for more screams. "What we need is a rope."

Kinzy gestured in frustration at her soaking wet leather trousers and tunic, as if to say, 'see? no rope here'. "Do you have one hidden under your petticoats?"

"No." She gnawed her lip thoughtfully. "But you have leather pants. If you would be willing to temporarily divest yourself of them, and I wrapped one leg around my arm and held on, and you grabbed the other leg, between you climbing and me pulling, we might be able to get you out."

Kinzy unbuckled her belt and stripped off her woven leather trousers. "I like this plan. Come, I will boost you. See if you can grab the lip of the well and pull yourself up."

"You do realize how short I am."

"Then I will try to heave you up and over. You are light enough, if you remove some of that wet clothing."

"But then I'll be practically naked!"

"As you see, I've already removed my pants. Would you prefer naked or dead?"

Esme rolled her eyes. "Well, when you put it that way." Stripping off her outer garments until she stood in just the bloomers she wore under her walking skirt and her camisole, Esme lifted her foot into Kinzy's hands and reached up, ready to be launched to freedom.

Chapter Twenty-Eight

Kinzy heaved with every ounce of effort she could and tossed Esme toward the edge of freedom above. Her knee wobbled and she stumbled, landing on her backside in the cold water. With an anxious glance above, she watched Esme scramble over the edge in nothing but her bloomers. Kinzy breathed a sigh of relief.

Once up and over, Esme looked down at her. "Do you always grunt like a cow in labor when tossing a woman into the air?"

"Only when I toss your large posterior." Kinzy purposefully grunted in pain as she stood up again, wet from head to toe.

Esme's voice became more concerned. "Are you okay? Hurt anything more than your knee? That really was a Herculean effort."

"Only bruised my backside, which is now very cold indeed."

"Toss your pants and the rest of my clothes up to me then and we can get you out of there, too."

Kinzy could hear Esme's teeth chatter with the cold as the woman reached down to grab the leggings. Kinzy shivered herself. She needed out of the icy water and to walk off the cold to get feeling back into her feet. Esme lowered one leg of the pants, and Kinzy, using one foot to brace herself against the stone wall, climbed hand over hand, her biceps straining. By the time she reached the top, she was at the limit of both strength and energy. Heaving herself over the lip of the stone cistern, she lay on the cold floor in the flickering torchlight and caught her breath. Esme swore at her swollen and now raw hands as she dropped the pants beside Kinzy.

It took them a few moments before they had enough energy to redress, the whole time alert for any dangers. The screaming ahead of them had stopped.

In the middle of putting on her second boot, a flap of gold wings appeared in front of her. Startled, she fell on her backside. *Again.* Her knee throbbed and burned now, despite the cold.

Trell gave a happy warble, a drakkeki form of laughter, as he landed next to her.

She swept him into a hug. "Light Bless, I thought you were dead!"

Trell purred in her arms, then squirmed with excitement until she let go. He stuck his back leg out toward her, a small scroll in his leather strap. Kinzy unrolled the message as Esme held up the lit torch Reynard had left for them.

Trust me, I trust you. ~A

Esme crouched behind her to read over Kinzy's shoulder. "Well. A mysteriously enigmatic queen, isn't she?"

"She can be." Kinzy held out her hand and Esme helped her rise and balance on her good leg. She tested her weight on it more fully. Painful, but it would heal later. The cold water had at least brought down the swelling. "But if she trusts me, then your Plan C is a go, though it's still a bit vague for me. Fill me in?"

Esme paused, glancing around, perhaps for inspiration. "Erm, defeat the bad men and the spirit warriors of the Inca, stop Reynard, and grab Atahualpa. Go home. Have tea. Simple."

Kinzy raised a cynical eyebrow. "Great plan, but perhaps a tad short on details."

"Details are in that direction." Esme pointed through the doorway leading deeper into the mountain.

"Forward for details. Trell, stay close."

Trell leaped from her shoulder and fluttered ahead, refusing to settle around her neck once he knew of her injury.

I am grateful you finally returned, what took you so long? We could have used your help.

You have used me as "another option" far too long, young faeleath.

Kinzy snorted as Trell sounded much like her Master spouting rules at her. *Lead on to Atahualpa, my friend, but I am afraid the Spirit Warriors have found Reynard and his men somewhere up ahead.*

We have other options for them now.

Kinzy pressed him, but he remained silent on the issue as they moved carefully forward.

Torch light flickered ahead as the tunnel took a turn. Gruff yells and shouts echoed. The shadow of a man on the tunnel wall crumpled to the ground. Kinzy could make out Miguel's shouts to hold fast amid the men's panicked cries. Kinzy and Esme watched three more shadows fall.

As she could easily see the Spirit Warriors, Esme crept up to peek around the corner. She turned back to Kinzy with a terse whisper. "Four Inca guardians with spears, focused on the last man standing. I think it's Miguel."

"I wish I could see these spirits myself. Trell, can you banish so many?"

In answer, Trell jumped up and stooped on her arm. She looked into his eyes expecting to communicate with him on a plan, but he reared back and spit in her face.

Kinzy dropped her arm and shook him off in disgust. She wiped her tearing eyes and shot an angry glare at him as he settled into a crouch nearby with a soft smug bark.

He hopped toward the corner and then looked back at her. *Other option. See now.*

She stuck her head around the corner and discovered Trell had done it. She could now see the spirits ahead. Four Inca warriors with headdress and spear, all in a hazy green glow. They circled Miguel. He screamed and swung his machete wildly at enemies he could not see. The warriors all thrust their spears together and Miguel dropped his blade, clutching his chest.

His body frosted over as he fell with a strangled cry. The shell of ice cracked and shattered as Miguel hit the floor.

"They just—" Esme started to whisper.

"I can see them now, thanks to Trell's spit." She glanced at the pleased-with-himself lizard. "Would have been polite to warn me, first, though. When did you learn that trick, my friend?"

Trell raised himself up and strutted around before settling into a regal squat before the two women. He trilled demandingly.

"Queen Airmed, eh? Remind me to thank her when we get home." Even as she spoke, the warriors turned in their direction and advanced, spears once again raised. Kinzy was certain Trell could handle them, and now that she could see, maybe she could help. Trell cried a challenge and prepared to launch himself down the tunnel. Esme grabbed a rock from the floor and Kinzy readied herself for the imminent attack, the two women shoulder to shoulder. They would face this together, live or die.

The warriors abruptly halted as one, spear ends swinging down to rest on the floor by their sides. They pounded their spears against the ground and Kinzy felt small rhythmic tremors through the tunnel floor. Then the spirits faded away and the tunnel ahead was dark once more with only a weak flicker of light from the floor where the men's torches had fallen.

"They're gone, Kinzy. Just gone." Esme looked at Kinzy, blinking. "Are they letting us pass?"

"It seems so, but why? Trell, how long will my spirit sight last?"

Trell gave a concerned chirp. *Long enough?*

"That short? Let us grab what we can from the fallen and find that mummy."

Trell gave an ominous chirp.

"No, I have not forgotten Reynard."

Kinzy found her knives and the oddly large pistol she had examined on the airship, the one Esme warned her was highly dangerous. Esme stripped a warm coat from one icy gentleman who would no longer need it, then took the weapon Kinzy handed her and examined it.

Esme grinned. "They carried it loaded. Dangerous."

"Might come in handy."

Esme snorted. "Only if we want to bring the mountain down on top of us."

"*Always have another option*, my Master says."

They checked the rest of the dead but did not find Reynard among the fallen.

Armed and somewhat warmer, they moved quickly through the tunnel. Kinzy wondered how these men could have followed Reynard and not known he would sacrifice them to reach the mummy. Esme, thankfully, felt no need to bury these men, so Kinzy hobbled on, still pushing away the pain. They could not let Reynard reach Atahualpa first, or he would acquire the abilities of the mummy and France would become undefeatable.

A shout in the distance sounded like the Frenchman, but the echoes made it difficult to determine how far ahead. They soon caught the dim light of his lantern, on the ground at his feet. He kept a warrior spirit at bay with a cross on a chain, almost as though he could see the guardian. Perhaps he could, Kinzy knew he clearly had access to more magic than most humans, thanks to his Fae affiliations.

The Inca warrior shied away every time the cross came near. It must be a blessed relic to have such an effect, it worked almost as well as Esme's holy water. In Reynard's other hand, Kinzy recognized Esme's missing bracelet.

As they snuck up on the Frenchman, Kinzy's blades firmly in her hands and ready to strike, the Inca turned their way with a snarl. Just as quickly, the warrior's expression changed. He stood tall and pounded his spear butt on the ground, just as the others had earlier, and nodded gravely at them before he faded away. The unhappy spirit had left them to take out Reynard, but why?

Reynard stepped back as his opponent vanished. He looked at the cross, then at the bracelet in his hand and grinned. "Ha! No match for the one true faith. *Eh bien.*" He held up the bracelet triumphantly.

Kinzy leaned over to Esme, mouthed, "What do we do?"

Esme shrugged, then whispered, "Let him lead?"

Reynard remained unaware of them. His rucksack hung askew on his back, Hieronymous's containment net hanging half out and rippling like a live thing, clinging to his back and legs. If Reynard noticed, he gave no sign. He shook the bracelet around himself. "*Alors*! Now, you piece of British nonsense, show me the way!" He waved the bit of jewelry in front of him and paused. After a moment he shook it again, his expression changing from triumph to frustration.

"Work, damn you. This is what you were made for. The magic is here, it must be so close, but there is no door in this wall. There is nothing here!" He cursed, a long rapid string of French epithets. Hurling the bracelet to the ground, he spat upon it. "Burroughs is a cretin! Nothing he builds works right!"

Kinzy inched closer, keeping Esme behind her. They were silent until her foot landed on a rock, throwing her balance off enough to make her stumble.

Reynard spun, eyes wide, amazement changing to smugness. "How annoyingly persistent you both are, and no one left to do the dirty work but me." He slid a pistol from his belt and took aim at Kinzy, a look of pure satisfaction on his face as he squeezed the trigger.

Chapter Twenty-Nine

Esme raised her pistol at the same time as Reynard, knowing she'd be too slow to save Kinzy. A flash of gold streaked past her from behind. A solid little body bumped her arm and careened toward Reynard as she aimed and pulled the trigger.

Amidst a flurry of motion and flash of iridescent wings, Reynard reared back. His gun went off, but the shot went wide. Esme's own missile from Hieronymous's special gun missed its mark and slammed into the stone wall to the left of Reynard's head.

Esme heard a deep, resonating rumble. Oh, no. She threw herself across Kinzy's body as the back wall and ceiling of the tunnel collapsed. A cascade of shattered stone blocks rained down around them. Esme covered her head with her arms and shielded Kinzy's prone form with her own.

Once the clattering of stones ceased, she rose to her knees. Debris tumbled off her back, where her existing bruises were now developing bruises of their own. Pulling her weapon free of the rubble, she aimed at where Reynard had been, but only a four-foot high pyramid of rubble marked the spot. Behind that, through the jagged opening the missile had created in the tunnel wall, she saw an enormous chamber, glowing as though lit by a thousand fires and filled with glittering golden objects.

Esme stood, transfixed. The logical side of her brain attempted to calculate the worth of the treasure that glinted and shone in the chamber beyond. The magpie part wanted to gather it all up and run away with it.

Beside her, Kinzy struggled to her feet. "By the Light!"

"Are you all right?"

Kinzy nodded, staring through the opening in the wall, clearly as fascinated as Esme.

The warmth of the light drew Esme forward. What they sought, she knew, lay within that chamber.

Kinzy grabbed her arm. "What are you doing?"

"He's in there. Atahualpa."

Kinzy remained motionless. "Yes, but we should approach with caution."

Esme took a step forward, compelled, although whether by avarice, curiosity or something else, she did not know. "It's safe," she heard herself murmur. As she neared the pile of rubble that lay on top of Reynard, she paused, bit her lip in remorse. "Should we try to dig him out?"

"He cannot have survived. Trell attacked him to save me." Her voice caught.

Kinzy looked at the pile of stones that served as Reynard's burial cairn and, Esme realized suddenly, Trell's as well. Her heart ached. "Maybe the little fellow flew off in time."

Kinzy's eyes shone in the light, glittering with tears. Esme saw her swallow hard. "He died valiantly, saving us." With a final blink, she bent down and scrabbled through the debris at her own feet, finally locating her curved blades.

"I'm so sorry."

Kinzy's face hardened. "It was a worthy end." She brushed dust from her leather jerkin. "Come, let's finish this."

The girl strode forward on those long, leather-clad legs toward the opening to the glowing chamber. Esme hurried to catch up.

Entering the tomb of Atahualpa felt like walking into what she imagined Aladdin's Cave must have looked like. The tomb chamber had been constructed of enormous, close-fitting blocks of stone. Against the far wall sat the mummy of the king. Rotting textiles wrapped his shriveled remains, positioned in death on a throne made of solid gold. A gold circlet from which sprouted ancient feathers crowned his skull, and a beautiful gold pectoral rested on his chest atop a capelet made of more feathers. As Esme moved inexorably closer, she could see a circular amulet in the middle of the pectoral stamped with an image of the sun god Inti. The mummy appeared ready to crumble to dust if touched and she wondered, even if the containment net hadn't been buried with Reynard, if the cadaver would have survived transport home.

Light flashed and twinkled around her, drawing her scrutiny away from the fragile remains of the Inca Emperor. Everything in the chamber seemed to be made of gold or silver. Gold foil covered benches. Hammered gold drinking vessels and plates filled with dessicated offerings sat on a textile rug in front of the throne. Even the sconces that held long dark torches had been cast from that most precious of metals. Wooden chests lined the walls, filled with a myriad of objects. Figurines, intricate pieces of gold jewelry, Spanish coins, gemstones.

Everything glowed, glinted and shimmered. Esme had never wanted for anything in her life, at least nothing of a material nature. She had been most fortunate in that regard. Yet the value of the items in this chamber sparked a little flame of greed even in her. No wonder the conquistadors had been maddened by lust for riches.

Forcing her attention from the treasure, she sought the source of light that reflected back her own distorted shape from every brilliant, shiny surface. Above her revolved a glowing golden orb from which rays of light speared down like sunbeams. Shading her eyes, she saw the face of Inti staring down at her, over and over, as the orb revolved.

"Dear Lord." Esme broke the silence. "Poor Pizarro. Knowing that all this escaped his clutches must have driven the man insane." Hands on her hips, she smirked. "Take that, you heartless pig."

Esme spun back towards the throne at a noise, like paper rustling. Kinzy whipped her blades up in front of her and Esme raised her gun towards the gilt chair. Something shimmered before the mummy, a filmy haze. Esme braced herself for another spectral warrior, but the figure who materialized exuded imperial splendor. Standing before his throne, he loomed tall even by European standards, with broad shoulders and a narrow, high-cheekboned face. An enormous pectoral covered his bare, well-muscled chest, identical to the one that hung on the withered mummy sitting on the throne behind him. He wore a short, white kilt-like garment around his hips, a long, feathered cape that fastened around his neck. In his strong hands, he held a tall spear tipped with gold instead of the more utilitarian iron. Gold rings, fitted with ruby and emerald cabochons, adorned his fingers, and broad gold and silver bracelets and arm cuffs molded around his corded biceps.

From his throne on the raised platform, he regarded them coolly. In a rich, mellow baritone that dripped with pride, he said, "He was indeed a heartless pig. Even his men despised him."

Esme found herself agog. Kinzy recovered first. She drew

herself up and gave the ghost of the Inca Emperor a formal bow. "Your Highness."

Atahualpa waved her gesture away. "There is no need for that. I am the ruler of no one now, nor have I been for centuries."

His mummy seemed to disappear as the spirit of Atahualpa sat heavily on his throne. To Esme, he looked weary, his dark brown eyes filled with sorrow. "The empire of my people is gone forever. This is how it was meant to be. Despite the horror inflicted by the Spanish, they have brought wonderful things to this land as well. The descendants of my people have flourished, and despite their European overlords, seem happy, well-fed, even prosperous."

Esme finally found her voice. "My leaders call that progress." She wrinkled her nose. "Although sometimes I wonder at the cost. Not all cultures benefit from contact with the so-called modern world."

"You are a wise woman, and a kind one." He rested his hands on the arms of his throne. "I have watched and listened. You have both vowed to not use the power of my magic to benefit your governments and their desires to conquer."

Esme looked to Kinzy, who nodded. "That's true. That power should belong to no one."

Atahualpa inclined his head. "Long ago, I had hoped that my brother, Ruminahui, would return and use my power to vanquish the foul invaders who brought such pain and sickness to our lands, but that is all in the past." He sighed. "Our time is over. The world has moved on." He leaned forward, his fingers gripping the armrests. "It is your world now. You must see to it that my power cannot be misused. I grow weary."

Esme took a step forward. "What would you have us do?"

Atahualpa gestured at the room around him. "All this must be lost to time." He stood, stepped aside, and stared balefully down at his fragile mortal remains. "And this. This must be destroyed." The spectral figure appeared to waver.

Esme looked over at Kinzy, raised her eyebrows in question. What should they do? Kinzy shrugged.

The warrior king walked towards them, and Esme found herself automatically backing up. He stopped in the center of the chamber, underneath the glowing Inti orb. Glancing up, he pointed at the orb with his staff. "Use the power of the orb. Cleanse this place with the light of Inti. I cannot bring myself to do it. I beg you, please, bring this nightmare to a close."

The King of the Inca grew more translucent. Esme blinked, but nothing changed. Atahualpa was fading.

Kinzy frowned as she examined the revolving orb. "How does it work?"

"I must go." His voice grew faint, receding into the distance. He extended his arm, pointing with his staff to space behind them. "Do what must be done."

The figure of Atahualpa vanished, leaving them staring at the pathetic bundle of his mummy.

There came a sudden flapping sound and Esme and Kinzy both spun around. Esme, expecting to see Reynard, brought up her pistol to fire another disastrous shot. She would not let Reynard have Atahualpa's mummy or his treasure. She'd collapse the ceiling on top of them to prevent it. But it wasn't Reynard.

The pint-sized dragon flew across the space from the rubble pile to Kinzy's shoulder. He landed, wrapped his tail around her neck and rubbed his face along her jaw, making a sound reminiscent of a cat purring. Kinzy wore an expression of pure delight. "Trell!"

The lizard gazed up into his mistress's eyes and silence fell as they communed in that mysterious way they had. If tears slid down Kinzy's cheeks, Esme would never speak of it to anyone.

Kinzy turned shining eyes towards Esme, blinked a few times, then cleared her throat. "Trell says we must destroy the orb."

Above them, the sphere spun slowly, pulsing like a real sun. "Yes, I understand that. The question is how."

Kinzy pointed at the pistol Esme still clutched. "Trell thinks that will do nicely."

"It'll bring the whole mountain down on us!"

"Exactly."

Esme frowned. "I had hoped we could do this *without* having to die ourselves."

Kinzy chuckled and grabbed her arm. "We can. But first." She went over to one of the smaller latched casks, which to Esme's surprise opened easily. Even more surprising, it did not crumble into dust at a touch. Inside were pieces of golden jewelry, small idols of gold, and other objects that glittered. "We will take some of this back. For the families of those who lost their lives. For Mani, Tomàs, and the others." She hefted one side of the box, straining under the weight. "Come. Help me carry this and let us leave this place."

With the treasure chest between them, they left the burial chamber. Maneuvering carefully over the pile of rubble, they crossed the cavern beyond until they stood in the entrance to the tunnel that led back the way they had come. "Are you sure about this?"

"Trell says he can shield us. Can you hit the orb from here?"

They lowered the cask of gold to the ground and Esme crouched down with her pistol, checked her aim, judged the distance. "It'll be just like knocking wine bottles off the backs of the sheik's camels."

Kinzy stared at her for a moment. "A sheik's camels?" She shook her head. "How many bullets do you have left?"

"Should be at least two." She frowned. "But if I miss, I

might not get a second chance. Especially if the whole cursed ceiling collapses."

"Then you better not miss."

Esme shot her friend a sideways look. "I can never tell when you're joking and when you're serious."

"I never joke," came the deadpan response.

Esme inhaled, steadied her pistol on her forearm, and aimed carefully. "Can Trell really shield us?"

"I've never before seen him do it, but he's surprised me often on this trip." She shook her head. "If he says he can, I believe him."

Trell gave a little chirp and wagged his own head.

"I guess I'm going to have to trust you. And him."

Kinzy grinned. "That is what friends do, is it not? Trust one another?"

"I like you more and more all the time." She took aim again. "Very well then. One. Two."

On three, she squeezed the trigger, closing her eyes against a blinding burst of light. The world shook, and it felt like the very ground beneath her gave way. She fell into darkness, dropping like a stone into a lake of nothingness.

They heard a loud pop and a jarring thud that shook Esme from her tail bone to her neck.

Something damp spattered across her face. She opened her eyes, surprised to see an overcast sky above her with the pale circle of a faint sun peeking through the rapidly scudding clouds. Next to her, on slick, Inca paving stones, Kinzy pulled herself into a sitting position.

"By the Light, I hate that sensation."

Esme's stomach roiled, bile burning her throat. Unable to stop herself, she turned and retched on the pavement. When she finally sagged back against the chill, damp stones, she took in their surroundings. "Where are we and how the hell did we get here?"

"Trell ported us. I don't know how. He's not supposed to be able to do that for other living things. We're still in the Inca city." She paused and looked around. "I think."

Esme groaned. Her head throbbed, her stomach churned and her right hand, the one that had held her pistol, the one that had already been swollen and painful, felt as though it were on fire. Red, weeping blisters covered her palm. "My pistol." She scanned the pavement but couldn't locate it.

Trell, who sat on Kinzy's shoulder, trilled and Kinzy translated. "He says the weapon melted in the explosion. There was no way to save it. Consider it sacrificed to the sun god Inti."

Esme eyed the little beast. "Well. I guess I owe you my sincere thanks." Refusing to let the experience get the better of her, she pulled herself to her feet to take stock. They rested on a high promontory paved with Inca stone. A few feet away, at the edge of the plaza stood a large, oddly shaped stone with a vertical notch jutting up out of it. Beyond the plaza lay nothing. A steep drop-off to somewhere far below. A thick mist occluded the ground, which had to be hundreds, maybe thousands of feet down. She didn't remember them being quite so high up, and she definitely didn't remember seeing a plaza like this. Plus, the air felt different, smelled different.

She staggered back, dizzy, afraid of slipping off the edge.

"Kinzy, is Trell sure we're in the same city?"

Kinzy turned to look at her reptilian companion. The lizard chittered and ducked his head. He and Kinzy stared at each other for a long moment. Kinzy frowned as she returned her attention to Esme. "He says he ported us to the nearest place he could find with what he calls stone magic." She pointed to the large stone with the peculiar notch. "That must be similar to a Fae portal stone."

"That's not exactly what I asked."

Kinzy frowned. "I think that this may *not* be the same city. He says the orb exploded and completely destroyed the other city."

"So where are we then?"

Trell flew off Kinzy's shoulder.

Kinzy stood, brushed off her leather leggings, and sheathed her two curved blades. "I don't know, but Trell says the path down is that way." She faced Esme. "Are you too injured to walk?"

Esme stiffened her spine in true British fashion, ignoring the throb in both her head and hand. "I am quite capable of walking, thank you."

"Then we should get started. There is apparently a group of locals not too far down the trail." Kinzy hefted one side of the chest of riches they'd gathered for the families of Mani and Tomàs and Esme grabbed the other. "They are herding llamas and may be able to shelter us for the night."

Esme had to double step to keep up with her long-legged friend. "When we get back to Quito, I am going to take the longest bath in human history. And I'm not going to feel guilty for one instant as the poor maid keeps fetching more hot water."

Trell, perched again on Kinzy's shoulder, gave a derisive snort. Kinzy chuckled as she strode down a steep set of stone stairs. "Quito will be a long way indeed. Trell says we are now in the country called Peru."

Esme groaned. She thought this 'porting' to an entirely different country was the beast's idea of a practical joke. "Peru? Good heavens! That's nearly a thousand miles from Quito! I don't suppose he could just port us somewhere close to London."

Kinzy shook her head. "He is exhausted. It cost him greatly

to get us away alive. He siphoned off energy from the explosion in order to save us. He believes Atahualpa's magic helped him."

"How interesting." Esme picked up her pace, coming abreast of her friend, a tight grip on her side of the chest. "I can see that travelling with you will never be without surprises. So what now?"

"As I said, we walk until we find the llama herders."

"No, I mean, what will we do when we both get home? I can't exactly tell Victoria I blew up her mummy."

Kinzy shrugged. "I too will have to face my queen." She sighed as they picked their way across a level terrace and then started down another set of steep stone steps. "I cannot lie to her, but I'm not sure how she will take the news. This may be my last mission."

"Oh, surely not!" The idea made Esme's stomach churn again, and not from nausea. "We make such an excellent team! Just think what we could accomplish together."

The other woman's face remained impassive. "It is not up to me."

The thought discomfited her. Esme felt certain Victoria would be unamused, but Esme had no fear for her own safety. The queen might not ask her to perform any more missions for her, but the world was a big place and as Cooper always said, Esme had a talent for finding trouble no matter where she went. Even without the queen's errands, there would be excitement enough if she looked for it.

Still, she found she'd rather have exciting times with her new friend than on her own.

"Perhaps I can speak with Her Majesty, and she could speak with your queen. Does Victoria even know about your kind? About your queen?"

Kinzy's face took on that guarded expression. "That is not something I can speak of."

"Oh, come now. We've already shared so much, surely—"

"Do not ask again."

The Fae woman's tone reminded Esme of Cooper in a churlish mood. "Well, I will have a word with Victoria and we shall simply make this work out right." She spoke confidently, hoping she could make it so. "I shan't let anything happen to you. I shan't."

Kinzy said nothing. For a long time, they carried on in silence, traversing countless terraces and stone steps until they saw a handful of men dressed in colorful ponchos and knit caps far down below them. They were encouraging a group of llamas down a narrow street between ancient Inca buildings. Esme paused to catch her breath and Kinzy turned back to her.

The Fae woman's manner remained somber, and she tilted her head as she considered Esme. "You would do that? You would speak with your queen on my behalf?"

"While things may not have turned out exactly as Her Majesty desired, I did succeed in my mission. The mummy is destroyed, and Napoleon has been deprived of his relic. That is largely thanks to you." She nodded as Trell chittered. "And you as well, Trell. A success of this magnitude should be rewarded commensurately." Esme grinned broadly at Kinzy. "Besides, it's what friends do."

Chapter Thirty

In the antechamber of Queen Airmed's throne room, Kinzy nervously adjusted the tightly buttoned cuffs of the emerald green tea gown Esme purchased for her in Cuzco. Kinzy had come directly to the throne room from the portal to beg an audience with Her Majesty, with no time to change from human garb to her formal silks. Her fingers itched to fiddle again with the cuffs but she stopped herself.

Show no weakness, Trell admonished her and tickled her ear.

Easy for you to say, flying stomach.

The trip home from Peru had been a delightful time. She and Esme played Senet and other esoteric games. Kinzy had learned about dinner parties and shopping. Despite strange human concepts regarding polite social behavior and ways to pass the time, Kinzy felt a kinship with the British woman she'd never felt before. Esme taught her more about being a human woman than any of her teachers had before sending her out on her first assignments in the real world. They were all Fae, though. Esme had been born to the upper caste. She lived and breathed it, happily sharing her knowledge in exchange for Kinzy's help with fighting and knife work. Esme invited Kinzy to her home in London for the season, and Kinzy wanted to go and experience such a totally different way of life. She hoped Queen Airmed would allow it.

She also hoped the queen would accept her attire. But uppermost on Kinzy's mind was that the queen might still order Lady Esme's death, for her knowledge of the Fae that Kinzy had given the woman. Kinzy's own life could be taken as well.

She'd waited outside the throne room for some time now, wondering at the delay. The queen could be showing her disapproval with the outcome of the mission by keeping Kinzy in the antechamber, staring at the Queen's Guard who glowered in their dangerous way. On the other hand, something important may have come up and the queen had no choice but to delay their meeting. That worried Kinzy greatly. She knew the Houses plotted and schemed, and the throne was the center of it all, both good and bad. Something might have happened in her absence, and she had no time to catch up.

Trell chittered softly in her ear. She reached up and scratched under his chin as he tightened his tail around her neck. Her small friend was correct, she was not alone. Their bond was stronger than ever. Perhaps the queen would be in the mood to explain why Trell was gone so long just when she'd needed him in the Andes. Trell would only—or perhaps was only allowed—to say that it had been difficult to get to the queen. Right now, the longer Kinzy waited, the more her fears rose. She quieted her mind and centered herself.

She ran through the litany of her transgressions for the hundredth time. Humans had seen Trell in his natural form. She had not brought the mummy home. Esme now knew all about Kinzy being Fae. Finally, she had collaborated with the human to achieve the destruction of the mummy. None of this would endear her to the queen, and any of it could be deemed treasonable in the face of the primary instruction to keep the knowledge of the Fae a secret.

She stood, stiff and prepared for anything, as the Queen's Guard stared through her, as though she weren't even there. Like she was human. It was the dress. It must be. She stood straighter and stared at them, with all the haughtiness of Lady Esme at her worst.

The throne room doors swung open and the guards turned sideways to let her pass between them. Kinzy swept forward into the brightly lit room, determined to show full confidence in herself and her completed mission. The queen had said to trust her. Let that be her guide now.

No one sat on the throne at the end of the room.

Belaron, the King's Right, stood halfway down the carpeted walkway and gestured to a side passage that led to the queen's private study. Kinzy had never before been invited there. This could be a good thing or a very bad thing.

The door at the end of the hallway was painted with ivy and flowers that seemed to move in a subtle wind. She could sense the magic on the door, spelled to allow only certain people to enter. Belaron did not follow her down the hall. Kinzy knocked on the door and waited for admittance. She was back in Tír na nÓg now. A faeleath did not barge in anywhere uninvited.

The door opened on a sitting area with couches on one side and a large conference table and chairs on the other. The queen sat on the far side of the oval table, a small meal laid out before her. Two more doors led off to other areas of the apartment. Kinzy knew this suite of rooms was a place for the queen to go for privacy, for meals with small groups, and meetings with important advisors. She struggled a moment to keep the awe from her face. *A faeleath was serene and focused in all things.*

"Please come in, Kinzalynn. So you are certain not to faint, I have asked them to bring food for two. Sit." Queen Airmed wore the ghost of a smile and gestured to the chair across from her, already set with a carafe of juice, a plate of meats, cheeses, and bread. In the center of the table between them sat a large bowl of exotic South American fruit, clearly the result of Kinzy's trade agreements. "I do not hold to ceremony here. The throne is for position and posturing. This room is made for getting real work done with those I trust. Try the mango juice, it's excellent."

Kinzy bowed, flushed with relief at such a benign, even generous, welcome. The queen continued eating quietly as Kinzy chose a few tidbits for her own plate. It wouldn't do to be greedy in front of her liege, though she had not eaten for many hours. She sipped in the same dainty fashion as Airmed, acutely aware that her queen studied her.

The queen chittered exactly like Trell, and the drakkeki scampered down Kinzy's arm and across the table, to sit attentively before the queen. She picked up a piece of dragon fruit from her plate and held it out for Trell, who took it gently. He gave a quiet warble in thanks and sat back on his haunches, munching with satisfaction. Kinzy was astounded he was so well behaved. Trell presented his eye ridges for scritching. The Queen of all Fae obliged him.

"Your Majesty has made a friend." Kinzy sipped her cup of mango juice.

"Trell is my friend as long as I feed him well and take good care of you. He made it very clear that you were special and should be encouraged."

"Thank you, Your Majesty." Something had transpired

between the queen and Trell, and Kinzy would give a lot to know that story. "I don't know what I would do without him. I owe him much for his services during our adventure."

"I think you owe this Esmeralda Eggerton much as well. I found the final reports Trell brought to be most interesting."

"I do owe her my life, Your Majesty."

"This woman knows much of the aristocracy of Britain. The peerage, they call it. She has traveled the world, working for Victoria, Queen of England, much as you assist me."

"She does, Your Majesty."

"I would like to know if you parted on friendly terms." The queen leaned forward and lowered her voice in a menacing way. "After telling her about your origins. About the Fae. Allowing her to see Trell's true form. Revealing your mission to her."

Kinzy froze. The room grew cold, and the queen's expression pinned her in place like a butterfly on a collector's board. A hundred answers sprung to her lips, none of them satisfactory. Nothing she could say would make a difference. Kinzy had knowingly broken their cardinal rules.

Trell scampered up Kinzy's arm and sat on her shoulder, chirping adamantly.

"I agree, Trell." The queen leaned back, once again genial and smiling. "She did what was necessary for the completion of her mission. She showed good judgement for when to follow the rules and when to bend them."

Kinzy let out a slow breath. When Queen Airmed set her napkin on her plate and pushed it away, Kinzy did the same. Back straight and head bowed slightly, she waited for the queen's pronouncement.

"It is time for this human monarch and I to meet. You have shown me that cooperation and allies in the human world have a place. I wish you and this Esme to work in concert, so you are better able to understand the influences upon this queen of theirs, and the peerage that supports or undermines their crown."

Kinzy kept her chin down but spoke quickly. "Your Majesty, you do not mean to ask her for public audience? Such an event would have so many security issues, not to mention—"

"Of course not, child. She and I will meet alone, privately. It's being arranged. You will simply continue to send Trell to me with reports. I shall feed him from my plate and he shall grow fat, so you must keep him with you and active. Raise your head, Kinzalynn, I'll not be killing you today."

Kinzy risked a smile as she glanced at the queen. She scratched under Trell's chin and he settled behind her neck. "I would truly enjoy working with Esme. I trust her, Your Majesty."

"Good, then you shall work with her to develop a story that befits your new station as a lady of their peerage. Esme will be given freedom to discuss this with her monarch, and we will be able to send you on mutually beneficial assignments. You shall be our representative to their court, but only Esme and her queen shall know of your true origins. Any treaty that develops between our court and theirs will include emissary status for you. It will be clear that you are *my* trusted subject, not hers. You will receive a stipend and regular messages through Trell. No one here shall be told of your status or placement." She paused, fixing Kinzy with that glare again. "No one."

"Master Shabao—"

The queen cut her off with a laugh. "The old meddling fool probably already knows. He is also one I trust. I've sent him to assist with a situation. He will not return before you leave. Establish yourself quickly in your role before the Eggerton creature is sent on her next assignment."

"As you will, Your Majesty."

"You will not be allowed to use the London townhouse for this role, except in case of emergency. Travel through the Salisbury portal stone for now. There is no need to return to me unless or until I send for you. Do you understand?"

Kinzy nodded with a solemn face, but within she felt pure joy. She and Esme would be allowed to work together. It was a brilliant plan if the queen was after closer ties to the British monarchy, and she could not wait to find her place in Esme's world. The restrictions made her wonder about the need for such secrecy and if it was related to events she had missed in her absence.

The queen tossed a large envelope across the table to her. "Inside is a letter of introduction to a legal firm in London, as well as other businesses, and a letter to the bank to access your starting funds. You have free access as needed, as well as an account under your own name, Lady Kinzalynn Quinn. You will comport yourself as befits a member of the British peerage and more importantly, as my emissary."

Kinzy sorted through the various papers, pausing on one. "Your Majesty? If I may ask, where did you get that human surname? Quinn."

"It is your human hereditary name. I thought it appropriate that you should adopt human ways and acknowledge the human side of you. You don't like it? It can be changed."

Kinzy was dumbstruck. Faeleath did not have last names, family names. They never knew family, only the other young faeleath of the *creis*. A faeleath was given a house affiliation and nothing else. To be told her human surname came as a shock. Kinzy had no idea how to feel about that, but she kept her spike of emotion under wraps. "I can work with that, Your Majesty."

"Be about your business then." The queen resumed her meal and opened a small book beside her plate.

Kinzy stood and bowed once again. "Thank you, your Majesty."

With Trell purring smugly on her shoulder, she went back the way she came. The guards closed the throne room door behind her, nearly clipping her heels as she left.

Chapter Thirty-One

"This was not the outcome We were expecting." Queen Victoria pursed her lip and narrowed her blue eyes.

"I understand that, Your Majesty." Esme knew better than to use the word 'but'. "It was either destroy Atahualpa's mummy, which I might add was what the poor old sod, I mean, soul himself wanted, or allow another sovereign government access to it and its associated powers."

Victoria leaned forward ever so slightly. "You were truly able to communicate with his spirit?" Both doubt and hope resonated in the queen's voice.

"Indeed. A most remarkable experience." Although not the first time she'd communicated with spirits, she thought ruefully, it would likely remain the most memorable.

"As you know, We are most interested in genuine spiritualism." She cleared her throat, changing the subject. "We are afraid We have another matter to attend to, but perhaps in the near future you can come for tea and We can have a more in-depth discussion about this experience of yours."

The thought of having tea with the queen made her squirm. "I look forward to that, Your Majesty."

Victoria assumed her rigid posture again. "It is unfortunate that you were not able to bring the mummy back with you. However, better it be destroyed than in the wrong hands. Especially hands that We have little familiarity with." She inclined her head at Albert, who stood waiting for her. "Perhaps it is time to attempt a more formal relationship with the royal Fae Court."

Esme poured as much sincerity into her words as she could. "If Kinzalynn is representative of who they are and what they stand for, then I think that would be a marvelous idea."

"You have made a connection with this woman."

"Yes, ma'am."

Victoria nodded. "That is most reassuring. We, and here We refers to both Albert and Ourselves, have a great deal of trust in you, Esmeralda. You have performed a number of valuable services to the Crown, and with exemplary results despite difficult circumstances."

Rare praise indeed. "Thank you, Your Majesty. I am honored to be of assistance." God, would this appearance never end? Not that the prospect of her next errand overly excited her. It would be even more egregious than this one, but just as necessary.

Victoria gave her a regal nod.

Albert, always in the background, but most assuredly present, quietly cleared his throat and looked at his pocket watch. "It is nearly three o'clock."

"Thank you, Albert." The smile she sent her husband, before returning her attention to Esme, transformed her plain face. "We are most pleased with this outcome, Esmeralda. We look forward to your continued service."

Esme nearly sighed in relief. "I am your devoted servant,

Your Majesty." She gave a curtsy and removed herself from the room as quickly as was decorous. Once out in the hall, with the doors closed behind her, she sagged a bit and sucked in as deep a breath as her tightly laced corset would allow.

Old Carl gave her a wink. "You've still got your head, so it can't have been that bad."

"No, not bad at all." Butterflies fluttered in her stomach. "I don't suppose you can tell me where Doctor Navarro has his apartments?"

The man's bushy white eyebrows went up knowingly. "I believe Doctor Navarro has lodgings above his surgery in Harley Street."

Harley Street. Of course he did. She scowled. "Do you—"

Carl grinned. "I will arrange a carriage for you, my lady. A driver will take you there and then home afterwards."

"Oh, that's not necessary."

Carl gestured to a young man in the royal livery. "A carriage for Lady Esme, please, to Doctor Navarro's surgery in Harley Street. It is to wait and then take her home."

"Yes, sir."

It galled her that everyone in the Palace would know where she meant to go next, but there was no help for it now. "Thank you, Carl. If you could then, please let my own driver know he can head home."

She made her goodbyes and soon found herself in a carriage with the royal seal, clopping her way towards Harley Street.

The persistent February drizzle, shoppers, and clusters of other wet fools jostling about with their umbrellas caused a fifteen-minute trip to take over half an hour. By the time the footman helped her down from the carriage, Esme wanted to turn around and go home. She'd spent the whole journey rehearsing what she needed to say to succinctly express both her sorrow at the loss of Rafael's cousin, and a level of detachment.

When she saw that Rafael himself answered the door, instead of his man, it completely derailed her.

"Esme!"

"Rafael," she stammered in surprise. "I was not expecting you."

He raised his hands palms up. "Who exactly were you expecting? This is my surgery, after all." He opened the door wide, stepped back and gestured her inside. "Please, come in, won't you? Such a nasty day outside."

She entered the white and black tiled front hall, glancing around for a footman or boot boy.

Rafael reached for her coat and hat, looking amused. "I am afraid it is only me at the moment. Young James, the boy who normally answers my door and escorts my patients into the waiting area, had to run to the hospital to deliver some medicine for me. I was not expecting any other appointments this afternoon. Imagine my surprise when I looked out my window to see a royal carriage pull up outside."

She surrendered her damp outer garments, watched him hang them on a rack. "You have no one to do for you?"

"*Frau* Strasse, my housekeeper, has the afternoon off." He cocked his head, still looking smug. "Do you feel the need for a chaperone? If so, I can ask Her Majesty's coachman to come inside."

Her nervousness evaporated, replaced by irritation. "That smugness always was your most unfortunate quality."

He had the audacity to laugh "And you your viper's tongue." When she did not laugh with him, he sobered a little, gestured at the carpeted stairs. "Please, won't you come upstairs? The ground floor houses my surgery," he explained.

"My living quarters are on the floor above. I can offer you tea, if you like."

As she had long since stopped worrying about her reputation, regardless of Cooper's constant vigilance, she nodded in agreement and allowed him to usher her up the sweeping staircase and into a drawing room that faced the street. It reflected him perfectly, masculine but elegant. A pair of leather armchairs flanked a cozy fireplace, fronted by a matching leather divan. Off to the side sat a small round table that held the remains of a light repast, probably breakfast, given that she could see uneaten triangles of toast and a jar of orange marmalade. Beyond that, abutting the heavily draped window, a drinks cart bore a silver tray with a couple of decanters, one filled with a tawny liquid she knew had to be his favorite port. The other contained a clear amber substance, either whisky or scotch. She perched on the edge of one of the leather chairs, smoothing her skirts. Was it warm in here, or just the effect of his rapt attention. "Perhaps a whisky instead of tea? That is still your drink of choice, yes?"

Words flew out of her mouth before she could stop them. "It is when Cooper isn't around to grouse about it." God, it was so easy to fall back into their old rhythms.

He splashed some whisky into a cut crystal tumbler and after filling an aperitif glass with a his port, brought the drink to her. "Ah, the inimitable Cooper. How is the old girl?"

Very little of Spain graced his speech now. He'd spent more than a little time in England these past five years. "Still Cooper," she responded, examining the room, the view out the window, the flocked wallpaper in a masculine bronze. His eyes sought hers and she could not risk the contact.

He sat on the divan, knees slightly spread, and rested his arms on his thighs. Watching her. "It may sound ridiculous, given how she disapproved of me, but I miss her." His voice dropped and his next words tore into her. "I miss you."

Esme picked at the jet beading on her burgundy skirt. Anything to avoid getting lost in those brown eyes again. She started to speak, squeaked, cleared her throat. "I am afraid I have another engagement this afternoon, so I need to make this brief."

He waved his stemmed glass of port at her. "By all means then, get right to the point."

Venom laced his words and stung when it shouldn't have. Let him be angry. She did not care what he thought any longer, damn it. She needed to bury this. Time to truly be done. She took a sip of her whisky, let the strong drink burn her emotions away before meeting his eyes again. "I wanted to say how sorry I am about what happened to your cousin, Tomàs.'

He looked down again into his port. "Thank you. It was a shock when the Spanish consulate in Quito telegraphed me." He cleared his throat. "I appreciate, however, the effort you have made in conveying your condolences yourself and, of course, for providing directions for the authorities to retrieve his body." He stared into the fire for a moment. "I could not quite believe it. Tomàs was a survivor. Cunning, brave, resilient. It was why I thought he would be the perfect guide for you. I knew he would do whatever it took to keep you safe."

A lump formed in her throat and she wanted to reach out, lay her hand on his. "He did, Rafael. He endured horrific abuse and never betrayed us. You and your family should be very proud of him. If not for his efforts, we might have been unsuccessful, and you know the ramifications of failure would have been monumentally disastrous, not only for England but for Spain, as well."

The fire reflected in his eyes, sparkled in the tears that he quickly brushed away. "You take too many chances, *mi corazón*. It could easily have been you buried under that cairn of rocks."

She shook her head. "Don't start. I'm not here to rekindle anything. I just wanted you to know that Tomàs acquitted himself bravely. He did everything anyone could have expected." She stood, set her glass down on a table, clasped her hands in front of her. "Well. That's all I wanted to say. I should be going."

He hurried to intercept her, laid his hand on her arm. "*Querida*, please. Let me at least explain what happened in Malaga."

She yanked her arm away, his touch like fire on her skin. "I told you before, I want no explanations. You made your decision, and now I have made mine."

"But it wasn't my decision. Not really. If Victoria's life were in danger, would you not move heaven and earth to save her?"

She stared at him. She had thought, at first, it had been another woman. Then she had believed he'd simply balked at the commitment. Finally, after a year, she had determined that he loved the game of politics that he played more than he could love her. She had never dreamed it had been about his queen. "Are you saying Isabella's life was in danger?"

"No, not her. Alphonso. *Don* José came to me that morning, told me of a plot to waylay Alphonso in Vienna. I had to go, had to stop it. If Alphonso had been killed, Spain would have fallen into chaos. I had no choice, Esme. My duty was to my country, my king—"

"Your future king."

"Fine, yes, mince words if you will. We grew up together. I love him like a brother. How could I live with myself if I let him be murdered?"

She had walked in here determined not to have this conversation, but she could not stop herself now. "And no one else in all of Spain could have done the job?"

"That is unfair."

"No, Rafi. Unfair was leaving me standing on the deck of that airship, waiting and waiting, and believing that you had decided I was not worth your time or effort. That all those pretty things you said to me, all the promises you made me about us leaving the spying and skullduggery behind, about going somewhere where we owed nothing to anyone, that all those pretty words were just lies. *That* was unfair."

He took her hand, held it to his breast. "Esme, please. I had to save him. *Don* José would not let me send you so much as a note. Secrecy was of the utmost importance." He peered into her face, and she did her best to keep her emotions locked down. "You cannot believe I did not love you. Not after everything we shared, after what we planned. Esme, I *still* love you."

Her head spun, the old squeezing pain in her chest renewed. Breathing became impossible. "God damn you, Rafael. No. You don't love me, and you didn't then. If you had, you would not have left me there."

"That is not true! I do love you. *Dios mio*, I have spent the last five years trying desperately to reach you, but you have spurned my every attempt. When I saw you today at my door, I hoped that finally you were here to listen, and we—"

"Stop!" She shook her head, yanked her hand away. "It doesn't matter, Rafael. It doesn't matter if you still love me. It wouldn't even matter if I still loved you."

"What do you mean? *Do* you still love me?"

She turned away, fixed her eyes on the sitting room door. The crushing pain she felt in her chest staggered her. The same pain that plagued her for months after she'd been abandoned in Spain. For six months, she'd cried herself to sleep. A year before she could think of him without feeling the blade of a knife twisting in her heart. "Love is for fools and I am no longer one. I cannot go through that kind of pain again." Her voice no longer shook, and she found she could look.him in the eyes. "No, not cannot. I will not. Not for you, nor for any other man."

He took her by the shoulders. "Esme, please—"

Calmly, coldly, she pushed his hands from her shoulders, kept her tone matter of fact, formal. "I'm sorry, *Señor*, but that is all I have to say." She turned, opened the door, and stalked out of the sitting room and down the stairs.

Acutely aware he watched her, she put on her coat and hat, and retrieved her umbrella from the hall stand. At the door she paused for one final look. Stricken and pale, braced on the upstairs railing, he gripped the rail like a sailor in a storm.

"I truly am sorry about Tomàs."

He said nothing. His knuckles were white against the dark cherry of the bannister.

She nodded at him coolly. "Goodbye, Rafael."

Before she could run back up the stairs and fling herself into his arms, she opened the front door and marched out into the blustery spatter, her only comfort the knowledge that the coachman wouldn't be able to tell her tears from the raindrops on her cheeks.

Chapter Thirty-Two

Kinzy felt a wonderful kinship with her human companion once again. Café Central, a bustling mecca of coffee and pastry in the midst of Vienna, did not normally allow women among the marbled columns and pressed tablecloths without being escorted by an impeccable gentleman of a certain standing. Esme had a brief discussion with the manager and magically they were welcome to spend all the time they desired at one of the small tables out front on the sidewalk. In such places as this, over the past months under Esme's tutelage, Kinzy learned all the different ways to have coffee and tea, in between Esme's grand tour of the city.

Last night had been a wonderful Royal Birthday Ball celebrating the 42nd birthday of Austrian Archduke Karl Ludwig. Esme and Cooper had trained Kinzy well enough that she could perform any of the waltzes and courtly dances she'd been asked, and oh, she and Lady Esme's dance cards had been quite full.

Kinzy shopped in stores she would never think of walking

into alone, with the proper funds and bearing to order the best in high fashion and accoutrements. In the past, she'd been constrained by the highest strictures of the Fae to never interact much with humans beyond immediate needs. Now, she learned the joys of living from Esme. Unfettered, independent, and often indulgent. Their last few assignments together had taken them all over the more affluent portions of Europe.

The wait staff laid out their coffee and cake with efficiency, and Kinzy added cream and sugar. She sipped from her porcelain cup as she and Esme watched people walk by and listened to the gentlemen playing chess next to them.

Lady Kinzalynn Quinn, companion to Lady Esme, was an enthusiastic student in "How To Be A Lady", but she desperately wanted to take her knives to the corset she was forced to wear. She'd worn them before, but never this particular fashionable style and never this tight. Cooper's mechanical strength made tightening a corset a true form of torture. Kinzy was certain the automaton enjoyed it.

Esme, reading the local paper, suddenly leaned forward, intent on one of the articles. "Well, well, did you hear that someone broke into the vault at Wegelin and Company Bank in St. Gallen, Switzerland yesterday? It says a Gainsborough was stolen, among other items."

Kinzy smiled in satisfaction. She'd known it would catch Esme's eye. "Trell arrived with a note about it this morning. Other trinkets were stolen, very important ones to my people, though everyone seems to just mention the Gainsborough. As the oldest bank in Switzerland, it would seem it had a *very special* clientele." Kinzy did her best to sip her coffee and look nonchalant.

Esme folded up the paper and considered her companion closely. "I have not visited St. Gallen in ages. I propose we take a small side trip there. Shall I book us a sleeper car on tomorrow's train?"

Kinzy took another sip of coffee from the fragile porcelain cup, pleased she'd been right about Esme's interest and assistance in the matter. Queen Airmed's message ordered her to find or account for a list of Fae items taken from the vault as soon as possible. "I would be grateful for your help."

Esme clapped her hands in delight. "You already booked us a berth, didn't you?"

Kinzy laughed, causing a few heads to turn, and the gentlemen playing chess next to them grumbled under their breath. "I'm a fast learner, Esme. Cooper agreed to have us packed when we return. The train leaves at six. I made reservations in the dining car as well." Kinzy grasped her fork and took her first bite of the layered chocolate torte she'd ordered. Chocolate was not found often in Tír na nÓg, and hardly ever given to the faeleath. It was a pity she had not learned about its delights sooner.

"Esme, do you think they will have chocolate desserts on the train?"

Her friend stole a forkful of Kinzy's decadent dessert and grinned. "My dear, I'll make sure of it!"

~~ The End ~~

If you enjoyed the book, please consider leaving a review. Reviews help authors like us find new audiences, and other readers like you find new authors and series to love.

Keep reading to continue the next Harrogate Chronicles adventures with the Novella *Teacakes and Kraken Bait*

Teacakes and Kraken Bait

A story in The Harrogate Chronicles set between book 1 and book 2.

Lady Kinzalynn Quinn jumped out of the carriage as it jerked to a stop at Scotland's Harris Island docks on that calamitous winter morning. Eager to stretch her legs, she didn't bother to wait for the driver's assistance as did her shorter friend, Lady Esme Eggerton, wife to the earl of Harrogate.

The driver helped Esme down the folding steps he placed for her. "Be careful on yer voyage, my lady. Taverns last night were crawlin' with salty ol' sailors so scared o' sea monsters that few ships be willin' ta set sail today. Harris Mining is nae sayin' much, but we all ken they've lost two subs in the North Sea this past week, an' all those poor souls aboard, save one."

"It's more likely a malfunction than a sea monster," Esme assured him, settling her ermine-lined stole and bonnet and smoothing her long skirts. "Don't accept hearsay and rumors of mythical monsters just yet."

"Beggin' yer pardon, ma'am, but sometimes tales be true." He tipped his cap and climbed back up on the carriage. "Just you be careful." With that, he left them on the unusually quiet docks.

"The world *can* be extraordinary, Esme. 'There are more things in heaven and earth, Horatio, than are dreamt of in your philosophy.'" With a sly smile, Kinzy buttoned up her hooded grey cloak against the bitter cold.

"Yes, but neither of us is allowed to let anyone know just how extraordinary, are we? Until I am face to face with one, sea monsters do not exist and aren't to blame. I fear it is Hieronymous's latest invention gone bad, as they often do."

Esme scanned the docks, settled on a direction, and took off with a brisk step. "Come along now, you're going to love this next bit."

Kinzy followed, excited to finally meet the portly, white-bearded gentleman pacing coatless at the end of the weathered stone dock. She was less excited to see the top half of a pearlescent white underwater craft the size of a small steamship, moored behind him. Esme had mentioned an unusual form of transportation to the mining station Queen Victoria wanted them to visit, but she'd been short on details. Now Kinzy knew why. Airships were one thing, but somehow, being submerged beneath the frigid waters of the North Sea made Kinzy's heart race. Not that she'd ever let Esme, or anyone else, know that.

As an agent to the Fae queen, Airmed, and being a faeleath or half-Fae, Kinzy spent a great deal of time suitably incognito in the human world, but her assignments had never before taken her to the raw, blustery Hebrides islands. Walking down the pier, she was surprised by the biting cold. Perhaps something akin to her friend's fur-trimmed outerwear would have been a better choice than Kinzy's simple winter cloak. She brushed back a stray lock of red hair that had escaped from her braided bun and reconsidered. The cold didn't affect her as deeply as it did her human friend. The cloak would do.

Ahead, Esme struggled to keep her bonnet from being snatched off her dark curls by the stiff wind. Kinzy lengthened her stride and neatly caught Esme's stole just before the wind whipped it away. Esme twirled, one hand on her head and the other clutching empty air, relieved to see the item had not been sacrificed to the sea. Kinzy offered her a steady arm, and they proceeded down the dock together, Kinzy now certain she'd made the right choice with her cloak and its tightly buttoned hood. Much easier to fight in, if necessary.

The man waiting for them, the famous - and often infamous - Royal Inventor and mechanical genius, Professor Hieronymous Burroughs, looked up from his pocket watch. He waved madly, as if they might miss him. "Esme!" he called. "I had almost given up on you!"

Esme gave Kinzy a conspiratorial smile. "Be prepared. He's a passionate fellow, at least in regard to his machines. He'll talk your ear off if you let him." Still clutching her bonnet, Esme took Burrough's pudgy, wind-chafed hand in her other and pecked the man she had known since childhood chastely on the cheek. "We came as quickly as we could. The ferry from the Isle of Skye only arrived five minutes ago." She turned to Kinzy. "Hieronymous, this is Lady Kinzalynn Quinn, my friend and traveling companion."

The man nodded at Kinzy and gestured toward the gangplank to the top of the submarine. "Pleased, I'm sure. Let us board quickly. There's no time to lose! That insufferable Captain Fillius of the Harris Mining Company has threatened to blow her up." He whacked his hand against the hatch as he gesticulated and winced. "Imagine, believing my machine is responsible for destroying their mining subs and killing all those men."

Kinzy could hear the polite smile in Esme's voice as she tried to soothe the agitated inventor. "My dear professor,

Queen Victoria has sent us to review the situation. You know this ore is needed for her new battleships. Surely, as an esteemed and learned scientist, you understand that we must examine the damage for ourselves, gather the facts, and assess all sides of the situation in order to arrive at a workable solution. If it indeed proves to be your machine--"

Burroughs harumphed. "*Her* name is DORA. DeepOcean Ore Recovery Automaton. DORA for short."

Esme carried on. "Do you believe you can fix DORA, even if she sits at the bottom of the ocean?"

Esme had told her he was passionate but neglected to mention he was *this* eccentric. Kinzy found it disturbing when humans gave objects names, genders, even personalities, but she could overlook this in such a brilliant man. He needed a proper assistant, though, if he was going to be out in this weather without a jacket.

He continued to the hatch on the side of a wide tower amidships. Burroughs offered a polite hand to them as they stepped aboard and down a set of stairs done in elaborate metal scrollwork. Inside, the vessel reminded her of one of the better London hotels with soft, teal-green and blue carpet underfoot and lustrous teak paneling on the interior bulkheads. Carved phostone sconces shaped like dolphins bathed everything in that alchemical substance's signature yellow glow. The only hint they were on a submarine was the length of gleaming brass railings which continued down each of the passageways.

"Of course I can fix her. I can fix anything! This submarine, the *Aspidochelone*, is my latest creation, and designed specifically for underwater repair. Isn't that right, Captain Gregg?"

The gentleman addressed waited patiently at the bottom of the stairs, offering his hand to Esme and Kinzy for the final two steps. He was a fit man in his middle years, with a silver-streaked dark beard and green eyes similar to Kinzy's own. His black uniform jacket, with its bright brass buttons and epaulettes, along with his sharply creased trousers, gave Kinzy confidence that this man, at least, was competent in his position. He wore a benign expression that Kinzy was sure rarely changed. It hid anything from boredom to exasperation, helpful if the captain had been working with the professor for a long time. Kinzy practiced that same face when facing any Fae lord or lady.

The captain bowed. "Yes, sir, Professor. We can handle anything needed." Gregg turned his attention to Esme. "Welcome aboard the *Aspidochelone,* my lady, and...?" He paused with an inquisitive look at Kinzy.

Kinzy, remembering the human social etiquette she'd been learning from her friend, deferred to Esme, who waited for Burroughs to make the proper introductions. When the man stared at them blankly, obviously unable to remember Kinzy's name, Esme stepped in. "Captain Gregg, this is my traveling companion, Lady Kinzalynn Quinn."

Gregg inclined his head towards Kinzy. "It's a pleasure. Any friend of Lady Esme's is welcome aboard my ship."

As Kinzy returned the nod and removed her hood, her ill-mannered drakkeki, Trell, lifted his head and chittered at them from his accustomed place around Kinzy's neck. She sent him a nudge through their telepathic bond to remain disguised as a mongoose on their trip, and not to make a nuisance of himself. Trell snuggled up and snorted in her ear.

Gregg's brow wrinkled. "I was unaware there would be pets included amongst our passengers. May I assume he does not like to dine on furniture legs? Or ship's wiring?"

She liked the man immediately. Trell snorted again. "Trell is very well-trained, Captain, have no worries. He is much more than a fancy pet." *Don't make me order you to perform for them, iguana-brain.* The shape-shifting drakkeki licked the side of her neck, a small tickle.

Gregg peered at the mongoose. "As long as the professor is happy, and I have your assurance he will not be in the way of my crew, he is welcome aboard."

Burroughs had begun to pace during the exchange. Now he threw his hands up. "Enough pleasantries! We have business to be about. Gregg, close the hatch and let's get moving before Captain Fillius finds a way to destroy my masterpiece." He hurried off down the corridor, muttering to himself.

Gregg almost smiled. "The professor will have gone to his study." He pointed along the passageway. "First door on the right, my lady. I'll arrange for tea. Just ring the bell should you require anything else."

Esme nodded, and with that flirtatious wink of hers, took off after the professor. Kinzy followed until she heard the captain close the hatch. She glanced back to see him spin the wheel with a series of clanks and a ping, locking them inside a giant metal bubble that would travel far beneath the waves. It was incredible to think that as far as she knew, she would be the first faeleath to travel so.

Burroughs's study in the submarine resembled the library at The Lady Explorers Club. There was a central table surrounded by a number of comfortable leather club chairs and a secured bar cart against the wall. A carved ebony escritoire stood in the corner with electric brass lamps bolted to the gleaming surface, and a plethora of cubbies and drawers. Overhead, beyond the paneling and crown molding, the ceiling was composed entirely of phostone, bathing the room in a steady yellow glow.

A rumbling vibration built beneath her feet, and the room lurched. The overhead light dimmed briefly as the engines engaged and the vessel began to move. Kinzy shivered with excitement. It was human magic, this science that allowed them to travel underwater.

The engine vibration eased into a predictable rhythm, and Esme removed her bonnet and coat and settled into one of the leather chairs. Burroughs retrieved a rolled-up tube of paper from a drawer and spread it across the table. He grabbed a few books and a heavy inkwell from a desk drawer to hold down the corners. Kinzy read DORA in the upper corner of the paper, and when she leaned closer to see more of the sketch, Burrough's eyes widened as he glanced up at her.

"My goodness! Is that a weasel aboard my submarine?"

Trell was wide awake now, stretched out from her neck to see the sketches for himself.

Amazed that the professor had missed Trell's introduction earlier, she poked the drakkeki's shoulder. "Trell, manners!"

Trell straightened up and gave Burroughs a bob of his head and a chirp of greeting.

"He's well-trained and harmless, Professor. More of an assistant than a pet."

"She is quite right about the little fellow," Esme told him. "He's a mongoose of extraordinary intellect, and *mostly* good manners." Trell flicked his tongue at Esme, and Kinzy had to laugh. She scritched his chin to ease any hurt feelings.

"If you say so, Esme. Now, come learn about DORA! She's magnificent! How can they even think about destroying such a creation? There is nothing like her anywhere. Look here." He stabbed his finger at the design showing a large cylinder with five mechanical arms extending out. "The scoop and vacuum attachments at the end of each flexible arm maneuver through the sand of the ocean floor. They are designed to assess the hardness of the material through which we must drill to reach the ore." He drew their attention to another section of the diagram. "This arm has a burrowing screw, and this one a hammer and pick combination that can make short work of any solid rock layers in the way."

"Or tear open a submarine and drown the crew." Kinzy could not help but see them as the weapons they could be.

Burroughs's lips thinned. "My DORA would not harm them in any way. Tell her, Esme! My inventions do what they are designed to do, and DORA knows how to mine ore, not destroy a submarine."

Kinzy considered some of the professor's more outrageous and wildly unsuccessful inventions Esme had told her about and wondered if he had ever used them himself.

Esme, clearly thinking the same thing, pressed her lips together before continuing. "Indeed, Professor. We understand it's needed to bring up enough ore for the queen's new fleet. However, if it has gone rogue, we will have to discuss our options, per Her Majesty's instructions."

"Well, yes, the queen, yes." He took off his glasses and polished them, then stuffed them in his pocket. "Now, where is that blasted fellow with our tea? I heard Gregg promise tea."

"Here, sir." A young man in uniform entered the room pushing a tea cart. He rolled it to a particular spot on the carpet and flicked his foot to secure it to a locking ring set in the floor. Kinzy marveled at the ingenuity. A silver tray on the cart held a porcelain tea set and a tiered display of teacakes. On the shelf below was a small bowl of water. "Does the mongoose require more than water? Some kind of treat? We don't have extensive food stores, but perhaps a bit of salmon or quail?"

Kinzy shoved the salivating Trell back behind her neck. "Thank you, what you brought will suffice."

"Will there be anything else then? Lady Esme? Lady Kinzalyn?" The young man glanced at Esme, then Kinzy. Burroughs had returned his full attention to his schematics after snaffling two of the teacakes.

Esme smiled at the seaman. "Thank you, that will be all."

"Aye, my lady. Just you ring the bell if you need anything further." He closed the door behind him.

After brushing crumbs from the schematics, Esme convinced the professor to roll up the papers and allow her to properly serve tea. He absentmindedly tucked one teacake after another into his mouth as he extolled the latest gadgets and device upgrades that could help them in their assignments. Kinzy was intrigued by the auto-lighting candle holder, the rocket-propelled skates, and the self-climbing rope grip, but she was most excited to hear about a firearm that could shoot a bullet around corners. That would be handy.

He pointed at the two suitcases strapped in next to the desk. "I have my latest prototypes in these cases. I can't let them out of my sight. Perhaps when this is over, I can demonstrate--"

The voice of Captain Gregg came from a speaker mounted alongside the hatchway. Next to it was a brass-adorned speaker tube, like they'd had on the airship Kinzy and Esme had taken to Quito the previous fall. "We'll be arriving at Berneray Mining Station in under an hour, Professor. Would you and your guests care to come to the bridge at four bells - that's ten o'clock - to watch the docking maneuver?"

Since the professor had just stuffed another teacake in his mouth, Esme replaced her napkin and teacup on the cart and crossed to the speaking tube. "Thank you, Captain, that would be delightful." She replaced the tube and gave the professor a stern look. "My dear Hieronymous, that is your seventh cake. They will have to cut the ship's hatch wider if you continue on in this fashion."

He harrumphed but put aside his plate and pulled the napkin away from his collar. "Fine." He shot Kinzy a glance. "She doesn't bully old Eggerton like this."

Kinzy leaned toward him. He was beginning to grow on her. "As thin as he is, I'm sure I don't know where Lord Harrogate would even put seven teacakes."

At the mention of her elderly husband, Esme smiled indulgently. "Old Egg does enjoy his sweets. Looks like Trell does, too."

Trell snatched his fifth teacake off the cart. *You'll be too heavy for my shoulder at this rate*, Kinzy told him silently.

His response through their bond was clear; she was being a bully, too. She ignored him.

She also ignored Esme when her friend winked at her. It was a wonder her eye didn't spasm with all her winking.

Esme smoothed her winter-blue voile skirt. "Now, why don't you show us more of this magnificent submarine you designed? Perhaps introduce us to the rest of your stalwart crew?"

Burroughs clapped his hands. "Splendid idea. I know you'll be impressed with some of the new conveniences I've had installed. Have I demonstrated my waterless depilation station? The crew has had mixed reactions, but they simply need to get used to the device."

The professor didn't wait for a response as he hurried out of the room.

Kinzy wrinkled her brow. "Why does that sound dangerous?"

Esme shrugged, then followed the professor, giving Kinzy little choice but to join them. She left Trell alone with the last of the teacakes and felt his satisfaction.

At ten o'clock, they entered the bridge at the front of the submarine. The ship now traveled on the surface, and an enormous window that curved along the width of the prow showed an island with a long sturdy dock and rail system that extended into the ocean waves. Behind the dock, on a rocky hill, sat a cluster of sad and dreary buildings. There was nothing fancy about mining ore in the North Sea.

As the submarine edged closer, the professor explained that the rail system brought the ore cars from the refinery out onto the dock where the mining ship would unload the ore, and where the great cranes along the dock would load the delivery ships bound for the factories and giant smithies building the British Empire's new fleet. The design was the work of one of his students, he said with pride.

"Of course, he got his best ideas from me. The cranes are a variant of one of my own designs as well, which I allowed my students to study in my advanced engineering class."

"Ladies, Professor." The captain turned from his station. "If you would please take a seat along the back wall and strap in, we can prepare for docking."

They settled themselves into the indicated padded chairs, Esme assisting the professor to fasten the buckle over his round belly. Kinzy felt a rumble and a judder through the soles of her feet as the submarine slid up and along the stone pilings of the massive dock. Through the window, they could see three people headed toward them.

Kinzy paused in front of the captain as Esme and the professor went up the stairs to the entry hatch. "Thank you for my very first submarine ride, Captain Gregg. It felt magical to be gliding through the seas in such a fashion."

Trell added his own excited chitter.

Gregg's lips twitched. "Always a pleasure to escort the professor and his guests, Miss."

Burroughs disembarked and turned his back on the group headed their way. He adjusted his vest, wiped his face—twice—

with a wrinkled monogrammed handkerchief, then adjusted his vest again. Kinzy wondered at his nervousness.

"Professor!" The man in front marched toward them, black boots thudding on the wooden boards, his long, brown, salt-stained coat unbuttoned and flapping in the wind. "I told you not to come. We have to blow the blasted thing up. It's not safe to go down there, certainly not safe to get close enough to fix her."

The professor leaned toward Esme and muttered, "That's Callum Fillius, the captain of the mining ship. You must talk sense into him."

Esme patted his arm as she whispered to Kinzy. "Captain Fillius is a North American colonial. You'll find his accent deplorably un-British and his turn of phrase rather blunt. I find the colonials to be quite charming, but most of our countrymen find them gauche and improper."

Kinzy watched Esme slip her arm through the professor's and drag him with her to meet the approaching storm. "You must be Captain Fillius! I am delighted to make your acquaintance. The professor tells me you run this whole mining operation out here in the middle of nowhere. We're here at the Queen's request to see what can be done to help the situation. I am Lady Esme, and this is my companion, Lady Kinzalynn." Esme waved a hand toward Kinzy, and Fillius gave her a glance that turned into a much bolder gaze.

Kinzy gave a slight bow of her head to acknowledge him without responding to the twinkle in his blue eyes. She figured he liked redheads, as many human men seemed to.

"Welcome to Berneray Station. This here's my second, Zaidee, and Jacob, my gunner and muscle. Is this..." He waved at the *Aspidochelone* with a look of incredulity. "Is this all you brought? We asked for warships to blow this contraption out of my waters, not a tarted-up narrowboat on a Sunday picnic. No offense, ladies, but we have mining submersibles in pieces, and debris strewn from here to Harris Mining Home Office. This is no place for women."

The tall, dark-haired woman behind him, Zaidee, also in a long coat and breeches, loudly cleared her throat. "You might want to rethink that last bit, Captain. Perhaps we can discuss this onboard the *Halcyon*?"

The two exchanged a silent look that Kinzy figured meant they'd speak about the woman's words later.

"Thank you, Zaidee, you're right as usual. It's cold enough to freeze a chimney pipe. Where are my manners?" He turned his back on them and headed to the other side of the dock where a large steamship, wide and metal-hulled with a wooden deck and two large cranes, was moored. "On the ship, people!" Then he paused and glanced sheepishly at Esme and Kinzy. "And ladies."

His crew followed in his wake, and when Esme looked at Kinzy with wide-eyes at his impertinence, Kinzy could only shrug. She'd learned that response from Esme, after all.

Esme sighed and looked grim. "On the ship it is, then."

As they climbed the gangplank up to the steamship *Halcyon*, the grinding creak of metal brought Kinzy's attention to the small rust-pocked submersible hanging from the davits on the side of the ship. Something had crumpled the stabilizing side fins and dented the back end, shearing off a propeller and knocking the screw off center. The warp in the top hatch allowed the wind to whistle through the sub with a mournful whine. Amazing that the vehicle had made it to the surface, and eying the damage, Kinzy worried about what kind of monster Hieronymous had built that could cause such abuse. She was beginning to dread what they would face down there.

They walked into a large room with a long trestle table and, based on the fact that crockery and food tins were lined up on the counters against both of the long walls, Kinzy assumed it was the galley.

The captain held a simple wooden chair for Kinzy, but as she made herself comfortable, she realized Esme, a woman of higher social standing, still stood. She glanced back at the captain, concerned about the violation of intricate social manners she knew the humans depended on. At times they were even more elaborate than Fae customs.

Fillius's smile faded as realization struck. "Show some manners, Jacob, and get the lady's chair." The other tall, muscular gentleman in their greeting party, Jacob, held Esme's chair for her. Zaidee, it appeared, could sit on her own just fine.

"Cap'n, if you don't need me, I'm just gonna go polish up Velma." Jacob eyed Kinzy and Esme in an appraising way that made Kinzy's hand twitch toward her knives, concealed in the special pockets of her skirt.

"Good idea, Jacob. Your ogling is making the ladies uncomfortable. Go." Fillius crossed his arms and glowered as Jacob backed out of the room with a grin and a sloppy salute. Fillius then turned back to the table. "He means his harpoon gun. Velma."

Esme, ignoring the by-play, removed her gloves and coat, and got straight to business.

"Now, Captain. According to communications shared with me, a submersible was deployed for a normal run to get a load of ore from DORA then turned up as debris. You subsequently sent down a scouting team, and that vessel, too, was found wrecked and all but one of the crew missing or dead. You believe DORA is responsible for destroying the submersibles and 'eating,' your exact word, the crews aboard. You requested a warship of the Royal Navy to come destroy it so you can resume bringing in the ore we need so badly. Is this correct?"

Captain Fillius nodded and slouched in his chair. "The Queen wants ore flowing, I make the ore flow, get my meaning? Whatever we have to do, we do. Now you can't just fix it, that's too dangerous, so I gotta make it go boom. Clear the way for new diggers. That new equipment don't come here 'til we have some sort of resolution and replace the crew to do the job. Now what can you do in that toy you came in?"

The professor clasped his hands together on the table. "Those crews were simply ill-trained for this kind of malfunction. DORA is not difficult to shut down and repair. I designed her so that even a child could fix her. You've obviously mishandled her during operation. Did you tinker with her?"

"I wouldn't touch a gear on that homicidal little gizmo's head, Professor. What I want is to blow it up from a reasonably safe distance. Did you bring me some missiles or munitions we can use? Maybe a doctor as could fix poor Tom Pond, our only survivor from that last scout sub?" Captain Fillius shifted forward, fists on the table, his face inches away from Burroughs's. "Your infernal mechanical beast drove the man mad!"

Burroughs drew back, but Kinzy had to give it to the professor; he was a stalwart champion of his work. "The man is clearly suffering from the effects of being too long on the ocean. Or perhaps his derangement is a result of exposure to extreme pressure when he was at the bottom of the sea. Either way, it could not have been DORA that caused this."

Kinzy could see the captain's jaw clenched in frustration. Before it could escalate further, Kinzy laid a hand on the captain's arm to distract him from whatever he was about to yell. "Please, Captain Fillius. We need to know the details to understand what's possible here. We have been given a writ by the Queen to make an attempt to fix or salvage DORA. We wish to determine if this is feasible and keep Professor Burroughs and your remaining crew safe." She looked him in the eyes until he calmed down and resumed his seat, his long legs stretched out once again, fingers laced on his stomach.

"Thank you, Kinzy." Esme lifted her chin and gazed steadily at Fillius. "Captain, what exactly does this survivor say happened to the vessel he was on?"

Zaidee frowned and was about to speak, but the captain cut her off with a raised finger.

"I think these nice people need to meet Pond. Ladies, would you come with me? You can meet with Tom, then we'll get on with it."

Esme smiled as she stood. "Thank you, Captain, yes. Your cooperation is appreciated."

They followed the captain to the ship's sick bay, where he introduced them to Dr. Lamb.

The doctor scowled. "I'm sorry, I don't care who you are. I won't let you upset my patient."

Esme stood her ground. "I understand your concern, Doctor, but this is important. We *will* see him, and we *will* hear what happened to him down there." Though softly spoken, Esme's words had steel in them, much like Kinzy's mentor, Master Shabao. It worked on the doctor just as well as it Shabao's authoritative tone had worked on Kinzy.

"Fine. But if he is in danger of tearing out my sutures, I'll sedate him and remove you. Is that clear?"

"Perfectly, thank you. Kinzy, come along and take notes, please." Esme strode after the doctor, his long white medical coat flapping about his knees.

Tom Pond, a thin young man in his early twenties with a shock of red hair and a beard to match, lay on his side on a cot in the small, locked room. As they all crowded in through the narrow door, he whipped around to face them.

Dr. Lamb approached slowly. "Easy, Tom." The doctor encouraged the young man with a smile, his voice low and crooning, the way one might talk to a frightened child. "These are important people, Tom. The Queen sent them." Dr. Lamb shot Esme a glare before looking back at Tom. "This is Lady Esme. She'd like to ask you a few questions, if you're feeling up to it?"

Pond nodded, although his gaze skittered away, and his fingers plucked in a staccato fashion at his bedclothes.

Esme stepped close to Tom's narrow cot. "It's nice to meet you, Tom." Her tone took on an uncharacteristic softness. "I'm so very sorry to hear you suffered such a harrowing experience. Do you think you could please tell us what happened down there? How were you able to survive?"

Tom flicked his sunken gaze from the doctor to Esme and back. "You want to know about The Beast?" He sat up, pulled his legs to his chest and rocked. "It's got arms of liquid iron, strong enough to crumple a sub like a paper boat!" Tom's pupils were dilated, and his breath came fast and ragged. He fixed a hollow gaze on Esme. "You believe me, right? I ain't going back there! Never, you hear me?!" Spittle flew from his mouth to glisten on his ginger beard.

Kinzy felt a touch of sadness from Trell, still huddled around her neck like a fur collar. He seemed to think the man was insane, and Kinzy had to agree. While Pond's mind appeared to have been pushed beyond human limits, it sounded to Kinzy as if DORA had truly gone rogue.

Tom grabbed Esme's arm in a vise-like grip, a haunted look in his eyes. "The Beast is alive, I tell you! It's gonna kill us all!" He shook her to make his point. "Tentacles of death! Beware!"

Dr. Lamb snatched up a pre-filled syringe from a white ceramic tray on a counter and plunged the needle into Tom's arm. A few seconds later, the sailor's hand fell limp onto the sheets. With a set jaw, the doctor herded them out of the room and shut the door on their heels.

Professor Burroughs took a deep breath. "Captain, it is clear that I need to go down immediately and investigate. It's the only way to discover what has happened to DORA. Once I understand the malfunction, I can affect the proper repairs."

Fillius crossed his arms over his chest. "Too dangerous. I've no mind to see your pretty little sub ripped open and your body chewed to bits. You heard Tom. DORA's a beast and needs to be put down."

Esme stepped in once again before the two men came to blows. "Captain, we *do* need more information. We don't even know if munitions will take care of the issue. I agree with the professor. We need to go down ourselves and get to the bottom of this."

Fillius scrubbed at his scalp, then appealed to Kinzy. "You look like a more reasonable woman, Lady Kinzy. Please talk them out of this insanity. Besides, we can't waste any more of our vessels, the company won't stand for additional losses."

"Nonsense!" Burroughs puffed up his chest. "There is no need to waste your obviously inferior equipment. The *Aspidochelone* is the top of the line and imbued with superior abilities not found in other submarines. I will repair DORA and you will see how wrong you are about her."

Fillius's face darkened, and the veins in his neck stood out as his jaw clenched. It was now Kinzy's turn to defuse the situation, much as she'd seen Esme do with the professor. "I am afraid I agree with Lady Esme, Captain. We do need to know more, and this is the only way to do so. We will use caution, I assure you." She shot Esme a glance. "These aren't the first dangerous waters we've been in."

"Use all the caution you want, but going down is bound to get someone else killed, Miss. I surely hope it won't be you."

Kinzy had to look away from the intensity in his blue eyes.

Captain Fillius stood on the dock with his arms still crossed, obviously unhappy, as Kinzy and Esme followed Burroughs back to the *Aspidochelone*. The sub's crew closed the hatch behind them, and they made their way to the bridge.

"Gregg! We're going down there, I have your coordinates. Get your engineer ready on the mechanical arms." The professor strapped himself in as he spoke.

The two crewmen on the bridge looked to their captain, who gave them a sharp nod. "Prepare to get underway!"

As the crew scattered to do their work, Esme and Kinzy quickly took their places beside Burroughs.

Kinzy could not look away from the viewing window. The gray, white-crested waves stretched away to the horizon, high and rolling. Once the captain gave the order to submerge, the sea churned. The submarine sank below the surface, and the world outside turned dark.

"Set a course for DORA. Running lights, please," the captain called out as they headed for open water.

The murky panorama lit up in front of them. Kinzy peered into the expanse, saw nothing to see but a gloomy greenish hue where there should have been underwater creatures. Perhaps the light frightened them away. Trell sat comfortably on her shoulder, also alert for any signs of fish, his favorite food. *Always thinking with your stomach, eh?*

"Are there not fish down here?" Kinzy finally asked Esme as the time dragged on.

Esme leaned toward Kinzy with a grin and whispered, "Perhaps DORA ate them all."

Kinzy thought that unlikely. "Maybe the mining operation keeps them away."

"All Slow!"

Gregg glanced over his shoulder at them. "We're coming up on the coordinates they gave us. Keep a lookout for any movement or debris."

Kinzy finally had her first glimpse of the ocean floor, and it was nothing like she'd imagined from reading Jules Verne. Esme had suggested his book, *20,000 Leagues Under the Sea*, and she'd loved the wonders described, but this was not fiction. She scanned the sandy seabed for any sign of the rogue mining machine. The mud-colored bottom, with its occasional scuttling lobster and scatterings of barnacle-covered rocks and cold-water coral, slid past the window in a never-ending parade of sameness. She had just nudged Esme, who slumped in a doze, when Kinzy saw a glint in the spotlights.

"Captain! Look, off to the left." Kinzy pointed.

"Good eyes, Lady Kinzy. Helmsman, adjust our heading."

Ahead, partially buried in the silt, was a mechanical arm, similar to what had been on the professor's schematics.

"Captain, may I approach the window to assist better with the search? I have always had keen vision." Kinzy's faeleath eyes saw further into the dim light.

The Captain glanced at Burroughs, who waved his hand. "Certainly, Miss. Please mind you stay out of the way of my crew."

She unstrapped and walked right up to the window. "I believe I see more debris further left."

She directed them along a line of small pieces. Next was the top of a mechanical arm, and a large gear that the professor identified as a shoulder joint where the arms hooked onto DORA's main housing. One of the giant scoops and more small bits of crumpled metal were jumbled together in a pile. A few more feet and they came upon the rotor of a mining submarine, half buried in the sand, followed by a line of torn hull sections.

A larger jagged sheet of metal reached out forlornly toward them, though Kinzy could not quite make out the configuration. "That looks oddly twisted."

Esme squinted into the gloom. "Possibly a piece from one of the other submarines?"

The spotlights followed the breadcrumb line of debris until they reached the bulk of what had once been DORA. By then, even Burroughs could see she'd been smashed beyond repair, as had the submarines.

Esme spoke gently. "Hieronymous, I am so sorry, but I'm afraid that DORA appears unsalvageable."

The professor sniffed, then snatched off his glasses and wiped at them busily. "This is just terrible. Those idiots have ruined my DORA."

Kinzy returned her attention to the window as Trell chittered sharply. She saw something incredibly huge uncoil from the wreckage. "I see movement!"

Stunned, she took a step back from the window as the vessel continued to move closer. Trell jumped down to stay in place, silent for once. The others raced forward to better peer into the murk. She could just make out the portion of the thing, the beast, closest to them. Big. Much bigger than their vessel. A looming bulbous hulk that faded into the darkness even her sensitive eyes could not pierce. She counted eight long tentacles slithering through the larger pieces of DORA.

One snaked out to pick up DORA's core, wrapping around it in multiple coils. It sheared off a piece from the main body and brought it to a dark void that Kinzy realized was a mouth. It popped the piece in, and the maw closed with a silent snap.

"We must flee!" She turned to plead with the captain. "Unless you have weapons that can fight a leviathan?"

Gregg cursed under his breath and shouted orders to his crew. The bridge tilted as the submarine swerved from the beast, and Kinzy felt the rising thrum of the engine through her feet. Trell raced back up her arm and behind her neck.

"Professor, are there views to the rear?" Esme demanded.

"Come with me."

The shaken inventor led them to a large circular port window in the aft of the sub, but they could see nothing of the beast behind them.

Esme released a slow breath as she peered into the dimness. "Perhaps it didn't follow?"

The professor turned from the window and leaned wearily against the bulkhead. "It ate my DORA, Esme. Ripped out her heart and ate it!"

They returned to the bridge and attempted to console the heartbroken man during the tense trip back to Berneray Station.

The argument on the *Halcyon* grew heated. Kinzy pushed herself between Professor Burroughs and Fillius, who were close to blows. "Gentlemen! I swear to you, there *is* a real kraken, a monstrous leviathan of the deep. I saw it with my own eyes."

The captain crossed his arms and raised skeptical eyebrows. "Nonsense. Me and my crew are sensible folk. We don't hold with sea tales, Lady Kinzy. Kraken don't exist."

She looked straight into his disdainful eyes. "I beg to differ, sir. Kraken do exist, and one of them is down there. Stubbornness will not make it go away. We must deal with this beast. It threatens this whole operation, your ship included."

Fillius frowned but didn't immediately dismiss her again.

Kinzy appealed to his professional integrity. "Let us examine this in a more practical manner. Just how did you intend to blow up the automaton? Perhaps it will also destroy the beast and clear the way for mining again. Queen Victoria wants the ore moving faster to the shipyards for the new fleet. We need to remove the impediment."

Fillius stuck his head out into the corridor. "Haley! Haley, get up here!" He sat down at the galley table. "You need to talk to our Chief Engineer. She has a few ideas."

A young woman with a messy ponytail and dressed in grease-stained overalls raced into the room. "You bellowed, Cap?"

"Come in here and regale us with your plan to kill the thing down there. This is Lady Esme, her friend Lady Kinzy, Captain Gregg of the *Aspidochelone*, and Professor Burroughs, the man who brought us the mechanical monstrosity we've been babysitting."

Once introduced, Haley's bright eyes never left the professor's face. Kinzy saw worship there.

"Oh! Professor, it's...it's just incredible to meet you!" She rushed up to Burroughs, a brilliant smile on her pixie-like face. She stuck out her hand to shake his, realized she still held a wrench, and stuck it in a pocket before pumping the professor's hand. The professor warmed to the greeting as Haley waxed poetic about all of the papers of his she'd read.

"Why, Miss Haley, you're a wonder. I don't see many females in my line of work." Burroughs beamed at her praise.

"More than you'd think, Professor! Though I did have to work harder than the boys and—"

"Haley!" Captain Fillius raised his voice over his engineer's. "These nice people need you to focus on blowing things up."

"Oh! You mean they didn't bring no warships or munitions?"

"No, so just get to your brainwork. We're dealing with a kraken, it seems, not DORA. Don't matter, still needs to get removed from our mining operations."

"Aye aye, Captain. A kraken, seriously?" Her eyes widened at his nod. "Well, I think it would work the same for a beast as it would for DORA."

Hayley sat down next to the professor, tapping her fingers on the table. Kinzy thought that if there were gears in the young woman's head, like Cooper, Esme's automaton at home, they'd be spinning madly amid puffs of steam and whistles. Hayley cocked her head to the side. "Seems to me that since it likes the taste of subs, we ought to fill one with an alkaloid fragmenting compound, mixed with a bit of phostone, ground up into a powder and packed into a brick. Mix in a delayed acid trigger that heats it all to a high temperature, so the phostone becomes unstable as soon as it chows down and hits the stomach. Coat the thing with some smelly fish guts to make it extra tasty, then when it eats it, BOOM!" She flung her arms up in the air. "That's assuming the kraken has a mouth and swallows and all?" She trailed off, looking at the professor, and then the larger group.

The professor nodded vigorously. "Excellent idea, young lady, though maybe an alchemical trigger. Do you have an alchemy lab?"

Burroughs' hands fluttered about while the two talked back and forth. The particulars were lost on Kinzy, and wondered if she should add science and alchemy classes to her education in the human world. Magic, she understood.

Haley voiced concern about the creature's size, and timing issues of the detonator, as well as their limited stockpile of phostone, but the professor brushed those aside and lectured on like the highest mage of the Fae court. Kinzy realized the two no longer knew the rest of them existed.

Everyone else looked relieved, since it appeared their experts had a plan to save the day, but Kinzy wondered about one particular point.

To the others, she voiced her concern. "You realize the only vessels we have available to us are the one we came in and that tiny wrecked one hanging from the davits on deck."

Esme turned to face Haley. "Professor? Miss Haley?" She had to call them three times before they looked up at her. "Would the damaged sub work as bait? Is it small enough for it to eat whole? The others were twisted wrecks."

Haley considered. "Don't see why not, it already took a liking to it. Professor? Is it small enough?"

"I believe so. The small scout sub is comparable to the--"

Fillius interrupted. "There's no propeller left, and the thing can't even be sealed. It's a miracle it made it to the surface. We had to pry the hatch open to get poor Tom out."

Captain Gregg cleared his throat. "It could be towed down to the beast. The *Aspidochelone* could do it."

Burroughs nodded. "Yes, yes. Tow it down there and drag it past the beast. A tasty little treat."

Fillius's jaw clenched as Burroughs and Haley continued

chattering to each other about their plan of attack. "Hang on." Fillius raised his hand, and everyone went still. "You take that fancy submarine down there, Gregg, and after it takes your kraken bait, it'll come after you. I'm telling you, it isn't safe." His eyes shifted to Kinzy, stayed there, his brow furrowed in concern.

Zaidee leaned forward. "Haley, you sure this plan will work?"

"I'm almost certain, ma'am. There's just a wee concern about the timing."

Zaidee looked at Fillius. "They tow the bait, but we shadow them from above. When that thing goes after the scout sub, they cut the cable and surface, then we bring them aboard. Something goes wrong, we're at least on the spot to help out."

Fillius didn't look happy, but Kinzy saw some of the tension leave the tall man's shoulders. He shifted toward Captain Gregg. "It's your ship. You willing to risk this?"

"We have an obligation to Her Majesty. If this will solve the problem, I can do nothing else." He nodded briefly. "If you will excuse me, I will inform the crew and begin preparations."

It was afternoon by the time Haley and Jacob had loaded several crates of the odd-looking bricks of explosives, now called PFC by the proud Professor and Chief Engineer, into the waiting mining sub. The professor wrung his hands and supervised from the deck until the top hatch was welded shut as best they could.

During a rushed lunch of pasties, Zaidee painted "Kraken

Bait" in bold, black letters across the side of their small and, hopefully, tasty bomb. Jacob christened it with chum for added flavor.

Kinzy approached Professor Burroughs at the railing, where he'd been staring at the small sub for some time, a flask in his hand. "I am so sorry, Professor. None of this was your fault."

"None of my creations have ever ended up as kraken treats. DORA was special. I don't believe I can ever bring myself to create another like her." He dabbed at his watery eyes with his handkerchief.

"Was DORA like Esme's housekeeper, Cooper? She is the most amazing automation I have ever encountered. I swear Cooper loves Esme just as much as Esme loves her. That is a special type of magic you have achieved."

He tucked the now-sodden cloth into his pocket and studied his outstretched hands. "These are my instruments, along with knowledge of physics, engineering, and more. That's not wizardry and the stuff of fantasy, that's science, my dear. Science is my power."

"Esme says you designed the *Aspidochelone*, as well. I think it is as wondrous as its namesake. And now, it is indeed a shield for us all against the deep."

Burroughs turned to her in amazement. "You *do* understand her name and relationship to the monsters of old."

"I do, Professor, but she was no monster. Rather more akin to her namesake. She will be the 'shield turtle' that defends us."

"I really must find out where Esme found you. You have an exceptional education." He regarded her intently. "Esme always did choose her friends wisely. Perhaps, someday, you'll share the tale of how you met."

Lesser folk might have cracked under that scrutiny. Kinzy kept her expression benign. "I don't know how much we're allowed to divulge. Sometimes our work is full of secrets. When this is over, you'll have to ask Esme."

Her friend joined them at the railing and handed the professor a clean, dry handkerchief. "If Victoria allows it, then perhaps one day."

Kinzy very much doubted that day would come. The Fae lands of Tír na nÓg must remain merely a fairy tale. Still, she nearly laughed at the thought of Burroughs and all his gadgets faced with the magic of the Fae. Or worse yet, the Fae faced with his gadgets.

"Hmph. You rarely tell me anything these days, unlike when you were younger. I often worry about you, my dear, but when the Queen commands, we do what we must."

Trell snorted, and the little drakkeki bobbed his mongoose head in agreement.

"This creature is enchanting, Lady Kinzy." He leaned closer, adjusting his spectacles to see better.

Trell leaped from her arm to race up around the professor's shoulders. He rubbed his furry head along the delighted man's cheek. Then the little trickster actually let the man scratch around his ears with a purr of contentment.

Do mongooses purr? Kinzy asked, but Trell neither stopped nor answered.

Kinzy sat buckled into the passenger bench aboard the *Aspidochelone* as the submarine slowly sank again beneath the choppy waves. They descended slowly this time, towing the little scout sub, now known as Kraken Bait, behind them via a metal cable. Gregg took care to maintain enough forward thrust that the dead weight of the sub didn't drag them down or off course.

Time seemed to stand still as they descended into the darkness, and Kinzy found herself holding her breath. It was almost startling when Gregg gave the orders for the forward lights, and the rocky, silty bottom appeared again.

Gregg stood erect, hands clasped behind his back, but Kinzy could sense his concern - a tautness in his shoulders, the grip of one hand on the other, the slight strain of his neck as he peered out the viewing window. "We should be close now to where we encountered it last time."

Pausing with her hand on the clasp of her restraining straps, she remembered her place. "Captain, if I may, I'd like to come forward for a better look."

He nodded in consent. "You've got the eyes for it."

She disengaged her strap. "Thank you. I shan't get in the way."

She moved to the viewing window and peered into the dimness with her sharper faeleath vision, trying to see shape and substance beyond the limits of the forward lights, as the sub eased its way ahead. Finally, she spotted the same scattered bits of wreckage they'd seen earlier. "I see the debris field, Captain."

He squinted and after a moment, as they moved closer, nodded. "As do I." He leaned forward. "I can't quite make out..."

The *Aspidochelone* rocked. Kinzy grabbed onto a railing to keep from toppling over.

Gregg's voice was terse. "Ahead, half speed! The damn thing hit us broadside." He scowled. "Well, at least we know where the accursed thing is. We need to get the bait in front of it. Lady Kinzy, please return to your seat."

The sub surged forward, and Kinzy stumbled back to the bench. There was another jolt. Even as she buckled herself back in, the captain shouted more orders.

"Release the cable!"

"Releasing cable, sir."

There was another jerk. Esme put a hand on Kinzy's knee. "I want to go aft. I want to see that the thing actually takes the bait."

Gregg's tone was sharp. "You'll stay put." Then he amended, "Your Ladyship."

Esme, never one to back down to anyone, asked, "Then how will we know--"

Gregg picked up his speaking tube. "Aft station, report."

"The shark has taken the seal, sir."

Gregg grinned. "*That* is how we know, my lady." He faced forward again. "Set course for the *Halcyon*. Mission accomplished."

The professor wiped his brow with his damp handkerchief, and even the unflappable Esme breathed a sigh of relief. "Well, now, that was unexpectedly easy."

Kinzy grimaced. "Perhaps too easy?"

Esme gave one of those sanguine shrugs. "Surely we're allowed easy once in a while."

As the submarine turned and began its ascent to the *Halcyon*, Kinzy could only hope she was right.

The *Aspidochelone* bobbed alongside the *Halcyon* while late afternoon clouds scudded overhead, and the wind whipped through even Kinzy's warm, woolen cloak. She, Esme, Professor Burroughs and Captain Gregg huddled on the *Aspidochelone's* conning tower, searching the waves for signs of the explosion.

Fillius, his long coat flapping around his boots, shouted down at them from *Halcyon's* deck. "Well? When does it explode?"

Burroughs pulled out his pocket watch and wrinkled his brow. "Soon, Captain. Very soon."

"Is it your intention to stand around and get water-whipped until it does? I say let us winch you up onto the *Halcyon*. We can wait on our deck just as easily. Lady Kinzy—I mean, the ladies should get out of the cold."

Gregg, who had his spyglass trained on the waves, nodded. "That is an excellent suggestion, Captain Fillius. Professor, ladies."

Burroughs waved him to silence. "Nonsense. It will just be a matter of moments. In fact, I believe I see bubbles now. Look there." He pointed astern.

Gregg turned his spyglass in that direction, and his mouth gaped open. "Mother of Pearl."

Kinzy saw a huge tentacle curl up into the air from beneath the waves. It towered over them for a moment and then splashed below. The submarine rocked violently. She watched in horror as one tentacle, as thick as three men, wrapped itself around the sub, then a second, then a third.

Fillius hollered down at them from the deck of the *Halcyon*. "Get up here! Jacob! Ladder!"

Gregg shouted into the hatch. "Abandon ship! Abandon ship! All hands to the hatch!"

The sub shuddered again. Kinzy felt cold water slosh over her shoes and realized the sub was being dragged under.

A rope ladder flopped down, and Gregg steadied it for

Esme first. As soon as her friend was climbing, Kinzy rushed the Professor to go next, then followed him closely.

"But I...I can't...It's so far..." He froze. "Wait! My suitcases! My prototypes! I must fetch them!"

Kinzy nudged him gently. "Professor, there is no time."

"No. I cannot leave without them."

Below her, she heard Gregg call out. "We've got them, Professor. Now climb!"

Kinzy glanced down and saw Gregg hadn't lied. Two of the crew lugged the leather suitcases up through the hatch. She gave Burroughs a prod. "I'll be right behind you, Professor. You can do this. But time is of the essence."

She chivvied him, urged him, encouraged him as he hesitantly moved up one rung after another. After a glance below, she started pushing. The *Aspidochelone* was disappearing beneath the waves. Gregg struggled to keep from being sucked down with it, and his last three crew members hung on the bottom of the rope ladder as it swung wildly above the waves.

"A little faster, Professor, if you please."

He grunted, heaving his bulk upwards. As they approached the deck, both Fillius and Jacob dragged the portly inventor over the railing. Fillius left the professor to Jacob and spun to help Kinzy, but she'd already climbed aboard. The rest of the crew scurried up the rope behind her, and by the time Kinzy had assured herself that the professor was safe, even Gregg had managed to clamber over the rail.

The *Aspidochelone* had completely vanished. Kinzy leaned over the railing, peering down into the swirling waters.

Esme came to stand beside her. "Why do I get the feeling this isn't over?"

Something moved beneath the frothy waves. "Because it's not." Kinzy raised her voice. "Captain Fillius! It's coming back!"

Fillius took one look at her face and started shouting orders. "Jacob, get Velma ready! Haley, kick those engines into high gear and turn us around. Kraken's coming to dinner!"

Zaidee leaned out of a hatch and shaded her eyes as she stared at the tentacles and bulbous head that slowly emerged from the sea two ship lengths behind them. "I don't remember sending that invitation. I thought we just blew it to hell."

"Zaidee, get everyone rigged for storm and check the lifeboats!"

The professor and Esme raced to the prow and watched in horror as the leviathan surged toward them, a trail of spray on either side of the huge gray-blue head.

"Hieronymous?" Esme looked to him for answers, but the man was silent, fascinated by the creature. "Professor, why hasn't it exploded?"

Kinzy scanned its body to see if there was any damage. What she saw was not good. "It did swallow the sub! I can see the outline of it, and it seems entirely whole."

"Perhaps the alchemical reaction was too weak," Burroughs muttered. "Or perhaps kraken stomach acid wasn't strong enough to generate the proper degree of heat. That must be it. The alchemy was perfect, but this solution has never been tested against a kraken before. The beast really does look bigger than the Palace of Westminster, doesn't it? Do you suppose we've disturbed the thing with our mining? Does it have intelligence? Speech? It certainly resembles a giant octopus, and they are highly intelligent, you know. Amazing problem solvers. I wonder ..."

"Professor!" Esme grabbed his arm. "We must get inside. It will be on us soon and we have no defense against something this size!"

Though he followed Esme, Burroughs gazed curiously over his shoulder. Kinzy caught Esme's worried glance and motioned that she was staying on deck to help if she could. Esme could take care of the professor.

The ship swung around and plowed through the waves at top speed, away from the creature. The mining station was miles away, but directly ahead, Kinzy glimpsed a small island, no doubt Captain Fillius's intended destination.

Jacob raced onto the deck with a harpoon gun like she'd never seen before. Over his shoulder, he carried a barrel at least five feet long, with a hose on the back end that he twisted off. He ran toward a metal pipe and box bolted to the deck near the stern of the ship. Kinzy had seen a few of them situated around the deck. Now she would find out what they were for.

He connected the hose to the pipe and turned a valve. The contraption reminded her of a fireman's spray nozzle, but it was much too big for that. She watched in fascination as he loaded his gun with long metal harpoons and hefted the five-foot barrel onto his shoulder.

Captain Fillius spun Kinzy around by the shoulder and pointed toward the nearest hatch. "Get below! There's nothing you can do here!"

Kinzy shook her head. "I'm staying. I can help."

He frowned. "Then put on a life jacket and clip yourself onto a line, it's gonna get a mite turbulent!" Even as he spoke, the ship lurched and swayed. The bulk of the large beast was below the waterline, but the long tentacles were already reaching for them.

She donned the jacket he shoved at her, and Trell, despite being unhappy to be stuffed inside the vest, appreciated the warmth and security.

The captain checked that her vest was secure, then turned back to his crew. "Jacob, you better have good aim!"

"Aye, Captain, Velma and me can hit the bucket!"

"Then stop jawin' and puncture the beast!"

Jacob whooped as he pulled the trigger. A deafening whistle screamed as a harpoon burst from the now steaming front of the gun. At the same time, the beast raised two tentacles high above them, both the length of the mining ship itself and covered in suckers like those on an octopus. They started their downward swing.

"Incoming!" yelled Fillius, even as Jacob fired another harpoon from Velma.

One of the tentacles smashed down onto the aft with a thunderous roar, tearing away the portside railing and splintering a good portion of the deck. The ship shifted and rocked, but Kinzy held her ground, a firm grip on the starboard railing.

The second and third harpoons pierced the mantle of the giant cephalopod, but they didn't penetrate deep enough to harm the beast. The entire ship lurched sideways and ceased moving forward as the engines shut down. The second tentacle crashed into the stern of the boat. Jacob toppled over and skidded across the tilting deck on his back. Velma flew from his shoulder, still attached to the steam pipe.

Kinzy grabbed his arm and heaved him further up the tilting deck before he went over the side. He caught the rail, then stretched out his hand to Velma. The entire ship pitched and heaved. The beast rose over them, swamping the deck as seawater rained down, and wrapped multiple tentacles around the ship.

"All Hands!" The captain's voice cut through the din of the steamship's destruction. "To the lifeboats! Make for the island!"

Jacob raced with Kinzy to the bow. He lifted her one-handed, like a rag doll, and tossed her into a small dinghy. She saw the other two lifeboats. One held the crew of the *Aspidochelone.* The other held Haley, the doctor, and Zaidee, who carried a limp Tom Pond. Esme and the professor dragged his two suitcases over the railing and dropped them down to Kinzy.

She settled the luggage behind her and helped her friends aboard.

Fillius shouted to Jacob. "The *Halcyon* will hold long enough for you to get away! For once, her heavy size'll actually work to our advantage. Row as fast as you can for the island. Shallow water should make the beast uncomfortable and it should lose interest." Fillius shoved Jacob toward the chains that still connected them to *Halcyon*. "Get your butt down there! Time to row!"

Kinzy frowned as Fillius stepped back. He wasn't getting in.

"Captain! Here!" Jacob tossed Velma up to him, then leapt over the railing and down into the boat. They rocked when they hit the roiling water, and Jacob pushed them away from the ship. Kinzy watched in horror as the kraken shook the *Halcyon*, hull dented, now listing heavily to starboard. The giant cranes on the deck fell toward them with a screech of metal.

"Row!" Fillius shouted. "Like your life depends on it!"

"I'm thinkin' it does!" Jacob grabbed the oars and heaved, slowly pulling them clear.

As the cranes crashed to the deck and tumbled into the sea, something metal flew through the air. Jacob cried out in pain and toppled backward into the bottom of the boat. Blood seeped out from between the fingers that clutched his shoulder.

He couldn't row anymore.

Kinzy shifted to the rowing position he'd vacated, and Trell returned to her shoulder, tense and alert.

"Esme, see to Jacob. I'll get us ashore."

The professor looked at her in shock. "You can't think you're strong enough to--"

Kinzy set the oars and stroked hard. The boat lurched ahead, and the professor closed his mouth.

Soon Kinzy found her rhythm. As she pulled, she witnessed the kraken strike the ship again. The captain set Velma to his shoulder and aimed. He fired again and again as the lifeboats moved further away.

The beast did not scream, but the air filled with the thunderous smash of tentacles, and the ship's stern broke away with the drawn-out shriek of shearing metal.

Fillius was nearly swept from his perch, but he clung to the base of the destroyed crane at the prow. Kinzy saw no way out for the brave man. He fought to the last, firing a barrage of harpoons at the beast.

What remained of the ship pitched up above the waves. Tentacles curled around the *Halcyon*, and the metal-clad frame of the ship groaned and buckled. Kinzy watched in horror as what was left of the ore carrier vanished into the churning water, taking Fillius with it.

"Look!" Esme pointed toward the lifeboat containing the rest of the *Halcyon's* crew, lagging behind them. Whoever manned the oars was, after all, only human. A tentacle rose from the waves above the small boat and crashed down, missing, but the boat swamped and rocked. Tom Pond cried out as he was flung into the cold sea.

Kinzy was ready to alter course and row back to the others to help when the beast abruptly shivered from bulbous end to tentacle-tip. A terrible roar drowned out the cries of the crew. The kraken's distended mantle swelled, then burst in a flash of light followed by a concussion that rolled over them in deafening thunder. They hung on as the boat was tossed by a tremendous series of churning waves.

The boom of the explosion faded, and chunks of kraken flesh fell down, plopping into the water around the small lifeboat in a gory rain. The carcass of the beast slipped below the waves and back into the blackness from whence it came.

Haley's whooping cheer broke through everyone's shock and Kinzy watched in relief as they pulled Tom Pond back into their lifeboat.

Esme rose from her crouch over Jacob, who clutched her stole to his shoulder. With her talent for dry understatement, she said, "I believe the kraken is dead, Kinzy."

"Yes. But the captain..." She searched the flotsam and jetsam for any sign of Fillius, even knowing he could not have survived.

She saw nothing. Just the sloshing waves and bits of debris. The other lifeboat rowed past them, heading for the island, and Kinzy set her oars in the water to follow. She looked back one last time. A shadow moved beneath the water. It splashed as it broke the surface. Was it the kraken? Or something worse, come to feed on its corpse?

Kinzy sucked in a quick breath as a hand shot above the water, grasping for a bit of floating debris, followed by a sputtering head. She began to row furiously back toward the spot where the last of the *Halcyon* had gone down.

"Kinzy? The island is *that* way." Esme jabbed her thumb in the direction the other boats were heading.

"But Captain Fillius is *this* way, and he's alive!"

Trell snorted in her ear.

By the ruddy light of sunset, they wrestled the lifeboats up onto the shore and dragged everyone out of the surf. There wasn't much but rock and sand on the lump of land Fillius had been aiming for.

Chilled by the biting wind, members of both crews gathered driftwood for a fire, while Esme and Kinzy helped Dr. Lamb bandage Jacob's wound. Haley dragged the professor's suitcases out of the surf and kept an eye on the morose Tom Pond. A wet and bedraggled Trell scampered off into the rocks, with a quick flash to Kinzy that he would scout around. Kinzy was certain he just wanted to shapeshift into something less wet and furry for a bit.

When the fire was laid, the professor dug into his dripping suitcase and removed a foot-long canister and nozzle. "Here, let me show you my new fire lighting device! It's a little big, but it contains enough fuel for a week-long journey in the wilderness. I just switch this on here and--" He leaned over the wood and pressed a lever. Flame shot out the nozzle and engulfed their pile with a roar that caused everyone to scramble back with startled cries.

Esme snatched the gadget out of Burroughs's hands. "Thank you, Professor, but your inventions are far too valuable to risk damage." She placed it back in the suitcase and snapped the lid shut.

"True, true." He settled back on his rock near the flames. "Captain Gregg, do you think the *Aspidochelone* can be retrieved?"

Gregg kept his tone neutral. "She's a fine ship, sir, but the damage..."

"We'll have to mount an expedition, now the beast is dead." His gaze grew thoughtful. "Do you suppose there are more like it down there?" He paused, a faraway look in his eyes, then shook his head. "Well, in any case, I will need to rebuild DORA. Obviously, my machine wasn't the issue at all, just as I said. The problem is that it didn't have the proper defenses against undersea leviathans."

No one had the energy to argue. The professor swept an

area of sand clear of stones and footprints and drew lines with his finger. They all watched as he mumbled something about DORA needing a harpoon gun. Trell scurried up to him with a small stick in his mouth, carefully stepping around the drawing to drop it by the professor's hand like a dog ready to play. Trell looked at Kinzy and waved his tail in the air as he caught her thought.

Burroughs picked up the stick, nodding. "Yes, yes, thank you, now get out of the way." Using his new writing implement, he continued to scratch his design in the sand.

"You should call the harpoon gun Velma 2.0," Jacob suggested, and Burroughs wrote Velma 2.0 on the sand in the corner.

Haley squatted down and studied his drawing. "That compression ram busts, it's gonna rip a hole in the plating and your machine will be no better'n drifting garbage. Better add an emergency shutdown sequence and a secondary coil here." She pointed and drew a mechanism beside the current plan.

"Splendid! I say, can we get a cup of tea or--"

Burroughs looked up, and Kinzy saw him realize they were nowhere near a kitchen or a tea cart. Still in helpful mode, Trell dropped a flopping fish at the professor's feet.

"Well, that's a fine fish. But it's no teacake." Burroughs pushed the wet fish away with his stick.

Esme used thumb and forefinger to pick up the creature by its tail. "An excellent offering, Trell, thank you. I'll just take that over to the fire, shall I? Please, grab more fish for everyone if you can."

"Will we get rescued soon, do you think? I really need that cup of tea." The corners of Burroughs's mouth drooped.

Fillius inched a bit closer to Kinzy, making room for Zaidee on his other side. "Might be awhile, though I'm sure someone will be along eventually." His assurance was directed at Kinzy herself, and her stomach felt like she was back on the rolling waves. Faeleath did not do relationships. Kinzy turned to Esme, who gave her a wink and whispered for her to go ahead, the water was fine now, whatever that meant.

"Come on, Cap'n, you can't think --" Jacob began, then looked on in stunned disbelief like the rest of them.

Trell dropped a coconut at the professor's feet.

Esme dusted off her skirt as she stood and picked up the coconut from the sand. "Oh, Professor, it'll be all right. Look, we've got you and a coconut. We'll be off the island in no time."

~ The End ~

Continue the adventures of Esme and Kinzy in Book 2, Merlin's Tomb

About the Author

Nan Sampson has been creating new worlds and peopling them with quirky characters since she was old enough to hold a crayon. Convinced she was an alien, she spent her adolescence reading SF/F, watching Star Trek, and waiting for her real family to arrive in a spaceship and take her home. Since that didn't happen, she now happily lives through her fiction, where she can time travel, pilot spaceships, cast powerful spells, ride clockwork horses, and find magical macguffins, always finding love and friendship along the way. When forced to exist in the mundane modern world, she is an avid history nut, a terrible but earnest gardener, and consumer of many cups of tea and coffee. She likes to imagine she lives in Roger Zelazny's Amber, but it looks remarkably like the suburbs of Chicago. Who knew?

Sign up for her newsletter for info regarding new releases, fun historical facts, and a free short story featuring Esme at
www.nansampsonauthor.com
Or chat with her on Facebook
www.facebook.com/nansampsonauthor

Also By Nan Sampson:

The Coffee & Crime Mysteries

Restless Natives

Office Heretics

Forest Outings

Fringe Benefits

The Magical Underground Series

Your Goyle and Mine

A Djinn and Tonic

That Old Plague of Mine (Coming Soon)

Love and Larceny Historical Romance Novellas

The Christmas Caper

The Valentine's Day Deal (*Available Feb 2026*)

The Gunpowder Plot (Coming Soon)

The New Year's Eve Assignment (Coming Soon)

About the Author

Susan Wachowski almost became an astrophysicist but decided to go back to her true love of stories, poetry, and art. She lives in Huntley, Illinois with her husband, daughter, son-in-law, and dear Mom. Hair going gray, eyes are blue and get greener the more she laughs. She's won awards for short stories and done some anthologies. Most mornings she can be found with a cup of hot chai firmly in hand, talking to her character friends and pushing forward on her science fiction, fantasy, cozy mystery, and short story projects. Or maybe painting miniatures. She is also the minipainter known as Paintminion.

Discover more about these and other projects by signing up for emails and info at
http://www.susanwachowski.com

Reviews are the lifeblood of a published author,
so please consider leaving a review.

That makes a *Universe* of difference and is much appreciated.
Your Readership Stats gain +3

Or keep up with Susan on Facebook
https://www.facebook.com/AuthorSusanWachowski/
Your Readership Stats gain +2

Also by Susan Wachowski

The Harrogate Chronicles

Atahualpa's Mummy

(now includes Teacakes and Kraken Bait Novella)

Merlin's Tomb

Aztalan's Idol

And wherever these characters take us next!

The Co-Author Dynamic:
A few more words from Sue

This series began at a convention, at a table in the hotel lobby, with drinks, lunch, family and friends chuckling. Alternate timeline discussions happened, and then, hey, let's toss Fae in there too! Esme and Kinzy were born.

Working with my co-author can be the most fabulous form of upward spiraling energy between us! It can also crash down a mountainside when neither of us wants to work on the manuscript. There are squirrel projects always, and we wanna chase 'em! Eventually, though, one of us regains a glimmer of adulthood and draws the other back into the fray.

It's an interesting dynamic for my unofficial sister and I. We have different ways of handling issues, different ways of writing. We both love "towards" and screw single spaces after a period. I tend more towards (see!?) the Oxford Comma, and she loves those -ing words.

We didn't fight, but I could tell when Nan really wanted a change made, and she backed off when something didn't matter to her as much as it mattered to me. We remain Pantser and Planner, Push and Pull. (We have buttons declaring that, btw!) We both love our world and its characters. We hope you do, too.

∞∞∞

Amusing Outtakes

For your amusement and chuckles, we give you a smattering of our outtakes and commentary while writing this book.

* * *

"Time for morning tea and cakes. The maid can draw a bath, and the Wardrobe Automaton has picked out a lovely lavender frock for the day." ... *One lump or two, is next, right?*

"What's that, Trell? Kinzy's fallen down the well?"

"Can you see the rope?"
"See it and taste it."

"That thing they do in Spanish countries - they elcome people."

We don't need no stinkin' map!

ick pick, the Vatican, and the coca thing.

"Let's never do that again." She massaged her upper arm, wincing a little. "I'll probably never be able to do crewel again." She chuckled.

Kinzy gave that gimlet stare that meant Esme had said something she didn't understand.

"You know, crewel. C-R-E-W-E-L? Embroidery?" Kinzy was still staring at her. "Never mind. Just a thing Cooper always tried to teach me and at which I was abominably awful. I used to tell her that making me do crewel was just cruel." She shook her head when that failed to get a response.

fneshid! ... I didn't know Esme was learning Fae words from Kinzy. --gah, I meant finished!

We have brains. We fill in blanks that aren't even there.

Governments's ... Governments'... gah, just rewrite to get rid of the word!

Amusing Outtakes

Gold Trell...
Red Trell...
Blue Trell...
White Trell...
...seriously if the beast can shape-change he can be any color at any time?!

Diego has Faedar? Really? Superpowers!

"Help me, Kinzy-kenobi, you're my only hope."
--Nerfherder.

So these guys are Red Shirts? Do 1800's Inca wear red?

Trell has to beam over to the Queen every now and then.

She can't go out to do her urgent business and not do her business. You said she was having stomach issues and there's no Immodium in her pack.

Ones who canCAN stop it. --No

Why did the chicken cross the rockfall? To get through to the other side.

He can't be hanging from trees in a forest when there are no trees this high up the mountains.

"I am NOT amused." said Queen Victoria haughtily.

∞∞∞

www.ingramcontent.com/pod-product-compliance
Lightning Source LLC
LaVergne TN
LVHW100510110826
845146LV00002B/587

* 9 7 9 8 9 9 4 9 9 1 1 1 4 *